ADVERSARY

KEVIN KNEUPPER

CHAPTER ONE

NO ANIMALS WOULD GO NEAR it, the thing that crept closer towards them day by day. It was moving; they were sure of that. It was almost imperceptibly slow, but it was happening. Each morning they'd wake to find it a few yards nearer, pulling the forests inside it and changing them into something else, something they couldn't quite make out through the slimy film that ran across its surface.

Some thought it was a liquid, and it looked like one, dripping and foaming with a light red tinge. They hadn't an inkling as to how large it was. Miles, at least, from what they'd been able to discover from trying to walk the length of its borders. They could tell it was spherical, a wall touching the ground and curving as it moved upwards into the sky, ending up above who knew where. There were things inside it, and they could see them from time to time, blurry black shadows behind the barrier. Some were shaped like people, but they could never quite be sure. The shadows would come close to the edge, staring at them from the other side, but never doing much else. It was possible to cross the barrier, that much was certain. But it wasn't clear whether it worked both ways: while animals and birds had gone in, nothing had yet come out.

Three boys stood before it, keeping their distance. They were all distraught, tears on the face of one, fear on the faces of the others. They stared at the black shapes dancing before them, giant Rorschach blots that moved and swayed behind the barrier, appearing and fading of their own accord. They couldn't look away, no matter how much they tried. Not with what had happened, and not with what was inside of it now.

They heard shouting from the trees behind them, the voices of adults who'd come as soon as they'd heard. They'd sent a fourth boy to run for help, once they'd realized there was nothing more they could do. He'd found his way back to the camp, deep within the forest, and he was running back towards them with an entourage of concerned adults following along behind him. At the forefront was a woman, the only one of them willing to lead. She was the one who'd shepherded them all away from their former home and into their new existence as nomads, wandering in the woods and never staying in a single place for long. And she was the only one who might be able to help them now.

Her name was Cassie, and she'd been one of them back in their tower, though not for long. She'd come from outside, and opened the door to others, and then it had all come crumbling down. She ran towards the boys, a bow and its quiver of arrows strapped to her back, the better to hunt for food without attracting unwanted attention from above. She wore a cloak of grey, the same as they'd once had in the tower. Her hair was jet black, mostly. A few strands of white had crept into the edges, and her face had a few more lines than it had borne just months before. But heavy is the head that wears the crown, and trying to help the helpless to survive was a constant stress. She couldn't abandon them, not to certain death, but the chore of keeping them alive despite themselves was taking its toll.

She stopped her sprint just short of the boys, and the men who'd followed her crowded around them in a circle. She looked down at the scared, confused children, and then at the dark blotches floating behind the surface of the barrier. "Where is he?" said Cassie. "What did you do?"

The boys all stood silent and stared at the ground, too stunned to say a word in response.

"What did you do?" said Cassie, her voice a little firmer.

"He went in," said one of the boys quietly. "It wasn't our fault. He went in. We didn't think he'd do it. But he did."

"It was a dare," said another, the dirt on his face turned to mud by his tears. "We dared him. And then he just ran through."

A loud thunk came from behind the barrier as shadows massed at its edge, attracted by their presence. Cassie stared at them, wondering if one of them was the boy, or if they were something else entirely. The shapes were dark and indistinct, and they made her feel nauseous the more she watched them. They didn't look like people, not exactly. But it felt like they were intelligent somehow, clambering against the wall and just waiting for their chance to push through.

It put her to an awful choice: she could leave the boy to his fate, whatever it was to be, or she could try to get him out and risk them all in the process. She'd never wanted to be the one in charge, and she'd rather that anyone else have done it but her. She certainly hadn't been a leader before the Fall. Back then she couldn't even find a direction for her own life, let alone for someone else's. She'd worked a series of odd jobs, from serving coffee to sitting at a reception desk to shelving books in a library. Then the system had come crashing down, and she'd gone from aimlessly enjoying her days to scrambling just to survive.

She'd been thrust into the role of leader rather than choosing it. The government had set up camps in the aftermath of the Fall, training their citizens to be fighters in a last gambit to win a hopeless war. She'd joined for safety, more than anything else, the same reason the people she was with had chosen to serve the angels instead. But a decade later, she was the only one with any survival skills, the only one with any courage, and she found herself leading those around her by default.

It wore on her, the longer she had to make life and death decisions for others. More and more she thought about throwing up her hands, abandoning her duties, and letting things be as they would be. But indecision was just as much a decision as anything else, and she knew that if she left these people to their own devices, they'd all be dead inside a month. She took a breath, summoned all her strength, and racked her brain for what to do about the child who'd wandered into a danger none of them were equipped to handle.

The first move was easy; there was no doubt in her mind about that one. Little boys didn't need to be there, not for whatever came next. She turned back to them, her eyes narrowed and her voice firm. "Get back to camp. Now." The boys needed no further encouragement. They took off into the woods at once, and none of them looked back, not even for a moment. As for the men, they all stepped as close to the wall of red as they dared, trying to see behind it while keeping themselves at a safe distance. There was nothing much else they could do. The boy was lost to them now, wherever he was, and deep in her heart Cassie knew they didn't have any choice but to leave him.

"It's getting closer," said one of them, a gaunt, older man whose haggard grey cloak was covered in rips and tears. "Every day it gets closer." His name was Herman, one of the servants who'd escaped the tower along with her. He was almost entirely bald, with a nose resembling a buzzard's beak and rows of lines across his forehead from a perpetually furrowed brow. He'd been of the servants' upper caste in the tower, such as it was, and considered himself above Cassie in rank. He was constantly questioning her judgment as a result, riling up the others and second guessing her every decision. The tower's collapse had been the worst thing to ever happen to him, at least socially, and he blamed Cassie for where he'd found himself in the aftermath.

"We're going to move camp again," said Cassie.

"Further into the woods. Away from this. Far enough that none of the children can wander near it."

"It'll just come there, too," said Herman. "It'll just keep getting bigger."

"Then we'll move downstate," said Cassie. "And if we have to leave cover and live out in the open, we'll do that, too. We keep going until we don't have any place left to go."

"We should have stayed in the tower," said Herman. "We never should have made them mad. The angels made this thing. To punish us. This is all because of what your friends did. And because we didn't stop them."

The men started to grumble, and a few looked at her with blame in their eyes. She knew she had to cut them off at the pass or their complaints would just spread. And if that happened, someone was bound to do something stupid. The only thing keeping her in control was what had become of all of the other servants who'd tried to break out on their own. It happened from time to time, whenever enough of them got up the courage. Most found their way to camp again within a matter of days, starving and dehydrated and begging to be taken back into the fold. Some they'd found dead, and a few had simply disappeared. She knew the odds of survival if one of them left, and she felt a pang of guilt every time it happened. So she puffed out her chest, tried to sound tough, and did her best to reassert command.

"The angels have always done whatever they wanted, whenever they wanted," said Cassie. "And they never much cared about any of us. If you're tired of following me, you're welcome to start fending for yourself anytime you like. Just say the word, and I'll make it happen."

She waited, and they didn't. Idle complaining was one thing; taking responsibility for themselves was quite another. Even Herman held his tongue, though not without an exaggerated series of grimaces.

"The camp moves," said Cassie. "Tonight. At least a mile, towards the south. And we're going to work on portable shelters. No more tents. I want something that moves when we do. Any of you ever seen a camper?"

Herman looked away, while the rest just gave noncommittal grunts. She knew they'd probably have been gone long ago if they'd thought they had the skills to survive on their own. Sometimes it felt like she was leading a pack of sullen teenagers, eager to rebel but well aware that they'd get themselves killed if they actually tried.

"Campers," said Cassie. "We'll build something close to one. I'll show you. We have woodworkers, and that's all we need."

"People are sick," said one of the men. "People are hungry."

"Then the healthy just have to take care of them," said Cassie. "We're not like the angels. We have to be different. They're down here because they didn't care for anyone but themselves. They were supposed to show mercy. Their hearts went cold instead. Any of you want to be like them? Any of you think we should turn ourselves into the things they've become?"

None of them could bring themselves to respond. She'd learned how to control them, not through force but through tone of voice and strength of will. They were all conditioned to bow to authority, and if she said things firmly enough, and met their eyes directly, it was almost painful for them to oppose her. They were lucky she was a shepherd; they could have just as easily found themselves led by a wolf.

She started to walk away, to lead them back into the forest, when she heard a loud thump. First one, then another, again and again. She turned to see a thick shadow approaching the barrier from the other side. It danced around at first, formless, and then they heard the thumping again as the shadow brushed against the barrier. They could see it more clearly, now: two hands, pressed against the red film, the rest of it indistinct. The hands kept pounding and pounding until something else formed behind it: a human shape, the size of a child, staring back at them from the other side.

"Hello?" said Cassie. "Can you hear us? Hello?"

"Don't get too close," said one of the men.

"We have to get him out," said Cassie. "He's trapped in there. We have to get him out."

"We can't," said the man. "There's things in there. Don't get close."

She looked around on the ground, picking up a nearby stick. She approached the red film, holding the stick out in front of her with one hand, stretching it out as far as her arm would go. She pierced the barrier with the tip of the stick, and as she did the liquid film began to run along the sides, enveloping it inch by inch. The shadow behind the wall moved closer, standing just in front of her. Then she felt a pull, and her arm jerked forward with a sudden force.

She let go at once, but she lost her footing, stumbling forward and holding out her hands instinctively to try to stop the fall. It felt like she was in slow motion, and she could see the bubbling red liquid coming nearer and nearer to her face. The stick was already covered in goo, poking out of the barrier and twitching back and forth as it was gradually sucked inside. Her knees hit the ground and she pitched forward, her face stopping just inches before it collided with the wall.

She teetered back and forth, waving her arms at her sides to hold her balance. Finally the men came to their senses and pulled her away, dragging her onto her back, but a chemical stench still lingered inside her nostrils. It smelled like she'd rummaged beneath some kitchen sink and sprayed the air with an armload of cleaning fluids, and they'd all come together to form the red mass in front of them.

As she pulled herself to her feet, she could see a shadow looming in front of her from behind the film. It was the size of a child, and she could make out a face, its mouth open in what looked like a scream. She yelled back to it, as loudly as she could. "Hey! Can you hear me? You have to try to get out. You have to push. Put your hand against the wall if you can hear me."

But the figure gave no response. From further behind it she could see something else approaching—more shadows, growing larger as they came nearer. Two more shapes. And both the size of children themselves.

"There's more in there," said Cassie. "We've lost

more kids. We have to get them out. We have to figure out some way to help them."

But as she spoke, the shape in the center vanished, dragged off into the distance by something behind it she couldn't quite see. The other two shapes moved closer, standing there just at waist height, looking out at her impassively. "Get out," said Cassie. "Get out. You have to try." They didn't respond, but she thought she could see something happening to their heads, the shadows twisting and reforming themselves over and over until they were nothing but a blur of motion.

"Just push," said Cassie. "Put your hands against the wall, and push." But they didn't. Something was happening to them, and more shadows were appearing at their backs. It took her a minute to process what they were, and by the time she did the shapes were already gone. But by then she knew exactly what she'd seen. She was certain of it. There'd been feathers in the shadows, and they'd been attached to tiny little wings.

CHAPTER TWO

Jana stood at the center of a field, its yellowed grass grown wild with disuse. Once it had been a farm, lush and green with rows of crops patching the plains around it. Now all that was left was a rotting barn and broken fencing, surrounding a charred pile of ash where a house once stood. But she didn't care for agriculture, and she didn't care for history. All she cared for at the moment was the skies.

She'd been watching the heavens for days, and doing little else. She ate when she could be bothered to, and drank when she had to, and if it weren't for Thane pestering her to take care of herself she would have fretted away into nothing. But she was eating for more than just one, and however frazzled her nerves she knew she had to force the food down and catch what sleep she could.

The problem wasn't the war between the angels, though the battle at Suriel's compound had given her nightmares for weeks. And the problem wasn't the pregnancy. That was something new, and something stressful, but she thought she'd handled it well enough given the circumstances. The problem was Rhamiel. The problem was that he was gone, and she hadn't a clue when he'd be coming back.

It had taken them a month to get there, maybe two, far from the battlefield and far from Suriel. They'd driven on roads when they could, and Rhamiel had flown them when they couldn't. It was nothing for one of his kind to carry a vehicle below him, and he took so much care to keep from jostling her that it was almost as if they'd stayed on the ground the entire while.

She'd felt safe, then, though she'd been in more danger than ever. Suriel wanted their child, and so would others, if they ever learned who he was. Thane was constantly troubling himself over the threat, and he was convinced that patrols were following close behind them, if not Suriel himself. But Jana wasn't concerned, not even a little bit. Having a guardian angel at her side had silenced all her worries, leaving nothing but her dreams of a quiet life with no one to threaten her or order her about.

And now he was gone, and she was alone with only Thane to look after her. Thane was protective, to be sure, but it wasn't the same, and it never could be. He hadn't the strength to fight an angel, even if he had the spirit. Still, he checked in on her again and again, bringing her fruits and nuts or simply watching from a distance, and she was more than grateful for it. But she longed to know where Rhamiel was, and she knew there wasn't much time left before her child would come.

It was a month at most, maybe just weeks; she hadn't

properly kept count, and she couldn't be sure. She'd grown as the days rolled past, and her stomach was large enough that she thought it might burst if it got any bigger. She could feel kicking inside, and a warmth from within that surged through her entire body whenever her nerves got too frazzled. It helped keep her calm, or close to it, even without her angel at her side. But staying calm was growing more and more difficult to do the longer she was forced to wait for his return.

Rhamiel had said he'd be searching for something, a way out of the quagmire they'd found themselves in. He'd promised he wouldn't go far, and that he'd be back before she knew it. He'd scouted the abandoned farm, decided it was safe, and ordered them to stay inside the old barn until he came back. He meant to keep her hidden, if only for long enough for him to find whatever he was looking for.

Thane had promised him that they wouldn't leave the barn, not even for a moment. But hours had turned into days, and in any event there wasn't much anyone could do to convince Thane to abide by anyone's rules but his own. There was nothing inside the barn to entertain them but dirt, piles of rotting wood and rusted tools, along with a few overly curious field mice. Soon they were wandering outside, just for a bit of fresh air, and it wasn't long after before they were ignoring the precaution entirely.

It wasn't the sensible thing to do, but Jana was under more stress than ever. Each night of fitful sleep left her a little more tired and a little more anxious about what might have happened to Rhamiel. Strong as they were, angels could be hurt; she'd seen it with her own eyes. They could even be killed, if it came to it, and no angel was a bigger target than hers.

There was nothing to be done but to wait for him to come back, and every second was a torture. She'd plopped herself atop a little hill overlooking the farm, scanning the skies each day until the sun slid below the horizon and it was too dark to see. Even then, she'd sometimes stare at the moon for hours more, hoping against hope to see the shadow of an angel pass before it.

This day had been no different. She sat against an oak tree, its gnarled branches spreading above her, taking advantage of the shade in the afternoon heat. She didn't even know which direction to expect him from, and so she stared to the west, off towards where she'd watched him disappear days before. She'd spent most of the morning thinking about her child, and what he'd be like when he finally came. She wasn't even sure if she'd get to name him; from what she could gather, he had one already. She wondered if he'd be able to talk, and if he'd remember who he'd once been so many years ago.

Would he be who he'd been before, or would he be a blank slate as Suriel had said, a newborn babe with the soul of a king? And would he love her the way a child loved his mother? Or was she just a tool, a doorway back to a world he'd left long ago? All she had in the end were her speculations. She didn't even know how an ordinary baby was supposed to be; what a divine one would be like was entirely beyond her.

"Seen anything?" She turned behind her to see Thane, carrying a skewer of freshly roasted meat of origins unknown. He'd been spending his days in his own way, scouting around the nearby wilderness and hunting or foraging for whatever he could. He was dirty and sweaty, his blonde hair grown out from weeks without a proper cut. He never roamed too far; he was too afraid to leave her there alone for long, so he stuck to places he could return from in a hurry.

It forced him to run back and forth between the farm and his foraging, leaving him exhausted at the end of the day, but there wasn't much she could do to ease his burden. She couldn't do the work of keeping them alive herself, not as far along as she was, and both he and Rhamiel had insisted she spend the last days of her pregnancy looking after herself before anyone else. Thane didn't look at all like he minded; he climbed the hill without complaint, dropped a backpack on the ground, and sat down beside her to join the vigil. "Anything up there?"

"Nothing," said Jana, staring back up at the skies. "But I don't know which way to look."

"He'll come," said Thane.

"What if something happened?" said Jana. "What if he doesn't come back?"

"He will, and we'll wait here 'til he does," said Thane. "Here." He brandished the wooden skewer at her, covered in blackened lumps of meat. "Eat somethin'. It's good."

"What is it?" said Jana, reaching her hand out hesitantly. She slid a piece of meat off the skewer, popping it into her mouth and rolling it around on her tongue. She liked the taste; juicy, and with more flavor than the things she'd eaten back in the tower. She'd had it better than most of the other servants on that front.

Servers at least got to sample the angels' leftovers, cold and picked over though they may have been. But this was warm and freshly cooked, and he'd sprinkled it with some kind of seasoning. A second hand delicacy from the tower was no match for whatever this was.

"It's squirrel," said Thane.

That wasn't of much help. She'd never heard of one that she could recall, and the blank stare she gave him told him as much. He thought a moment, then started gesturing with his hands as he tried to explain.

"Kind of a little rat," said Thane. "But with a big, bushy tail."

She knew about rats. They'd had those, hiding in the tower's walls and crawling over their legs at night when there was no light to see them by. This one tasted better than she remembered, and even if it hadn't, she was happy enough that there was one less of them running around.

"I like it," said Jana politely, reaching for another piece. She didn't have much choice, not if she wanted to avoid prompting another round of clucking from Thane about taking care of herself. She took more and more, the both of them eating their fill in silence. She would have talked, but she didn't know what to say. Thane was a little scary even now, long after his anger towards her had burned away. He didn't call her a traitor, not anymore, but he looked mad even when he was happy, and she was always worried that something she said would set him off again. Besides, he was so different. Everyone who'd grown up outside the tower was. The two of them didn't have much in common, and they didn't have much to talk about.

It was a barrier, but it was one neither of them knew how to pass. His culture was fading away, and faster than it should have, dying off and being replaced with something alien and wrong. The wheel had turned: weakness had replaced confidence, chaos had replaced order, and the world was burning as a result. The younger ones didn't know any better, and Jana was no exception. There was a gulf between them; he always thinking of the world as it should have been, she knowing nothing but the husk it was. They sat there quietly, passing the skewer back and forth until Thane finally broke the silence.

"We need us a radio," said Thane. "You ever hear a radio?"

"No," said Jana. She'd heard of them: little boxes that talked, marvels of a world she'd never seen. She wished she could have been there, back before the angels' Fall had torn the world asunder. She looked around at the ruined farmhouse, trying to imagine it as it had once been, but she didn't have anything to work off of. She thought the two of them had that in common, at least. She'd lost her own world, just as he had his, and they'd both found themselves tossed into an unfamiliar reality they just wanted to escape from.

"That's the worst thing," said Thane, staring away into the sky. "No music. No rock, no country, no nothin'. Just silence. That ain't how it's supposed to be. They ruined lots of things, but the worst was the music."

"We could sing," said Jana. "I know how to sing."

"It ain't the same," said Thane. "It'll never be the same."

She started to hum something anyway, one of the many simple tunes she'd learned back among the servants. She found common ground with him on that, at least: of all the things she missed from the tower, she missed music more than anything else. It had brought the servants together, their voices joining as one around the fire each night after their chores were done. She'd memorized every song she could, even if the words rarely made much sense. Most of them were holdovers from before the Fall, the last dying echoes of a world that no longer existed. But there was something primal about it, something that made her feel connected to the ones she sang with, and the feeling had been a release from the drudgery of her daily toil.

She hummed song after song, ballads from another time and place. Thane closed his eyes and listened, and after a few minutes he even joined in. They might never really be able to understand one another, not with the distance between the worlds they'd grown up in, but the rhythm gave them a common feeling all the same. They passed a little time in harmony, until the song within her died away and they went back to staring at the empty sky.

"Thane," said Jana. She hesitated; she thought back to his temper, and she wasn't sure whether what she wanted to talk about was safe to discuss. "Can I ask a question?"

"Shoot," said Thane. She gave him a quizzical look, and a puzzled moment of silence. It took him a bit to notice, but then he laughed and patted her on the shoulder. "It means ask."

"You told me about Heaven," said Jana. "You said that's where we go, if we're good."

"Yep," said Thane. "Be good and they let you in. That's the way it works."

"You said something else," said Jana. She stumbled over the words, trying to force out the question that had nagged at the back of her mind for months. "You said once an angel falls, they can't get back in. You said we'll go to different places when we die. Me and Rhamiel."

Thane gave a sigh, and his face went grim. He'd said the words in anger long ago, but they were out into the world now, and he couldn't ever take them back. It didn't stop him from trying, nonetheless. "What the hell do I know? Don't listen to me. People don't know shit like that. Not really. I was just makin' it up as I went."

"But what if you were right?" said Jana. "What if they send us to different places when we die? What if I have to spend all of eternity up there, knowing he's down below?" It was supposed to be paradise, the place up in the skies. But paradise without someone she cared so much for would be a hell all its own.

"Your angel seems like a good guy, as angels go," said Thane. "And this boy you got." He put a gentle hand on Jana's stomach, and she could feel a little kick inside as he did. "If it's him. If it's really him." A look passed across his face, one of awe mixed with a healthy dose of skepticism. "His whole thing was forgiveness. That's what he told everyone. Doesn't matter what you did before, you do the right thing, and he'll forgive. Rhamiel ain't that bad. He'll get a pass, I think."

But Jana couldn't help but wonder: what if he didn't? Every crime had its punishment, and the angels had punished her for even the slightest of wrongs. What if her son wasn't even the one who decided? Rhamiel was his father, in the physical realm, but they said he had another. And that father might not want to take back an angel who'd once spat in his face and turned a sword against him.

' She didn't know what she'd do if that happened. She couldn't spend an eternity without Rhamiel. She'd barely been able to tolerate the last few days. Dark thoughts flickered across her mind, thoughts of things she could do that would get herself sent down below to join him. It would be fire and brimstone, but it wouldn't be all bad. At least they'd suffer their punishments together. But she pushed the thoughts away, going back to her humming. The more she dwelled on it, the more it ate her up inside. She ran a hand down across her stomach. If she spent too much of herself on her fears, there'd be nothing of her left.

She hummed and hummed, and the day went on and on. She'd almost dozed away into a nap when her eyes caught something in the distance, a tiny grey fleck against a horizon filled with clouds. Her hopes rose, but not by much; they'd been dashed to earth too many times before, by birds or leaves or even bugs. It was what came of being too eager. The more she pined, the bigger the hole inside her was to fill. But this time the spot didn't disappear. This time it grew larger, and she could see the light reflecting off of it, a shiny bright point below the clouds. No bird looked like that, and this time she knew it was no false hope.

"There he is," said Jana. She jumped to her feet, starting to run down the hill, only to feel a hand at her shoulder. Thane had stopped her, eying the skies with his customary suspicion.

"It's one of 'em," said Thane. "Go wait on the other side of the hill. Just for a minute."

"I want to see him," said Jana. "I want to be there waiting for him."

"Go," said Thane. "You know what the other angels are like. You know what happens if it ain't him. Get over there and wait 'til I say it's okay." He must have seen the pained expression on her face, because his voice softened, if only a little. "Just for a minute. It won't be long. You hear me yell, you run over to that barn and you hide inside."

She knew he was right, but every fiber of her being said to ignore him. The anticipation was too much, more than she could handle. She ducked around the other side of the oak, huddling against it, and she started to shiver all over. If he was back—if it was him—she could finally feel at ease. She could feel safe again. She could put aside her worries, focus on the baby, and trust that he'd be there to worry enough for the both of them.

She could hear the sound of wings beating as the angel came closer, a heavy thunk, thunk as they pressed against the air. Still Thane was silent, even though he must have seen the angel by now. But he'd never call out, not this soon: he was entirely too paranoid, and he'd wait until the last minute, even if there wasn't any doubt. Thane might be able to wait, but she couldn't contain herself. If it was some other angel, she'd never get away anyhow, not if they were this close. She screwed up her courage, poked her head around the tree, and snuck a peek.

There he was, his wings spread wide, his golden hair blowing up behind him in the wind. His eyes flashed a sapphire blue as the sunlight danced across them, and his armor shined with a silver hue. He glided down from up above, growing larger and larger as the seconds passed. He looked as weary as an angel could be, as if he'd been flying the entire while he'd been gone. She took a step out from behind the tree, a wide smile on her face, and then she ran towards his open arms.

"Rhamiel," said Jana. "You're back."

CHAPTER THREE

THEY WERE COMING TO THE camp, if one could call it that. It wasn't much of one; few of the servants had mastered any skills beyond scrubbing and groveling, and those talents weren't of much help out in the wilderness. Cassie led them back, as always. There were no trails and few landmarks, and it took a certain sense of direction to find the way through the woods with nothing but their guts to guide them. The servants tended to get lost, if left to themselves, and they always ended up walking around in an endless series of circles. That had been wise back in the tower, with its maze-like halls on every floor, but it didn't do them much good out in the wider world.

Cassie weaved them through a dense patch of trees until it opened up into a clearing, the place the servants had been living for nearly a week. It had been a nice spot while it had lasted: the forest was thick around it, and the canopy hid them from prying eyes up above. Dozens of tents formed a circle at the center, lined up around an ashy fire pit they'd dug to keep themselves warm at night. The tents didn't look like much, and they weren't: they'd been quilted together from worn blankets and tattered pieces of clothing, and they were supported only by sticks and salvaged pieces of wood. But they protected them from the elements, they were better than nothing, and for many of the servants they were even an improvement over their accommodations back in the tower.

Four small wagons were lined up in a row behind the tents, carved from wood with bicycle tires attached, thin enough to drag them between the trees. The camp's food supplies were stacked atop them: assorted meats they'd smoked or salted, a pile of potatoes, and jar after jar of pickled apples. Women milled around the fire pit, forming a protective ring around a group of children playing with the ashes. A few young men tossed knives at an old log, their aim shaky from inexperience as they competed for what honors they could. The rest of the servants sat huddled in groups, looks of shock across their faces.

The camp was in an uproar. The boys had gotten back first, and they'd already told everyone what had happened. The servants were used to death, and worse, but that was from the devils they knew. The giant red bubble creeping after them was something none of them could understand, and it was all the more frightening because of it.

At the edge of the camp stood a woman all by herself. Her auburn hair was hung low over her shoulders, and she wore a dark green t-shirt several sizes too big. It looked almost like a dress, hanging down towards her knees, but the servants were happy to wear whatever they could scrounge. Her eyes were puffy and red, and her face was scrunched up in worry. She'd cried out all her tears, and all that was left was to stand there choking on the sobs, waiting for a final confirmation of the news that had already come. She started shouting as soon as she noticed them approaching through the trees. "My son. Where's my son?"

Cassie had been dreading something like this ever since they'd started the walk back. Part of her had hoped the boy didn't have anyone left to miss him, even as the rest of her was disgusted that the thought kept popping into her head. Most of the people there were on their own, their loved ones long gone. It would have made things easier if the boy had been one of them. There'd be no one to tell, and no one else to suffer.

She knew his mother was the one who'd feel the real pain, and that nothing she went through could compare to it. But she'd already had to have this conversation dozens of times before, and it wasn't getting any easier. It tore at her insides when she had to break this kind of news, and it took away little pieces of her every time she did. She worried that if she repeated the experience too often, there'd be nothing left of her inside but scars and callouses.

The woman stood there with accusation in her eyes, waiting for Cassie to say something. Cassie knew her from back in the tower—Laura, one of the weavers. They hadn't talked much, not back then, but the crafters had kept their heads down and kept to their work. Cassie had spent most of her time in the tower focused on Nefta, and on trying to find some way to help Holt with his plans to bring it all down. She hadn't had time for friendships, or for anything else but her work. The detachment made it easier to lead the servants now that they were free, but it made it hard to connect with them in moments like this.

"Laura," said Cassie. "Your son. He's alive, we think." The woman's face brightened with reckless optimism, and Cassie's heart sank as she had to finish breaking the news. "But he went through the wall. He's still on the other side. And we don't know how to get him back."

Laura choked on a moan, her face gone crimson as she squeezed out what tears she had left. "You left him there. You let him wander away. You let him go inside that thing. And then you just left him there."

Cassie stuttered for a few seconds, trying to find the words that would express her sympathies, the words that would show how much it hurt her to lose someone she'd been responsible for. But she didn't get the chance. Laura screwed up her face and balled up her fists, and then from nowhere she launched into a mad dash straight for Cassie.

Cassie found herself defending against a barrage of slaps and punches, holding up her arms to block the assault as best she could. She could have stopped the attack in a moment if she'd wanted to. She'd had some training back in the militia camps, in fighting as well as in foraging. But part of her felt like she deserved it. She could think of all kinds of ways she could have avoided this. She could have kept a better watch on the children, or even tied them all up if she had to. She could have done something, anything, and maybe Laura was right to attack her.

The voice of reason within her said it wasn't true. There were more than a hundred of the servants in their camp, and no one could keep track of them all. It wasn't as if she had any help. Some of the older servants had lived outside, but they'd all joined the tower soon after the Fall. They didn't know what the world was like, not now, and she was the only one with any experience surviving outside. She was also the only one who knew how to give orders, rather than just take them. She'd tried to turn some of the others into deputies of sorts, though the slightest deviation from her plans was enough to paralyze them. But whatever she'd done, it wasn't enough, and others were the ones who'd had to suffer the consequences of her failures.

Her face stung from the slaps, but they were wild and unfocused, and she took as many of them as she could. It felt like a penance of a kind, the pain on the outside dulling away the pain within. When it got to be too much, she backed away, then managed to grab hold of Laura's arms and lock them into place. "I'm sorry," said Cassie. "I'm so sorry." She couldn't think of anything else to say. She stood there as Laura raged away, sobbing and crying and trying to wrench herself free from Cassie's grip. Finally she collapsed to her knees, and Cassie let go of her arms. Some of the other servants rushed up to comfort her, and after a few soothing words they managed to pull her away to the other end of the camp.

Cassie wiped at her face, and her hand came away with a few drops of blood. Not much, and she thought she deserved worse. She pushed her cloak back into place, straightened her hair, and headed towards the fire pit. The children were there, surrounded by their mothers, if they had them. They were playing a game with some wooden dolls the crafters had carved for them, and she intended to have a good, long talk with all of them about wandering off on their own. But she didn't make it there. She was interrupted by a voice from behind her, seething with resentment.

"You're not ready to lead, I should think." She looked over to see Herman, a satisfied smirk on his face. "Maybe if you'd been a few levels higher up in the tower, you'd have been made of sterner stuff." A group of servants crowded behind him, giggling and snickering. They'd all served angels from the top few floors in the tower, and now they formed a clique, bunking together in tents of their own and keeping themselves apart. They even called the others names, but only to themselves, and only under their breath. Cassie didn't like it, but there wasn't much she could do. Every time she tried to confront them, they just denied things and went back to it the moment her back was turned.

"This isn't the tower," said Cassie. "Look around you. We're all on the same level here."

"Some of us are, and some of us aren't," said Herman with a sneer. "A purebred doesn't lose his pedigree simply because he's dumped in a cage with the mongrels. The tower may not stand, but class isn't shattered so easily." He turned to his cronies and gave them a wink. "Perhaps it's time for the lower class to stand aside in favor of the upper. Perhaps things would be better if one of your betters were to lead."

"I don't want to lead," said Cassie. "I have to lead. There's no one else."

"So you say," said Herman. "So you've said since we started off from the city. It was always you, you, you. And yet leadership comes from the top. The head leads the body, not vice versa. And you were a few floors down from the top of the tower, if I recall."

"You think you should lead us," said Cassie skeptically.

"Me," said Herman. "Or one like me." He gave her a snide smile, exchanging knowing glances with the servants beside him. "It's not a matter of ego, dear. It's a matter of talent. And if you'd had any talent, I think you'd have made it to the top."

"Talent," said Cassie. "Let's talk about talent." She marched over to a log near the fire pit, a hunter's catch laying across it: a few dead rabbits, waiting to be prepared for the evening's dinner. She grabbed one of them by the legs and strode back over to Herman, dangling it in front of his face. "Skin it. Now."

"Skin the thing," said Herman, his nose wrinkling in disgust. "I can't, and I shan't. That's work fit for a crafter, I should think."

"Then grab a bow and some arrows, and hunt us up another," said Cassie. She slung her quiver from off her back, holding it out in front of him. "Go on. I'm not the best shot. I'll admit it. Let's go on a little hunt. You take point, and show us how it's done."

"Dear," said Herman, his face wrinkled up in smug disgust. "Leaders are meant to think. They can't waste their time with the trivialities of implementing the things they've planned. It's all about brains, and nothing to do with brawn."

"Then tell me where to go to find some deer, brains," said Cassie. "Tell me where to hunt. Show me the path. Lead me there." Herman sniffed, but he didn't respond, and she continued on, pressing the point. "Show me where to find water. Tell me how to purify it. Tell me the way out of the woods. Tell me how to make a tent. Or how to make a fire. Tell me anything useful. Anything at all." His cheeks reddened, but he stayed silent. She felt a twinge of satisfaction inside. She could tell by the fury in his eyes that he wanted to respond, and badly. But he didn't have anything to say.

"Leaders need to be down in the dirt with the ones they're leading," said Cassie. "You spent too much time around the angels. Getting things done isn't about ordering people around. It's about guiding them. You have to find the path yourself before you can take someone else down it."

She thought he was done, at least for now. He'd be back at it as soon as he found the courage, but the look on the faces of the others told her she'd won the day. She started to walk away, and then she heard him calling after her. "You were pledged, weren't you? To Nefta?"

She stopped in her tracks. He couldn't prove himself with action, so now he'd gone back to words, playing one of the parlor games the upper classes had obsessed over back in the tower. That was his arena, not hers. But she had to indulge him, or she knew he'd tell everyone she'd walked away out of fear. And no one would follow a leader who publicly gave into their fears.

"I said the words," said Cassie. "But those were the angels' rules, not mine."

"I was pledged, myself," said Herman. "To Jehoel. Something I took seriously. Something I honored. He treated me fairly, and justly." His lips curled into a sneer, and his chin jutted up into the air. "I, for one, would never have turned on someone who cared for me. Even if I'd had cause, I'd never have done it. It makes people wonder about whether you'd turn on them someday, too."

"He treated you like a slave," said Cassie. "They all treated us like slaves."

"They took us in," said Herman. "When the world was collapsing, they took us in. They gave us food. They gave us a home. They raised us up so high, when everyone else was down so low. I was always grateful for that. And we gave them our word. It's a bond, someone's word. If you don't know if you can keep it, you shouldn't give it quite so freely."

"They're the ones who tore the world apart in the first place," said Cassie. "Them. I didn't owe them a thing, and neither did you. Now get back to your tents." The servants all smirked at her, refusing to move. But she knew how to handle that. She lowered her voice to a growl, anger spreading across her face. "Get."

That was enough for men with wobbly spines. The show was over, and they scrambled apart. She knew they'd be back. Their kind were always filled with discontent if they thought there was anyone else above them. She didn't care about who was better than whom, but that didn't stop them from making her into an enemy she didn't want to be. She watched them scurry around the camp, reassembling in two's and three's whenever they'd gathered back their courage.

It was all so frustrating, and sometimes it made her want to cry. That was the worst part about being a leader: she couldn't cry, not anymore. She couldn't show any emotion, in fact, not in front of the others. No matter how scared she was, or how much someone had hurt her, or how much she wanted to throw up her hands, she had to keep it all bottled up inside. Anytime she let any of them see something like that, they just poked at her all the more. Some days she had to sneak out into the woods alone, bawling to herself in private just to let things out where no one else could see. And the more Herman schemed against her, the more she thought this might be one of those days.

As she watched Herman's clique spreading about, her eyes caught something behind them. It was something in the trees, just a little hint of movement down towards the ground. She heard the rustling in the leaves, and thought it must be an animal: a rabbit, or maybe even a deer.

But then it came closer, and she knew it was something else entirely.

No animal would brave their camp, not with this many people up and around. It couldn't be an angel; the trees were too dense to let them through without their wings slamming against the branches and giving them away. But there were still plenty of things that could be out there. Another person who'd stumbled onto their camp. Maybe a servant who'd found their way back, or maybe just someone hungry and desperate enough to wander into someone else's territory unannounced. Maybe a criminal, or maybe even the Vichies. Cassie drew her bow, slowly, and gave a short, loud whistle.

The other servants rallied around her with what weapons they had. Mostly that meant clubs, but some had knives or sticks sharpened into crude spears. They were servants, not soldiers, but there were enough of them that Cassie was sure they could put up some kind of fight. She motioned for them to spread apart, forming a pincer as they moved in towards the sound from both sides.

They inched towards the forest, Cassie at the very front. She couldn't help but smile a little at Herman and his cronies, hanging at the back of all of the others in relative safety. They were big and strong when it was so many of them against one of her. But put them in danger, and they huddled behind her for safety. It felt satisfying, even if part of her wanted to dump them all into the woods for a few days to try fending for themselves without her. But there were others to think of, and others to protect, and everyone was safer if they stayed together.

She crept towards the place she thought the sound had come from. She couldn't see anything unusual, just trees and brush. She paused, holding up her hand for silence. Then she heard it again.

It was closer, just a few yards away. She could see it, something moving around behind a bush, just glimpses of shadow in the green. It disappeared before she could see what it was, and then it flashed out of the bush and vanished again behind a copse of trees.

"It's a deer," shouted one of the servants. "I can see it. It's just a deer."

There was rustling again, and then more movement. Something stepped out from behind the trees, walking into the open. They had their first clear look at it, and the thing standing before them was no deer.

It was shaped like a person, though it had nothing else in common with a human being. It was the size of a child, and it could have been one, but for its skin and but for its eyes. Its skin was pure black, a void so colorless that if one caught it from the wrong angle, it made the creature look almost flat. Its eyes were worse. They were two shiny dots of red, fixed at the center of its head and glowing out of the blackness. The thing moved forward, but it didn't seem to walk so much as its limbs changed size, stretching and contracting as it moved. It was more shadow than substance, and the more Cassie looked at it, the more she noticed something else: it cast no shadow of its own.

"Mommy," said the thing.

It couldn't be, but there it was. Somehow the boy had come back from beyond the barrier, and whatever magic had been done to the world behind it had been worked on him as well. Cassie felt her stomach curl. She didn't know if the thing was child or monster, or perhaps a little of both. She nocked her bow, holding the arrow steady and pointing it towards the ground, just to the side of the creature. If the boy was still in there, she couldn't kill him, no matter what had been done to him. And she didn't want to think about what would happen if he wasn't.

"Son?" said Laura. She stepped forward from the frightened servants, walking hesitantly towards the creature.

"Stay back," said Cassie. "Keep talking. But keep your distance."

"Mommy," said the thing, and it took a few steps closer. The grass sizzled beneath its feet, leaving behind smoking brown footprints wherever it tread.

"Don't get near him," said Cassie. "Both of you, stay away from each other. We don't know what's happened to him."

"You're alive," said Laura. "What matters is you're alive. You're the only thing I had left. The only thing I cared about in this world anymore. And you're alive."

"Mommy," said the thing. "Come live with me." Its eyes glowed bright and its arms stretched apart, its limbs jerking as it moved. It seemed to smile, somewhere in the darkness where its face should have been, and then it sprinted towards her.

CHAPTER FOUR

THEIR EMBRACE LASTED ONLY A few minutes, but to Jana it felt like hours. She nestled there in the warmth of Rhamiel's arms, the safest place she could imagine and the only place she'd longed to be for days. Neither of them spoke. She stood watching the sun drift towards the horizon, resting her head against Rhamiel's chest as he ran his fingers through her hair. She didn't want it to end, but she knew she couldn't stand there beside him forever. Still, she waited as long as she could before breaking the silence between them.

"You were gone for so long," said Jana. "I was worried you wouldn't come back."

"Nothing could have stopped me," said Rhamiel. "My absence was a price, but one worth paying in the end. I found something. A place we can go. A place we may find friends, if we approach in peace."

"Friends of yours, or friends of ours?" said Thane. He'd disappeared behind the oak, but he hadn't gone far. He leaned against the tree, eavesdropping, and he looked entirely unenthusiastic about the prospect of trusting someone on Rhamiel's word alone.

"Enemies of Suriel," said Rhamiel. "And so friends of us both."

"More angels," said Thane. "You sure that's smart? I know you ain't all bad." He looked at Jana, and his eyes dropped to her stomach. "But you really think they're going to be happy to see her? Or her kid? He's the one y'all were fighting about up there. What happens if they try somethin'?"

"Then they face me first," said Rhamiel. "But they won't. I know some of them from before the Fall. They don't live the life they thought they would when we rebelled. The presence of the Son changes things. We wanted him to come back down here all along. That was the entire point of the rebellion, after all. And they'll want the change he offers, now more than ever."

"I don't trust 'em," muttered Thane. "I don't trust any of 'em."

"I trusted you," said Rhamiel. "You tore apart my home, my family, and my life. And yet I've trusted you alone with the two things I care about the most, in this world or any other." He put a hand around Jana, sliding it down to her stomach, caressing her and feeling the warmth of the child growing inside her. Then his eyes narrowed, and he looked across the farm towards the empty barn. "And perhaps I shouldn't have. You gave me your word. You were to be hidden the entire while I was gone. And yet here you are, out in the open, with nothing but a tree to conceal her from the skies."

"We were fine," grunted Thane. "And we were

hungry. Can't expect us to sit there for days in some rotten old barn with nothin' to do."

"Still, I trusted you," said Rhamiel. "Trusted you to care for her, and for my son."

"And I did," said Thane. "There's a big difference between me and them. All you had to worry about was me doing somethin' stupid. Those buddies of yours might hurt her just for fun."

"The ones I want us to speak to are beaten and broken," said Rhamiel. "They have no hope. They need her alive, even if they don't yet know it. The birth of the Son will reset things the moment it happens. It means the end of what we have now, and the beginning of something else."

"Kinda matters what that somethin' else is," said Thane.

"What will come, I cannot say," said Rhamiel. "But something other than this. The ones we'll speak to, they'll be quite eager for anything other than this."

"Where?" said Jana. "Where are they?"

"Close," said Rhamiel. He pointed off into the skies towards the direction he'd flown from. "A day's flight at most. In a tower of their own."

Jana's thoughts flashed back to the home she'd left behind, now turned to ash by a weapon she couldn't even comprehend. Part of her missed the tower, even if she hadn't been entirely happy there. It was what she knew, and she'd felt safer there than she did wandering around in the wilderness in an unfamiliar land, pursued by unfamiliar enemies. She wondered what this other tower would be like, and whether it would be anything like the place she'd left. She wasn't sure she wanted it to be. Then again, she wasn't sure she didn't, either.

"Are we going to stay there?" said Jana. "Live there?"

"The hell we are," said Thane. "We oughta just run. Just run and run, and never stop until he's born."

"We'll have to keep running until he's grown," said Rhamiel. "For years upon years. You know what Suriel planned. And you know how many angels are in his service. There's no cave so remote that we can hide from him forever. If Suriel finds him while he's a boy, he'll raise him as his own. He'll be no savior, then. Not with what Suriel would teach him. But I think they can help us, if we can but convince them to."

"And what if one of these guys gets the same idea?" said Thane. "Or has some other crazy thing pop into their head?"

"We have no choice," said Rhamiel. "We cannot survive alone. We'll be found, and we'll be killed. It's only a matter of time. Time we do not have. We must take a leap of faith." He flexed his knuckles, blistered and scarred by the heat from his fall. "Sometimes it's the only choice one has."

"Fuck it," said Thane. "I'll go get the truck ready. Better pray you're right, if you still do things like that." He trudged off into the distance, towards the rotting barn and the place they'd hidden their truck and all their possessions.

The two of them were left there alone, Jana gazing up at Rhamiel, and he gazing down at her. His wings fluttered in the wind, the feathers mussed out of place from the long flight. She had so many things she wanted to talk to him about. Conversations with him she'd had in her head, alone, while he'd been gone for so many days.

But there was one thing that nagged at her mind more than anything else. One thing that kept tormenting her, and one thing that only he could answer. She wasn't sure she really wanted to know. But she also wasn't sure she could keep going if she didn't. She screwed up her courage, stumbled over the words, and blurted it out.

"What happens?" said Jana. "What happens when you die?"

A look of concern crossed his face, and he bent down towards her, running a hand across her cheek. He paused, taking a moment to gather his words. "I will not die. You shouldn't speak of such things."

"Some of them died," said Jana. "Back there." Her thoughts were drawn to Suriel's compound and to the battle that had raged around it. Angels had been dropping right and left, slaughtering each other with ease. If they could die, then so could he. He might not want her to think about it, and maybe he was right that she shouldn't. But she couldn't help herself. She cared about him, and it wasn't as if there was anything around to distract her from her worries. There was no work, no play, no anything, and with nothing to focus her she couldn't control the places her mind wandered into.

"My kind can live on until the end of creation," said Rhamiel. He put an arm around her, and she burrowed into his embrace. Something about being next to him made her feel safe. He was big, and he was powerful, and he could have killed her or anyone else in an instant if he'd wanted to. But he was comforting her instead, a giant turned gentle when she was in his arms, and it was almost enough to calm the anxieties inside her. "Don't worry over things that need not come to pass. You could waste an eternity fretting over things that will never be. So calm your worries. I will not die."

They were nice words, and he might even have been right. Neither of them knew the future, and neither of them could control it. But she couldn't help but worry. She could see something off in the distance, something inevitable that would come between them, and she couldn't just shut her eyes and pretend it wasn't there. "Maybe you're right. Maybe you won't die. But I will. Someday I'll be old. Someday I'll die, and you won't."

"You cannot worry over things you cannot change," said Rhamiel. "You'll live a long and happy life. You'll be safe. I promise you'll be safe. I'll be by your side until the end of your days, and nothing will harm you. Not you, and not our son."

"I'm not worried about dying," said Jana. "I'm worried about where I go when I do." She didn't want to speak it. There was a fear in her that if she said the words, it would make them real. She knew that didn't make any sense, but she still felt it. She pulled together all her courage and started to speak her fears aloud. "What I heard…. What I heard was that I go up. Back to where you came from."

"I know you will," said Rhamiel confidently. "You needn't worry about that, I can tell you that much. I know people, and better than you might think. I watched over many, many different people over the centuries. I saw good, I saw bad, I saw everything one could imagine. You have a kindness to you. And an innocence. The kind and the innocent don't go down below. It simply isn't heard of."

"But when I go up," said Jana. "What happens to you?"

"Me," said Rhamiel. He shook his head, a grim look on his face. He was silent for an uncomfortably long moment. He stayed inside his thoughts, gripping her in his arms, and then finally he spoke. "It doesn't matter what happens to me. I fell, and by my own choice. I tainted myself. I threw away my paradise, and I don't deserve another chance at it."

"It matters to me," said Jana. "We'd never see each other again. That's what they say. I'll die, and you won't. And then you can't go up. You can't ever see me again. You'd live, on and on and on. And I'd have to go on without you. Forever."

"But you would be safe," said Rhamiel, his voice wavering. "And you would be happy. Even if you think you wouldn't. And even without me. I've been broken, though you cannot see it. There's a darkness inside me now." His eyes flashed a glistening blue, and he went quiet for a moment. She could see pain written across his face, and she hugged him close, resting her head against his chest. He ran a hand through her hair, and finally he spoke. "It's something we never really understood when we were up there. Fault, and sin, and corruption. We had none of it in us. But I understand it now. I was corrupted when I fell. You haven't been. And I won't let you suffer the fate I've brought upon myself. That judgment is mine to bear, and mine alone."

"You're wrong," said Jana. "You're wrong about yourself." She knew he was, deep in her heart. The angels had done many things when they'd fallen, and many of them were just as awful as what he was describing. But she'd never seen him act like any of the others. And she couldn't imagine that he ever had.

"You know why I care for you so much?" said Rhamiel. "Why I fell so hard for you, and why no other woman and no other angel would do?"

She didn't, not that she hadn't wondered from time to time. Rhamiel was near perfect, and he could have had anyone he'd wanted. Any of the female angels would have had him, and certainly any of the women among the servants. He'd said before that he saw something in her, something only one of the angels could see. A perfection of form, a perfection that matched the essence of who she was. But she could tell there was more to it than that.

"Why?" said Jana. "I know why I fell for you. I was so nervous even being around you. I didn't know what to do, and didn't know what to say. You were so high above me. And then you saved me from Ecanus. You came out of nowhere, and you saved me. I knew if you'd protect me once, you'd do it again. I knew there was good in you, no matter what the other angels were like. But I was just a servant. I wasn't anything. Why would you ever fall for me?"

"Redemption," said Rhamiel. "I've thought about it so much. About what drives how I feel for you. And it comes down to redemption, I think. It's the secret dream of any who've sunk to lows from which they can never recover. And especially for my kind. We whispered about it back in the tower sometimes. Some of us. But only among the ones we trusted. Some of us regret what we did. Some of us wish we'd made peace instead of making war. And I saw a hint inside you of what I could have been."

"But we're not anything like each other," said Jana. "That's what I don't understand. I was so low. Just a servant. All the other angels thought I was dirt. And you were so high up. Why love me when I'm nothing compared to you?"

"You can't even see yourself, can you?" said Rhamiel. He smiled, and kissed her forehead. "Calm your worries. Few can. I loved your innocence. I loved the way you hadn't been corrupted. Not like us. We served once, too, and I was in quite the same position that you were. A servant to others, tending to their needs before my own. We let our service wear on us, and in the end that tore us apart. But you didn't. You were like a mirror, showing me what I should have been. What I wish I could be still."

"You can be whatever you want," said Jana. "And I like you the way you are."

"I'm afraid I can't," said Rhamiel. He sighed, staring off at the sun dipping into the horizon. "I can't be what I once was. I can never have the innocence I used to. I did things. And the memories of them tear at me inside."

Jana shuddered, pulling away involuntarily. An image of Ecanus flashed in her mind, gleefully slicing away at the servants with his dagger. She wondered if he'd ever been like Ecanus, so twisted and cold. Rhamiel must have seen it in her face, because he jumped to reassure her.

"Not like that," said Rhamiel quickly. "Not like some of them. But I did unpardonable things, and others I watched were still worse. I watched all manner of things, and I didn't lift a finger. I told myself at the time that I couldn't have stopped them. We were an army, after all, and one warrior cannot stand alone against such wild pillaging. What I guarded for so many centuries, I stood by and watched them destroy. I know why my brothers are so tortured inside. I feel the same myself, though it hasn't warped me the way it has some of them."

He seemed so strong on the outside, so in command of himself and everyone around him, and she almost couldn't believe he'd be suffering that kind of pain within. It touched her, making her heart feel warm and sad all at the same time. She wanted to comfort him, to soothe away all the pain he was feeling. But she didn't have any idea how.

"Even the slightest sin was something new to us," said Rhamiel. "None of us were prepared to handle it. Back when we cared for you, we thought of you as mere children. Too simple to even know the good from the bad. Now I think we were the simple ones. We knew the good, but we couldn't fathom the bad. We'd never tasted it, and we didn't know what it took to deny ourselves the temptation. And if one has never known sin, they haven't known guilt, either. We dipped our toes in sin, but even the slightest bit was too much. We'd never felt guilt, and many of us couldn't handle it. The more it nagged at us, the more we reveled in violence to drive the pain away."

"You aren't like that, now," said Jana. "I don't believe you ever really were. Whatever you saw back then, you aren't like that now."

"That may be true," said Rhamiel. "But it weighs on me. It likely always shall. All there is for me to do is keep going. To try to be what I'd have myself be, instead of what I found I'd become. And just living with you is a redemption for me." He tucked a strand of hair behind her ear and ran his hand softly along her neck. "We never understood redemption. We thought we did, but how could we? We hadn't any sins, and hadn't anything to redeem ourselves from. But I see what it is, now. It's wanting to make yourself better, that you may do better for someone else."

Her stomach did a somersault insider her. It was what she loved about him more than anything else, more than looks, charm, or how the other angels deferred to him. It was the way he cared for her, the way he could be so soft even wearing a warrior's armor and bearing a heavenly sword at his side. But the better things were, the worse it would be when she was wrenched away from him. "But it ends. That's what frightens me. We have such a wonderful thing, and they're just going to snatch it away. And all because of something that's in the past."

"You mustn't think of such things," said Rhamiel. "You must think of the now. If you dwell on an awful past, or dwell on an awful future, you're dwelling in an unpleasant place. And why? This moment, this very one we're living, is one of the most wonderful I've seen in eons."

"I just don't think I can handle it," said Jana. "The two of us being separated. I'd be up there, and all I'd be able to think of was you. Of what was happening to you, and where you were. It's eating me up the more I think about it."

"Would you give up what's between us?" said Rhamiel. "If you knew it couldn't last forever?" A pained look flashed across his face, and he ran a hand through his hair. "Would it hurt you that much to keep going, if we were fated to be apart at the end?"

"You can't go up," said Jana. "But maybe I can go down. Maybe—"

He grabbed her by the arms, gripping her with a fury in his eyes. It frightened her, even though deep inside she knew he'd never hurt her. He must have seen it in her face, because his expression melted into one of intense concern. "Don't ever, ever say that. Never again." He pulled her close, holding her tightly, and after a few moments he began whispering in her ear. "I don't want you to even think it. You don't know what it's like down there. A soul lost in Lucifer's Pit. There's emptiness. Things that would torture you, and worse. Promise you won't do anything foolish. Promise you won't follow me, if that's where I'm fated to go."

"I don't think I can spend forever up there alone," said Jana. Tears welled in her eyes at the thought of it. She'd gone a lifetime without love, not from anyone. And not just the kind between lovers. She didn't know her parents, and she'd been nothing more than a slave for her entire life. She felt close to someone, finally, and it burned inside to think of being ripped away from him. "I just don't think I can do it."

"Promise," said Rhamiel firmly. "You're still my pledge, you know. You made a promise once. That you'd obey whatever orders I gave."

"And you promised you'd only order me to do what I liked," said Jana. "You promised you wouldn't be like the others. Like Nefta."

"I want you to remember something," said Rhamiel. "The next time your thoughts turn to something so rash. You think of me, and you think of giving everything up for me." He ran his hand across her belly, and she felt a warm kick inside her. "But wherever I go, whatever happens to me, he'll be up above in the end. He'll be your son, too, you know. Part of him is part of you now. Remember that. Remember that if you did the thing you're thinking of, you wouldn't just be following me. You'd be abandoning him."

She felt another kick within her, and her heart melted at the thought. She was being pulled in all directions at once, the needs of the ones she loved competing with needs of her own. Part of her still wanted to try some mad scheme for the sake of love. She wanted to know Rhamiel, and what it had been like for him to fall. But he was so certain that she shouldn't, no matter how strong the bond of love was between them. In the end, it came down to trust. She trusted him, and trusted that he wanted what was best for her. She knew that, even if she didn't know anything else. She didn't know what it was like down below, or what it was like up above. But if he needed her to stay with their son, then that was what it was to be.

"I won't try to go down there," said Jana. "I promise."

"And I promise you," said Rhamiel. "I promise I'll move Heaven and Earth to keep us all together. I'll storm the gates if I must, come what may. The ones up there are still my brothers, even after all that's been done. They may let me in, they may let you out, or they may kill me. But I don't think they'll have the stomach."

She heard an engine rev from down near the abandoned farm. Thane was sitting in the cab of their truck, a battered brown jalopy he'd rescued from the side of the road. It had once been a delivery truck, and the back was big enough for Rhamiel to ride inside with room enough to stretch his wings. Thane leaned out the window, shouting and gesturing at the two of them.

"Let's go, boys and girls," said Thane. "We're burnin' daylight. And I'm burnin' gas. So let's get this show on the road."

"Come," said Rhamiel, holding out his hand to her. "You've given me much to brood over. But we're together now, and now is what matters. So let us focus on the moment, and on the things we know how to change. And that means finding safety for you, and safety for our child."

CHAPTER FIVE

"Move," said Cassie. "Move!" She shouted at Laura, trying to pull her attention away from the thing that was rushing towards her. But Laura was entranced by it, by a second chance with a son she'd been sure she'd lost. She'd barely had any time to grieve, and now he was back. He'd changed into something else, but she didn't seem able to process it. She just kept stumbling towards the creature, her arms open to embrace it.

Cassie knew it was no boy, even if Laura couldn't accept that. She knew how much it must hurt her, and how impossible this all must have been to handle. But she couldn't endanger the rest of them for the sake of any one person. She was the leader, and she had to make the choices, no matter how hard they might be. She had to fight the thing, to stop it in its tracks before it did who knew what to the woman who used to be its mother. She already had the burden of letting one child wander from her flock; she wasn't sure if she could take the pressure of losing even more of them.

She aimed her bow at the thing, targeting its legs and praying she could cripple it before it went any further. One arrow whistled through the air, then another, and both of them found their mark. There was a little snap as each of them struck, poking out of the thing's leg but not slowing it down a bit. It just kept coming, a trail of smoke sizzling behind it wherever it touched the grass. The shafts of the arrows caught fire where they'd impaled it, blackening and snapping away as it walked.

"Mommy," said the thing. "Everything's better on the other side, mommy. There isn't any pain over there."

"There isn't?" said Laura. Her face was awash with confusion. One moment she seemed to believe it, taking a hesitant step forward. The next she'd grimace in disgust. The conflict within had trapped her there, unable to fathom the danger she was exposing herself to. It was admit the truth, that her son was gone and hope along with it, or cling to fantasy even if it was all darkness underneath. She couldn't decide which was worse, and couldn't force herself to choose between the two.

"Everything's the way it's supposed to be behind the wall," said the thing. It was just a few feet away from her, walking through a shower of rocks and sticks hurled by any servants brave enough to throw them. It didn't pay them any mind. It just kept heading towards her, its arms stretched wide. "It's wrong over here, mommy. It's all got turned around. But they're making it better. All you have to do is walk across, and it'll all be better. We did. And we're so much happier."

Cassie didn't register the 'we,' not for what it meant. At first she thought something had gone wrong with the boy's head, just another weird defect of personality to go along with what had happened to his body. But then she saw the shadows, creeping closer in the forest, and she could see what was coming if they stayed there much longer.

"Everyone run," said Cassie. "All of you. Don't fight. Just move." None of the servants did. They all looked around in confusion, eyeing each other indecisively. They clung to the safety of the group, and if the group wasn't leaving, then neither were they. Cassie had to resort to shouting, trying to project command in her voice. "Move!" That got them going. They obeyed almost out of reflex, streaming away from the thing and off into the forest.

"Laura," said Cassie. "Let's go." She grabbed her by the arm, pulling her along with the others. But after she'd dragged her a few yards, Laura jerked her arm free. The stalemate within her was over, for better or for worse.

"I'm going to stay and talk to him," said Laura. "Maybe I'll go see what it's like. On the other side."

"That's crazy," said Cassie. "Look at him." The thing's eyes were growing wider, bright red orbs that never let up their stare. And others were stepping out from behind the trees, other blackened child-sized things that each looked exactly like the first. The angels had done this to them, she was sure of it. And anything the angels had touched, Cassie didn't want any part of.

"He's my son," said Laura. "I can't just leave him."

"He's gone," said Cassie, grabbing her arm again. "I'm sorry. But he's gone."

"No," said Laura. "No." She pulled away and ran,

charging through the grass towards the thing that claimed to be her son.

"There was a plan, mommy," said the thing. "A plan for all of us. For everything. It's all gone wrong, and nothing's the way it's supposed to be. But they're going to fix it. The little angels, and the big, big man."

Laura ran to within a few feet of it, slowing down as she approached. Tears rolled down her cheeks, and she stumbled towards it, half-hesitant, half-ecstatic. She came to within a foot of the thing, paralyzed again by indecision at the last moment. All she could do was stand there in front of it, sobbing, too afraid to take the final step and enter its embrace. But the thing had no reluctance at all.

"Mommy," said the thing. "You're going to come and live with us now."

The thing wrapped its hands around her back, and her skin ignited into a dull blue flame wherever it touched her. She screamed, writhing beneath its hands and struggling to pull free. But it had her, and it wasn't letting go. The flames died away into blackness, dancing across her and spreading all around her body. Parts of her started to flicker and fade, slowly replaced with the same darkness that had consumed her son. The two of them seemed to merge together in their embrace, until finally there was nothing left of Laura but shadow. She turned back towards Cassie, cocking her head and taking a few tentative steps forward.

"You can come with us, too," said the thing that had once been Laura, staring out at Cassie with eyes like smoldering coal. "I can see it, now. What they were trying to tell us. Everything really is wrong. But we'll make you better. We'll make it all better. All you have to do is come with us."

"No," said Cassie. "No, no, no."

She turned and ran, fleeing off in the same direction as the servants. She didn't even stop to look behind her. She knew what was there; she could hear them, their feet crackling against the ground wherever they stepped. She weaved between the trees, trying to disappear among the leaves and the brush. But they were still somewhere behind her in the distance, thumping against the ground and corrupting everything they touched.

She came to a creek, winding through the woods in her path. She didn't know if it would stop them, but she could hope. She leapt into the water, splashing across it. The bank on the other side was high, too high for her to scramble up. She ran along it, looking for a way up to safety. She thought she wasn't going to make it, and her gut lurched up and down as she went. It felt like she was about to have an anxiety attack. Dying was one thing. She could handle that, if it came to it. But losing herself, losing the core of what she was? Turning into one of those things? That was something else entirely.

She was about to just run along the creek wherever it took her and pray for the best. But then she saw the roots to an old tree, snaking out of the muddy bank and forming the perfect handhold. She grabbed hold, dragging herself up the bank and rolling over the top to the other side. She turned her head to see a line of the things, standing there on the opposite side of the creek.

None of them were moving. The mud seared beneath their feet, and all of their eyes focused on her.

Their voices rose together in unison, sounding out as one and bombarding her from all around. "Don't run. Come back. We only want to help you. You can't see it now, but you will."

"Go to hell," said Cassie. For all she knew, they might have come from there already. But whatever they were, and wherever they were from, they didn't belong out in the world. "Just go back to your bubble and leave us all alone."

"You shouldn't be alive," said the things. "You shouldn't even exist. None of this was supposed to be. Everything was supposed to end. We're only trying to make things right. To put the plan back into place."

"I don't care about your plan," said Cassie. "None of us do."

"It wasn't our plan," said the things. "It was the Maker's plan. You think we're oh-so-very-bad. But there has to be an order to things. Someone has to do something if he won't. Nothing works out when we let the plan turn to chaos, not for anyone. But we'll make everything right. You'll see." A shrill sound hooted at her from all around. She wasn't sure what it was, not at first. But then it clicked. Laughter. Or whatever passed for laughter among the things, a nasty, horrible sound that made her cringe just to hear it.

She couldn't stay there any longer. She ran forward through the woods, not waiting to see if they'd follow. She couldn't hear them, and though she turned her head a few times to check, she didn't see anything following behind her. Maybe they could cross the water, and maybe they couldn't. Maybe she just wasn't important enough to be worth the chase.

It was ten minutes, maybe twenty, and then the woods began to thin. She could see open space up ahead of her, and she heard voices. The servants. They were standing there in a crowd out in the open, a hundred or so people huddled together in a ball of feverish chatter. They were all completely ignoring the woods and looking at something, though she couldn't see what it was. She felt nervous, and the stress was almost more than she could bear. Those things were still back there, and now the servants had stumbled into something else for her to worry about.

She stepped out of the woods and saw what they were obsessing over at once. It was easily visible off in the distance, spiking up into the air and touching the clouds, black and gloomy and forged from metal.

A tower.

A tower still standing, and presumably still occupied.

The thing was jet black, a thin pillar stacked atop a fat mound of metal that made up its base. The base looked gooey, scraps soldered onto scraps with angelic swords until they'd crusted into a foundation sufficient to hold the rest of it in place. Looming above it was a shaft of smooth metal, story after story stacked atop one another until it clawed at the skies themselves. The top of it was all spires, branching out in all directions. Some extended horizontally, and from them hung pods, strange fruits borne from a stranger tree.

Everything around the tower was waste. Dunes of

ash rolled atop old buses, overturned and left to rust. Flocks of grackles scavenged here and there, pecking at the dirt for scraps, their feathers dyed grey with the ash. Skeletons of a few old buildings rose through the ash, but mostly they'd been leveled, leaving only piles of debris to mark where they'd stood. The tower looked down on it all, but there wasn't an angel to be seen.

"Home," said Herman, awe in his voice. "Another home."

Murmurs rose from the servants, and looks of joy flashed across their faces. Most of them hadn't taken to life outside, and they hadn't taken to Cassie as their leader. They stumbled towards it, some of them breaking into a run out into the wasteland surrounding the tower, and Cassie had to shout at the top of her lungs to herd them back into some semblance of order. "Hey! Get back here! Get down!" The runners stopped, but they weren't happy about it. They slowly made their way back to the group, hovering at the edges and gazing at the metal oasis off in the distance.

"We're not walking into that death trap without knowing what's inside," said Cassie. "There could be angels in there. There could be who knows what. And how long before that red bubble creeps its way over here? We'd just be running all over again. Assuming whoever's inside the tower lets us leave."

It looked like home to some of them, but she had to stop them from being drawn like moths to the flame. And not just for their safety, but for her own sanity. If they went in, she'd be going in after them. She knew herself well enough to know it was true. She felt bonded to them, responsible for them no matter how foolish their years as slaves had made them. Their dream would wisp away to reveal a harsh reality beneath, just as Laura's had. They'd need someone to help them, then, and if it wasn't her, it wasn't going to be anyone.

But she knew it was no small thing to ask of herself. If she went inside another tower, she wasn't sure she'd survive it. She'd only managed to live under Nefta's thumb because she had a job to do. A task to focus on, and the hope that if she held out long enough, she'd bring it all down upon her tormentors' heads. There'd be no one coming to the rescue if they went inside this tower. It would be home, forever, and she wouldn't be coming back out unless she found the way herself.

"Angels," said Herman. His voice rose as he called out to the crowd around him. "They could protect us. Keep us safe from the things we just saw. We could stop running, and start living once more. Back to the routines that made us who we were. Back to the life your friends took from us."

"Back to slavery," said Cassie. "Back to wondering whether you'd survive from one minute to the next. Whether you'd drop a glass, or say the wrong thing, and someone would chop your arm off for it."

"Back to the top," said Herman. "Back to luxury. Back to the devils we know, instead of the devils we don't."

Some of the servants clapped in response to his words, and there was even a cheer or two from the back. The most vocal support came from Herman's cronies, but she'd lost the rest of the crowd as well. She could see it in their eyes. They weren't even listening, not really. They were just staring longingly at the tower, waiting for someone else to decide what they were to do. But it was clear what command they all wanted to follow, if only someone were brave enough to give it.

"We're going," said Herman loudly. "Whether you like it or not. The angels helped us once before. And they'll help us again, provided we're sufficiently apologetic. We can redeem ourselves. Become the servants we weren't before. Loyal and obedient. Worthy of their love."

"You really want to go back to that?" said Cassie, addressing the crowd. "To a life under their thumbs? To tyranny?"

"To safety," said Herman. "To protection." He looked back and forth around him, shouting and waving his arms. "Can she protect us from those things we just escaped? She hasn't any way to fight them. She doesn't even know what they are. She just let Laura die. And she'll let the rest of you die, too, if they come back. They could be on our heels even as we speak."

He marched off in the lead, heading into the wasteland by himself. He went slowly, pacing himself and cocking his head every few steps to make sure he didn't go too far on his own. But one by one, his followers went after him. And soon the trickle turned into a flood as the herd made its collective choice and they threw their lot in with him.

Cassie sighed to herself, watching them all stream back towards the hellish life she'd fought so hard to save them from. She couldn't decide what to do. What she really wanted was to wander away on her own, to try to pick up the pieces somehow and rebuild what she'd once had. But she didn't have a life out there anymore.

Her life from before the Fall was long gone. She missed it, but she couldn't bring it back. The funny thing was, she hadn't even realized how wonderful it was until it was gone. She'd felt restless, a wanderer going from job to job to avoid having to narrow her choices down to the point where she'd no longer be able to change them. She'd thought she was miserable, bored with her life and with the drudgework she had to do to earn enough to survive. But now she knew better. She hadn't even had a taste of misery back then, and no minimum wage job could compare to life as a slave to the angels.

She'd been alive with possibility, even if she hadn't known it. She'd simply been too young to realize how good things were, and how bad they could get without a social order to protect her. She'd dreamed of being a writer, a dancer, an artist—but she'd never settled on one path. She thought she'd have all the time in the world to work things through and chart a course for the rest of her life. Part of her thought she could have it all, as silly she'd known as it was, and have every single one of her dreams at once. And now those dreams were dead, along with nearly everyone else from the world they'd all left behind.

The scraps that were left of her life paled in comparison to what she'd lost. She had friends she'd met from after the Fall, assuming any of them were still alive. Holt and all the other fighters she'd worked with long ago were probably wandering around somewhere, still trying to kill off the angels. But she'd never find them. She knew what things would be like if she threw up her hands and left the servants to their own devices. She'd just end up farming turnips in some dirt patch, struggling to survive without any reason left for surviving in the first place.

Taking care of the servants had given her something. A purpose, a reason to keep on going. It was frustrating at times, intensely so. But still, it made her feel better about herself. There had been moments of loss, but moments of hope as well. She thought back to the good parts, the memories that sustained her when things went bad. The time she'd marched through the rain for miles looking for a sick little girl, finding her under an old highway bridge and leading her home. The time she'd followed a rumor in search of a doctor, coming back with a vial of freshly cultured penicillin just in time to save a man's infected leg. She'd helped people countless times, and every time she did it kindled a little fire inside her that kept her going no matter how dark the world became.

And what she'd done had salved the guilt she felt for tearing down the servants' home, even if she knew in her head that it was something that had to be done. Now they were rushing back to the fate she'd delivered them from, and it made her wonder if any of it had been worth it. Maybe some people were too domesticated to ever live in the wild, off on their own with no one else to guide them. She'd lost so many of them, and they were all so scared.

But going into another tower was mad. They'd probably all be killed, and she would, too, if she went along with them. Still, she didn't see any other choice, not one she thought she could live with. So she trudged into the waste behind them, picking up her pace to catch up with Herman.

They walked in silence between the small hills of dirt and debris that pocked the landscape around the tower. Whatever this place had been when man had ruled it, it was nothing now. The soil was dead, and she couldn't see any plants or any other signs of life. Herman didn't say a word, and he let her edge ahead of him as they walked, taking the lead once more. She could tell he didn't want the responsibility, no matter how much he claimed to. All he wanted was the credit, without having to bear any of the burden that came along with it.

They inched closer to the tower, and Cassie kept an eye behind them, watching for any signs that the shadowy things had pursued them. They hadn't, at least as far as she could see. Everything was empty, and everything was silent. But then something caught her eye, something moving just a bit ahead of them.

It was a person, and a human one. Whoever it was, they were wrapped up in a brown cloak, bound tightly enough around them that there couldn't be any wings beneath it. Cassie stopped in her tracks, Herman beside her, and the servants bunched up behind them. They were too close to flee if there was a threat, and all Cassie could do was draw her bow and wait as the figure approached.

It was a woman; that was clear when she was a few dozen feet out. She strode confidently towards them, standing before the servants and blocking their path. Auburn hair wisped out around her head from beneath her cloak, and she stared at Cassie and Herman with fierce brown eyes and a smirk on her face. She cleared her throat and nodded back towards the tower. "You shan't be welcomed if you simply walk up to the door unbidden. I'm afraid the Seraphim have little tolerance for unwanted intrusions."

The servants huddled together in front of her, waiting for Herman to say something. But he looked just as frightened as all the rest of them. It was one thing to talk of leadership; it was another thing entirely to stand up and lead. And this woman was something unfamiliar, something strange. She could be dangerous, and her voice was strong, the kind they felt compelled to listen to. None of them knew how to respond, not until Cassie broke the silence.

"I know you," said Cassie. It had taken her a minute, but now she had it. She knew exactly where she'd seen the woman before. "You were Holt's friend. Part of his cell. We met, back in the tower. Before they brought it down. And then back in the city. In the subways." They hadn't been around each other for long, and she had to rack her brain for the name. Holt had sent Cassie messages for nearly a year, and he'd talked about his team almost as much as he did his battle plans. Then the name popped into Cassie's head, bubbling up from somewhere in the depths of her memories. "Faye. You're Faye."

"That's right," said Faye. "I am, indeed. A friend of your friend, and thus a friend of yours. And as a friend, I must warn you. You've grave dangers in front of you if you approach this tower alone. But you need not face them by yourselves. Let me lead. Let me show you the way."

She was right about the danger, and Cassie knew it.

If she had any choice, she wouldn't approach the tower at all. It was all danger, no upside. And she'd already lost so many of them. So many of the people she'd tried to help. She'd bond with them, begin to feel connected to them, and then they'd get snatched away by the dangers hovering all around. And here was someone offering to take away a little of that burden. To lighten the load that was constantly bearing down on her shoulders, threatening to crush her beneath it.

An inner voice still nagged away at her, telling her that no one could really be trusted, not the angels, not the servants, and not even friends. It told her she was safest if she just held onto the reins despite the stress. Something seemed off, something about the way Faye smiled. Her expressions looked different somehow than the way Cassie remembered them. But she hadn't known her for long, and she hadn't known her well. Besides, this was a world that changed people. Cassie knew that, more than anyone else. Faye seemed to sense the inner conflict. She leaned in close, taking Cassie by the hand and pointing her towards the tower.

"I can help you," said Faye. "I can arrange a safe entrance." She smiled a warm, friendly smile, her eyes aglow with possibilities. "Trust me, and I can assure you we'll each be of help to the other."

CHAPTER SIX

THE THING IN THE DISTANCE looked more tree than tower, but it was clearly an angelic work. At its base was a billowing mound of dark metal, soldered together by the angels' swords. Atop it was a thick central pillar, with girders branching out from its sides supporting blocky black pods suspended in the skies. They were rooms for the angels who'd lived there, though now both sky and ground were barren and empty of life. The only sound for miles around was the grunting of a beat-up old delivery truck trudging its way across the sands surrounding the structure.

The truck stopped far from the tower, its engine dying away and leaving the wasteland in total silence. Thane stepped out of the cab, and from the back came Rhamiel, lifting Jana in his arms and lowering her gently to her feet. No one came to meet them: not angel, not servant, and not anyone else.

"I don't think anyone's here," said Jana nervously. "Maybe we should go back." The tower was so dark, and so lifeless. It didn't look like a home, not one she'd like to live in, and not even a place she'd like to visit.

"Afraid, are you?" said Rhamiel, with a wry smile. "I thought you bold, when I asked you to take the pledge."

"I'm not afraid," said Jana indignantly. She looked up at the dark, jagged metal spiking out from the tower, and at the cavernous entrance gaping at the bottom. She couldn't see anything inside no matter how hard she peered at it. It was a blackened void, and she shuddered at the thought of what might be skulking there in the darkness waiting for them. "Perhaps I am. Just a little."

"Boldness is best seasoned with a pinch of wisdom," said Rhamiel. His voice turned somber, and he took a few steps forward. "But they are my brothers, the ones who live here. Whatever they might think of you, they are my brothers. They will honor the pledge and what it means."

"What if they're the wrong kind of angel?" said Jana. "What if they're friends with Suriel?"

"They would be off bowing and scraping to him already if they were," said Rhamiel. "I met some of them outside the tower before I turned back. They were in a sorry state. But they were friendly, and eager to parley. They spat Suriel's name when they spoke it." He craned his neck to look above them at the pods looming away in the distance. "They must be up there, now. Their ranks will have been depleted. Uzziel's army took most of the Seraphim with it. There will be plenty of room for all at the top."

"What'd they say about us?" said Thane. He slung a rifle over his shoulder and wedged two pistols into his belt, then stood beside Rhamiel, eying the tower with suspicion. "And what'd they say about the kid?"

"I didn't speak of you," said Rhamiel. "Not then. I thought it imprudent. Dangerous. She wasn't by my side. She wasn't where I could protect her. I couldn't take any chance that one of them would beat me back to her. I simply couldn't." He strode confidently towards the entrance, a vast yawning opening at the tower's base, and he held a hand back towards Jana. "Come. Stay behind me. Take my hand, and don't let go. It may be dark, but there are darker places, and more dangerous ones."

She grabbed hold of it and followed him into the darkness. Rhamiel led the way forward, using his sword as a torch to light the way. "Stay close," he said, squeezing Jana's hand. "Stay behind me, where I know you'll be safe." She clung to the warmth of his grip and held on tight. Walking alone through a tower was frightening enough, but this place was so black she'd never find her way out on her own. She couldn't see in front of her, not past his wings, and Thane kept up the rear. All she could see was what they passed on their sides, illuminated by the flickers of fire from Rhamiel's sword.

Mostly what she saw was trash. The place was empty, the servants long gone. Garbage had been dumped about in piles, and the filth had been left to fester. There were heaps of ragged clothing, shattered dishes, and empty crates. Now and then she'd catch a whiff of a rotten smell, or step in something that squished beneath her shoes. She was glad she couldn't see it, but she expected they'd all be wiping their soles clean before they left.

"You have wild goose chases up in Heaven?" said

Thane. She couldn't see him, but she could hear his voice from somewhere behind them, following along in the darkness. "Ain't nobody here. And if they are, we don't wanna talk to 'em."

"Uzziel's army was a host of warriors," said Rhamiel. "Many faces I knew were among them, but many were not. The Seraphim weren't all warriors, and many would have stayed behind. Some of them survived the cherubs' treachery. The two I spoke to said there were others. They must be here somewhere, and we must find them."

"Fine for you," said Thane. "What about us? They look at us and all they see are dogs. Dogs they need to put down."

"They will be as desperate for help as we are," said Rhamiel. "I would not bring her here if I thought it unsafe. I would not bring my child here. Trust in that, at least."

"I don't trust anybody with wings," grumbled Thane.

"You will have to," said Rhamiel. "I brought us here to search for a miracle worker, and not just for my own purposes. This entire journey, all you could speak of was your lost friend. She was felled by a miracle, and only a miracle worker can help her. You've only two choices: you may come with me and search for someone who can help, or you may speak to Suriel on the matter."

"I don't trust your miracles, neither," said Thane. "Not after what your friend did to Faye. Not after how he got into her head." He kept muttering, but it died away into an indistinct griping that only he could hear. They inched along in the darkness until finally they came towards the center of the floor. Jana looked up, expecting to see all the way to the very top. She would have been able to, if she'd been back in her old home. But the creators of this tower had opted for their own design.

A metal ceiling ran just a few feet above her, as far as she could see. Here and there were wide holes, big enough for an angel to fly through, and against one of the walls she could see a staircase leading up. It was nothing like the tower she'd lived in, with its vast open space all the way to the top. These angels had traded room to fly for floor space, and from the volume of junk they had to weave through it looked as if this floor had once been crammed with servants.

They headed towards one of the staircases, the vast floor silent and empty. "Mind the steps," said Rhamiel, sweeping away a bit of debris from the stairs with his boot. He pulled his wings in tight around his back; the staircase wasn't meant for angels to tread, and at his size he could barely squeeze through to the next floor. Jana kept close, his hand her lifeline in the dark. Her nerves grew more frazzled the further they went. She knew that the higher up one went in a tower, the more dangerous things would become.

"Got a lot of ground to cover," said Thane. "And this place could have a lot of floors. Could be here all day if we walk. Maybe you head up top, take a look, and come back down and let us know how things are. Maybe talk to some of your friends before they have to meet us in person."

Rhamiel turned behind him. He saw Jana's body quiver with fear, even in the dark. He felt her hand squeezing his, and he dismissed the suggestion at once. "We must stay together. I will not leave her side, not down here in the darkness. The two of you would be defenseless on your own."

"Defenseless my ass," muttered Thane, noisily rattling his rifle. But bravado aside, he followed along behind, letting Rhamiel take the lead. Jana felt a rush of relief; she didn't want to leave his side, not in here. If he'd flown away on his own, her nerves might have forced her to take flight herself.

They ascended more floors than Jana could count. They all looked the same to her; just pile of junk after pile of junk. If angels still lived here, they'd let their home turn to a dump. She wondered what they'd be like, and if they'd really be friendly. They were so inscrutable with their motives, and the ones she'd known had whiplashed back and forth between moods so often she wouldn't be surprised no matter how they were received.

She turned her head to the side as they walked, stopping in her tracks. There was someone there, someone standing in the dark and watching them from the shadows. She let out a loud, involuntary shriek, wrapping her arms around Rhamiel's waist and holding on tight. He whipped his sword from side to side before him, sending waves of light all around. Then he saw it, too, standing next to one of the walls in silence.

She'd thought it had moved, but it was just a trick of the light. As the shadows danced back and forth across its face, she could see what it truly was: one of the cherubs' golems, an artificial servant gone silent without its masters to guide it. Its back was ramrod straight, its arms hanging down to its sides. But its head was bowed low, and its eyes were dark. She could see her reflection in its bronze skin, and the image of Rhamiel's sword shined across its chest.

"It's nothing," said Rhamiel, putting an arm around Jana and pulling her close. "Just a construct. No threat to us, and no help to the ones who lived here. Not once its true masters left it to rust."

"Maybe he's sleepin'," said Thane. "We fought enough of these things at Suriel's compound. I don't want one of 'em sneaking up behind us."

Rhamiel answered with a quick swipe of his sword, lopping off one of the golem's arms. It clanged to the ground, but still the golem didn't move. With another swipe, the golem's head rolled away. All that was left was an empty husk standing at attention, its wounds dripping trickles of molten metal along its skin.

"He's no threat to us," said Rhamiel. "Not without someone to guide him."

They made their way ever upwards, and each floor was more of the same. All were empty, save their piles of trash and a few more scattered golems. All the golems had gone silent, and none objected when Rhamiel removed each of their heads in turn. Finally they came to something different, something that made Rhamiel tense his wings and wave a hand to stop them.

There was a light ahead of them, a stack of logs lit with flame heating a copper pot strung up above the fire. They could see a shadowy figure standing beside it, tending to the pot and stirring it with a long spoon. Rhamiel squeezed Jana's hand, and then he let go. She was gripped with fear until Thane came up beside her, pulling her behind a pile of wooden crates. Rhamiel advanced on his own, and after a few steps it was clear why. The figure stepped away from the pot, and wings fluttered along behind him. It was an angel, stalking between the piles of junk and holding a tray of food in his hand.

Rhamiel crept towards him, the angel blithely ignoring him as he went about his business. Jana peeked around from the crates, watching as he went nearer. The angel was so much smaller than Rhamiel, barely bigger than she was. But he was still dangerous. All of them were. If she'd met him alone, he could have overpowered her in an instant. She tried to focus on Rhamiel instead, rolling his sword around in his hands as he approached. It calmed her worries to know he was there, throwing himself in between her and the threats that lay ahead of them.

Rhamiel's boot crunched against something on the floor, and the angel snapped his head to the side. "Who?" said the startled angel. He dropped his tray with a clatter, then reached to his side for a sword that wasn't there. He was thin, nearly to the point of emaciation. His eyes were sunken, with deep black furrows beneath them, and his scars were heavy, covering virtually every inch of his skin. Jana had never seen an angel look like that, not in all the years she'd served them.

He was sickly and weak, worse so than any angel she'd ever known. Their scars aside, even the smallest of angels in her own tower had been pictures of health. This one's feathers were loose on his wings, falling away in patches all across them and leaving only leathery skin beneath. Even his demeanor was unlike them. He cringed before Rhamiel's sword, his head dodging back and forth in a panic at the sight of him.

"I don't think we're acquainted," said Rhamiel, pointing his sword towards the floor. "Or if so, my memory fails me. I am Rhamiel. I was one of the guardians before the rebellion."

But if the angel heard him, he didn't wait to listen to Rhamiel's entreaties. Instead he turned and ran, bolting towards a hole in the ceiling and leaping up into the next floor. Rhamiel started to follow after him, but thought better of it. Instead he stepped back towards Jana, welcoming her into his arms as she rushed towards him from the darkness.

"That's who's gonna help us?" said Thane. He walked over to the angel's fire, leaning in for a whiff of his cooking. "That guy's what's left of your warriors? Suriel's gonna eat him up."

"He's a seraph, if an unhealthy one," said Rhamiel. "He's been neglecting himself. But there will be others. Perhaps we can rouse them to action. Inspire them to become what they were. Perhaps—"

He was interrupted by loud thuds from all sides. They could see them in the shadows: more angels, dropping to the floor through the holes up above. The alarm had been sounded, and they found themselves very unwelcome guests. The new arrivals were bigger than the one who'd fled before them. They all had swords, not of fire but of metal. They wore pieces of armor, all earthly ones, and the craftsmanship wasn't up to standards of old. None of the pieces matched, and their surfaces were covered with cracks and trickles of hardened metal. Whoever had forged them had been learning the skill anew, and they'd have a long way to go before they could call themselves armor smiths in public.

"Brothers," said Rhamiel. He pulled Jana behind him, lifting her up with one arm and depositing her next to Thane and the cooking fire. "We come with dire news, news of the fate of the Seraphim. We come seeking help. We come—"

"You come to die," said one of the angels, the top half of his face pristine and handsome, the bottom half a mess of reddened blisters. "You've no invitation, and no excuse for barging into a home that isn't yours."

"I spoke to some who said they were your brothers," said Rhamiel. "I told them of my presence, and told them I'd return."

"We've heard no such thing," said the angel. He nodded towards Jana and Thane, his tongue slithering across his permanently chapped lips. "And we've certainly heard nothing of any new servants. Whether we shall keep them or whether we shall kill them, I cannot say. But I know what's to be done with you." He nodded towards the others, and the angels closed in on them from every side. They were bigger and stronger than the one who'd fled, and their eyes glowed orange in the darkness from the flickering of the fire.

"A moment," said Rhamiel. He sheathed his sword, knocking away the logs beneath the cooking pot with a sweep of his foot. In an instant the room was plunged into darkness. Jana clutched his hand, as tightly as she could, and she felt a reassuring squeeze in return. It lingered for a few seconds, and then she felt his hand slip away. Her stomach dropped, and she backed away until she felt Thane somewhere behind her. Then she crouched down to the ground, hoping the other angels were as blind in the darkness as she was.

She heard the clang of metal, swords battering against armor, and then the sound of weapons clattering to the ground. She heard groans and muffled shouts, and wings jostling back and forth in the dark. She heard a nasty crunch, followed by screams of pain, and then more pounding and thudding. Finally it all went quiet, other than a few soft voices whimpering incoherently. Then the room was suddenly aflame again.

Rhamiel stood there, sword drawn and waving slowly at his side. All around him on the ground were battered angels, the worse for wear for choosing conflict over diplomacy. They had scars, but most of those were from the Fall. A few of them had acquired new wounds from their scuffle with Rhamiel: some were nursing twisted limbs, and one was clutching his hand to a busted nose, blood trickling through his fingers as he struggled to breath.

"Told you she'd be safer outside," said Thane. "Should have gone up and talked to these guys first. Told you."

"As I told you she'd be safer with me," said Rhamiel, kicking at one of the angels hunched over by his feet. "Now is the time for explanations. Why do you skulk around in the dark, drawing weapons against a fellow seraph?"

One of the angels looked up at him, angry and

impudent despite his position. "You invade our home, without invitation, and you demand to be treated as a guest?"

"Invade?" said Rhamiel. "You have no doormen stationed to greet your visitors. In point of fact, you have no door. I came seeking succor from my brothers in time of need, and they strike at me instead. I spoke to two of you first, and I was led to believe I'd be welcomed. And yet here I stand, before a battered militia posing as an army."

"My words cannot bind this tower, and neither can those of any of my brothers," said the angel. "And they should not have claimed to, if they spoke to you outside. Their lips were loose, and their promises vapor. You should have spoken to the one who leads us now. You should have spoken to Ambriela."

CHAPTER SEVEN

SHE LOOKED ALMOST LIKE SHE was crying, with what the scars had done to her face. Splotchy red blood vessels covered the surface of her skin, spreading down her cheeks from the bottom of her eyes. The rest of her face was porcelain pale, and from beneath her armor another network of vessels crawled upwards across her neck, merging into a pink mass around her throat. Her hair was dark black and hung down over an angular silver battle suit, her shoulders covered in epaulettes fringed with golden tassels.

She sat in a high-backed silver chair, sipping at a glass of wine. Rhamiel, Jana, and Thane stood before her, waiting in silence for her to speak. But she greeted her guests with an aloof air of indifference, staring off into the distance without acknowledging their presence, finally speaking only after Rhamiel gave an insistent cough.

"Rhamiel," said Ambriela. She turned to face them, setting her wine on a tray held by a nearby angel. "Handsome Rhamiel, now homeless Rhamiel. Come to beg for room and board during his exile. It would cheer me to think of it, if you hadn't emptied out my home as well as your own."

The room was far from empty, at least as angels went. There were more than a hundred of them, many lounging about on couches or chairs of their own. But something was off, at least compared to the tower Jana had lived in. The space they were in looked like a ballroom, a vast chamber designed for parties and celebrations. The ceiling was covered in elaborate fresco paintings, depictions of crystal towers and golden fortresses surrounded by wisping clouds. Light shined inside the room on all sides from wall-sized windows made of colored crystal, bathing them in a rainbow that shifted along with the sun.

But while there were scores of angels there, they weren't nearly enough to fill the room. It could have held hundreds more, and what angels were left in the tower looked none too healthy. The few at leisure were in fine shape, but they were the exception. Emaciated angels trouped around in plain brown attire, rushing back and forth between their idle betters with trays stocked with food and wine. The stronger ones seemed to revel in their position. Now and then one of them would snap at their angelic butlers, or slap away a tray if a cringing seraph came too close. It was just as things had always been for them, and only the species of their servants had changed.

"Ambriela," said Rhamiel. He stepped towards her, standing in the center of the room atop a seven-pointed star, its thin lines of gold melted into the scorched metal that made up the floor of the tower. He leaned forward in a polite bow, then rose back to his full height. Jana and Thane followed close behind, sticking to Rhamiel's side as every eye in the room fell upon them. But Rhamiel just smiled and kept up a friendly front. "It's been some time since we've spoken. Time enough for hostilities to brew, I fear."

"Hostilities, no," said Ambriela. "Suspicions, yes. Our former leaders chose to follow the banner of Uzziel. The banner of your tower. Of your battle." She waved a dismissive hand around the room at the remnant angels of her tower, such as they were. "And here I am, left to pick up the pieces. We've space, that I can't deny. But you cannot stay here." She cocked her head to catch Jana peeking around Rhamiel's wings, and she gave her a cold smile. "Perhaps your companions may, if they'd serve. We've many here who'd be eager to take them on."

"One is pledged to me already," said Rhamiel. "The other would make a poor servant, I can promise you."

"Pity," said Ambriela. "But in that case, you must go, and you must do it soon. This is no place for you, and certainly no place for them."

"We come not merely to beg for refuge," said Rhamiel. "We come for help, and to rally the Seraphim. All of them. To continue the fight against Suriel, as best we can, for as long as we can, with as many soldiers as we can."

"Soldiers?" scoffed Ambriela. "There are no soldiers left among the Seraphim. You yourself saw to that. We have singers. We have chefs. And we have smiths. But soldiers? You'll find none here. Look around you, Rhamiel." She nodded towards the other angels, seated around the room on chairs and cushions or rushing about with trays of food and drink. None looked fit for combat. The majority of them were female, and the males who were left were sickly and thin, far from the stuff warriors were made of. "Any seraph with an interest in battle left with all the others to fight in the cherubs' war. Not a one of them has returned, and the news that's reached us is dire. Where do you expect to find soldiers when you've reaped them all and tossed them into the thresher?"

"You'll be soldiers soon enough, and you've no choice in the matter," said Rhamiel. He sauntered towards her, and Jana followed as closely as she could. She tried to hide in his wings as Thane marched behind her, enveloping her in a little bubble of safety between the two of them. She could still see angels leering at her from all sides, peering with eyes alit with curiosity. She didn't like it, not a bit. She could tell from their faces that they coveted her, and that pledge or no, this tower was desperate for any servants it could find.

"We'll be soldiers?" said Ambriela. Rhamiel stopped a few feet before her, and titters came from angels all around, mocking his entreaties. "We'll be nothing of the sort. We'll be here, comfortable in our own home. And we won't be a part of a war with Suriel or anyone else. We've chosen neutrality, and we won't be swayed from our choice. It's the only sensible course in a war whose outcome one can't change no matter what one does."

"What was it you were up above?" said Rhamiel. "No soldier, and no guardian. I seem to recall it was something else."

"I worked miracles," said Ambriela with a thin smile. It twisted the blood vessels on her face into a red cobweb, creeping down along her cheeks. "I was quite good at them, in fact. Now parlor games are all the use that's left for that particular talent. Water into wine, and by the bucketful." She rolled her glass in her hand, lifted it to her nose for a sniff, and then took another drink.

"We've more use for your talents than you can imagine," insisted Rhamiel. "It's a miracle we ask for, and to best an archangel, we shall need one. We lack men, we lack weapons, we lack everything. We need you, and we need your help, if any of us are to survive."

"Another thing we lack," said Ambriela, "is servants. Proper servants." She snapped her fingers and an angel rushed to her side, holding out a tray of candied fruits. He cringed before her, his eyes dipping low and avoiding so much as a glance at her. "We had many of them before the angels of your tower came. We were induced to slaughter our servants with promises of a better way. We traded them for constructs, little golems that were to work for us night and day. That was the promise, at least."

"Uzziel's promise, perhaps," said Rhamiel. "And one I was not a party to."

"He was a fool, and so were we," said Ambriela. "The Cherubim promised him the perfect army. They promised us the perfect slaves. Machines with no interests of their own. But their makers had interests, even if they did not. They were a sham. They turned on us. Mere days after the cherubs had left, their creations turned on us."

"As did Uzziel's own golems," said Rhamiel. "And as did the cherubs."

"Some simply stopped where they were, never to move again," said Ambriela. "Others stalked the halls, falling upon us in our sleep. Jolting us with electricity, or stabbing at us with strange weapons. Tearing apart our property. Pulling at the very foundations of the tower. It was a night of terror. There were three deaths, and scores of injuries. Now all we're left with are rusted golems, and no one else to support us. Seraphs make poor slaves, you know. They chafe against their manacles, no matter how loose they may be."

"We'll all be in manacles if we let Suriel reign," said Rhamiel. "Servants, one and all. We cannot let him rule, Ambriela. You must know that."

"We answered the call of war against Suriel once," said Ambriela. "A foolish choice. And the fools who made it are dead, slain on the battlefield by the ones who promised them victory laurels. Treacherous cherubs, who came to our home and tore apart our way of life." She spat the words as she said them, and her lips curved down in disgust. "We won't make that choice again. We've committed to neutrality. We shall neither aid Suriel nor oppose him. We shall simply stay out of his way."

"No one can stay out of his way," said Rhamiel. "He won't be content with the rule of man alone. Suriel sees himself not as king but as god. He won't be content until every creature on this world is his slave."

Ambriela sighed, rolling a piece of fruit between her fingers and studiously ignoring Rhamiel. She waited, letting the seconds tick by, and finally she spoke. "Do you remember how you came to rebel? I certainly do, myself. I had no quarrel with the Maker, and I was content with my service. Many of us were. But I was seduced. Seduced by sweet words dripping from the mouth of a handsome angel." She looked up at him, her expression a mixture of admiration and suspicion. "We were in the Ethereal Gardens, a group of us, breathing life into plants that had long since died away. And who do you think came upon us?"

"Someone like me," guessed Rhamiel. "One of the guardians, perhaps."

"Not a guardian," said Ambriela. "A warrior. Fresh from a battle in Lucifer's Pit, the blood of some foul creature staining his tunic. He spoke to us of things he'd seen. Of the freedom of the creatures that lived down there, and how they simply did as they pleased. No rules, no labors, no obligations. They were old words. Old treasons, recycled from the first rebellion. But we hadn't heard them in so long, and they had a force to them, coming from one so strong." Her eyes went up and down Rhamiel's armor, taking him in from head to toe. "Coming from one so powerful."

"It's not the power of the speaker that matters, but the power of their words," said Rhamiel.

"They're one and the same sometimes, for the listener," said Ambriela. "Who was I to decide the prospects of a rebellion? I wasn't a fighter then, and I shouldn't have let myself be drawn into someone else's battles. It was foolhardy. And now look what's become of me." She ran a finger underneath her eyes, and a tear dripped along the swollen arteries running down her face. "I've learned something, at least. To let others fight their battles for themselves, no matter how their tongues drip with honey. We've stained ourselves with corruption, and we can't change that. But I won't be made a fool of twice."

"I seek no fools as allies," said Rhamiel. "You can ignore a war, but you cannot expect it to bypass you when you find yourself in its path. I was no partisan of rebellion, though I fought under its banner. It was one side or the other. I knew that, and I chose the side I thought best. But I chose, and so must you."

"And how, Rhamiel?" said Ambriela. "How came you to rebel, if you had no heart for it? If you felt that both sides were comprised of fools or madmen, why draw your sword at all?"

"I wasn't even there when the warriors fomented their discord," said Rhamiel. "I heard grumblings over the years, of course. I was in and out of Heaven. All the guardians were. A decade or two protecting one of our charges, and then another decade spent back home in prayer and song. I was off on an island, watching over a sick little boy who hadn't much longer to live. The years went, his time came, and I brought him up where he belonged. But everything was different. The place was in an uproar."

"It was like that for years," said Ambriela. "A pot filled to the brim with water, and they simply let it boil and boil."

"We wavered," said Rhamiel. "My friends whispered among themselves, going back and forth in circles, but it was the Loyalists that flipped us more than anything.

They wouldn't bend, not on anything. They wouldn't even let us petition the Maker. Wouldn't even let anyone talk to him. They demanded loyalty, and demanded that it be absolute. The Son could question the Maker, and yet we couldn't even speak to him. Even a hint of disagreement and they wanted us tossed out of Heaven for all eternity. It drove so many of us away, the fanaticism. In the end, we were simply tired. Weary. The Loyalists made us pick sides, and so we did."

"You chose the wrong side, it seems," said Ambriela. "And look where it's landed you."

"And if I hadn't chosen," said Rhamiel, "I'd have been tossed out of Heaven all the same. But we are where we are, and I am where I am. We cannot change our past. We can only change ourselves. We were about others, once. And we were happier then, servants though we might have been."

"Slaves," said Ambriela. "We were slaves." She stared at Jana, then at Thane. "And have you slaves of your own, Rhamiel?" It made Jana feel uncomfortable every time she looked at her. There was something cold in her eyes, something predatory. She looked at them like they were pieces of meat, just waiting there to be devoured. Jana clutched at Rhamiel's feathers and ducked behind him, but she could still hear Ambriela, and she knew her stare was still upon her. "They huddle under your wings for safety. Do you prod us to fight for our own benefit, or for theirs?"

"They are something more important," said Rhamiel. He tensed up and put one hand behind him, offering it to Jana. She took it, eagerly, and felt him squeeze against her palm. "Something worth dying to protect."

"Something important?" said Ambriela. "I'd thought they were merely your servants when you first arrived." Jana snuck a peek, only to see Ambriela's eyes peering at her over the mess of blood vessels beneath, and all of the rest of the angels staring at her just the same. She worried they were about to come for her, to rip her away from Rhamiel's side and turn her into a servant once more. But Ambriela just smiled and turned her gaze back to Rhamiel. "Pets, perhaps? You talk of change, but you certainly weren't one for humans, once. Not after your fall. In fact, I recall a quite different Rhamiel than the one I see before me today."

The words stung Jana's ears. Rhamiel had told her that he'd been corrupted by his fall, and that he'd joined the other angels in their newfound sin. But he'd never said precisely what he'd done. Ambriela clearly knew, and that hurt a little all on its own. This woman knew things about Rhamiel that she didn't, that he wouldn't even talk to her about. It was hardly surprising; he was thousands of years old, after all. But it was still painful, knowing he'd kept something from her. Now Ambriela was toying with her, and her comments couldn't have been directed at anyone but Jana. She knew the angels' penchant for verbal games, and she was more than familiar with how they played them.

The surface of a sentence was whatever it was, but there could always be some hidden meaning beneath. The angels delighted in toying with one another, hinting at things without actually saying them. They played their games with their servants, too, making up the rules as they went. Jana knew that all too well. Once a pair of seraphs had wandered into the kitchens unannounced, and then they'd simply stood there, watching from the middle of the room as Jana and all of the rest of the servers prepared their meal. They'd gone on and on about how much they admired one of the dishes, about how fresh it was, and how they'd soon be carving it to pieces.

She'd been too young to read anything more into their words than what they'd said. She'd paid extra attention to the vegetables she was chopping, so sure that the angels would be carefully tasting every bite. The others had known better. They knew the games fallen angels played, and they were on edge until the two of them finally left for the dining room. The servers followed, trays in hand and fear in their eyes. And when they'd come back, one of them was missing: a little boy named Abe, about her age and one of her closest friends. No one would say a word about what had happened. He'd simply disappeared, never to be spoken of again, and she'd never looked at the angels quite the same.

Ambriela had the same tone in her voice they'd had, a soft mockery that never admitted what it was. She'd said Rhamiel wasn't one for humans, and she must have meant something by that. Jana leaned out from behind Rhamiel's wings, trying to read what she could from the expression on Ambriela's face. Sometimes the angels gave things away with their emotions, dropping hints about the nature of the game as they played it. Ambriela just watched her, and it took everything inside Jana not to turn away. It didn't help. Ambriela knew now that she was curious, and it was all the bait she needed to smile and speak to Jana directly.

"He was a slaver, of sorts," said Ambriela, leaning aside in her chair to get a better look at Jana. "Did he tell you that? I can't imagine he would have. The towers needed servants from the moment we built them. And not all of us could be counted upon to bring a servant home undamaged."

Jana let out a little gasp. The corruption of the angels had taken many forms, but she'd never imagined Rhamiel doing something like that. Maybe she just hadn't wanted to. Slavery. She'd been called a servant, but slave was just as apt a name, even if she'd only started to see that near the end. The tower had relied on a constant stream of new servants as replacements for the ones the angels had worn through. They'd been mostly volunteers by the time Jana was there, but there'd been a time when the servants had to be forced inside and forced into their labors.

And Rhamiel had been involved somehow, if Ambriela spoke the truth. She wondered about her own parents, and how they'd come to the tower. She didn't even know them, or what had happened to them. Perhaps they were slaves once. Perhaps they still were somewhere. She'd never know even if they were, and she wasn't sure she'd recognize them if she saw them. She felt Rhamiel's grip tighten, but she pulled her hand away. Her mind was whirling, and it was all she could do to keep herself steady. She'd gotten so close to him, close enough to bear his son, a mingling of life that meant they could never truly be separated again. But it had all happened so quickly, a rush of love that had washed away reason and left only passion to guide her. She'd thought she'd known his character from his actions, but now she wasn't sure she truly knew a thing about him.

Ambriela leaned forward in her chair, smirking as she eyed Jana through the gap in Rhamiel's wings. She'd heard Jana's gasp, and she could see the horror written across her face. "He was ruthless, dear. Whatever he is now, he was ruthless towards your kind in the beginning. How many of them would you say you rounded up for the towers, Rhamiel? Dozens? Hundreds?"

"Thousands," said Rhamiel quietly, his eyes dropping to the floor. "Thousands at least, and perhaps more."

"He was one of the first," said Ambriela. "One of the first to see that your kind could be more than mere toys. That we could make some use of you instead. He pushed us to do it, in fact. A cruel thing, though. You were free creatures, once, if stupid ones. And now what has he turned you into?"

"They're alive," said Rhamiel. "Perhaps they're no longer free. But they're alive."

"Were," said Ambriela. "I'm not sure many remain, not after the cherubs' promises. But you saved them from our slaughters, at least for a time. You gave them life, such as it was. I suppose there was some good in that."

"Ambriela," said Rhamiel, his voice dropping to a low growl. "Enough games, and enough talk of old scandals. You think it impossible to defeat Suriel. I know it's true, else you'd take up arms despite your words. But there is hope, yet."

"Hope," spat Ambriela. "The drug of choice for fools. It blinds one to reason, and blinds one to the truth."

"The girl," said Rhamiel, raising his wings into the air and revealing Jana for them all to see. He put an arm around her and held her close, looking around the chamber, daring anyone to challenge him. "My Jana. She's with child."

"All the more scandalous," said Ambriela in mock horror. The room erupted in whispers and soft laughter, and every angel around them bore a leer or a smirk on their face. "Lying with one of them, only to raise its bastard offspring as your own. You've gone soft in the head, dear Rhamiel. Even a guardian wouldn't have done such a thing, not in days of old."

"I said she was with child," said Rhamiel, his voice firm. "I did not say she was with a child of man."

The room was silent for a moment, then urgent chatter rose from all around. Ambriela scoffed, her face contorted in disbelief. "You cannot think what you hint at. You cannot think it could be yours."

"It is a child of my own loins," said Rhamiel. He scanned the room, speaking loudly and cutting off the nervous whispers around him. "The Son is coming back. Something has happened up above. Things up there must still be in turmoil, political or otherwise. But this much is clear: we have not been abandoned, as Lucifer was to his Pit. The Son is coming, for one reason or another, and he is coming here."

Ambriela leaned forward in her chair, her expression oscillating between suspicion and wonder. "If what you say is true… And I do not concede that, Rhamiel. I do not concede it for a moment. But if what you say is true, what can it mean?"

"It means things will change," said Rhamiel. "What changes they will be, none of us can say. But it means we have a chance once more."

"A chance at what?" said Ambriela.

Rhamiel turned behind him, looking down at Jana, and then he turned back. "A chance at redemption. At building something new instead of living in a pile of ash of our own making. Perhaps the Maker would even take some of us back, if we truly wanted it. Stranger things have happened, and darker souls than ours have passed through the gates of Heaven. You all know that."

"Human souls," said Ambriela, musing to herself. "And not without quite a bit of contrition first. We'd be slaves once more if it came to pass. And even if we wanted such a thing, would the Maker take us? Or does he send his Son to cast us into Lucifer's Pit, down with all the rest?"

The chattering began anew, and all around the room angels were sneaking anxious glances at Jana. They didn't stare at her, not anymore. They didn't seem to have the courage to. There was something new in their eyes, something more than the scorn she'd felt when she'd first arrived. It was something she'd never seen on the face of an angel, not when they were looking at her. Something she wasn't even certain angels could feel, not until that very moment.

It was fear.

"I do not believe it," said Rhamiel. "The Maker could have cast us down there long ago. He could have done it when he quashed our rebellion. And you know well why the Son came, the last time he was born."

"To purge the world of guilt for its sins," said Ambriela. "To clean the slate. To fix a broken world, and put it back on course. Until the day he'd come once again to reap the harvest he'd sown."

"We weren't part of it, then," said Rhamiel. "His redemption. But back then, we didn't have any sins of our own to purge."

"Perhaps this is the reaping we were promised," said Ambriela. "The very thing we rebelled over. He wouldn't come, not then. But now he's seen the error of his ways. It's all been pointless. We took up arms because he wouldn't end things, and now he's come to end things all the same."

"Perhaps," said Rhamiel. "Or perhaps things are just as they were before. Perhaps it is not mere ending, but the beginning of another cycle. Another birth, and another redemption."

"You think things will be different this time," said Ambriela hesitantly. "That this time it won't just be man he comes for. That we'll start anew along with all the rest. That having bitten the apple, we'll spit it out and overcome its taint?"

"I hope we will," said Rhamiel. He turned, looking back at Jana, huddling there behind him. "All I have now is hope."

"What do you ask of us?" said Ambriela. "We've our neutrality to think of. It's a foolish thing, to cast one's lot on such murky promises."

"A month, at most," said Rhamiel. "That's all I

require. Enough time to birth my son into the world and see him to safety. All I ask is shelter until then. And a minor miracle. A glamour, to hide him from Suriel's eyes."

"A glamour," said Ambriela. Jana didn't know what they were talking about, but Ambriela must have caught something of her ignorance from her expression. "A sort of spell, dear. A mask. To hide you from prying eyes, and make you appear to be something that you aren't to those who'd harm you."

She held up a piece of fruit to the air, then waved one of her hands before it. And suddenly what was in her hand was a leg of mutton, juicy, steaming, and freshly cooked. She waved her hand across it again, and the mutton had turned to a handful of fat brown nuts. She smiled, closed her hand around them, and shook it in the air. When she opened her fingers, there was the fruit again, just as it had always been.

"Just a trick, girl," said Ambriela. "One that would require me to expend great effort and energy, if I did as you asked. And one that Suriel would surely see through."

"In time," said Rhamiel. "But his servants would not. And I don't need long. I'll protect my son once he's come. Trick or no, it's a simple choice for you, I should think. Suriel wants the child for his own, and that is something none of us can tolerate. A son of mine might redeem you. But a son of Suriel's would surely press his boot against your necks."

At that Ambriela snapped her fingers, and a seraph rushed to her side. He leaned down towards her, his withered wings twitching behind him. "Review the abandoned quarters. Find something that can be made suitable without too much work." He jumped to attention, launching himself down the hallway as fast as he could run. Then Ambriela turned back to them, her eyes ablaze with curiosity.

"You may stay, for a time," said Ambriela. "Long enough for us to ponder what's to be done about the news you've brought. And long enough for us to speak among ourselves. In private." She smiled at Jana, nodding to a half-dozen angelic servants assembled at the entrance to the chamber. "We'll grant you quarters to live in, for now. But do not make yourselves too comfortable. You've brought opportunities here, but also danger. And all of us need to think on what's to be done about it."

CHAPTER EIGHT

THE SERVANTS TRUDGED THROUGH THE wastes, following Faye as she led them towards the base of the tower. The wind blew gusts of dirt around them, and they had to step gingerly to avoid jagged chunks of torn up old cars or iron girders ripped from the insides of demolished buildings. But despite it all, their faces had brightened and the collective mood had turned to one of optimism. Cassie could hear them whispering among themselves as they walked, speculating about what the angels would be like or about how the new tower would compare to the old.

"Is this really safe?" said Cassie, stepping over an overturned telephone pole as Faye led the way forward. "And is it really wise?"

"Of course it's safe," said Faye. She waved her hand dismissively, keeping up a brisk pace without even looking behind her. "These angels are quite unlike any you may have met before. Quite friendly once you've been properly introduced, and quite the hosts. Perhaps they'd even take you in on a permanent basis." That last comment was louder, broadcast to all the servants nearby. "They've room enough. I'm sure of it. Why, I've even spoken to them on the subject. They're in want of servants, and they've a different attitude on the matter than many of their brethren. They're kinder masters than you may have been used to."

"Kinder," said Herman. He turned to the servants, crowding behind Faye and hanging on her every word. "I told you. I told you all. There's a home for us yet, and it isn't out in the trees or down in the mud. It's up in the skies where we belong."

' "Up top," said Faye. She smiled, her voice warm and friendly. "Everyone would be up top. It's a wonderful place." She pointed up at the hundreds of black pods hanging from the tower's sides. "Much safer than it is out here, that much is certain. Only a seraph can protect you from the things that roam about outside the walls of a tower."

Cassie looked on, watching the murmurs of delight spread as Faye spoke. She didn't know her, not well. But there was something so wrong about what she was doing. Faye had been part of a cell dedicated to killing off the angels, one by one and at whatever the cost. Cassie might not have known Faye, but she knew Holt. Fighting the angels had been all he'd ever talked about. Faye had followed him, and now she was pushing the servants back into the very serfdom she'd worked so hard to free them from.

Something must have changed her, something she'd gone through. Cassie knew how that could happen, more than anyone. Maybe Faye had seen the servants in the same way she had: as slaves freed from their bonds, but not from their habits. They knew a certain kind of life, and they didn't know any other. She'd tried so hard to change them, but they were old dogs with no interest in the new tricks she was trying to teach them. Maybe it was all just a fool's errand. Maybe when someone spent so much of their life living as one thing, they were too invested in it to ever be anything else. Too comfortable with their routines, and with too little energy to drag themselves up mountain after mountain of changes even if they'd be happier people at the end of the journey.

Or maybe it was something else. She knew she had to get Faye alone, and the two of them had to have a talk. Faye was eager to help the servants back into the comforts they'd left behind, such as they were, and Cassie needed to know why. Maybe these angels were different. It was at least possible. She knew the angels hadn't always been the fallen things they'd now become.

"Faye," whispered Cassie in a low voice. "Is this some kind of guerilla operation? And where's Holt? Where are the others?"

"Why, they're inside," said Faye. She smiled, beckoning Cassie forward and picking up her pace. "Everyone's inside. You'll see. Simply follow along, and everything will make sense once we arrive."

"But the angels," said Cassie. "Is Holt going to kill them? What are we going to do?"

Faye stopped, turning around and locking eyes with Cassie. There was an intensity to her stare, a strength of will that made Cassie reflexively look away. But she forced herself to look back, no matter how uncomfortable it felt. She'd learned all about eye contact while leading the servants; the simplest way to get them to do what she wanted was often just to match their eyes in open challenge. It was a primal test of strength of sorts, and Faye just smiled when she managed to pass. "Do you trust him? Your Holt? For this is a matter of trust. Do you have trust in the ones you're looking for?"

"Of course," said Cassie. She'd worked with him for years, and she knew what kind of man he was. He'd do what he thought was right; she didn't have any doubts about that. "Of course I trust him. What kind of question is that?"

"Then trust," said Faye. She waved a hand at the servants behind them, their eyes agog at the imposing structure looming up above. "There isn't any other choice, after all. These followers of yours are in no mood for suspicions. Their path is chosen, and all one can do is help them along the way."

Cassie thought back to the first time she'd gone into a tower, back in New York more than a year ago. She was scared now, but then she'd been terrified. Holt had bribed a caravan of Vichies to smuggle her inside, telling them she was an angelic sympathizer who wanted to spend the rest of her life basking in their reflected glory. It wasn't that implausible a story; despite how far the angels had fallen, some still loved them. Some even worshipped them, biblical injunctions aside. Holt had paid off the Vichies, and then a fat man with a white bandana and a mustache dyed to match had shoved her into the back of an old ambulance stuffed with luxury goods, bound for the tower that stood where a city once had.

The trip there had been just as nerve wracking as actually meeting an angel. The Vichies were thugs to a man, and they were as volatile as their masters. She hadn't been allowed to bring any weapons, and it wouldn't have mattered if she could have. There were more of them than there were of her, and every time the fat man leaned back to leer at her from the driver's seat she'd thought of all the things he could do to her if he wanted to, from beatings to rapes to simply killing her and dumping her body on the side of the road.

But leers were all she'd suffered, at least until the tower. The convoy had made it inside, and she'd been tossed into a pen with all the other new servants, waiting for days until one of the angels decided what use they wanted to make of her. There hadn't been much of a plan, other than for her to get as high up in the tower as she could. Holt wanted her to meet servants, important ones, and to befriend anyone who might help when the time came to smuggle in the rest of them.

The first part had turned out to be much easier than the second. She'd sat in her pen for a few days, waiting in darkness, constantly brushing against the arms or legs of the others who were packed in with her. Now and then a torch drifted towards them, and someone would come to either drag one of them away or pack someone else in along with them. No one spoke to anyone in the pen, no one listened to them when they called for food or water, and no one cared a bit about them. They were just livestock to everyone else in the tower, bleating to themselves in the dark as they waited their turn to find a place in the society the angels had built.

And then Nefta had come.

She'd appeared from nowhere, two servants at her back carrying torches to light the way through the bottom floor of the tower. Her face flashed through the bars of the pen, half of it mangled and scarred from her fall, the other half beautiful and pristine. The others in the cage had cringed and cowered, piling into the corners to avoid drawing her attention. Nefta hadn't said a word. She'd just nodded to one of the servants and pointed a finger at Cassie. Then they opened the door and pulled her out.

Cassie knew at once why she'd been chosen, and why Nefta had left the other servants to whatever their fate would be. She wasn't the only one who'd seen Nefta's face. But she was the only one who hadn't looked away.

She'd been terrified then, and she was just as scared now, even though this time she knew what the inside of a tower was like firsthand. They were coming to the entrance, a cavernous opening that revealed only darkness beyond it. It was quiet, and that was strange. The other tower had never been silent, not for a moment. Fulfilling the whims of a tower full of irritable fallen angels was no easy chore, and only an army of servants could keep them anywhere close to happy. But she couldn't hear anything from inside, and she couldn't see anything, either. This tower was more dead than alive, and she wondered whether there were really any angels in there at all. She certainly wouldn't complain if there weren't.

They all stopped short of the entrance, waiting just

outside of the shadows. All of them but Faye. She wasn't afraid, and didn't even seem to care. She just kept on walking, stepping into the darkness alone.

For a moment, Cassie couldn't see any sign of her. But then a light flickered in the distance, the flame of a torch, and it slowly drifted back towards them until Faye emerged again into the sun. "Come. There's no bottom here. Not anymore. You'll be living at the top, every one of you. It's dreary at the beginning, and dark. But once we've gone a few stories up, you'll all see the light."

"Where the people who matter are," said Herman. "Where the power is." He looked happier than he had in months, and only the wrinkles from his permanent scowl gave any sign of his usual ill temper.

"You'll be one of them," said Faye. She waved the torch at the entrance, sending a shower of sparks into the air around her. "And all you need do is follow me."

She turned away and stepped back into the darkness, her torch bobbing up and down before them. The servants hesitated, and for a moment Cassie thought they might change their collective mind. It was a momentous decision, and the fear among them was palpable. Fear of what waited up above, and fear of what waited out in the wilderness. It was an impossible choice, and a cruel dilemma for people who weren't much equipped to make choices at all.

"Let's go," said Cassie. She started walking away, pulling her cloak around her and trudging back into the wastes. "Let's just turn around and go. We'll run, as fast as we can. We'll get away from here. Let the angels stay to fight their wars. Let them fight those things from behind the wall when they come. We'll be long gone, somewhere else."

"No," said Herman. "No, we shan't. You've led us too long, and led us poorly. It's time for another to take the reins. The way for us is up. Back to where we came from, and back to where we belong." He put his chin up and strode into the darkness, following the light of the flame and disappearing after it.

That was enough for the other servants. There was another moment's hesitation, and then the choice was made. They all rushed forward, chasing after the dimming light before it flickered away into nothing.

"Crap," said Cassie. "Crap." She was left there all alone, standing just outside the entrance. It was now or never. The longer she stayed there, the greater the risk. She was just outside an angelic tower, and she wouldn't stay undiscovered for long, especially not once the servants started talking to any angels who lived there. If she wanted to leave, she had to run, and fast.

Her body was screaming at her that she was in danger, and that she shouldn't stay for even a moment longer. But as much as she wanted to run, she couldn't. The guilt gnawed at her more than the fear, and the pain of it was far greater. She thought of the debt she owed to the servants, and how they'd suffered from the war she'd waged. They wouldn't be here if it wasn't for her, and if she left, she'd be abandoning them to whatever would come.

And she thought of Jana, who should have been off in a college somewhere reading books and planning her future. Instead she was naive to the point of helplessness, one of the first generation of humans to be raised in a culture that deemed them good for nothing but servitude. Cassie had led her up to the top on Nefta's orders, tossing her in among the angels as chum. Then she'd just dumped Jana in the outside world with a group of people the girl didn't even know and hoped for the best.

She'd relied on Holt to take care of Jana, doing what she would have done herself if she hadn't had the other servants to manage. If he was really here, then maybe Jana was, too. She looked up above at the gloomy black pods hanging there and blotting the skies. Even if there were angels up there, there had to be some plan. Holt had to be up to something. And if Faye was here, then he had to be there, too. There was only one way to find out. It was either take the chance, or wander off and live by herself for the rest of her days.

She didn't think she could make it as a hermit. And she'd never been afraid of the unknown before: she'd managed unknown jobs, indefinite dreams, and the life of a double agent in an angelic tower. It couldn't get much worse. So she screwed up her courage, locked her eyes on the torch far ahead of her, and ran towards the sound of the servants chattering among themselves as they followed along behind it.

She nearly tripped a half dozen times as she went, stumbling on things she couldn't even see and flailing her arms to keep her balance. But still she ran, chasing after the dwindling ball of light. It headed upwards, rising towards the ceiling, and then it disappeared. The room was plunged into total darkness, but she could still hear them. The servants, mumbling to themselves as they walked. The sound grew louder and louder, and finally she slammed into someone, nearly knocking them both to the ground.

Whoever it was made it back on their feet, though not without a stream of profanity. She still couldn't see the light, but she stuck close to the servants, pressing a hand against one of their backs and going wherever they did.

Where they were going was up. There was a staircase there, and once she'd gotten to the top she could see the light again, leading them still higher. She pressed forward, mingling among the servants until she was closer, until she could actually see. And there was Faye, the torch lighting up her face, completely expressionless as she walked them all forward.

Faye led them up one staircase, then another. The floors all seemed to blend together into an endless procession of steps and darkness. Cassie let herself fall towards the back of the group; she didn't have any light of her own, and she was sure some servant would get lost along the way if she didn't watch them like a hawk. But they huddled together in a tight mass, clutching one another for safety and security, and this time none of them were foolish enough to wander off alone.

Finally they came to one of the middle floors, one important enough to merit windows for its occupants. It was still dark, but not impossibly so; here and there light shined in and revealed their surroundings. The place looked abandoned. From what Cassie could see, it must have been a floor dedicated to the warriors. Pieces of rusting armor littered the ground, and at one end she could see the outline of a giant cage rising to the ceiling, an arena for the angels to test themselves in combat. At least she hoped it was for the angels.

"Just a little further," called Faye from the front of the group. "We're almost there. You'll all be quite pleased with the place. And you'll never regret your decision to join this tower, I promise you that."

She led them up another few floors until finally they came to the upper levels. The place was lit, and well maintained. The ground had been swept clean, the junk was gone, and everything looked much as it had back in the tower the servants had come from. Faye hung her torch on the wall and led them onward, curving around and around until they came to a long hallway, a white light shining in the distance from an area that opened to the outside.

Cassie could see someone standing at the end of the hallway, the outline of wings spread out from their sides. The light nearly blinded her, and she had to put a hand to her eyes to get a better look. The figure wore armor, and she thought it was male, at least until she took a few steps closer. Then the light faded around her, and Cassie got a better look: it was a female angel, her face covered in red lines of arteries that had permanently blistered beneath the surface of her skin. The angel walked down the hallway, stopping a few feet away from Faye and greeting her with a smile.

"Zuphias," said Ambriela. "You've returned." She eyed the train of servants, huddling together in awe at the sight of unfamiliar angels. "And you've brought payment for my services along with you."

CHAPTER NINE

J ANA SAT THERE ON THE metal floor, scrubbing away at a nasty brown patch of dirt and rust. She was locked away in a suite Ambriela had provided them with, one of the pods that had once been assigned to a seraph who'd gone away to fight against Suriel. The room was long empty. The stain she was wiping at had been left there to fester by the prior occupant, a grimy blotch that marred the appearance of what otherwise would have been some of the tower's most luxurious lodgings.

No one had asked her to spend her day cleaning. In fact, Rhamiel had insisted that she shouldn't. He thought the work was beneath her, a chore better suited to one of the lower ranking seraphs than to the woman who was soon to be the mother of his son.

But she wanted the chores, as hard as it was for him to believe it. She hadn't done anything in nearly a month. It was driving her mad, the lack of anything to do. Something about the work gratified her, even if there was no real point to it. No one minded the stain, no one but her. Both Rhamiel and Thane were men, and they each had a man's attitude towards tidiness. They seemed perfectly content to live amid dirt or even piles of sludge, so long as they could step around it. It didn't even enter their heads to complain.

But Jana noticed, even if they didn't. The stain was there, and so was she, and the only alternative she had to working away at it was to sit there quietly with her thoughts. She preferred trying to make the place look a little better, even if it was only for herself, and even if she hoped they wouldn't be staying there for very long.

The work wasn't comfortable, and she had to rise from time to time to walk around the room and stretch her legs. Sitting on a hard metal floor would have been a strain even in the best of times, but it was especially so with a child growing inside her. One of the seraphs had given her a bucket of water on Rhamiel's orders, and she'd scrounged around in a storage closet in the back of the suite until she'd managed to find some rags and a few old bars of soap.

The suite took up the entirety of the pod, hanging out in the air with a perfect view of an imperfect landscape, a brown wasteland edged with the scraggly trees of a dying forest. A large foyer dominated the center space, committed to the entertainment of guests. Windows opened to the skies beyond, letting in light from all around. Along the sides were a series of smaller rooms, tucked away where they wouldn't interfere with any social gatherings.

The other rooms were filled with the belongings of the angel who'd lived here, and it felt a little like living inside a forgotten tomb. Thane was snoring away in the darkness of a nearby bedroom, a rifle clutched across his chest. The bed was surrounded by trophies of war: breastplates hanging from wooden mannequins lined one wall, and a display case on the opposite side held rows of single feathers mounted beneath the glass, the spoils of battles past with other seraphs. The room was a perfect fit for Thane, but to her it felt cramped and violent.

Jana preferred the foyer: lots of open space, and lots of open windows. The decor wasn't to her taste, but the room was meant for the public, and it didn't feel quite so much like she was squatting in someone else's home. Thin benches made of bronze ran along the edges of the room, set a few feet away to provide space for wings to stretch. Crystal vases stood on end tables beside them, and the wall opposite the windows was covered in tattered green banners, rotting away in disuse. It looked nice, like it had once been elegant and could be again if someone were to spend the time to maintain it. She meant to try; she was on her own, and she didn't have anything else to busy herself with.

Rhamiel had allowed himself to be dragged away to politick with the other seraphs, now that he was comfortable that she and Thane could be safely left on their own. He didn't trust the other angels, not exactly, but he needed their support if he was to convince Ambriela to work her miracles. He'd locked the door behind him, and he'd promised again and again that he'd stay within shouting distance. She could hear him outside from time to 'time conferencing with anyone who'd speak to him, forcing them to come to him so that he could stay close to her.

He was consumed with worry that someone would sneak inside in his absence to harm her somehow, but she didn't think it possible. A single shot from one of Thane's weapons would be enough to draw Rhamiel there from anywhere in the tower, and the doors were thick enough that even an angel would struggle to break through them. But if it made him feel better to stay nearby, she wasn't going to complain.

With Thane asleep and Rhamiel prowling the hallways, Jana was left there all by herself, alone with her work. She tried to sing to herself, quietly enough that it wouldn't wake Thane, but thoughts kept coming back to her, ones she didn't want to think. Thoughts about things Rhamiel had said, and things Ambriela had confirmed. She'd known there was a reason he couldn't go back to the paradise he'd come from. All of the angels were rebels, and Rhamiel was no different. But she'd once believed that was the extent of his fall.

She kicked herself inside for being so foolish. He'd as much as told her there was more, even if he'd held back the details. She'd only seen kindness in him, even when he'd insisted there was corruption. Nefta had been sure of it, too, but in the end Jana had dismissed that as the ravings of a lovesick admirer who was more than a little unbalanced. Now she knew there was truth to it, and the truth was awful. Rhamiel had gathered slaves for the other angels, ripping them from their families and locking them away in the towers for the rest of their lives. Maybe that was why he was so sure he couldn't be redeemed. She'd seen the horrors that servitude brought with it. And if he ever came before the Maker again, Rhamiel had his own part in that to answer for.

There had been a darkness in him once, even if she couldn't see it there now, and she wondered if he'd turn to it again. He was stronger than she could imagine, both in body and in will. It was part of what drew her to him. She'd spent most of her life feeling weak, like she was a complete nothing who didn't matter to anyone. She'd probably been right, on reflection. But then Rhamiel had flirted with her, and he'd protected her, and he'd proven by his actions that he valued her. Ecanus had been about to kill her, and Rhamiel could have let him. He could have loved her and left her, and no one would have said a word. Instead he'd risked his social standing to be with her, and then he'd risked his life.

He didn't seem anything like the person Ambriela had described. A slaver. Someone who had it in him to round up people like her and imprison them in the darkness, toiling away forever on behalf of ungrateful fallen angels. But he'd admitted that he'd done it, back when Ambriela had spoken the words. He hadn't corrected her, and he hadn't fought back. That meant there was truth to what she'd said. And it meant the person she loved the most in the world might be damned for all eternity, chained up far away from her no matter how hard he worked at redeeming himself.

Jana scrubbed at the stain harder and harder, trying to wash it away and bring the floor back to what it must have once looked like. Smooth and pristine and inviting, the kind of place where an angel would want to live. But the stain wouldn't fade, no matter how hard she pressed the rag down against it and no matter how much soapy water she sloshed over it. The rust had eaten its way into the floor, damaging what was beneath and etching the mark into it permanently. The stain was still there, and it would always be there, and there wasn't anything she could do about it. She tossed the rag to the side in frustration, sending it into the bucket of water with a plop and a rain of suds.

Tears ran down her cheeks, and she felt a rising urge to break down in sobs. Once she would have let it all out. Once she wouldn't have had the strength to keep any of it in. But the things she'd seen had changed her. She hadn't had control of herself, not for most of her life. She'd let others order her about, and she'd obeyed them without question. There hadn't been any choice, not if she'd wanted to survive.

But now things were different, and she knew she had to be stronger than that.

Now she had a child inside her, a child who was about to be the most important thing in the world to her. And maybe the most important thing in the world to everyone else as well.

Everyone around her seemed to think he was something special. Something that awed them, and something they were more than a little frightened of. They knew him as whatever he'd been up above, and as whatever he'd been before. But to her he was a warmth, a part of her, a precious little life she was nurturing into its own existence. It didn't matter what part he was to play in the course of the world, or whether he even had one.

All that mattered was having someone who loved her, someone who'd care about her no matter what. Someone she could trust to be there to the end of her days, and if the stories were true, for long thereafter.

She sat there on the floor, leaning against the wall in exhaustion and running her hand across her stomach. She loved Rhamiel, and she was in awe of him. She knew there was good in him, even if there was something dark mixed in as well. But she had to be able to trust him. And the idea that she'd gotten him all wrong truly frightened her.

Love was something she felt, not something she thought. The feeling had overpowered her, plunging her into a relationship she hadn't been at all prepared for. And in the end, it was only her feelings that had guided her. There was more to Rhamiel than what she knew. He'd been around for thousands of years before she'd even been born. It would take him a lifetime just to tell her of all the lifetimes he'd lived. Maybe that didn't matter, and maybe his past wasn't who he was. But he was the product of his past, and the way he'd acted before might be the way he'd act again. And who knew what else he might have done that she didn't even know about?

She heard a click at the door, and she scrambled to her feet. The lock moved, and the door heaved inward to reveal Rhamiel standing there, a broad smile across his face as he confidently sauntered inside. "We've allies here, it seems, ones I'd never expected. Ones who'd turn back the clock if they could. And they see our son as their one chance at redemption. Their one hope to make things as they should have been, or as close to it as possible." He went on and on, telling her of this angel or that, and how one by one they'd pledged renewed allegiance to their son.

She tried to listen politely, but she couldn't bear it. She couldn't pretend nothing was wrong. He might have been happy with his political conquests, but she couldn't sit there and act as if they were what truly mattered to her. She'd been miserable the entire day, and it was consuming her. She turned away from him, her arms folded across her chest. She didn't want to speak to him, not yet. She wasn't sure she could. The hurt was still fresh, and it hadn't had time to fade.

"What's wrong?" said Rhamiel. He walked up behind her, putting his arms on her shoulders to comfort her. "Something troubles you. Let it out, and let me help."

"It's nothing," said Jana. She started to sit down, intending to quietly go back to her scrubbing. She didn't want to talk about things, not now. She'd barely had time to process what Ambriela had said. And she didn't want to fight with him, not about this, and not while they were on the run. Not while he was working so hard to protect her, whatever his faults might have been. But Rhamiel wasn't to be denied, not when he was intent on something, and not when it involved her.

"It isn't nothing," said Rhamiel. He took her by the arm, holding her in place even as she tried to push herself away. "It's something deep inside you, and it's welling to the surface. Tell me. Tell me, and I shall fix it."

She looked up at him, summoning all the courage she had in her. She was confronting an angel, and it was frightening, even if he was the one person she felt closest to in all the world. His kind were so dangerous when they were mad, and though he'd never shown a hint of temper towards her, she still had memories of how his brothers had acted when they'd lost control. She was nervous, but she had to know the answers to the questions that were nagging at her. She had to, if there was to be any chance for the two of them in the long run. So she summoned up the words and forced them out. "It's true, isn't it? What Ambriela said?" Rhamiel went silent, and his expression turned to stone, but she kept going. It was out in the open now, and she needed her answer. "That you put people into slavery? People like me?"

He winced at the words, and this time he was the one who looked away. He paused, staring out of the window and off into the distance. Then he turned back, his eyes glistening blue as he looked down into hers. "Ambriela spoke the truth. It shames me to say it, but on that point at least, she spoke the truth."

"Slaves," said Jana, shaking her head. She felt like she'd been sucker punched, and she couldn't help herself. She blurted out her thoughts without any concern about how much they might sting. "You didn't even care about them. All those people, and you turned them into slaves."

"Jana—" said Rhamiel.

"Is that what happened to my parents?" said Jana. "Is that what happened to me?"

Horrible images danced through her head, pictures her imagination had spent the last few hours concocting. Images of her mother and father, locked away in a cage in some angel's chambers. She wasn't even sure if it was what they'd really looked like. She'd been too young to remember more than scattered fragments of them, and she didn't have any pictures to go by. But still they were there in her mind, a man and a woman, angels with swords of fire driving them forward like livestock and snapping them into their fetters. And no matter how hard she tried to push the image away, she couldn't help seeing a twisted version of Rhamiel flying above them, taunting and laughing just as any of the other angels would have.

"You know that wasn't what happened to you," said Rhamiel. "You'd have known. Those were different times. And we had few choices. I did what I thought was best. What would help people. What would keep them safe from—"

"Help them?" said Jana. "That's how you help people? By locking them away to do your chores?" She couldn't control her fury, not anymore. She reached down and picked up a sponge, hurling it at him and sending it against his chest plate with a soggy slap. He wiped it away, moving towards Jana with open palms and sorrow on his face.

"It had to be done," said Rhamiel. "You must understand, and you must believe me. It was easy when we were up above, simply following orders. We didn't have to make choices for ourselves. We did what we were told, and there was never any sin in it. But once we fell, we were on our own. Sometimes we had to choose between sins, and choose what we thought was the lesser of the evils before us. And I was hardly the only one to make the choice I did. Any angel who cared for humans did the same."

"That's not caring," said Jana. "You don't know what it's like to be a slave. You never could. It's not like being someone's guardian. They could kill us whenever they wanted to. They did things. Just for fun. Hurting people, like it was a game. We were servants, but not like you ever were. You know that. You saw it."

"I know," said Rhamiel. He ran his hand through his blonde hair, digging furrows into it with his fingers. "I more than know. But that's the thing with being forced to choose between evils. It blackens you on the inside. Just a tiny bit, but it was enough for one who'd never sinned before. And once the spot is there, it spreads. I didn't know how to handle it. None of us did. We distracted ourselves with drink and frivolities. I buried myself in preening and the attentions of others. And we all turned a blind eye to what was around us. We should have cared, but we didn't. It would have hurt too much to."

"That's not an excuse," said Jana. "To make someone a slave."

"I didn't want to enslave them," said Rhamiel. "I had to. There were so many other things that would have happened if I hadn't. Horrible, horrible things."

Jana could feel something rising in her, unchecked emotions she'd never be able to control. Anger. Frustration. A feeling of betrayal. He didn't seem to get it. Maybe it wasn't his fault. Maybe he couldn't understand. But she had to make him. She had to make him understand what he'd done, if there was ever to be any hope for him to redeem himself. She started to vent, letting it all out at once in a burst of passion. "There couldn't be anything more horrible. The things I saw—"

Something interrupted her before she could finish, something from beyond the door: a rising din of shouts and screams from somewhere off in the distance. Rhamiel's hand went to his sword and he charged towards the door, pulling it open just a crack. The sound grew louder, coming from the direction of the ballroom. It was a cacophony of voices, blending together in excitement and panic.

"Something is wrong," said Rhamiel. "Something has happened."

Thane emerged from the bedroom, wiping sleep from his eyes with one hand and leaning the rifle against his shoulder with the other. "What's goin' on? I'm tryin' to sleep, and there's all this yellin'. First you two, and now them."

"What it is, I do not know," said Rhamiel. "A disturbance of some kind, and I aim to discover the source."

"Let's go," said Thane. He slung his rifle across his back and drew a pair of pistols from his belt, checking their chambers before heading towards the door. "If someone out there wants trouble, they're gonna get it."

"Her," said Rhamiel, looking over at Jana with concern across his face. "Someone must stay here with her."

"I'm not staying anywhere," insisted Jana. "I'm going to see what's happening. If you go out there, I'm going, too."

A low grumble rose from Rhamiel's throat. He turned back to Jana, his eyes a fierce azure. "That simply will not happen. You carry our son, and he goes where you do. Stay here. Do not leave this room, do not open that door, and do not speak to anyone but Thane. I will confront whatever is the cause of this disturbance. And you will stay in this room, for now, until I have absolute confidence that it is safe for you to leave."

"This isn't what you promised," said Jana. "You said I'd be free. You said you wouldn't give me orders."

"When the life of our son is at stake, as well as your own, you will do precisely as I say," said Rhamiel. "That is what it means to be guardian. To guard. Neither of you will be put into danger. Not for a moment, not while you are in my charge."

"It could be just as dangerous in here," said Jana. She didn't want to be alone, not there, and not anymore. She felt safer by his side, even if there was darkness in him, and even if his path led towards something dangerous instead of away from it. She pulled at his arm as he walked, trying to drag him back towards her, but he gently brushed her aside. It didn't stop her. She kept following as he headed for the door, dogging his footsteps as he went. "I'm not going to stay here by myself. I'm simply not. What if something happens? What if you don't come back?"

"She could be right," said Thane. "We might have to split, and fast. That's easier if we're all in one place."

Rhamiel turned back towards her, his eyes burning with passion and holding her prisoner where she stood. "I can be back here in moments, and I will not compromise where your safety is concerned. On this matter, you will do as I say. And on this matter, I have already spoken."

"Is that all I am to you?" said Jana. Her voice quavered with hurt, the pain of a lover who was beginning to doubt where she stood with her beloved. "A slave, like all the others?"

Something cracked in him. She could see it in his face. It looked like her words had wrenched his heart from his chest, leaving him bloodless and broken. His wings drooped, and it took him a few moments to recover himself before he could speak again. He stammered and sputtered, and finally he forced something out.

"You are no slave," said Rhamiel. "Do not use that word about yourself. Do not speak of yourself that way ever again."

"It's what I was," said Jana. "It's the truth."

"It is what the others thought you were," said Rhamiel. He pulled her close, wrapping his arms around her so tightly she thought he'd never let her escape. "It is not what you are, and not what you are fated to be. You've freedom, now, and you must savor it. Do not let your prior servitude define you. We did, and look where it landed us. Enjoy being free, instead of dwelling on what once was."

"If I were free, I could choose where I wanted to go," said Jana. "I wouldn't be locked away someplace I didn't want to be."

Rhamiel hesitated, his fingers tapping against his sword as he stared into the distance, listening to the sounds coming from outside of the chamber. Something in him clicked, and he made his decision, turning back to Jana. "If you truly wish to come, then come." He pulled the door open wide, stepping into the hallway and waving at her to follow. "Stay behind me, and stay within my sight." The sound of shouting grew, and he tensed as he stared down the hallway. "And if I order you to safety, then promises or no, you will not hesitate to obey."

That was good enough for her. She walked through the door, letting it shut behind them. Then she headed after Rhamiel and Thane, following behind them as they led the way towards the growing commotion in the distance.

CHAPTER TEN

"**P**ull," said Ecanus. "Lean into it, and pull."
He strolled through the furrows of a freshly plowed field, the soil tilled in thin lines across it. Before him were a few of the Seraphim, the ones who'd survived Suriel's massacre. He wasn't sure whether to consider them the lucky ones, or whether they would have been better off if they'd fallen at someone else's hand during the battle.

He wasn't sure he cared.

It had been Suriel's decision, in the end, and he'd chosen to let them live. They were Suriel's own little playthings, and not ones he was particularly interested in. He'd spent a few weeks testing their loyalties and ordering them about, and then he'd tired of them, retreating to the greater pleasures of his private harem. Now he'd left them to be managed by Ecanus, still in his toy box though in the care of another, and the experience had ensured that they'd never be the same again.

There were hundreds of the surviving seraphs working in Suriel's fields, bound by heavy chains lashed around their chests and looped beneath their wings. Weights dangled all along their bodies, heavy leaden spheres that anchored them to the earth. Behind each of them was a plow, one designed to be dragged by an ox. But on this farm they were pulled by angels instead, soldiers turned pack animals, servants once and now servants once again.

"We'll make something of you yet," said Ecanus. He stepped atop one of the plows, riding behind a seraph, his feet pressing down upon the metal and driving the blades into the soil. The seraph struggled against the pressure, trying to drag both plow and master, but the force of it was too much for him. He was weak, too much so to struggle against Ecanus's boot. For all his exertions, the best he could manage was to drag it a few feet before slumping over in exhaustion.

Ecanus cursed at the angel, driving a foot into his back, barraging him with angry slaps and insults. He sounded furious, but in fact he was the happiest he'd ever been. It was one of life's greatest pleasures, torturing those beneath you, and he meant to savor every moment. He hadn't had any of this in him back in Heaven. Not that he knew of, at least; he'd never thought about the matter, not back then. He'd simply toiled away at things, a soldier in a mass of other soldiers, drilling and fighting right beside all the others. He'd been far from the strongest, and far from the best, but it hadn't mattered. They'd treated him the same as everyone else, as a brother-in-arms and as a friend. But that had been before he'd rebelled, and before he'd been tossed down among a mutinous army with no taste for the moralities that once bound them.

They'd all been peers up above, or at least that was what they'd told themselves. In truth, they'd been arranged into rigid castes, with only the thin veneer of nominal equality to connect them across the lines of class. The Fall had changed things. There was an order to life up above, and slights against one's brothers were unheard of. But once they'd fallen, the angels were suddenly free to sin, and Ecanus was one of the first to be sinned against. It was the way of the weak to be preyed upon by the strong, and the old rules no longer restrained them once they'd been tossed down to Earth to fend for themselves.

"Say it," said Ecanus. He stood atop the plow, his scarred face lit with glee as he watched the beaten angel sweat beneath the scorching sun. "Say it, or get the whip." He was going to give it to him anyway; he'd already decided that. But all the fun was in the process, in fanning the distant hope that perhaps this was the day he'd show one of them the mercy he'd never been shown himself. Sometimes he even did, just to keep their hopes alive. This wasn't to be one of those days.

"Suriel loves me, and I love Suriel," muttered the seraph, forcing out the words with all his strength. But it wasn't enough for Ecanus, not that anything would have been. The air crackled with flame, and a fiery whip snapped across the angel's back. His wings twisted and convulsed in pain, and he managed to pull the plow forward a few more feet in a burst of newfound energy. "Suriel loves me, and I love Suriel!" shouted the seraph.

"Good," said Ecanus. "Quite an improvement. A shame you couldn't manage your devotions on your own.

Most of the others have, you know." His eyes scanned the field, taking in other seraphs lashed to plows of their own. "But I'll be here to prod you onwards whenever you need it. I'll wring every ounce of sweat from your body, and every ounce of love from your soul. It pleases Suriel, and I must say it pleases me as well, if not for precisely the same reasons." He slashed his whip across the seraph's back again, leaving a thin line of smoke along his wings. Then he cackled to himself, reveling in the pain he'd inflicted and riding along as the angel slowly pulled the plow through the dirt.

It was a fortunate thing that the seraph could still think properly at all. Most of them couldn't. Many couldn't even speak, not anymore. Not after what he'd done to them. They might recover themselves, if the stress of his tortures was removed and they were given time to heal. But he didn't plan to let that happen. They'd treated him much the same in days past, and now the wheel had turned. As far as he was concerned, this was their just deserts.

He wasn't sure whether this was one of the angels he truly hated, one of the ones who'd treated him so badly after their Fall. There had been so many slights coming from so many others, and he couldn't possibly remember them all. Some had merely mocked his scars, a network of burns across his skin that was more extensive than most. Others had shoved him in the dirt, or played tricks upon him, or pointedly excluded him from whatever entertainments they'd concocted to pass the time.

And things had only escalated from there, once the fallen angels had begun testing the boundaries of sinfulness. No lightning had struck them, and they'd heard no words from on high in reprimand. They'd had their fun with the humans, but when they'd tried taking out their frustrations on the weakest among them it had practically become a sport.

For Ecanus that meant nearly a decade of indignities, each compounding all the others. He'd been a dullard back then, in retrospect. He'd kept following the rules for far longer than any of the others, in spite of his rebellion. An attitude of servitude had proved easier to purge than his habits, ones he'd built up over millennia. And he'd still believed in the other seraphs' constant professions of brotherhood, no matter how obvious it became that none of them followed that code any longer, not unless it was to their own advantage. The others had poked and poked at him, and he'd quietly seethed inside as the bitterness grew and grew.

But for years, he'd done nothing. Nothing but simmer and burn, feeling a far sharper pain than he ever had from the fire that engulfed him during his fall.

The turning point had been the day Nelchael had ruined him in front of all the others. It came a little while after the Fall, before he'd known the others for what they truly were. He'd had suspicions, and he'd had hints, but still he hadn't seen.

It was before the towers had been built, back when he and his kind had roamed aimlessly about the planet, playing at war with an enemy that was virtually helpless against them. His war party had been camping around a fire, weary from a day of flying about and tearing apart the remnant armies of man. It was all they'd done since the Fall. Hunt for sport, engage in a little casual butchery of the ones they'd used to serve, and then rest for the night and start the whole thing over in the morning.

They'd spent the evening talking amongst themselves, just as they always had. Most of them, at least. Ecanus had been left at the fringes of the group, his usual position, sitting quietly in the darkness and ignored by all of the others. He'd been lost in his own thoughts, dwelling on the injuries of the past, with little interest in social games he wasn't allowed to play.

And then one of them had spoken his name.

"Sing, Ecanus," Nelchael had said. He was a big one, his body taut with muscle, a true warrior whose scars were but mild compared to the others. Just a little redness under his thick brown beard, and a few patches here and there where the hair hadn't grown back after his burns. His chain mail shined silver beside the fire, and he was smiling broadly, so full of mirth. They'd all seemed that way, a circle of angels huddled around the warmth in the dark, laughing and clapping and urging Ecanus on.

A song wouldn't have been an unusual request, not up above. But the others had fallen faster than he had, and farther. He was their fool, and he couldn't even see it. He'd closed his eyes and sang softly, sincerely, a paean to the Maker of the sort they'd all once sang together, each and every night. He'd thought they'd finally begun to accept him after months of fighting by their side. He thought they might let him sit by the fire, and that even if there was no beauty in his face, there might still be a little left in his voice.

But this hymn brought no hallelujahs. At first he heard snickers, just a few, and then they rose to a chorus of laughter that drowned away the song and left him standing there by the firelight alone, pelted by pieces of food and handfuls of trash.

He still remembered the words, the ones Nelchael had sputtered out between his cackling. "There's still loyalty in him, even in these dark days. Look at him. There's nothing of his face left, and still he sings the praises of a tyrant. A blighted little blister the Maker couldn't quite pop." The others had joined in, slinging jeer after jeer along with their missiles. He saw the hatred in their faces. Some of it was for him. Some of it was for themselves. And the closer they were to the edges of the group, the more enthusiastic their taunts, and the more their hate was mixed with something else: relief that Ecanus was the butt of the evening's jibes instead of them.

Something had snapped in him, then. The scales fell from his eyes, and he saw what the other angels had seen long before him. The pointlessness of it all. The pleasure they found in the pain of others. The feeling of superiority, the thing they used to drive away their own insecurities, masking them beneath the deficiencies of another. He saw what they'd all become, and how they'd been using him for their own amusement for so many months. Using him as a sponge to absorb the venom that would otherwise flow towards them.

They looked so much like demons, the fire lighting their faces in the dark as they laughed. They were no brothers of his, and they never would be. He'd always be weaker, he'd always be smaller, and he'd always be the target of their cruelties. He always had been; he simply hadn't seen it.

But it didn't matter, in the end. Not to him. There were others still weaker than he, and what worked to salve the wounds of the other seraphs could work just as well for him.

He'd rushed off into the darkness, flapping his wings and taking to the skies, heading off at random. He'd wanted nothing more than to be away from them, away from those who called themselves his brothers yet treated him as an outcast. He'd flown and flown, gnashing his teeth together until his mouth bled, choking down one pain with another.

And then he'd seen them.

A little group of humans, probably soldiers on some futile mission. They were weaving between the trees, rushing along a narrow trail in the darkness in the hope no one would catch a glimpse of them from above. But see them he had, and they were exactly what he was looking for, even if he hadn't known that he was looking.

He dove down and landed before them, finding no soldiers. Nothing but women and children. They turned on their heels at the sight of him, fleeing into the woods in all directions. None of them had weapons, and there were no fighters among them. They were helpless. Defenseless. Weak.

They were perfect.

He'd spent the night taking out his frustrations on them, one by one. He'd hunted them like the animals they were, lapping up their fear and doing everything he could to enhance it. He'd stalked along behind them, bursting from the shadows and slicing at them with his dagger, then disappearing again just as quickly. He'd toyed with them again and again, burying his pain beneath their own, just as the other angels had done to him. Letting all his rage and frustration loose, proving to himself that there were others out there who were far, far beneath him. And it had felt marvelous.

They'd died at his hand, one by one. And he'd found that it was true what they said of predators. Once they had a taste of human blood, they could never again be sated. The towers had gone up soon after, and they'd proved both a blessing and a curse for one with his newly acquired tastes. He'd had so many people to torture, brought right to his doorstep without the need to flit off and search for them. Unfortunately his "brothers" had been there as well, and there'd been no end to their humiliations. He'd tried to leave at first, so many times, to live by himself untroubled by the rest. But he'd always come back. He couldn't handle the solitude, despite how they treated him. It was maddening, not being able to be away from those he hated so much, but it was what it was. He'd plunged himself into his tortures, and the hobby had been a fine means of coping with his predicament.

And now so many years later he'd been given his first taste of the blood of angels, and he'd found their suffering to be far more to his liking than the mewlings of mere chimpanzees.

It was an ordinary day in the fields, at least since Suriel's victory. The camp had grown, the forests around it stripped bare to make way for farms to feed his followers. A sprawling stone citadel had been erected in place of the compound, a palace sufficient to house Suriel and those who'd worship him. It looked like a ragged grey pyramid with no tip, and it was growing brick by brick, built by captured seraphs who'd been turned to masons in their newfound servitude. More and more people flocked to Suriel's banner; the sight of angels laboring away on behalf of humans had been a stunning propaganda coup, and everyone wanted to join the winning side.

The angel before him was just one of many, a beaten enemy, once so high and mighty and now dragging himself through the dirt. It made Ecanus feel so powerful, riding atop his plow, and he snarled at him as they went. "May I leave you to your own devices, and trust that your enthusiasm shan't wane in my absence? I've others to monitor, and the day is exceptionally hot. Cold water and some shade, that's what one needs in such heat. Groveling is a talent, you know, and one you'd be wise to practice. Perhaps if you apply yourself to it, you'll taste such luxuries again yourself."

"Suriel loves me, and I love Suriel," muttered the seraph as he dragged the plow forward.

"Good," said Ecanus. "Very good." He wasn't sure how much of what he'd said that the seraph understood. Some of them were beyond understanding anything but Suriel's mantras. But he slashed his whip against the seraph's arm all the same, prompting a sharp yelp of pain. It wasn't quite as satisfying as slicing away with his dagger, but there were limits to the damage he could do to the property of another. He hopped away from the plow to stretch his wings, sauntering off and leaving the seraph to his work. "You'll get it, eventually. Pride is for fools. You'd be so much higher up, if only you had the sense to be a little more shameless in your praise of the man at the top."

He strolled through the rows of tilled soil, strutting and smiling as he went. Occasionally he'd lunge this way or that, just to watch the shudders of pain ripple across the faces of the nearest seraphs. It was great fun, keeping them on edge and keeping them in their proper place. But it could be exhausting, and sometimes one needed rest even from the most joyous of entertainments.

He headed towards a nearby building, a squat concrete bunker that Suriel's followers had built as an overseer's residence. It wasn't a tower, but it was something, and it was more than what any of the other seraphs had. That was what mattered in the end, and it gave him a place to while away the time when he wasn't wandering about frightening Suriel's human followers or torturing his captive angels.

He was nearly to the end of the field when he heard a heavy beating in the air above him. He knew the sound by heart, and he bent down on his knee at once, dropping his head low to the ground. He didn't look up, not when he heard the boots crunching in the soil behind him, and not when he saw the shadow looming on the dirt in front of him.

"Such labors," said Suriel. He stepped in front of Ecanus, tapping him on the shoulder and signaling for him to rise to his feet. "Such devotion. It warms Suriel's heart to see it. He loves to see his followers at their tasks. In their proper places, each according to Suriel's decree. You've done so well, dear Ecanus. Overseeing your brothers was fitted to you indeed. But tasks must change. And Suriel has a new task for you."

Suriel stood so high above him, an archangel, a member of a different caste entirely. He was bigger than any of the other angels, covered entirely in black silk from his neck to his gloves to his feet. There were scars under there, and Ecanus knew it. But they weren't for the eyes of others, and even mentioning them would have been a death sentence. His face was near perfection, framed with a shock of silver hair that stole the attention away from the rest of him. He was so far above Ecanus, an angel who'd be a god. But gods needed servants. Ecanus was determined to be the most loyal among them; being second in rank might not have been perfect, but it was higher than he'd ever managed on his own.

"Suriel loves me, and I love Suriel," whimpered Ecanus. A nearby seraph muttered the words as well, over and over, until Suriel glared in his direction and Ecanus silenced him with a firm boot to the back and a series of emphatic prayers to his master. He had to make a show of things if he wanted to keep his authority, and as galling as it was to be beneath another, it was far better than being at the bottom.

"The Cherubim," said Suriel. "It's been some time since Suriel has heard from them. A curious thing, from creatures with so many promises upon their lips. One would think they would keep him apprised of their progress, if indeed they meant to deliver upon them."

"One would think," said Ecanus. "Perhaps the

cherubs' promises are as clouded as their rhymes. Perhaps they've run into trouble. They promised the universe, its foundations stripped bare and woven anew. The Cherubim are mechanics, not Makers, and this may be beyond their talents."

"Perhaps," said Suriel. "But Suriel has heard rumors. Word reaches him from all corners of the globe. And part of that globe is changing." He paced around one of the seraphs, running a finger along the open wounds on his back as the seraph did his best not to wince. "The Cherubim promised Suriel that they would unravel creation itself. That they would snip out the Maker, and replace him with a kinder master. A better one. One with more appreciation for the worship of his subjects. One who would show them a harder form of worship, but ultimately a more fulfilling one."

"Suriel loves me, and I love Suriel," said Ecanus with as much exaggerated eagerness as he could muster.

"And yet have the Cherubim chosen Suriel as that master?" said Suriel. "Or do they seek to elevate one of their own instead?" He rubbed his hand against his chin, towering over the angels and their plows and casting a dark shadow running the length of the field. "Suriel knows that the change has begun. He hears rumors of it from others. And he can feel it, deep down in his bones. Creation is not what it was, even mere weeks ago."

"Zephon always was a treacherous one," said Ecanus. "A fine trait, if one's a master of it. But the Cherubim blunder into their betrayals rather than plan them. They're daft, and always have been. They simply can't process why anyone would begrudge them a change in plans, if the change fits their peculiar logic. And they can't be bothered to ask permission beforehand."

"A possibility," said Suriel. "But there are others. Zephon styles himself a king already. And what king would be satisfied with the rule of a tiny little hive? He may want more, more than what Suriel has generously offered him."

"Poor servants, if you ask me," said Ecanus. "Give me a month, and a tiny whip, and I'll have their little brains in working order. They'll be proper servants, with a proper attitude."

"Suriel did not ask," growled Suriel. "And opinions which Suriel does not ask for will be kept to yourself, lest he tear your wings from their sockets."

Ecanus turned to sniveling at once, bowing his head and dropping his knee to the ground in submission. "Suriel loves me, and I love Suriel." He looked up, ready to repeat the line as often as needed to please his master. But Suriel just stared down at him, smiling with pleasure at his groveling. He idly ran a hand along Ecanus's scalp, mussing his scattered tufts of hair in all directions.

"You know that Suriel loves you, despite your outburst," said Suriel. "And Suriel needs loyal followers if he is to rein in the disloyal ones."

"I'm nothing if not loyal, to one who's given me what you have," said Ecanus. "Your leash is a long one, and a tolerable one. I've no complaints about my tasks, none at all." He rattled his whip against his belt, and the seraphs beside them cringed at the sound. "I'm quite fond of them, in fact. Quite fond of what you've asked me to do."

"Then Suriel asks something else of you," said Suriel. "He hears rumors of the cherubs. And he hears rumors of the Son."

"The Son," said Ecanus. He hadn't heard a word about him in months. But then, he hadn't exactly cared. He'd been preoccupied, and as much as he loathed Rhamiel, torturing one angel was as good as torturing another.

"Running away, hiding away," said Suriel. "But he shall be Suriel's to raise in the end. A king no more, but perhaps a prince. He hides himself, but poorly. Word spreads, and the Earth is a tiny globe on which to conceal oneself. He has been spotted, and in a tower, no less. Hiding from Suriel's scouts for a time, and searching for someone who'd help him."

"He's a fool," spat Ecanus. "And so are his parents, if they think any would risk themselves to aid them."

"There is an army here, if one that's battered and beaten," said Suriel. "Gather up the most obedient. Those who no longer chafe at their bridles. You shall visit this tower, and you shall find Suriel's son. He shall come home to Suriel's embrace, even if he would rather stay where he is." He looked up at the skies, a smile spreading above his broad jaw. "For who can resist Suriel, in the end? And if Suriel must rip his son from the womb to have him, then that is what Suriel shall do."

CHAPTER ELEVEN

"**S**O MANY SERVANTS," SAID AMBRIELA. "So many little lambs in need of a guiding hand." She stood at the entrance to the ballroom, smiling down at the people as they were ushered past her by scowling guards. Man, woman, and child alike shuffled inside, averting their eyes from Ambriela's heavily scarred face. "Come now. Come along. We've a place for every one of you. The perfect place. And we've many inside who're quite eager to see you."

Cassie was in the middle of the crowd, streaming along with all the rest of them. She didn't have any choice in the matter, not anymore. She'd come too far, and her freedom was gone. Maybe gone forever. She was at the angels' mercy, and they were salivating at the sight of so many healthy servants ready to be put to use. She could see Herman at the front of the line, an oblivious grin plastered across his face as he slapped the backs of his cronies and celebrated their turn of luck.

Cassie just shook her head. He thought he'd won. He really thought this was a moment of triumph, and that the angels would put him back in his proper place. Maybe they would, in fact. But she wasn't sure he'd agree with them as to where his proper place would be.

She caught a glimpse of Faye up ahead of her, strolling beside the servants as they went. She pushed her way through the crowd, struggling to the edge of it until she could get closer, trying to catch her attention in a loud whisper. "Faye. Faye!" Faye didn't notice, or affected not to. So Cassie tried again, louder this time, the nearby servants scooting away in terror at the thought that she might draw unwanted attention onto themselves. "Where's Zuphias? And how do you know these angels?"

"Hold your tongue," snapped Faye, whirling her head towards Cassie with a sharp glare. "You've a new home, and it's time you adjust to it. Authority out there means nothing in here." Then she turned forward, ignoring Cassie as she pushed the other servants aside on her way into the ballroom.

There was something about her. Something wrong. Cassie could see it, now. This was no freedom fighter. Maybe she'd switched sides, just like the Vichies had. Some people got that way. They'd called it Stockholm Syndrome before the Fall, a kind of empathy for someone's abusers that made them justify everything they did, or even want to become one of them.

Cassie could understand it, even if she couldn't excuse it. She'd been pledged to Nefta, and sometimes she'd felt close to her despite the expectation of servitude. Sometimes she'd even thought they were friends. When she was in a good mood, Nefta had been charming. She'd insist on braiding Cassie's hair, gossiping about the other angels as if the two of them were a couple of school girls instead of a grown woman and a thousand-year old supernatural being. Or she'd make Cassie gifts, little wooden sculptures of things from Heaven that had been dear to her. Strange musical instruments that looked almost like harps, and even a statue of Cassie herself. It was touching, and it had almost made Cassie want to call off her mission and plead with Nefta to find some way for angels and humans to live beside one another in peace. Almost.

But when Nefta was in a bad mood, things got very dark, very quickly.

She'd smash apart the carvings she'd worked so hard on, finding excuses to scream at Cassie over the slightest errors in her chores. She'd grumble and pout, muttering things that made Cassie's spine curl. Things about what she could do to a servant, if only the whim overtook her. Talk of violence and death, and slicing people apart with her sword if they offended her. The truly bad times were rare, but they happened often enough to poison the good. Anyone who thought they could befriend someone like that was a fool. And if Faye thought the angels had accepted her as one of them, she'd been touched with a special sort of madness.

The servants were all inside the ballroom, and the doorway was blocked behind them. Two heavily armored angels barred the exit, and the servants stood together in small groups, none of them sure as to what they should do. Cassie was just as lost as the rest of them. Angels sat around the room, whispering among themselves and looking the servants up and down as if they were prize pigs. She could see Faye, bold enough to stride right up to Ambriela and speak to her directly in a low voice. The two of them turned, both smiling, both looking entirely too pleased at the presence of so many guests in their home.

"Gather round," said Ambriela. She clicked her tongue at the servants, pointing at a spot in front of her in the center of the room. "Gather round, and let us take a look." She wandered past the assembled servants, poking and pinching and appraising them with cold eyes. "Too fat," she said of one, grabbing his belly between her fingers. "He'll have to go down bottom. Somewhere he'll work away his weight." The man nearly fainted, but she'd already moved on to another. "A fine looking girl. Very pretty." She leaned down towards a frightened little child, clinging to her mother's dress. "You'll stay up here and serve the fruits. And you'll learn to move so very quickly."

She put a hand on the shoulder of one of the taller men, turning behind her to a balding old seraph with a crooked nose and wings that had been charred to black. He looked more vulture than angel, perched atop a puffy brown couch. "Kemuel. Take this man. You'll need a strong one, if he's to handle a master as demanding as you. But don't wear him out, as you shan't get another."

"He'll survive my punishments," said Kemuel. "However much he may wish he hadn't."

Whispers started among the servants. Cassie could hear hushed voices, currents of doubt swirling around her as Ambriela went on with her inspection. The chatter came from all around, filled with apprehension and fear.

"We should have run."

"My hands. My back. I can't work a forge. I simply can't."

"I wasn't a house servant. I never talked to them. I can't be around them like that. All day, every day."

They'd finally realized what Cassie had known all along: that they'd traded a bad situation for a worse one, their remembrances of the tower clouded by the inevitable difficulties they'd been forced to endure when running their lives for themselves. Having someone else manage their lives for them had its upsides; there were no choices to be made, there was a certainty to their days, and any failure they faced wasn't truly their own. It was a difficult climb, from servant to another to a master of one's self, but they'd given up before they'd reached the peak. And now that they were back at the bottom, serfdom's downsides had become realities once again.

"Now, now," said Ambriela. "Quiet down." She walked in front of them, tapping the heads of servant after servant. "You, you, you, and you." She shooed them towards a thin angel in a red velvet vest, nodding at him to lead them away. "You'll man the furnaces. Dangerous work, but we must be warm. It's very important that we be warm, and you mustn't shirk your duties. We served you, after all, and you've at least a thousand years before the score is settled."

Ambriela kept making assignments, filling out positions without letting the servants speak a word. But one of the angels rose from his couch, his body young and virile, his scars wrinkling his skin enough to make his face look like that of an old man. He hesitantly stepped forward into the center of the room, a newly-assigned servant cowering in fear beside him. "Ambriela. A word."

"You're dissatisfied, Jeremiel?" said Ambriela. "You'd prefer another servant?" Her lips curled into a sneer, and she cocked her head and watched him approach. "You chose me as your leader, if you recall. All of you. Our Conclave failed us, and drove us to war. You wanted a single master instead of many. A burden I did not seek, and one I do not relish."

"And you've made a fine leader," said Jeremiel. "As we all knew you would. You counseled against trusting the cherubs when the rest of us clamored to join them. There isn't another who can take your place."

"Then instead of carping about my choices, I suggest you remedy your complaints by trading servants with another," said Ambriela. "I lead as best I can, but I cannot please us all. Not with such a limited stock. But we'll find more. This is just a start."

"It isn't that," said Jeremiel. "It's the entire enterprise, really. Perhaps we should discuss it in private."

"Perhaps you should state what thoughts you have, and quickly, instead of claiming time from me that I cannot spare," said Ambriela curtly. She stared at Jeremiel, and his eyes dropped to the floor, running up and down his feet as he withered before her displeasure. But after a moment, sound sputtered out of his mouth almost involuntarily. "The Son."

Jeremiel paused, clearing his throat, summoning all of his courage in the face of Ambriela's glare. "What will he think of all of this?" He warily nodded towards the line of servants being led off into the tower by their new masters. "Perhaps we should prepare a bit in anticipation. Moderate things, if only a tad."

"You fear Lucifer's Pit," said Ambriela dismissively. "You fear he'll toss us all down there and let us rot."

"I fear we'll be judged," said Jeremiel. "And not merely for our past rebellions."

"He may judge all he likes, but we cannot escape what we are," said Ambriela. She turned towards the seated angels, raising her voice so all could hear. "We cannot escape what drives us. The flaws the Maker built into us at our very creation. Some will always be on top. Some will always be on bottom. It's foolish to strive against something that's at our very core. And it's foolish to put a mask on things. Slaves will always be slaves, no matter what you call them."

"All the same," said Jeremiel, tugging nervously at the sleeves of his robe. "Perhaps we should tread carefully. Perhaps we should not put the servants quite so far beneath us. Purely as a precaution, you see."

"They put themselves beneath us," said Ambriela. "And of their own volition. We're so high above them, and we always have been. They put us on pedestals even when we were slaves to them. They cannot help it, and neither can we. Look at them." She waved a hand towards the frightened servants, ducking into themselves as much as they could. "They want something from us. Our power, our protection. The mere proximity to those as high as we are sends them into a state of thrill. They want us to lead. To make their choices for them. They'd lash that burden to our backs, and thrust their own responsibilities upon us. So who's to complain if we ask for something in return?"

"It's no complaint of mine," said Jeremiel. "But I fear it could be a complaint of his."

"He made us that way," said Ambriela. "Do you think I want to be down here, living as we are?" Tears welled in her eyes, but barely, and they disappeared almost as soon as they'd come. "I don't feel anymore. I can't feel anymore. Not with what's been done to me. Am I to be judged for who I am? For the way I was made to be? I cared, once. We all did. But the caring's been wrung out of me. I see things the way they are." She sniffed at the servants, turning her nose up into the air. "None of them gave a whit about our kind. They cared not for us but for what we gave them. It was all hollow, and now so are we."

"The Son will care," said Jeremiel. His voice wavered, his confidence fading as the angels around him murmured indecisively. "Perhaps."

"He does not feel for us," said Ambriela. "Don't you see that? He cares for them, but not for us. He never did, and he never will." Her voice dropped low even as the entire room was silent. "It hurt me. It hurt all of us. We sang so many songs to him. We did exactly as he said. But where was the love for me? For any of us? We were tools, and nothing more. Machines, all of us. And if we finally see the truth, who is he to complain?"

"But perhaps he'll help us," said Jeremiel. "Perhaps things will be different once he's here. Better."

"The Son isn't coming back for us," snapped Ambriela. "He's coming back for them."

Cassie's jaw almost dropped. It was inconceivable. They'd thought they'd been abandoned, all of them. And now maybe they hadn't. No one had ever had any real hope of defeating the angels. No one with any sense, anyway. She'd known it was a lost cause, and so had everyone else. She'd fought because it was the right thing to do. Because it was fight or bend your knee forever, and she didn't have any intention of doing that.

But maybe someone up there had finally seen the light. Maybe they'd noticed what a mess they'd created, and they were finally going to do something to clean it up. The angels certainly seemed to think so. Even a mention of the Son made them cringe. She knew exactly what they were thinking about. All the things they'd done, all the people they'd hurt. If there was a Judgment Day, any angel who'd fallen would be sure to be judged.

And she and all the rest of humanity had reason to hope.

The angels were another matter. Their hopes were mixed with fear, and as Cassie scanned the room she could see something approaching pure dread on the faces a few of them. Maybe a little guilt was mixed in there, too, but if so it didn't look like it. Mostly it looked like they were afraid for their own hides. She could hear scattered whispers from the other servants, from the ones who'd picked up on the import of the angels' discussion. The younger ones were a blank slate as far as religion went, but the older ones had at least heard the stories from before the Fall. They knew what was coming, and they knew the angels' nightmare would be a dream come true for them.

"I sacrifice enough of my days for the Seraphim, and I shan't be bothered to waste any more on the servants," said Ambriela. "You'd have me spend my days cleaning, or cooking, or on some other menial labor? My time, that I'd rather spend as I please on myself? Think on your words. One of us must be slave to the other. Either we labor for them, or they labor for us. There's simply no middle ground, not while we inhabit the same world. We were servants to the Maker and his Son, just as this lot are to us. And I won't stand by and listen to him fault us for sharing faults of his own."

The angels stood silent, and so did she. She looked around the room, from seraph to seraph, giving them each their chance to object. Whatever their thoughts, none of them had the bravery to voice them, and Ambriela went back to her assignments with renewed enthusiasm. Two servants to clean the trash from the lower levels. A boy to fix sandals, and his mother to tan leather. A manservant each for a group of female angels, seated in a row on a velvet couch and whispering idle gossip among themselves.

And then she turned to Herman.

He stood there looking up at her, a smarmy grin plastered across his face, primming his robe and preparing for his dreams to come true. Cassie knew exactly what he was expecting. A position at the very top. Probably he thought he'd be Ambriela's own pledge. She hadn't taken a servant, not yet, and the supply of unassigned humans was dwindling. They stood there for a moment, he looking up and she looking down, until finally she pressed a finger against his forehead and beckoned towards one of the guards.

"The furnace," said Ambriela. "Find this one a shovel, and find him some coal." His face drooped in shock, but she just continued down the line, tapping at each of the servants' heads as she went. "The crafting floor. The kitchens. The transport of buckets of water up and down the tower."

"Madam," said Herman insistently. He stepped forward, his hands clenched against the cloth of his robe, tugging it into position as he walked.

You could have heard a pin drop. Cassie's stomach tightened into a knot, and she wasn't even near him. She'd known Herman was stupid, but this was another level of foolishness entirely. He'd been caught up in his delusions, so much so that he'd forgotten his place, and he'd forgotten the dangers of leaving it. Anything could happen if Ambriela grew angry, and Cassie knew full well that the fallout wouldn't be limited to the fool who'd set off the explosion.

Ambriela strolled back towards Herman, her head bent as she took in this creature that dared to speak to her directly. She stood in front of him, not saying a word, her wings tensed up behind her. The other angels were all just as silent, watching from their perches as if he were carrion about to be devoured.

Herman cleared his throat, summoning up all his confidence. "With respect, madam, I'm not meant for menial chores." He cleared his throat again, his eyes darting from angel to angel. "I'm worth so much more than that. Why, I managed Jehoel's accounts myself, and I practically dressed him. No one's tastes are finer than my own, I assure you." He raised his chin high in pride, the gloomy lines across his cheeks contorting into something close to a smile. "My service was quite valuable. Jehoel would have been nothing without me."

"Nothing?" said Ambriela. Herman's expression turned to one of pained obsequiousness. Cassie could see that he'd caught his mistake, but seconds too late. And she knew full well that those few words could be enough to doom him. She wondered if he'd gotten too used to challenging her without consequences, and if she should have done something about it. Arrogance was expected among the angels; among their servants, it was unimaginable. Maybe if she'd slapped him down a little harder, a little sooner, his sense of self-importance wouldn't have grown out of control. But in the forests, he'd just been a nuisance. She hadn't known they'd be coming back to a tower. And she hadn't known how delusional his fantasies about what the angels thought of him had become.

All around the room the angels leaned forward in their chairs, eager to see what came next. They weren't used to servants this bold, let alone servants this cheeky, and they weren't sure whether they should be amused or angry. Ambriela circled around Herman, running a finger along his shoulders, then across the sides of his face. Her tone was teasing, nearly friendly, but beneath the surface she was all ice. "You took the pledge, and this is how you speak of your former master? You think yourself superior to the Seraphim?"

Herman's breathing grew heavy, and sweat rolled down his forehead as he leaned forward in an exaggerated bow. "Hardly, madam. I simply meant my services. I did what Jehoel couldn't. I'm quite valuable as a servant, more so than the others." He forced a smile, puffing up his chest and trying to feign confidence. "I fear I'd be wasted on a mere shovel. I can do what others can't."

"What we can't," said Ambriela coldly. She scowled, her wings twitching behind her in fury. "You think us helpless. Centuries of serving you, and all we ask is a few decades of your life in return. And you think us incapable of menial chores?"

"I meant I do what other servants can't," said Herman hastily. "What someone as high up as you shouldn't have to." His voice grew faster, more nervous, and he spat out his words like a machine gun. "You've more important things to attend to than I do, I'm certain of it. Things I couldn't fathom. Things…" He trailed away into indistinguishable muttering, unable to meet her stare.

Cassie tried to think of some way to intervene. Herman's eyes kept moving back and forth, casting about for support from his cronies. But none of them would so much as look at him. They'd edged away into the crowd, vanishing among the others and leaving Herman to face his fate alone. She felt sorry for him, if only a little. His toadying to the angels was so pathetic, and so transparent. But he'd only been doing what he'd been taught. He'd lived among them for so long that he was one of them in attitude, if nothing else. He probably even loved them, after his own fashion. But it was as one-sided a relationship as there could be, and the angels saw him as nothing more than dirt on the soles of their sandals.

Ambriela was staring Herman in the face, malevolence

flashing in her eyes. Cassie ran through her options in her head. The angels would just kill her if she tried to stand in the way of whatever punishment Ambriela had planned. She knew she couldn't persuade them. She didn't know any of them, and didn't have the clout. The only thing she could think to do was to beg Faye to calm things down somehow. Faye knew these angels, and she was the only one who had any chance of helping. Cassie pushed her way through the crowd to where Faye stood, watching the show with a broad smile across her face.

But she wasn't fast enough.

Ambriela grabbed Herman by the scruff of the neck, lifting him into the air, his feet kicking helplessly below him. He tried to sputter something out, but her hands choked the words away before they left his lips. She strolled over towards an open balcony, dragging Herman along with her. He grunted and groaned, but no one moved to help him. A few of the angels followed along, but only for a better view of what was to come. Some tugged at their collars, unsettled by the talk of the Son and clearly uncomfortable with the proceedings. But the majority were still firmly in Ambriela's camp, at least in public, laughing and snorting in support of her.

"Too good for the place we had for you?" said Ambriela. "A proper servant doesn't complain about his assignments. A proper servant knows to keep his mouth shut. And we've no need for servants who don't know their place."

"Please," said Herman. "I'm so sorry. I'm such a fool. I'll love the furnace. I'll love it so much."

But Ambriela wasn't listening. She just dragged him

towards a crystal door, thrusting it open and letting in a beam of yellow light amid the colored glow around the room. It opened onto a balcony, leaving Herman with a view of the clear blue sky beyond. He didn't even struggle. He knew better than that; if there was any chance to save himself, it was in obedience. Fighting back would only make things worse.

"I'll do whatever I'm told," said Herman, his body gone as limp as his words. "Please."

"Whatever you're told?" said Ambriela. She waved her hand with a flourish towards her audience, her smile widening as she held him towards the edge of the balcony. "He'll do whatever he's told."

"Anything," said Herman. The air rushed around him, blowing strands of grey hair back and forth across his face, and he looked down at the ground below with terror in his eyes. "Please."

"Then jump," said Ambriela. "Let us see if you're truly the servant you claim to be."

"Jump?" said Herman. He looked like he couldn't quite understand what he was hearing. Ambriela pushed him closer towards the edge, then plopped him on the floor. He leaned against the railing, struggling to keep his wobbling legs from collapsing. "Jump?"

"Do as you're told, and jump," said Ambriela. "You say you're a servant. You say you're loyal. Perhaps if you obey, the Son will save you. Perhaps one of us wishes to curry his favor, and they'll fly down and save you for him."

"Save me," muttered Herman. He stared at the

ground below, then back at Ambriela, his expression a desperate plea for mercy.

"Perhaps I will save you myself, as a reward for your obedience," said Ambriela. "But only if you jump, and by your own accord."

He looked over the side again, his eyes welling with tears. Then he closed them tight, grabbed hold of the railing, and tossed himself over the side.

Ambriela spread her wings wide, tugging them against her back and looking down over the balcony. She turned back towards her audience with a smirk. "Then again, perhaps not."

The room erupted into a noxious mix of screams and laughter. A few of the seraphs looked queasy with guilt, but the majority were delighted. They chattered away among themselves, some loudly proposing a repeat of the performance with another few servants—just to put their new guests in the proper state of mind, of course. They missed their old entertainments, and here was a fresh batch of fools to start the play anew. The servants, on the other hand, were horrified. Some covered their eyes and shivered in fright, but many couldn't help but scream together in horror. They'd forgotten what it was like, living under the thumb of fallen angels, and they'd just received all too vivid a reminder.

As for Cassie, she was paralyzed by shock. She couldn't move, she couldn't talk, and she couldn't even blink. She'd gotten a reminder herself of why she'd been so afraid to come up here, and of the life she was now consigned to. And all her hopes of ever escaping it had vanished along with Herman.

CHAPTER TWELVE

JANA COULD HEAR A VOICE echoing down the hall as they approached, bouncing back and forth off the blackened walls. She wasn't sure who it was, not at first. But as they drew nearer she could make it out: Ambriela, speaking loudly and drowning out the indistinct chattering of a crowd far larger than the gathering of angels they'd seen before. "A fine catch. A bounty, and a worthy one, to be sure. But you ask for too much in exchange. Far too much."

She was approaching the ballroom, with Rhamiel and Thane flanking her on either side. But as close as they were, Jana still couldn't see Ambriela, not through the doorway. There were angels crowding in front of it, blocking her view as their wings flexed up and down behind them. As they moved, she caught a glimpse of something else just inside the room, something she hadn't expected. The ballroom was filled to capacity, and it was filled with more than angels.

"People," said Jana. "There's people."

There was a wall of them, visible just inside the

room. They huddled together in the center, and two stern seraphs stood at the door, guarding the exit in case any of them were inclined to leave. None of them made any move to. All she could see were their backs, all of them focused intently on Ambriela as she spoke.

"What you want comes at a cost," said Ambriela. "An unsettling one, for whoever's forced to pay it. And we expect more from you if we're to pay the price you ask." Jana had gotten close enough to see her, so long as she stood on her tiptoes and stretched her neck. Ambriela was as dismissive and as aloof as ever, speaking to someone at the center of the crowd. "You've brought a hundred servants here at best. We've easily more seraphs than that. Who is to go without clean clothes? Who is to cook their own meals? And who is to stay a servant to whom? We need more, if we're all to be satisfied. Hundreds more. What you've brought us simply won't do."

She could hear someone else speaking in response: another woman, standing somewhere in the crowd of humans huddled before the angels. The voice sounded familiar, but she couldn't quite place it. "I want what was promised. You demanded servants, and here they are. Willing ones, in point of fact. I ask only that you uphold your part of a bargain you were once quite eager to make."

"You gotta be shittin' me," said Thane. His face turned cherry red and contorted in fury, a look Jana was more than familiar with. She knew what was coming from the sound of his voice, but she didn't have time to try to keep him from doing something rash. Before she could even say a word he'd slung his rifle from his back and was charging into the ballroom, ducking underneath the wings of the guards and waving the gun in all directions as he went.

"The fool," said Rhamiel, bolting after him with Jana in tow. But it was too late, and he didn't have a chance of stopping the confrontation. He wouldn't let go of Jana's hand, not with the other seraphs nearby, and Thane had already barreled past the guards and disappeared among the servants before they'd even made it to the door. Rhamiel pushed his way inside and pulled Jana along with him, but he was too big to follow Thane through the crowd; his wings alone kept him from making his way through the dense mass of people.

"Where's he gone to?" said Rhamiel, tensely scanning the room. Jana couldn't see him, either; there were too many people, and Thane had gone right into the center of them all. But then she heard a loud cracking sound, piercing through the air and slamming against her eardrums. The servants all dropped to the ground in terror; they looked like they wanted to run, but there was nowhere for them to run to. Thane had fired his rifle into the ceiling, panicking nearly every other human in the room. Almost all of them were cowering in fear. Everyone but Thane and two women wearing cloaks, the only two humans brave enough to face him.

As for the angels, they were more surprised than scared. After a few seconds of shock had passed, they burst into laughter, leaning forward and hoping the turn of events would prove an entertaining distraction. It was a dangerous reaction, as Jana well knew, but Ambriela's was worse. She just sat in her chair and scowled, looking extremely displeased at the interruption of her affairs. It made Jana's stomach churn. Happy angels might allow a servant to survive their follies, if they were sufficiently entertained. An unhappy angel wouldn't hesitate to cut the entertainment short, and the servant's life along with it.

"Rhamiel, one of your little pets is off its leash," chided Ambriela. She gazed down at Thane from her chair, her face half smile, half sneer. "Control yourself, pet. Or you'll find one of us quite capable of controlling you instead."

"I ain't here for you," said Thane. "I'm here for her." He pointed at one of the two women, staring at him with cold eyes and a look of intense displeasure. Jana didn't recognize her, not at first. But then she looked closer, and there she was.

Faye.

She didn't look like herself, not exactly, not with an angel's expressions written across her face in place of her own. Zuphias was still inside her, still pulling her strings as if she were a puppet. If there was anything left of the woman who'd once tried to comfort her and guide her through the early days of a pregnancy she knew nothing about, Jana couldn't see it. And apparently neither could Thane. He'd been talking about finding Faye the entire trip, but now that he had, he sounded none too happy about their reunion.

"I'm here to settle things up with her," said Thane, waving his rifle around as he fumed. "Or him. Or whatever you want to call the asshole who's squatting inside my friend's body."

"Involuntarily," sniffed Faye. "I'd be free of my cage, in fact, if this sorry lot had any honor. They owe me the body of one of their own. Whether your friend regains hers once the transaction is done is no concern of mine."

"You in there?" said Thane skeptically. He stepped towards Faye, gritting his teeth and eying her up and down. "Can you hear me? Can you talk? You gotta try and talk." He reached out a hand to touch her face, but she just slapped it away.

"She's quite buried," said Faye. "Down deep, where you'd never find her." Her lips turned up into a smile, if something with so much viciousness and venom could be called that. "Your friend could hear, I think, but I suspect she doesn't want to. That way lies madness. Easier to rest inside one's dreams, waiting for it all to end no matter how long it takes."

"I'm gonna kill you," said Thane. His nostrils flared, his eyes grew to plates, and he spat into Faye's face and let out a frustrated roar. "I'm gonna tear you apart." He'd lost control of himself, and he almost made good on his words, leaping towards her with a hand aimed at her throat. But the servants' cowering had finally cleared a path for Rhamiel. He rushed between them and yanked at Thane's shoulder, spinning him to the floor and leaving Faye smirking down at the victim of her words. She looked up at her rescuer, comfortably housed in his own body and looming several feet above her. "Rhamiel. Dear Rhamiel."

"Zuphias?" said Rhamiel. He searched her eyes for something behind them, something he couldn't quite see. "Can it be you? Your body was floating in a vat when last we spoke. And the things the Cherubim had done to it...." He shook his head, waving away the memories. "These people told me you'd reappeared inside their friend. I wasn't quite sure I believed it."

"I've escaped my prison," said Faye. "A miracle all its own. But now it's either live in this body, or live inside the void my body has become. No eyes, no ears, no tongue. Nothing to feel. Nothing but me and my thoughts for all eternity."

"So she's gotta live like that instead," said Thane, pulling himself to his feet. "She's gotta be stuffed down in the dark just 'cause you don't like the hand you drew?"

"Someone must," said Faye smugly. "And I promise it shan't be me."

"You fucker," said Thane. He thrust himself forward only to be blocked again by Rhamiel. Thane strained against his grip, waving his arms towards Faye's throat, his fingers grasping at the air. His spirit almost overcame his lack of strength, his wild lunges forcing Rhamiel this way and that.

He'd gone savage again, and there was nothing to be done about it. Jana backed away; she knew what he was like when the mood came over him. He couldn't control himself, even if it was his own friend he was trying to strangle, and she didn't want to be in striking distance until the beast inside him was back in its cage. She tripped over a few of the servants as she went, pressing a hand against one of their backs to steady herself and keep from falling. Then she heard someone whispering in her ear. "Jana. It's you."

She nearly jumped at the sound. This voice was one

she remembered, and one she remembered well. It was a voice that had scolded her when she hadn't done her chores, a voice that had called her away from her home and up to places she'd never imagined she'd see, a voice that had warned her of dangers to come. She turned and looked. Behind her was the other woman who'd stood her ground when Thane had fired his gun, and she recognized her in an instant.

It was Cassie.

She was standing there, either brave enough or foolish enough to stay on her feet, alive and well and in the flesh. She looked a little older than she had before, her face a little wearier. Her eyes flicked towards Jana, then went straight ahead, pretending she didn't see her. She bowed down a little lower, mixing back in with the other servants and whispering just loudly enough for Jana to hear. "Jana. I want to talk to you." She paused, then spoke again. "I need to."

"How did you get here?" said Jana, keeping her voice as quiet as she could. "And why?" She tried not to look directly at Cassie; she must have thought she was in danger, and Jana didn't want to frighten her any further. Instead she looked around at the other people, paying closer attention than she had before.

She found she knew some of them: she couldn't put names to any of the faces, but she was certain she remembered seeing them back in her own tower. There was a froggy little man with a protruding lower lip that almost rubbed against his nose; she knew she'd seen him carrying water through the hallways, and she remembered him once nearly spilling an entire bucket on her cloak.

A few feet away was a woman with a bent nose and thick wrinkles on her forehead who she was sure had worked near Nefta's chambers. She didn't see Sam or Peter or anyone she knew very well, but she had no doubt that they were all from the same place as she was. They'd come from her tower, and now they were seeking refuge here, just as she was.

Cassie stared straight ahead for a few more seconds, then whispered again. "We can't speak. Not now. But bring me with you. We have to talk. We have to help these people out of here."

Jana nodded as Cassie ducked down to the ground, blending in with the others while the room was still absorbed by the conflict between Rhamiel and Faye. Rhamiel had managed to restrain Thane, mostly, but he was still spouting threats and brandishing his rifle even if he was doing it from a few feet further away.

Faye just ignored Thane's grunts and growls, focusing her attention on Rhamiel. "Calm this creature, if you can." She looked down at herself in disgust, pinching at the flesh of her arm. "I've no intentions of staying in this condition. Locked inside a feeble body, and a woman's, no less. Ambriela has made me a promise. Stock her tower with servants, and she'll furnish me with the body of one of their own. A seraph's body. An immortal one, one the cherubs haven't tampered with."

"It's true," said Ambriela. "And if he'd only fulfilled his end of the bargain, I'd be working my miracles already."

"My end of the bargain is complete," said Faye. "Look around us. More than a hundred of them, and all I ask is a single body in return. I'd take the weakest among you, the truth be told. I want out of this skin, and I want out of it now."

"You promised me a tower full of servants," said Ambriela. "And we haven't even one for each of us. Not with this lot. We need more. And we still need you. You're of much more use to us in human skin, I'm afraid. They trust you. They listen to you. And it's far easier to acquire an intact set of slaves through persuasion than it is through force." She looked over to Jana, her eyes dark with malice. "Isn't that right, dear Rhamiel?"

It roiled Jana inside as she said it. She wanted to do just what Thane would have done, running around punching at people until they learned to keep their snide comments to themselves. Thane looked like he would have done it for her, in fact, if Rhamiel didn't have him by the scruff of the neck. But she had more control than he did. She took a breath, thought of her child, and held it all inside. She looked to the floor, ready to do or say whatever Ambriela wanted. Whatever it took, if it would only keep her child alive.

She might have been able to bring herself to bow for the sake of survival, but someone else couldn't. Rhamiel's wings spread wide, he dropped Thane to the ground, and he took a few deliberate steps towards Ambriela. He'd seen the way she'd looked at Jana, and he was very, very unhappy.

"You'll direct your words to me, unless you prefer to choke on them," said Rhamiel. "A threat to my pledge is a threat to me." His eyes filled with fire, his teeth clenched. "I won't hesitate, Ambriela. My patience is worn clean through. I'll kill you in a heartbeat if you make so much as a grimace at her again."

Jana was scared, but it warmed her inside to hear him speak. She wasn't strong, not compared to the angels, and that left her with little she could do to protect herself. She had to keep the angels happy, and that was that. But Rhamiel wouldn't let her bow. He'd set her free, and not just to see her chained up again by someone else. It made her feel safe. Watching him rattle his sword, watching the looks of fear on the faces of the other angels, and watching them drop their heads to him just as she once had to them. It made her feel like no one could hurt her, no one in the entire world.

No one but him.

He stood there, facing down Ambriela, facing down a tower full of enemies for the sake of her honor. It sent a wave of emotions through her, surging up and down and back again. She loved him, and she couldn't help that, no matter what he'd done in the past. But she feared him, too, if only because he was one of them. And she feared the truth. The truth about what he'd done, the truth about what he'd do again, and the truth about what would happen to them all when the Maker's plans were finished.

The only thing comforting her was that as afraid as she was, the other angels were finally showing some fear of their own. Ambriela in particular had gone from taunting Jana with every word to studiously avoiding any eye contact whatsoever. She slowly placed her wine glass on a tray held by a waiting seraph, holding her hands up in submission. "Calm yourself, Rhamiel. We've truly nothing to fight over. Perhaps I've grown too used to our parlor games, but they're meant as amusement, and not as a threat."

"I know your games," said Rhamiel. "I know them well. And I know the way they often end."

"I'll work the glamour you seek," said Ambriela. "Hide you away, as best I can. I'll even make the snarling one look a hapless puppy, if it pleases you. But you will have to go, and leave us to our business. We need you gone from here if we're to stay neutral. And Zuphias will have his miracle, once he works for it. Perhaps he'll set your friend free after that. But that is no affair of yours."

"You'd pervert the power you were given?" said Rhamiel. "Even with the Son coming here, and even with the chance of redemption it implies?"

"It's a folly, Rhamiel," said Ambriela. "There shall be no redemption. Not for us. Have you ever heard of such a thing among the fallen? No one ever came back from Lucifer's Pit. And no one ever shall."

"Any human can be redeemed," said Rhamiel, waving a hand around the room. "Any of them. Deeds cannot be undone, but their doers can change."

"Perhaps any human can be redeemed," said Ambriela. "But we are no humans." She glanced at Faye, and the room erupted in titters at Zuphias's expense. "Most of us, at least."

"Yet we live among them," said Rhamiel. "We've acquired their faults, and perhaps we've acquired other characteristics as well. A fallen angel has never been redeemed, true. But what angel had ever fallen to Earth before our rebellion? The others were locked away in their Pit. We were cast out of our Eden, but we were left free to roam this plane. We're just as free as humans are to make our own choices. Perhaps we simply haven't made the right ones."

"You're mad with love, Rhamiel," said Ambriela. "A fault all its own."

"I do not deny its truth," said Rhamiel. He ran a hand along Jana's back, wrapping his fingers around her waist as he pulled her close. "Though I deny that it's a fault." Jana could feel the eyes of the room upon her. It was embarrassing, but in this moment she didn't even care. She felt the old warmth for him, the same rush of adrenaline as when she'd been in his arms back in her tower. She knew she had to make things right with him somehow, no matter what he'd done. He was the father of her son, and he was the only one who could protect him. That was what mattered to her, more than anything.

The other angels around the room seemed just as entranced by Rhamiel's words as she was. He'd given them something they hadn't had in a decade: hope. Hope that if it were possible for them to change once, it might be possible for them to change yet again. Hope that they might save themselves, reversing their exile and returning to the beings they'd once been. But some of them didn't see it that way. They'd all chosen their fall, and some of them weren't quite as eager to go back to the way things had been.

"How sweet," said Ambriela. Her voice rose as she stood to address the room. "And how stupid. He'd seduce you all with promises of redemption, just as he seduced this foolish girl with his strength. But to fall is to fall. Rhamiel must believe this dream because he cannot bear to face the truth of what he is. The words he sells you are nothing but a fantasy."

"It is no fantasy," said Rhamiel. "It is a hope. I know what I am. The question is what I'd like to be."

"The question is whether we accept what we are, or listen to yet another self-righteous fool trying to peddle us a future we cannot have," said Ambriela. "The wise learn from their mistakes. We made war twice against an enemy we could not defeat. Once against the Maker, and once against Suriel. And now he'd have us make the same mistake yet again. He'd have us abandon our neutrality and face a foe whose power is beyond us. And for what? To warm our hearts before we die? We must tend to our own affairs, I'm afraid, and not to the problems of others."

"And you must tend to your bargains," said Faye. "I shall not work for free. Give me a body, a true angel's body, and I will harvest all the slaves you like. I could range further. I could drag them here one by one. I'd be far more efficient."

"You would lose all motivation, I fear," said Ambriela. "And I suspect you'd never find your way back."

"Can't you send him off to his own body?" said Rhamiel. "Just for a time? "

"Traitor," spat Faye. Her face contorted in fury, and she strode towards Rhamiel, poking a finger at his chest. "I thought you a friend. I fought by your side. I was the hound in your Hunt, sniffing out the very prey you now seek to spare. And how do you repay my loyalty? By locking me inside a living corpse."

"Zuphias," said Rhamiel. "What you do is far from just. It's not your body that's corrupted, but your soul. I cannot be a party to it."

"You've been a party to worse," said Faye. "To far worse."

"Once, when I had nothing but an eternity of exile to look forward to," said Rhamiel. "That time is past." He looked down at Jana, and then down to her stomach. "And now I have a future to be concerned with."

"It's a moot point, in any event," said Ambriela. She gently pushed herself between the two of them, all smiles and seduction, trying her best to soothe their anger before things spiraled out of her control. "We need a place to put Zuphias, and we have none. He'll be lost to us if he's sent away. The connection will be severed, and if he's off who knows where in his own body, we'd never find him again. I remind you that we need him, if our tower's to regain its former glory. And we will not give him up."

The two of them glared at one another across Ambriela's wings. Faye's face was as smug as any fallen angel's had ever been, and Rhamiel was barely able to contain his disgust. But then a voice came from behind them, drawing their attention away from each other.

"I'll do it," said Thane. He stepped forward from behind Rhamiel, pulling his rifle from his shoulder and dropping it to the floor. Then he set his jaw and stood before Ambriela as she sized up the creature in front of her. "I'll do it. Put him inside me, and let her go."

"I will not bounce from servant to servant like some unwanted house guest," snapped Faye. She ran a hand up and down Thane's arm, and he tensed at the touch. "This body will not do. It will age and die, just like all the rest of them."

"Thane," said Rhamiel, placing a firm hand upon his shoulder. "Be silent. Your proposal is as rash as it is foolish. You haven't thought through the implications. You do not know the things you'd endure."

"Bullshit," said Thane. He pushed Rhamiel's hand away, standing toe to toe with Ambriela. "He needs a body. I need to help my friend. And the rest of you want Rhamiel outta your tower before he kicks all of your asses to hell and back. So put him inside me, let her go, and let's be done with this shit forever."

CHAPTER THIRTEEN

"IT'S MY CHOICE," SAID THANE. "It's my body, and I get to do whatever stupid thing I want to it. Won't be the first bad decision I ever made, either. I spent a lifetime drinkin' too much, eatin' like shit. That angel's gettin' the raw end of this deal." He rubbed at the first beginnings of a paunch around his stomach, forcing a smile. "He keeps going like I did, this thing's going to wear out on him instead of on me. The guy's a sucker."

"This is different," said Jana. "It's not just a drink. You know that. You know it."

"You'll do fine without me," said Thane. "Better, I think. No more yellin'. And you'll have Faye back. She's a hell of a lot nicer than I am. You'll be fine. The two of you can help each other more than I ever could."

"I want you both," said Jana. Tears welled in her eyes, and she was as surprised by it as he was. For the longest time she'd hated him. She'd thought he was awful for its own sake, just like the angels were. But she'd gotten to know him, and he'd gotten to know her. He was angry, and more than any man should have to be. But the rage wasn't about her, and there was something else beneath it. A kindness that shined through sometimes, and that had appeared more and more often as they'd travelled side by side.

He didn't deserve the suffering he was volunteering for. Faye didn't, either, but no one should have to make that kind of choice. She thought back to the little things he'd done for her on their journey. An entire day spent hunting around in some old marketplace, searching until he found a puffy sleeping bag to make the truck they rode in a little more comfortable for someone as pregnant as she was. Losing sleep on countless nights to stand guard so she didn't have to, and carting back armloads of books from old houses so she'd have something to read as they went. He'd been sheepish at first, atoning for his old angers however he could. But then guilt had turned to caring, and before long he'd doted on her almost as much as Rhamiel did.

She couldn't hold the emotion inside. She tried to keep talking, but nothing but sad little moans would come out. He was the only person she really knew anymore, the only one besides Rhamiel, and now she was about to lose him. She turned away, putting an arm in front of her face and crying into it to keep the hurt from showing.

Thane's facade cracked at the sight. He wrapped her up in her arms, swaying back and forth as sobs burst from her lips. "It ain't that bad. I'll be back. He'll get his new angel's body, and then they'll bring me back."

"They won't," said Jana. "They'll give your body to the other angel. They'll have to."

"Someone's got to do it," said Thane. "If someone doesn't step up and do this, Faye's stuck, and I don't think she's ever gettin' out."

"Why you?" said Jana between the tears. "Why does it have to be you?"

"My daughter's gone," said Thane quietly. "I told you I lost her. I don't think you know how much that hurts. You may not get it, now, but you will pretty soon. Pretty soon your kid'll be all you ever think about." He looked down at her stomach, fought away a few tears of his own, and then managed to look back at her. "It's every day. I wake up and it's like a buncha knives in my gut. Then they twist, and the whole day I'm just tryin' to think of anything else I can. I go to sleep and it's nightmares. Melanie in the dark, and all these guys comin' at her. I wake up in a sweat and it starts all over."

"This won't fix it," said Jana. "It won't."

"I just don't wanna be here anymore," said Thane. "I need a break. And I need to feel like I mattered. Like I did something that mattered to somebody else before I went. I couldn't save her. But I can save Faye, and I'm not gonna let anything stop me."

"You'll be all alone," said Jana. She couldn't imagine it. Utter darkness, and not a single form of outside stimulation. "Just you. You and your thoughts." She shuddered. She wouldn't survive it, not if it were her. And it was hardly the escape Thane thought it would be. His demons would follow him in there, and he'd be locked away with them forever. "If it's bad now, what'll it be like for you then?"

"Maybe I need it," said Thane. "Just me. Maybe I need time to think." He didn't look like he believed it, but he kept spouting out the words, rationalizing the choice he'd already made. "And besides. It's me, or it's someone else. And I'll be damned if I'm going to let it be her."

"Don't," said Jana. "Don't do this."

"I have to," said Thane. "I can't leave a friend like that. I just can't. If it were you, I'd do the same thing. Might even do it for that angel of yours, too, if he asked me nice enough."

She heard rustling from behind them, and a little cough. There was Rhamiel, looking entirely unsure about whether this was the right choice to make. But he stood there silently, letting Jana cry it out and waiting until she'd had time to say her goodbyes. When she was done he turned to Thane, looking him up and down.

"Are you ready?" said Rhamiel. "You don't have to go through with this, you know. It's a noble decision, but in many ways a foolish one."

"Well, then I guess I'm a damned fool," said Thane. He looked over at Ambriela, balling his fingers into fists, and then closed his eyes. "Light me up."

Faye stood next to him, looking pleased as punch. Ambriela's eyes went back and forth between them, and after a moment she rose from her chair. "Very well. It might be for the better, in any event. Perhaps Zuphias will be a more efficient slaver in a stronger body."

"I'll be a happier one, at least," said Faye. "It's a step

up, if only a small one." She licked her lips as she eyed Thane up and down. "A strong body, but only a temporary one. I'm still expecting the one I was promised."

"Soon enough," said Ambriela. She stood between the two of them, placing one hand on Thane's forehead and the other on Faye's. "But first things first." For a time she was silent. Then her eyes snapped shut, her eyelids pulsing up and down. Her mouth moved as if she were speaking, but no words came forth. Not from her, at least.

It started with Faye. Her eyes rolled into her head, and the smug smirk vanished from her face, replaced with a loose jaw and a line of drool. Her mouth began to move, synchronizing with Ambriela's. At first all that came out were whispers. But then the sound grew, and soon she was standing there motionless and shouting words only the angels could understand. "Halah makurah shabazz atadah! Halah makurah shabazz atadah!"

Thane was next. He'd been looking at Faye, his nerves showing in his eyes, but then the life inside them slowly dulled away. Soon he was repeating nonsense just as she was, their voices ping-ponging back and forth until they joined together in harmony. The sound grew louder and louder, the chants distorting their voices until neither of them were recognizable as human. Then something clicked and it became a song, a single voice filling the room, somehow soprano and bass all at once.

It was the most beautiful thing Jana had ever heard. The angels didn't sing anymore, and they hadn't in years. This was what they'd been talking about, the choirs they now damned but that once had ruled their lives. She didn't understand a word the voices said, but the sound was dazzling, more perfect than anything she'd ever heard from human tongues. The two kept singing, louder and louder, and some of the angels even quietly joined in. She hummed along with it, trying to memorize the tune, but it was too complicated. There was too much to it, too many pieces merged together into one, and in the end she decided to stand there, close her eyes, and listen.

The song stopped all at once. Faye and Thane stood swaying on their feet beside one another, looking like blades of grass blowing back and forth however the wind took them. Their eyes were closed, the both of them moving in unison, wobbling in the same direction as if they were partners in some ritualistic dance. Jana thought they were about to fall over, but somehow they kept their balance, and after a minute or so their backs both went ramrod straight. They stood at attention, eyes shut and mouths open, not a sound passing from their lips.

It was Faye who spoke first. "What?" Her eyes were groggy, and her words were slurred, her lips barely her own to command. But something in the tone was different, and Jana could see something new in her face. She was recovering herself, but slowly, and she acted as if she were drunk, stumbling on her feet as she fought for her balance. "Where? How?"

"You will be fine," said Rhamiel, offering her his arm. But Faye just slapped at it, nearly toppling over as she lunged towards him. "Angels. Kill them. All you do is hurt."

"Shush," said Jana. She put an arm around Faye's shoulder, and after a short, angry glare there was finally recognition in her eyes. Jana led her towards the other servants, walking her discreetly towards where Cassie sat. She eased Faye to the floor in the middle of them all, leaving her where she knew she'd be safe, and then headed back towards Thane.

He was standing there as if he were in a trance, gazing off at nothing with his mouth agape. For a moment hope rose within her. He seemed more zombie than puppet. He wasn't himself, but he wasn't anyone else, either. Maybe Zuphias was gone. Maybe there was some way to get Thane back from where they'd sent him.

"Where is he?" said Jana. "Where did he go?"

"I haven't the slightest idea," said Ambriela cheerfully. "Off into Zuphias's old body, most likely. Or perhaps he's vanished into the ether, or gone down to Lucifer's Pit. It's no business of mine. This was what you asked me for, and this is what I've given you. This shell is the property of Zuphias to do with as he pleases."

"But he's not talking," said Jana. "Why isn't he talking?"

"Patience, girl," said Ambriela. "Don't question things you cannot fathom. You're a simple creature, with a simple mind, and some things are just beyond you."

Rhamiel looked like he was about to slap her. But she just smiled, turned back to Thane, and waited in silence. Minutes ticked by, and nothing happened. Then he gasped, sucking in the air as his eyes burst open.

Thane coughed, nearly hacking out his lungs before he finally pulled himself upright. He ran his hands up and down his body, pinching and poking as he made sure everything was where it was supposed to be. Then he smiled, a grin too satisfied at the situation for a man who cared about anyone but himself. "Better. Much better."

"Thane," said Jana. She knew it wasn't him, but still she reached a hand out towards him, grasping at one last touch, one last connection between the two of them. But as the man before her flexed his hands and felt his body, smiling and gloating all the while, she knew there was nothing more of her friend within him.

"It was his choice," said Rhamiel. He pulled her away and wrapped her in his arms, turning her head against his chest so she couldn't see. "It wasn't the choice any of us wanted, but in the end, it was his to make. We'll set things right. I promise you we'll find a way to set things right somehow."

"You'll be doing it someplace else, then," said Ambriela. "You've tortured us enough with your moralizing and your self-righteous posturing. It's unbearable, almost as if we hadn't left Heaven at all. You're leaving. You and your girl. And you must do it now."

"The glamour," said Rhamiel. "Work your glamour, and we'll be gone from your lives forever. And once the Son is born, we'll put in a word for you. Sins aside, we'll tell him what you did."

"As if I need your recommendation," said Ambriela. "Or want it." Her smile turned to sneer, and she ran a hand along Rhamiel's cheek. "I'm doing this to be rid of you, and that's that. The girl will look simply beastly. More toad than temptress. And you. I hope your vanity's a thing of the past, for your sake." She slapped a hand against his stomach. "You'll have the gut of an old man. Your hair will be thin. The light in your eyes, gone. Your—"

"Be silent," said Rhamiel.

"You dare," said Ambriela, her eyes flashing with anger. "We grant you what you ask, and beg only that you leave us in peace. You don't offer us a single thing in return. It's quite a bargain, but still you seek a quarrel. Think on the matter and you'll see I'm right. However can you hide if I make you both appear as beauties? Every eye you meet would be upon you."

"I said be silent," said Rhamiel. "I hear something." He raised a hand, and the room quieted. He closed his eyes, listening intently. Then the noise came again, and his eyes flashed open along with it.

Jana listened as carefully as she could, and soon she could hear it, too. A low buzzing bass that rolled towards them from somewhere outside. She couldn't place what it was. A braying animal, perhaps. She might even have thought it was someone blowing their nose, if it had come from the next room. But it was too loud. Too far away. They waited a few moments, and then she heard it again. Closer. Louder. More familiar.

It sounded like something she'd heard before. It sounded like something that had once filled the skies and thundered down upon them all, a portent of awful things to come.

It sounded like a chorus of horns.

"It cannot be," said Ambriela. She stood from her chair, stumbling towards the balcony in a daze. She shook her head, her words denying what her face said she knew to be true. "It simply cannot be."

"It is," said Rhamiel. "Suriel has come. And now we must go."

CHAPTER FOURTEEN

THE SKY WAS FILLED WITH little black dots, swarming towards them from off in the distance. They moved in formation, aligned in squares or rows that rolled through the clouds with military precision. Horns bellowed from somewhere behind them, deep guttural sounds that shook the air even as the steady thump, thump of hundreds of drums pounded against the walls of the tower. It was the battle call of the Seraphim, and an entire army was heeding its command.

"Leave, Ambriela," said Rhamiel. He stood at the entrance to the ballroom, holding Jana by her hand and calling behind him as he prepared to go. "Leave your tower, and do it now. If you do not lead your people out, there'll be no hope for them."

"He's coming," said Ambriela softly. She stood near one of the balconies, staring off into the distance at the approaching army, the network of scars across her face glowing red in the sun. "You brought him upon us. You dragged us into Suriel's war, and now he will destroy us all because of your folly."

Panicked voices reverberated around the room from human and angel alike. The servants stayed on the floor in the center of the ballroom, while the seraphs drifted towards the windows, staring out in fear at the swarm that blotted the skies beyond. All of them were shouting out at once, cries that bordered on hysteria. Ambriela paid them no mind; she just kept talking to herself and watching the army approach. "This cannot be. It cannot. We've done nothing to him. Surely he'll see reason. Surely he'll see that we mean him no harm and leave us to our own affairs."

"He'll force you to bend the knee, Ambriela," said Rhamiel. "Each and every one of you. And the seraphs of this tower are no fighters." He looked around at the flurry of agitated wings buzzing throughout the room. "The strongest of us could not beat him in the open field. The weakest of us have no option but to run."

The angels seemed to ratify his words with their actions. The ones carrying food had dropped their trays and abandoned their duties, blending in among those they were serving. All of them cowered in fear just as their newfound servants had, watching the events outside with resignation. Rhamiel called out one last time, waving Jana and Faye through the door as he went. "Ambriela. You've conditioned your brothers and sisters to bow and grovel in your service. And it's no more difficult to bow to Suriel than it is to bow to you. You cannot fight. And I cannot stay, not with what's at stake. Come with us or do not, but you've little time to choose."

She snapped at him, starting into a biting response. But a crashing noise from above cut her off, diverting the attention of the room. A dark shape burst through a window near the ceiling, shattering the colored glass and sending out a rain of shards. The shape rolled towards the floor, a tangled mess of metal and flesh.

Wings spread from where the thing had landed, and an angel rose to his feet. He was naked but for a ragged brown cloth at his waist, and the skin on his chest was covered in black gashes, the singe marks of his master's whip. His eyes were wild, the whites turned pink with blood. Heavy chains hung from his arms and ran around the back of him, looping over his head and ending in a horse's bit jammed into his mouth. His fall had gotten him nowhere; he was less than slave, no more than cheap livestock in an archangel's army.

The angel drew a sword from his belt, a thin rapier of fire. Then he let out an angry moan, muffled by the bit in his mouth, and charged towards Ambriela. She barely had time to reach for her own weapon before the seraphs around her had knocked the angel to the ground, rushing at him and stabbing away with their metal swords. They didn't do much more than nick him; the swords themselves bent or snapped against his skin before any real damage was done. But then the seraphs began kicking and punching, tearing at him with all their might. Weapons forged from earthly metals might not have been strong enough to hurt him, but fellow angels were. He struggled to rise to his feet, but as the blows rained upon him he grew weaker and weaker until he ceased to move entirely.

"Kill him," said Ambriela. She strode towards the angel and joined in with the others in the attack, sending her boot into the angel's side for good measure. "And toss his corpse from the tower."

But even as the seraphs around her pummeled the intruder to a pulp, another window burst inward, and then another. Angel after angel crashed into the room, each bearing Suriel's chains, and each bearing the scars from his whips. They rolled to their feet, more and more of them, adding to the melee and sending the room into chaos. Some of the seraphs kept trying to fight; others panicked and ran to the hallway. Soon the doors to the ballroom were a crush of seraphs and servants, pushing against one another and crowding the exit. A few seraphs managed to scatter out the windows themselves, buzzing out of the tower like bees from a damaged hive. The rest of them were trapped inside, flailing against attackers that came from everywhere at once.

Suriel's slaves had free rein inside, and only Rhamiel had a weapon to match them. He spread his wings and drew his sword, waving it before him and slicing a deep gash into one of the attacking angels who came too close. A kick sent the attacker reeling, spinning to the ground in a tangle of chains. Another charged him from behind, swinging wildly with his rapier. But Rhamiel heard the footsteps, dropping his head just a moment before the sword connected with his neck. The fire swept past his head, and he jerked his elbow behind him, dropping the angel to the floor with a blow to the stomach. As the angel wheezed, Rhamiel grabbed him by the chains, swinging him round and tossing him out the window and over the side of the tower.

He craned his head behind him, eager to check on

Jana. She was standing with Faye, both hovering to the side of the room's exit, avoiding the fleeing horde and waiting for him follow. He pressed towards them through the skirmish. An angel lunged at him as he went, a thin female warrior with matted brown hair that curved around her face and covered most of her scars. Her chains were made of silver and lined with jewels, a mock gift from her master, and she screeched through her bit as she swung her sword at Rhamiel.

He gripped her by the wrist, slamming her sword aside, but she kept clawing at him, aiming at his eyes with grimy black nails grown long as daggers. Finally he slammed her away with a blow to the shoulder, flipping her on her back and leaving her lying on the floor in a sputtering heap. He took another step towards Jana, but the angel grabbed at his legs, dragging him to the ground in a flurry of wild kicks and punches.

The crowd was thinning, and most of those who meant to leave had either escaped or found themselves entangled in the battle. But that left Jana exposed, tending to Faye as she gradually roused from her stupor. A thin scarecrow of an angel stumbled towards her, his skin red as an apple. His chains wound around his legs, forcing him into slow, careful steps. He was jabbering something at her, but the bit in his mouth made it come out as a garbled growl. But his eyes spoke what his tongue couldn't: they lit with glee at the prize before him, the girl his master coveted and his only hope for freedom.

She tried to move away, but Faye flopped to the floor, her legs only barely answering her commands. Jana pulled at her, dragging her away even as the slavering angel crept closer and closer. Someone knocked her aside as they fled down the hall, hurling her to the floor. Pain stabbed at her from her stomach. She didn't see whether it was a seraph or a servant she'd collided with, but in the end it didn't matter. She wasn't meant to be bashed about, not this late in her pregnancy, and she closed her eyes to absorb the agony. Then she felt an urgent kick from within. She flipped open her eyes to see the angel standing above her, film bubbling from his mouth and hatred pouring from his eyes.

He snatched at Jana's throat, choking off the air as she struggled against him. Faye pulled at his arm, but she'd have been too weak to stop him even if she weren't still adjusting to her own body. The angel slapped her face, sending her into the wall and knocking the wind out of her. All Jana could do was watch as the angel snarled down at her. He was thin and weak, relatively speaking, but he was still too much for any human to handle.

She'd thought Suriel wanted to capture her, and maybe he still did, but this angel was beyond anyone else's control. He was mad with rage, and he raised his sword above her, the fire flickering orange against the rainbow light from the windows around them. She felt a kick inside her again, but it was too late. She had nowhere to run to, and she was nothing against the monster standing above her. His sword swung down, sending a whoosh of heat towards Jana's face. Then all she could see was a solid wall of fire.

She was amazed to be alive. The flame danced up and down in front of her, just inches from her nose. Tongues of fire licked at her eyes, and she didn't dare move an inch. The fire pushed up, then down, then back again. Then she heard a deep, guttural shout, the fire flashed away, and the angel sank to his knees, blood gurgling out of his mouth.

There was Rhamiel, standing above her, pulling his sword from the angel's chest. He'd managed to parry the blow with his sword, and he'd been the stronger of the two of them. She could see a rapier of fire rolling along the floor next to the angel's feet, even as he collapsed headfirst to the ground.

"You must go," said Rhamiel, helping Jana to her feet. His armor was stained red, and his golden hair speckled with drops of blood. He ran a hand through Jana's hair, cupping her head softly in his fingers and speaking firmly into her ear. "Go. Now. The both of you. Into the halls, while I cover your escape. I will keep myself between you and any who'd do you harm. Do not stray too far, and do not leave my sight."

"We can't," shouted Jana, struggling to be heard above the din. "What about the rest of them?" There was still a group of servants lying on the floor in the center of the room, mostly women and children, all too terrified to make a move to flee. Suriel's angels were ignoring them for the moment, too busy slaughtering their brothers to bother with enemies who weren't capable of resistance. But a wild battle raged around them, and more and more of Suriel's army was pouring in through the balconies. The maddened angels were lashing out at everything around them with wings, including each other, and it was only a matter of time before they'd butcher everyone in the room.

"Just us," said Rhamiel. He eyed the helpless servants, then grabbed Jana and Faye by the arms and guided them towards the door. "Look at how many there are. I will defend the exit as long as I can, but we cannot save them all."

"My friend," said Jana. "We have to help my friend." She struggled against him, managing to point out one of the servants. It was a woman in a grey cloak, standing by the others, dragging them to their feet one by one and shoving them towards the door. She was doing her best to save them from themselves, but they were all so terrified that it was a nearly impossible task. They'd stumble a few feet while she was yelling at them, but collapse to the ground again the second she'd moved on to another servant.

Rhamiel squinted, staring at the woman for a long moment. "I know her." He scanned her face, searching his memories, and then it clicked. "I know her from the tower. And I met her outside, in the city. She told me about you. That you were alive."

"Cassie," said Jana. "We can't leave her here to die." She wrapped her arms around Rhamiel's neck, pleading into his ear. "She helped me get out. She helped you find me. We can't just leave her."

"And we cannot take her," said Rhamiel softly. He shook his head, looking away, then looked back at Jana. "I intend to fly us far away from here. I've one arm for you, and one for this friend of yours we've rescued from Zuphias." His voice wavered as he ran a hand across Jana's cheek. "I cannot risk you. I cannot fight them all, and I cannot risk you."

"We have to try to help Cassie," said Jana insistently. "We have to bring her with us. I won't leave her here."

"Jana," said Rhamiel. "It's a kindness that you ask, but a foolish one. Many will die this day. We cannot stop that. You are what matters more than anything. To me, and to the world."

"You said you wanted to redeem yourself," said Jana. "You said you don't want to be like you were before. Didn't you?"

"I meant every word," said Rhamiel. He puffed up his wings, his expression grim. "I won't let you go up there alone. I won't let my past consume me the way so many others have."

"Then don't," said Jana. She looked up at him as he stood there pondering the choices before him. She couldn't be sure what he'd do. He looked torn, forced to choose between saving the one he loved and saving what was left of his soul. All she could do was stare up at him, begging with her eyes and praying he'd choose what was right. She couldn't live with herself if she just left a friend to face her death alone, and all for the sake of her own skin. She couldn't live with him if he was the type of man who would. More than anything, she had to know there'd been a change in him. She had to know the spark of good she saw in him was more than mere illusion.

The moment was tense, and it seemed to last forever. Rhamiel was locked in a struggle with himself, and she knew it wasn't an easy one. He cared for her; she could see that, and she didn't doubt it. But she'd asked him to risk something he loved more than anything for the sake of something that was right. She'd asked him to prove the truth of all his words about redemption, and proof would come at a cost. She knew deep down in her heart that he wanted to grab her and flee, and for an instant she thought he was about to do just that. But then he whirled around, marching back into the ballroom and back into the thick of the battle. One of the enslaved seraphs charged at him, a hobbled old angel with bronze skin and a fat fiery broadsword. But Rhamiel just swatted him to the ground with a slap of his hand.

"Come," said Rhamiel. He waved his sword above his head, his shout piercing the commotion and drawing the attention of every servant in the room. "All of you! Make your way down the stairs, and do it at once!"

The servants didn't need any further encouragement. An order from an angel broke through their hesitation and made them do the only sensible thing they could: run, as fast as possible, and as far away from the invaders as their legs would take them. They streamed through the door, past Jana and off into the darkened hallways. But they didn't come alone. Rhamiel's shouting had attracted more than servants: several of the invading seraphs stumbled towards him, dragging their chains along behind them.

The first one went for Rhamiel's throat, lunging forward and jabbing at the air with his sword. But the angel telegraphed the blow; his arms were weighted down with bulky manacles that slowed the swing, and Rhamiel was too quick for him. The angel's head rolled away from his shoulders with a slash of Rhamiel's sword, even as a second angel shambled forward to take his place. Rhamiel pulled backwards, only to find another of the angels leaping onto his shoulders, clutching at him and entangling him in its chains. They both rattled to the floor in a heap as angel after angel fell upon him, grabbing at him from every side as he struggled to his feet.

"Run, Jana," said Rhamiel. He called to Cassie as she herded the last of the servants out the exit, scanning the room to make sure that none had been left behind. "Run, all of you, and I will follow."

"A poor host," came a shout from across the room. "Leaving so soon after his guests arrive? Whatever are we to think of you, Rhamiel? It took us so long to find you, and now you'd disappear before we've even a chance to talk?"

Jana could see him landing on a balcony, his lips curled up into a demonic smile. Suriel's angels put aside their battles to bow as he walked past them, ignoring whatever was going on around them. One of them found himself strangled by his own chains, choked by the seraph he'd been fighting. But it didn't stop him or any of the others from risking their lives to pay their respects. They were terrified of the being that walked before them, terrified of the things he might do.

They knew Ecanus just as well as the rest of them, and they all knew what their fate would be if they displeased him.

He saw Jana from across the room, and he smiled. His tongue flashed across his lips, a little brown slug that left them covered in a trail of slime. She didn't wait. She didn't speak. She didn't call for help.

All she did was turn, and run.

CHAPTER FIFTEEN

IT WAS A FACE CASSIE had hoped she'd never see again. It wasn't the scars or the blisters, though they were as frightening as they'd ever been. And it wasn't the craggy, nearly-bald skull, as battered and pocked as the moon. It was the darkness she knew was beneath the surface, just waiting to bubble up and drag everyone else down with him. He was the worst of any angel she'd known since the Fall, and that was saying something.

"I'll pluck her hair out, strand by strand," said Ecanus. "And that's just to start." He hunched his shoulders, spreading his wings above him and cocking his head to peer at Jana as she fled. "She won't go back to Suriel intact, that I promise you. She doesn't need her face to birth a child. I'll cut off what pieces I please, and scar whatever pieces are left. And when the child is born he won't need her any longer. She'll be mine, and I'll start the process all over again."

Cassie could see Jana shaking on her feet as she ran, fleeing away down the hall. The sight of Ecanus had made her lose it, and she didn't blame her a bit. She chased after her, and it wasn't difficult to catch up, no matter how hard Jana tried to run. She was too far along in her pregnancy to move quickly, even as afraid as she was.

The closer Cassie got to her, the worse Jana looked. She was pale, she was crying, and she'd broken out in a sweat. They could still hear Ecanus laughing from behind them as he advanced, his enslaved angels at his side. The sound of his voice had sent her into near hysteria. She was quivering all over, and from the looks of things she was on the verge of fainting. But this was no time for that. Cassie darted towards her, locking their arms together and holding her up despite her wobbly feet.

"Don't," said Cassie. She started to turn behind her, then decided she wasn't sure if she could handle another look at Ecanus herself. "Stay with me. Stay here. I need you on your feet. I need you with me."

Jana mumbled something under her breath. It sounded like "him," or maybe "help." Cassie couldn't tell. But Jana was swaying, and in a few more seconds she'd be a helpless heap on the floor. That wouldn't do, not for an escape, and not with an army of angry angels nipping at their heels. Cassie pushed at her, managing to get her turned around to face the hallway so she couldn't see Ecanus. Then she reached down and pinched at the skin on Jana's arm as hard as she could, sharp enough that she knew it would leave a bruise.

It was an old trick she'd learned from her grandma to get someone's attention, though back then she'd been on the receiving end of it. Her grandma had been impossibly old, her grandpa long passed, and she'd ruled her house with an iron fist. Cassie had sometimes lived there for weeks at a time whenever her parents had travelled, often enough that it was almost a second home. She'd thought the pinching had been harsh, back when she was just a child. But her grandma had grown up in a harsher time. A time when people were a little wilder, and a little meaner, and a lot more concerned with how they'd put bread on the table than with how they'd afford the latest in entertainment. She didn't understand her grandma then. She was just an old woman, kind sometimes, but a little too gruff for a rambunctious child. But now Cassie understood her perfectly well. More than she'd like to, if she were honest.

The pinching worked on Jana, just as it had always worked on her. She jumped to attention, rubbing her arm and staring at Cassie in shock. Cassie smiled, with as much encouragement as she could manage. "Sorry. But stay with me. I need you awake. It's going to be okay."

She heard a voice from behind them, deep and powerful and full of command. "You. The both of you." It was Rhamiel, nodding his head towards Cassie, then towards Faye, who'd stumbled into the hallway after them. A pile of angels lay on the floor behind him, battered and bruised, and he stood in the doorway guarding Jana's retreat. There was steel in his eyes, and anger. They looked like balls of blue flame, piercing the darkness of the halls as he blocked the door and shouted back at them. "You." He stared at Cassie, and for a short moment she felt as wobbly as Jana was. "They cannot escape without your help. You must lead them away.

Make it to the bottom of the tower if you can. Hide somewhere in the darkness if you cannot."

"What about you?" said Cassie.

"Go," growled Rhamiel. "And do it now. I cannot hold an army at bay by myself, not for long." With that he turned back to Ecanus, as more and more of Suriel's angels entered the tower. Rhamiel was outnumbered, and the odds were exceedingly poor. But it didn't stop him. It didn't even make him hesitate. He just waved his sword, let out a deep guttural yell, and charged into the middle of them all.

Cassie could finally see what Jana saw in him. She'd always thought he was as smug and as arrogant as the rest of them, a preening dandy preying on a foolish little girl. He had reasons for his vanity, she'd give him that. Perfect hair, perfect eyes, and a perfect body. But there was more to him than that. A sense of honor and selflessness that the other angels had mostly abandoned. It hadn't been obvious back in the tower, when all she'd ever seen him do was drink and carouse with his friends. Maybe Jana had done him some good. Maybe she'd brought out part of what he'd once been like, before they'd all turned into the fallen things they'd become.

"Come on," said Cassie, grabbing Jana's hand. Then she turned back towards Faye, shouted at her as fiercely as she could manage. "Come on!"

She regretted it the instant she'd done it. Rhamiel was brawling in the middle of a mass of angels, and she could barely see him. All she could make out were flashes of fire, whirling through the air as Suriel's angels pushed towards him. But there were so many of them, and at the edges of the battle were angels who couldn't even get close. They couldn't see Rhamiel, but they could certainly hear her.

Heads turned in her direction, wondering what this creature was who spoke with the authority of an angel, but had no wings and no power to speak of. She could see eyes staring at her from all around, eyes filled with pain and madness, the eyes of angels who'd been beaten down from posh heavenly servants into something closer to animals. Some of them ignored her, turning back to Rhamiel and keeping their gaze on the prize before them. But a few others walked towards the door, shouting unintelligible things at her from behind their chains and their bridles.

"Go," said Cassie. She slapped Jana on the back, and that was enough. She ran down the hallway, as fast as she could manage. Faye was recovering herself, but Cassie had to run back to help her, steadying her and helping her find her footing.

She'd gotten out of the ballroom, but Faye was too close to the door, no more than a few yards away. Two angels were already pursuing her down the hall, lurching slowly after her. A third followed them, but collapsed to the ground in a tangle of his own chains. His wings jerked up and down as he swung his sword all around him, hacking away at his bindings. It didn't do him any good, not against whatever the chains were forged from, and in his fury he slammed the sword into one of his wings, prompting an outpouring of feverish screams as the sword roasted through his feathers and came out the other side.

The angel's thrashings had blocked the doorway, stopping any of the others from following. But the other two were already through, and they were still coming. Faye managed to shake some of the dizziness away until she was moving on her own two feet, running after Jana as the hallway curved off into darkness. Cassie kept behind her, shouting encouragement and pushing her forward. She was a leader again despite herself, but this time she didn't have any choice. She wouldn't have changed things if she did. Her life didn't matter, not now. And she'd heard what the angels had said. That little life inside of Jana might turn things around, and what fallen angels feared might be the hope of mankind. If she was going to die, there wasn't any better reason to.

She heard something close behind her, an angry moan just a few feet away. She rolled to the side, then whirled around, hoping she could dodge whoever was behind her and then catch up to the others somehow. She could have made it, if luck had been with her. These angels weren't exactly fast, not with the way they'd been weighted down. But she was too scared, too desperate to escape. She lost her balance, her legs bumping into each other. She tumbled to the floor, and as she pushed herself back to her feet she heard the moaning again, closer than before.

She looked up to see an angel standing over her, his near-naked body a patchwork of swollen red lines. He held a flaming sword in one hand and dragged a chain attached to a heavy iron weight with the other. It wasn't exactly practical, not for a battle, but she didn't get the sense that this army cared much about its casualties. The angel raised his sword, a thin little thing that looked like a stick made from molten lava. He shouted something through the metal in his mouth, but all Cassie heard was "mmpf." She got the gist of it, though. He was mad, and she was dead.

His arm swung towards her, and she twisted her head to the side. It was a narrow miss, and she could feel the heat on her face as the sword bounced off the floor next to her head. She crawled past the angel's legs, maneuvering herself until she was behind him. He twisted to follow her, managing to wind his chains completely around his foot. He couldn't run, but it didn't much matter: neither could she. She'd trapped herself in the hallway, right between the two angels. She didn't have any place to go, and now the second angel was only a few feet away.

She snapped to her feet and danced back and forth between the two of them, trying to keep moving. The one behind her swung his sword, and she ducked below it. Then the other angel stabbed at her, thrusting his sword forward and aiming for her stomach. It was a miss, but only because of the circular weights attached to his forearm. They jangled in all directions, slowing down the swing and giving her time to move aside before it hit.

She knew she wouldn't survive for long. The angels were too close, and she didn't have any room for error. All she could do was draw things out for as long as she could and hope it gave the others time to escape. She kept herself between the two angels, bobbing up and down, weaving through attack after attack. Then the second one closed in, and she didn't even have room left for that. She dropped down to the ground, trying to crawl through the angel's legs, but he was wise to that. He planted a boot in her path, and then the game was over.

The angel raised his sword above her, and Cassie tensed up and waited for the blow. But it never came. The angel stuttered, stumbling a few feet forward, then stared down at his chest. A little black spot appeared on his skin, growing wider and wider. Fire poked through, the tip of a sword that jutted outwards from his wound. Blood dripped around the bit in his mouth, and he pitched forward into the other angel, knocking them both to the ground.

She lifted her head and saw what had happened. The third angel was still tangled in his chains, but he'd dragged himself towards them, close enough to strike at his brother, if not at her. He stared at Cassie with greedy eyes, mumbling to himself as he pulled his sword from the corpse of his comrade. He wanted the kill for himself, apparently, for whatever good it might do him with his masters.

She didn't intend to give him the time to do it. The two surviving angels were squaring off against each other, neither one willing to share the credit for their catch. She dropped to the floor as they screamed unintelligible insults at one another, crawling between the legs of the one who'd caught her in the first place. He made a half-hearted grab for her, but the other angel was on him before he could stop her, slamming their skulls together with a vicious head-butt.

She left them to the dispute, running as fast as she could, fleeing the tangle of wings and fire and rounding the corner at the end of the hall. She could see Jana moving down the hallway, holding a torch she'd grabbed from one of the walls. Faye followed after her, her legs jerky and slow.

She sprinted after them, the sound of her footsteps nearly sending them into a panic. But when they saw that it was her, they slowed, waiting for her to catch up. They looked winded, and Cassie felt the same. She'd burned through her adrenaline just getting over here, and she didn't have any idea how they'd make it to the bottom of the tower before someone with wings beat them there.

Still, they had to try. There wasn't anything to do but try.

"The stairs," said Cassie. "We have to find the stairs."

"I don't remember the way down," said Jana. "It was all dark. Just zigging and zagging."

"We'll figure it out," said Cassie. "Here." She grabbed the torch from Jana, shining it ahead of them. They ran forward, following the hall through turn after turn. They came to a window, and they could see angels circling the tower, diving up and down in aerial combat. They crawled along the ground to avoid being seen, and when they'd made it past they found themselves at an intersection in the halls. Cassie scanned from side to side, trying to remember the way they'd come, searching for anything she could recognize. Then she spotted it.

"There," said Cassie. She waved the torch to her right, and a few stairs leading down were barely visible among the shadows. She led them forward, keeping the two of them behind her, pushing through the trash and the junk. They were a few floors down when something came at them in the dark, a black shape stumbling forward from just a few feet away.

She nearly bashed its head in with her torch before she realized it was just a little girl, lost and alone in the darkness. "Come here," said Cassie. "Hold her hand." She reached over to Jana, taking the little girl's hand and pressing it into hers. Soon they were all holding hands, one after another, with Cassie leading them on. "Now stay close, and don't let go. Any of you."

They made their way down, floor by floor. Every staircase they passed they found more and more of the servants lost in the darkness. Their human chain grew longer and longer, all of them following Cassie as she lit the way with her torch. She kept thinking some angel would pop out at them from nowhere, but none of them did. They were long past the windows where someone might spot them from outside, and anyone with wings was up in the skies, not trudging around in the dark.

It seemed like forever before they made it to the bottom, but she could tell from the sounds outside that the battle was still raging. They could hear shouting, and screaming, and things clanging against the side of the tower. The world outside was visible in the distance, and she cast the torch aside, hugging the wall until they were nearly into the light.

"Stay here," said Cassie, and the others didn't argue. She crept out of the entrance to the tower, looking this way and that, sure that at any moment she was going to be spotted by one of the angels and they'd all be done for. But they were too busy with each other to scour the ground for missing servants, at least for the time being.

She could see the angels up above her, little black dots weaving between each other like a flock of agitated birds. And there were a few of them who'd fallen down into the dirt a little ways off in the distance: corpses from either side, battered and beaten, none of them moving. She caught sight of something else up in the sky: Rhamiel, she thought. It had to be him. It couldn't be anyone else. The invading angels surrounded him, diving at him and then pulling away, an entire army focusing its best efforts on a single warrior. And off to the sides she saw what looked like Ecanus, hovering away from the fight and waiting to swoop in whenever it was done.

She waved towards the servants, but none of them would come. Finally she ran back to them, grabbing Jana's hand and dragging the whole line forward. "Let's go. The fight won't last forever. We've got to be somewhere else when it ends." She didn't see much hope of that, but she wasn't going to tell them. The land around the tower was nothing but open wastes for miles. The only hope she could see was to spread them all apart, getting them into some of the old cars, or maybe underneath some of the pieces of rubble. The angels would probably find most of them. But maybe some of them would manage to stay hidden.

And if that didn't work, they'd just have to run.

She pulled them forward, weaving them through furrows in the dirt. The line of people stretched far behind her, holding hands and running one after another, and she knew they'd all be easily visible from up above. They crawled over an old billboard for a soft drink company, topped with a giant plastic can of soda faded to a light pink. Then she turned their human chain towards the sun. She thought it might make them harder to see that way, though she wasn't really sure. She kept them running, as fast as she could. But after a few minutes she felt a tug from behind her, and she heard Jana let out a little gasp.

"There's something coming," said Jana. "Something awful." Jana pointed off in the distance, towards a line of trees at the edge of the wastes. It was the forest where Cassie and the servants had come from. And the sight beyond the trees stopped them all in their tracks.

A slimy red wall bubbled across the horizon, covering the land as far as they could see. It rolled towards them, enveloping the last of the forest before sucking up yard after yard of the empty soil beyond the trees. It was moving faster and faster, accelerating the closer it came. It foamed over rusting cars and piles of trash, fizzing and popping as it absorbed the landscape into itself.

"That stuff," said Cassie. "There's monsters inside it. Little shadowy things." She shuddered, drawn to thoughts of Laura and what the creatures had turned her into. "And if you go inside, you never come out. Not the same way you were when you went in."

"We have to get away," said Jana. The line had broken apart, and some of the servants were already running. They'd seen the things that came out of it firsthand, and none were inclined to wait around and see them again. They knew just as well as Cassie did what could happen to anyone who went behind that wall.

"Where?" said Faye. "I still." Her voice sounded like she'd been drugged up by a dentist, her tongue too numb to form the words. But she pushed them out, struggling to gain control of herself again. "I still feel like shit. Can't hardly move."

"Anywhere," said Cassie. "We can't stay here. There's things, and they're going to come after us. I know it. And we can't be here when they do." She could see angels in the sky, fleeing off in the direction they'd come from. They wouldn't be looking for them, not anymore. But the things she knew were coming for them would be far, far worse. She glanced again at the wall, eating up yard after yard of the terrain. It had moved before, but not this fast, and not this far. It was too much for her to bear. They'd almost escaped, only have their hopes dashed yet again. She wanted to just throw up her hands and give up. But everyone around was looking to her, begging her to save them, wondering what they could possibly do to save themselves. So she told them the only idea she had.

"Run."

CHAPTER SIXTEEN

J ANA DIDN'T KNOW WHAT IT was, the bubbling red thing in the distance. It looked like a giant wave rushing towards the shore. But it was tall, impossibly tall, and she couldn't see the top of it no matter how hard she strained her neck. She wanted to stay and wait for Rhamiel, whatever this thing turned out to be. But Cassie said run, and so she did. It was good advice, and she knew that at once. All it took was one little peek at the fleeing angels up above.

She was looking for Rhamiel. She'd seen him up there as soon as they'd gone outside. At least she thought she had. He was nothing but a shiny silver speck, darting between scores of angry angels and struggling just to stay aloft as they battered him from all sides. Now she couldn't see him at all, but she could still see them. Suriel's angels, come to take her back to his compound. Come to hurt her and torture her and do things to her that she couldn't even imagine, all because they wanted her child.

But now the angels were running away, just like the rest of them.

They'd seen the red barrier, too, and whatever it was they didn't want any part of it. Drums from beyond the tower were sounding a retreat, and the angels had abandoned their fighting to flap away as quickly as their wings would take them. She whispered to herself as she ran, telling herself over and over that Rhamiel would make it out. He had to. Cassie was nice, and so was Faye. But they couldn't keep her alive. They were nothing to the angels, and they'd be tossed aside like rag dolls if they tried to stand in their way.

But she couldn't think about any of that now. She worked to keep her thoughts on what was in front of her. What was behind was terrifying, and so was what was above. She couldn't let herself get distracted by wondering what had happened up there. So she looked down at the dirt instead, watching the grey soil and the debris as she ran. She passed rusted pieces of metal, and she tried to imagine what they could have been long ago. She stared at the legs of the servants in front of her, pumping up and down and sending up puffs of dirt as they fled. Anything mindless, and anything to keep her going.

The barrier was coming closer, and it wasn't stopping. She didn't look, but she didn't have to. She could see it on the faces of the servants in front of her. They couldn't quit turning around to check its progress, and they were doing it more and more often as they went. All it did was slow them down, but they couldn't help it. Jana knew better. She just ran and ran, stuffing the fear down within her and staring straight ahead. She managed, at least until she heard the first scream.

She slowed down, sneaking a peek as she went. It was one of the servants, an old man who'd fallen behind all the rest. He'd tripped, and he lay there on the ground, the wall oozing over his legs. He was shouting for someone to help him, but no one even tried. They all just turned and ran faster. Jana wavered, taking a few steps towards the man, but then she felt herself being jerked away.

"No," said Cassie. She had Jana by the arm and was dragging her forward, yanking her back into motion. "He's gone. You aren't. Keep going."

Jana started to respond, but there wasn't anything to say. It was horrible, but she was right, and in any event she didn't have any choice. Faye had grabbed her by the other arm, pulling along with Cassie. She couldn't see anything of the man but his fingertips, clasping out through the red goo, and then even those disappeared. She turned back around, and this time she did as she was told. She kept running, for all the good it would do her. The barrier was faster than she was, faster than any of them, and they'd all be on the other side of it soon.

More and more screams came from more and more lagging servants. The voices were closer every time, and soon the screaming was no more than a dozen yards away. It wouldn't be long, at least. She didn't know what was waiting for them on the other side, or what it would be like. She didn't even know if she'd survive the passage through the barrier. But at least she could quit running, if only for a time.

"Keep going," said Faye, huffing as she jogged

alongside Jana. "I didn't make it back here just to drown in a bunch of rotten tomato soup. We'll be fine."

"We'll make it," said Cassie. "It's going to stop. It always stops."

She knew they were both lying. They had to. The stuff was just a few yards away from them, and it was still coming. There weren't many servants left besides them, and the ones that were had slowed their pace to a crawl. They'd given it their all, but it wasn't enough, and it was time to accept what was fated to be.

Jana started to slow, too; the running was too much for someone as far along as she was, and her insides hurt all over. Cassie kept pulling her by the arm, but they all knew they wouldn't make it. Then she saw a dark shadow on the ground before her. She thought it was the ooze, come to take her inside with all the rest, but then the shadow spread apart on either side of her. Wings. She heard flapping, and shouting, and she turned up to see him swooping down towards her.

Rhamiel.

He was in a deep dive, almost vertical, plummeting down to the ground. His face was grim, dripping with desperation. He wasn't sure if he was going to make it, and neither was she. She stopped, ripping her hands free from Cassie and Faye. She held them up into the air, reaching out to him, and then she felt his arms close around her, lifting her up and hugging her close to his chest.

He cradled her in his arms, pushing into the air and racing away as quickly as he could take her. She struggled, trying to tell him to wait, trying to convince him to go back down and help the others somehow. But his wings beat away at her words, drowning them in the wind. They were up in the skies before she could stop him, barreling away from the tower and away from everyone else. It was too late for them, and it might be too late for them all.

"It's coming faster," said Jana, shouting over the wind. Little bubbles were forming in the side of the barrier, popping out towards them in plumes that tickled at Rhamiel's feet as he flew. "It's like it knows. Like it knows we're getting away."

"We will escape," said Rhamiel. He snuck a glance at the oozing dome, the ruby red reflecting in the center of his sapphire eyes. "We must." He wrapped his arms more tightly around Jana, flapping his wings harder and pulling her higher and higher.

She could still see them down there on the ground, Cassie and Faye, little black specks running away from the barrier as quickly as their feet would take them. They'd seen Thane's truck and they were headed straight for it, probably hoping against hope that they could get it started and pull off a high-speed escape somehow. But they'd never make it. She didn't have any doubt about that; the thing was moving too quickly, and even at its fastest the truck had rocks and hills to maneuver around. She saw them disappear inside, she saw the doors slam shut behind them, and then she saw the wall of film rush past them all, absorbing them inside of it.

"We have to go back," said Jana. Rhamiel didn't even look down at her, so she shouted it again. All he did was shake his head, clutch his arms around her more tightly, and keep pressing forward. The barrier was impossibly high, and even from her vantage point in the clouds she couldn't see where it ended. It just curved and curved, heading up towards infinity as its base rolled towards the tower.

As for Suriel's army, it was in full retreat. She could see them in the distance, black spots forming and reforming like a panicked school of fish. They'd been positioned for another attack, and she could see how hopeless things would have been if they'd stayed. There were so many of them—hundreds, at least, and she worried that Suriel was somewhere among them. He'd been poised for a grand victory, and now it was washed away in a sea of red. She felt a shiver of satisfaction in that, at least. Whatever this thing was, at least Suriel wouldn't have her. At least he wouldn't do the things he'd threatened to do to her son, and the things he'd threatened to do to her. She remembered the women back in his harem, and she knew she couldn't survive for long as one of them.

Rhamiel veered to the south, avoiding the tower and avoiding the army beyond it. There were a few other angels in the air nearby, but none of them paid them any mind. They weren't even looking. It was everyone for themselves, and no one had any interest anymore in anything but their own hides. But it was too late, too late for them all.

The plumes were coming closer along with the dome. It was catching up to them, and now the tendrils weren't just brushing against Rhamiel, they were grabbing at him. She felt a sharp tug, and she looked back to see his boot snagged on a long tentacle of ooze, surging out of the surface of the barrier and holding them in place. The two of them whipped up and down as Rhamiel pulled against it, but more and more tentacles slithered up his leg, dragging him back even as he struggled forward. He cursed under his breath, but even with all his strength he couldn't pull away. She knew the game was over, then. She closed her eyes, held her breath, and waited for what was to come.

She felt it first on her feet. It was icy cold, and as it rolled up her leg everything it touched went completely numb. It was as if her legs were gone, as if they'd never even been there in the first place. But there was no escape, not now. They were caught like flies in a spider's web. Rhamiel's wings were already tangled up in strands of glop, and the two of them hung there in the air, suspended in the sky as the liquid crept around them. It went over her belly, and she let out a scream of anguish when she realized what had happened.

He was gone. Her son. He was on the other side, and there wasn't any coming back. She couldn't feel him. No kicks, no warmth, no movement. Just nothing. He was dead to her, and she dead to him. She'd rather they just killed her outright. Anything but this. It only lasted a few moments, but they were the worst of her entire life. It was pain and horror and despair, pounding at her from every side as she sobbed and sobbed. And it only ended when the liquid crept over her face and pulled the rest of her inside of it.

The world went red around her. Everything had a ruby hue—as if she were looking at the world through stained glass and all the light had gone wrong. The wall of film kept rolling past, and then it finally let them go. They plummeted towards the ground together, twisting and flailing, Rhamiel holding onto her and beating away with his wings. He struggled against the air, against his own weight, but finally he got control again. He managed to slow the fall, then stop it entirely, carefully weaving them to the ground below. He set her down, and the soil felt wrong beneath her feet. It fizzed, she thought, and she knelt down to put a hand to it. The ground was warm, and everything around her smelled of sulfur.

Her hands went to her belly, and for a moment of panic she was worried he was gone. But then she felt a roll and a wiggle from inside her, and she knew he'd made it. They were connected again now that they were both on the same side of the wall. A feeling of reassurance washed over her, and she choked out a laugh and wiped away her tears.

She could see the barrier a little ahead of them, its expansion slowing to a crawl. Rhamiel launched himself after it, lashing out with his sword and trying to cut their way free. But the flames died away as they touched the liquid, the sword forming and reforming itself with every swing. Finally he pounded at the wall in frustration, slamming his fists against it again and again. But none of it mattered. Whatever it was, even an angel's strength couldn't break through it.

They were trapped there, trapped inside a world turned upside down and inside out. Nothing felt right. Jana could hear sounds coming from the forest in the distance, shrieks and wails and something that sounded like a melody composed of shattering glass. And Rhamiel looked wrong. Everything did. She held up a hand before her face, and somehow it was off. At first she thought it was the light, turning her skin a light red. It took her a moment to realize what it was, but then she knew.

The shadows. It wasn't her hand that was off. It was the shadows her fingers cast across it. They pulsed, they moved, and they crept up and down her hand as if they were alive. She shook her hand back and forth, trying to knock them away, but it didn't do a thing. Maybe it was a trick of the light, and maybe not. But it sent shivers down her spine all the same.

She could see the tower. It had been pulled inside along with everything else, a big black thing that didn't look quite like itself. The landscape looked just as off as everything else did. It was the same, but somehow it wasn't. Everything felt wrong, even if she couldn't tell exactly why. She looked over at Rhamiel. He'd sheathed his sword and given up on escape, and she called out to him as he headed back. "We have to find the others. You shouldn't have left them." She felt more than a little furious that he'd done it. Cassie and Faye were her friends, as close to friends as she could have in a world like this one. He'd risked his life to get them out of the tower, and once they were safe he'd just left them to their fate without even giving it a second thought.

"It was save them, or save you," said Rhamiel. He leaned towards her, staring at her with eyes turned magenta pink from the light. It was so odd looking into them, bathed in that unnatural color. But they were still a window to what was inside him. The light didn't matter, not for that. She could still see him in there, still see the pain he felt at the thought of losing her, and it melted her anger away as he spoke. "I couldn't have helped them. There were too many people. I could only carry one of you. I had to make a choice, and there wasn't the slightest doubt in my mind as to who I would save."

She thought about it, and she knew he was right. She'd wanted to save that man back there, fallen down in the dirt and screaming as the barrier passed over him. She'd wanted to, but she couldn't. And Rhamiel couldn't save everyone, either, no matter how hard he tried.

"We're here now, though," said Jana. "We're inside. And so are they. We can't let them die. We can't let Ecanus or Suriel find them. We can't let them be turned into…." The word was out of her mouth almost before she knew it. She didn't mean to say it. But she couldn't help herself. "Slaves."

"Slaves," said Rhamiel. He finished her sentence for her with a look of shame, his head shaking as he spoke. "I hurt you, didn't I? It hurts to know how I sinned?"

"It hurt that you didn't tell me," said Jana. "And it hurt because I was one of them. I just couldn't quit thinking about it. About whether it was all a lie. About whether you really cared about any of us." She dropped her eyes to the ground, taking a deep breath and then lifting her head up again. "About whether you really cared about me."

"I care about you," said Rhamiel. "Don't ever, ever doubt that." He ran a finger across her face, and then into her hair, and even through the warped red light she could see the love in his eyes. "And I cared about the others. The people I brought to the towers. I only did what I did because I cared about them. We were so hardened after the Fall, but it melted me, watching what my brothers were doing to them."

"But slaves," said Jana. "You can't do that to people. It's awful to live like that. As bad as any of the other things they do."

"I had to choose," said Rhamiel. "Just like I had to choose whether to save you or to save your friends. And for better or for worse, that is the choice I made." He gave a heavy sigh, breathing in deeply as he spoke. "I don't need to tell you how my brothers were. How they still are. I told them to stop, at first. Ordered them. Many of them even listened. Status is a powerful thing, and for the first time I could remember, I had it. My face." He rubbed his cheek with his hands, and she could see why the angels had followed his orders. He had charisma, even beyond his looks, and even if looks were all that mattered to the angels in the end. "I was one of the beautiful ones, and they listened to me. When I was there. Most of them."

"Why, though?" said Jana. "Why couldn't you just talk? Just get them all to stop?"

"I tried," said Rhamiel. "Don't think that I didn't try. But it was hopeless. I learned that much. It was at one of the towns. A little one. We used to tear down buildings for the fun of it. Abandoned ones. There was such rage in all of us, then. There still is in many of us. But it helped to let it out. To rip things apart and leave them all in a pile of dust. We'd lost our war, and we'd thrown away our paradise on a lark. We resented mankind for winning the Maker's favor. And the works of man were a favorite target."

"It doesn't make sense, to tear things apart like that," said Jana. She didn't get it, whatever drove them towards destruction. It seemed so pointless, and she thought it had to have been just as bad for the angels as it was for everyone else. "You've got to live here, just the same as we do. And now the world's a mess for all of us."

"You've never fought in a war," said Rhamiel. "You don't know the thirst for destruction that comes over you. It wells up from within. It's not rage, exactly. More like lust." His eyes blazed with memories of old, and she was more than a little frightened. She'd seen him in battle, how he'd launched himself into the fight, and she worried he couldn't control himself even now. But he pressed a hand against her face, gently, and the fire died away as he continued. "It makes you run amok. Swinging and slashing. It doesn't matter who you hurt. Passion overtakes you, and there's nothing to be done but follow its current wherever it wends."

"Did you?" said Jana. "Did you lose control?" All her worries came rushing back. She could just see him in her head, mad with anger and letting his inner passions run free. She'd seen more than one angel like that. It was when they were at their most horrible. Sometimes they just yelled or raged. But sometimes they did more.

"It happened to me once, during the war," said Rhamiel quietly. "It kept happening to many of the others, even afterwards." He stared off into space, his eyes blank as he withdrew into his memories. "I haven't lost control like that, not since. When you're in the heat of that moment, when you're surrounded by enemies, by fire, by the beasts of war let loose from their chains. When you think your time has come, and it's all about to end. You do what you must to survive, and sometimes that means letting go of yourself. I'd been fighting, and it was complete chaos. One moment I was fighting shoulder to shoulder with my brothers. The next, I looked up and found I'd been cut off somehow. I was behind the lines of the enemy with no one to help me. I saw them coming towards me, hundreds of them. I saw my brothers, far away and locked in combat of their own. I thought it was the end. But then it all went black. When I opened my eyes again, I was all alone, my armor covered in blood, trudging through a field of golden flowers far from the battle."

"You didn't even know what happened?" said Jana.

"I don't remember a thing," said Rhamiel. "It was instinct. Something inside me that I didn't even know was there. A fire that burned through me and compelled me to do the things that needed to be done to keep myself alive."

"It scares me," said Jana. "That something like that might happen to you." She thought about other angels she'd seen, wild with rage and driven by their emotions. "That it could happen again."

"It won't," said Rhamiel. "It was all about survival. I've control of myself, and I don't intend to lose it again. But some of the others. The same thing happened to them, and they liked it. They remembered bits of what had happened, and they wanted to lose themselves in the feeling again. When we were tossed down here, they sated their thirst by fighting your armies. And when the armies were all gone, they had to find someone else to fight."

"People," said Jana.

"Innocent people," said Rhamiel. "The town I spoke of. It was supposed to be empty. That was what the scouts told us, at least. Now I think they hadn't even been there. There was little discipline left, and we were barely an army anymore. When we arrived, we found them. A few hundred people, eking out what life they could in the ruins of their homes. Most of them women or children."

"They didn't," said Jana. But she knew they had. The look on his face told her as much, his lips clenching together in pain.

"I told them to stop," said Rhamiel. "And some of them did. I told them we'd find another place, and another source of entertainment. But some of them were too eager. Or perhaps they simply didn't care. They listened, and they laughed, and then they flew towards them. The things they did. I'd drag one of my brothers away, and their place would be taken by another. In the end I couldn't do a thing. I couldn't even watch."

"I'm sorry," said Jana. She wasn't sure what to think about it, not yet. He sounded sincere, and he looked it, too. His eyes were filled with hurt, and he almost couldn't bring himself to look at her when he spoke of it. He regretted what he'd done; she was sure of that. But turning someone into a slave was an awful thing to do to anyone, and the fact that someone else was running around doing things that were even worse wasn't much of an excuse. He'd still sinned in a way she thought was nearly unpardonable. And if she couldn't forgive him, would anyone up there ever manage it?

"It was a massacre," said Rhamiel. "Not many survived. They dragged them to the center of the town and sat them down on a grassy square in front of an old church. They were going to kill them, one by one. It was just a joke to them. A game. Only a few of us still had our senses about us. There'd been talk ever since we fell about making mankind serve us for thousands of years, just as we had served them in turn. Mostly grumbling. But we needed a reason to keep them alive. A reason the others would listen to."

He stared up at the dome above them, lost in memories he'd rather have forgotten. But he kept going, reliving a moment he thought had died long ago.

"I walked out into the middle of the square, and I claimed them all as my own," said Rhamiel. "Every single human there. I told my brothers that we needed pledges, and that as the highest among them, I deserved them all." His frown turned to a wry smile. "That set them to arguing, and soon they were too absorbed in fighting one another over who owned those people to even think of killing them. They went on and on for more than an hour. About who was higher than whom, and how many servants each of them were entitled to. We ended up leading them all back to camp and dividing them up. Human servants became status symbols, but only so long as they were alive. In time some even begged to serve us. Entire governments bent their knee to us if it meant they'd be left alone."

"They had to," said Jana. "They didn't have any choice. We never had any choice."

"They were marked for death," said Rhamiel. "The ones we turned to serv...." His voice trailed off, and he couldn't bring himself to finish the word. He could call them servants, but it wasn't the truth, not really, and so he started anew. "We turned them to slaves. They'd been marked for death, all of them. Gruesome deaths. They were but playthings to those of the Seraphim with darker bents. And if I'd left them there, they'd have been nothing but corpses when the play was done. As the years passed I did the same thing, again and again. Convincing my brothers not to kill the only way I knew how."

"So you took them to the towers instead," said Jana. His teeth were gritted together, and she could hear every breath he took, deep and heavy and sad. She knew it, then, the thing she'd been desperate to know. He hadn't wanted to hurt people. She wondered what it must be like, having been so perfect, so utterly without flaw, only to lose it all because of a single mistake. She could tell that it weighed on him, and maybe more than she could ever understand. She put her arms around him, leaning her head on his shoulder, and after a long silence he finally spoke again.

"I should have told you," said Rhamiel. "I shouldn't have kept it back. Perhaps that was a sin all its own."

"I just wanted to know that the past is the past," said Jana. "The others. They scare me. They scare all of us. I didn't want to think you were anything like them."

"I can't say I'm nothing like them," said Rhamiel. "Not truthfully. We fought together and we fell together.

We lived side by side for centuries. I'm of them, even if I'm not the same as them. But then again, I've met many humans. Some bad, some good, and some thoroughly evil. But none quite like you." He kissed her forehead, softly, and then gave her his most persuasive smile. "None so fair, and none so kind."

It worked. It melted her to hear his words. The anger was gone, replaced with hope. No one was perfect, not even her angel. But she could live with that. She could live with someone who made mistakes, so long as there was kindness in his heart.

She didn't have long to savor the feeling. They were interrupted by something in the distance, a low growling noise from behind a dune of ash. An engine. She turned to see their truck heading straight for them, churning up a cloud of soot behind it. Cassie had found them, apparently, though it couldn't have been hard. The barrier had stopped, and there wasn't anywhere else they could have gone.

"Ask them," said Rhamiel, nodding towards the truck. "Your friends. Ask them what the world was like in the aftermath of our Fall. You might be too young to truly remember it, but things are quieter now. The towers calmed things down. They're an evil, but one I chose to support of necessity."

"They trapped people there," said Jana. "Trapped them inside the towers forever."

"A few of them," said Rhamiel. "But before the towers, my brothers roamed the entire planet, doing whatever they pleased. Anything to break up the tedium. It would have been a genocide, had things kept going the way they were. If you cannot trust me...." His voice choked on the words and he looked away, struggling to meet her eyes. "Your friends will tell you how it was. They'll speak the truth. They may not agree with my choice. But none will deny that I was forced to make it."

"It doesn't matter," said Jana. "It doesn't matter what they say. I believe you. I know it's true." A look of relief washed across his face, and he stood up taller, stronger, the vigor and life coming back to him. He pulled her into him, holding her there while they waited.

The truck pulled before them, its wheels slamming to a halt and sending up a cloud of dust. Cassie kicked open the passenger door and ran towards them, holding out her hand to Jana, her eyes pleading at Rhamiel. "You've got to help us. The servants. They're back there on their own. But there's things. We can hear them. And there's something in the forest, something bad. None of us know what to do. I don't know what to do."

"Please," said Jana. "Please help them."

"I don't know if I can," said Rhamiel softly. He looked at Cassie for a long moment, then back at Jana. "But I promised you I would redeem myself. I promised you I had changed. And I promised you I would do whatever it took to earn the right to follow you through the gates of Heaven. Now is as good a time as any to prove it."

CHAPTER SEVENTEEN

RHAMIEL WAS GOING TO HELP them. Them. A bunch of servants, lost in the wilderness with enemies all around. It was the last thing Cassie would have expected from one of the angels. She'd have guessed that he'd just leave them there, or maybe even kill a few of them for fun. But instead he was flying somewhere above them, following the truck with Jana in his arms. She'd never understand them, no matter how long she lived, but she wasn't one to turn down help when she needed it.

Maybe he was moody, like Nefta had been. She didn't know him well enough to know. Maybe Jana had him so wrapped around her finger that he'd do anything she wanted. Maybe this was just some game, and all he was doing was getting their hopes up before he turned on them just like the others. Or maybe he actually did care. It didn't seem likely, not with one of them. But she was certain about one thing. She'd seen it all over his face when he'd held off the other angels to let them escape. He cared about Jana, and he'd give his life for her. And if he cared about her, maybe he could care about someone else, too.

She was driving back towards where they'd left the servants, or at least where she thought they were. But she could barely see where she was going. Everything looked so strange. The sun was blocked out by the gooey film that covered the sky, and whatever light came through was tinged with red. She could barely make out what was in front of her, and bits of dirt that looked like rubies blew across the windshield. She kept wondering when she was going to plow into something, but she was thankful to be driving at all. If someone hadn't left the keys in the sun visor, she and Faye would have been entirely out of luck.

She looked over at Faye, sitting there in the passenger seat. She was staring at her fingers, flexing them back and forth, balling them up into a fist and then spreading her hand back out as far as she could. Every now and then she'd frown, pull her arm against her chest, and then start all over again. It must have been hard, adjusting after what they'd done to her. Cassie held the wheel in one hand and reached over with the other, touching Faye on the arm.

"You okay?" said Cassie. "You feel alright?"

"I'm alive," said Faye. She looked at her hands again, wiggling her fingers. She held one hand in front of her eyes: it shook uncontrollably, but just for a second, and then it was still. "I'm starting to get my body back. And he's gone. I think he's actually gone."

"Zuphias," said Cassie. "He's such an asshole." She shook her head, clenching her teeth as she thought of all the things she'd seen the angels do. "They're so selfish. They don't care about anyone. They don't even see us as people. You didn't deserve that."

"It could have been worse," said Faye quietly. "They can always think of something worse to do to you."

She looked so sad. So beaten. It tore at Cassie to see it. She wondered if this was how the servants turned into the kind of people they were. Hurt someone often enough, over and over, and eventually it just starts to feel normal. Eventually they accept it as the way things are. Maybe some of the servants were like her, once. Free, and able to decide things for themselves. She couldn't see it in them, not now. But she could see a hint of the servants in Faye. She was curled up in her seat, staring off into nothing. Zuphias might have left her body intact, but he'd done some serious damage to her soul.

And the worst of it wasn't even over. Cassie wasn't sure how much Faye knew about how she'd been set free. She wasn't sure whether she'd been conscious, or whether she had any idea what her friend had done. But she had to tell her. It might hurt her even more, but Faye had to know. It was going to hurt them both, because this wasn't exactly a message Cassie wanted to deliver. But if she didn't tell her, she'd find out from someone else eventually, and they might not be as careful about delivering the news. It had to be done, it had to be done right, and now was as good a time as any.

"Do you know what happened?" said Cassie. "Do you know how they brought you back?"

"I just woke up," said Faye. "I started hearing voices, and then I woke up."

"Your friend," said Cassie. "The big blonde guy. I wanted to make sure you knew." She'd lost enough friends of her own, and she knew what it was like. But the wondering was worse. It was always worse. She didn't know if Holt was alive or dead. She didn't like the odds, not with what had happened to Faye. But it was the wondering that gnawed at her. Truth was always better, in the long run. It hurt, but at least it healed. "Your friend made the angels a trade. His body for yours. He gave himself to Zuphias, and they gave you back to us."

"Thane," said Faye. Her voice shook, and tears welled in her eyes. "They took Thane."

"It was brave, what he did," said Cassie. "It was stupid. But he bought you your life. I wanted you to know that. You had to know that—"

"Where is he?" said Faye. Her voice filled with urgency, and her body tensed. "We have to find him. We have to get him back, and we have to get that angel out of him."

"I don't even know," said Cassie. "He was in the crowd when we fled. And he has to be around here somewhere. He doesn't have any wings. He couldn't fly. He had to come out the same way we did."

"Then we can find him," said Faye. "We have to. You don't know what it's like in there. The darkness. The nothing. The thoughts you start to have. We can't let that angel have him."

"We'll check the servants," said Cassie. "He might have come out with us." She nodded towards the windshield; they were nearly there, back where they'd left them. The servants were just standing around in a daze, all alone in the wastes. She didn't blame them. There wasn't anywhere to go, not anymore. They were trapped, all of them, and this time she didn't see any way out.

"We have to check them all," said Faye. "And if he's not here, we have to go back inside. We have to."

That wasn't happening. Cassie knew it, and so did Faye, even if she didn't want to admit it. But she had to keep Faye calm, and she had to keep her from doing anything rash. "Thane wanted to give you your life back. He wouldn't want you to throw that gift away. And Zuphias wants to keep him alive just as much as you do. He'll be fine. I promise." Neither of them believed it, not entirely, but Faye bit her lip and held her tongue all the same.

They pulled up in front of a group of servants, turning off the engine and leaving the truck. None of the servants spoke to them. It was just how they were. Cassie knew that. When danger came, they all turned into possums: playing dead was a far better idea than speaking up and sticking out your neck.

She looked up at the skies. There were angels up there, but none of them were nearby. She could see the army, or part of it, at least. They'd converged on the barrier and were trying to beat their way through it, for whatever good that would do. The angels from the tower had plans of their own. They were scattering in all directions, fleeing from the invaders while they still could, leaving any efforts to escape for another time. And then there was Rhamiel, turning in a gyre and slowly descending towards them.

Faye was busy pushing her way through the servants, lifting up their cloaks and checking the faces of everyone she passed. Cassie scanned the crowd: no Thane, not that she could see. She knew it at a glance. No one that big could hide among people so small. And she doubted Zuphias would have stuck around, even if he'd been with them. He had friends up there. He only had enemies down here.

She heard a crunch from the ground behind her and turned to see Rhamiel, lighting down on the ground and helping Jana to her feet. His eyes kept darting up above them, watching for threats in all directions. He was thinking the same thing as Cassie was, and he was right. They were sitting ducks, and if they were going to move, they needed to do it soon.

"We have to find a way out of here," said Cassie. "Or something. We need some kind of plan. You have no idea what's in here. These shadow things. They're so black. So awful. And they take people, and they change them. We saw it, all of us."

"I've seen such things," said Rhamiel. "And I've some idea what they are." He spat on the ground, kicking at the dirt with his boot. "Things from the Pit. Abominations from down below. Though how they would be up here, I cannot imagine."

"There's something happening," said Faye. "Something bad." She'd finished her search of the servants, or at least decided that there wasn't any use to it, and now she was trudging back towards them. "I could feel it. And I could hear things, sometimes. Angels, talking in rhymes. I was connected to that angel's body. Something's wrong with it. I was having these hallucinations. Sometimes it'd be dark, and sometimes I'd see these awful things."

"Zuphias's body was a mess, when last I saw it," said Rhamiel. "But I need you to tell me more, whatever you can. These rhymes. What did you hear? What were they saying?"

"They're going to change everything," said Faye. "The world. The universe. Heaven, Hell. Everything. There's going to turn it all upside down. They're poking around into how it all got created, and how it all works. I don't know what they're doing, but it's bad. It's why everything's red. This bubble is what they want to do to the whole world. It's just going to keep growing, faster and faster. And one day there'll be nothing left."

"That isn't possible," said Rhamiel, his brow knit together in confusion. "It simply isn't. No angel has that power. No angel can even understand creation, let alone rework what the Maker has done."

"Well, they think they can," said Faye. "All I know is it's what they were talking about. Not that I believe a word out of an angel's mouth." She looked up at him, then averted her eyes, suddenly sheepish. "No offense."

"It's foolishness," said Rhamiel, shaking his head and ignoring the slight. "It's madness."

"It's what's happening," said Cassie. "Everything in here." She held up her hand, looking at her skin, the color of it all wrong. "It feels strange. It looks strange. I don't know exactly what it is. But it's all different. Wrong. And the kids. They did something to some of our kids. Made them into something else. They were talking to me. About fixing things. About going back to the Maker's old plan."

"A reaping," said Rhamiel. "That was what was meant to be, before the Son had his change of heart. Collecting the souls of everyone and sorting them into their proper place. But this is more than a reaping. There's no way up. Look above us." He pointed upwards, toward the roof of the dome, the liquid swirling red and black above them. "We cannot leave, and I doubt a soul can, either."

"They didn't look like they cared about souls," said Cassie. "They didn't look like they cared about anything. And look. Over there." She nodded towards where she'd come from, the trees she'd led the servants through. "Behind the forests. Off towards the horizon. Do you see it?"

There was something there, something reaching towards the skies above. It was a pillar of black tar, flowing upwards like a river running vertically, ending in hundreds of tendrils grasping at the sky until they merged into a cancerous mass bulging out of the red liquid dome above them.

"What is it?" said Jana, pulling her cloak around her and staring up at the thing in awe.

"The center of the corruption," said Rhamiel. "And judging by the direction, it lies somewhere near the home of the Cherubim." He breathed in deeply, choking down an angry growl. "The cherubs are strange creatures, conducting strange experiments. I've seen it myself. Little hands must have been meddling to bring about such a mess."

"We have to do something," said Faye. "Get over

there and shut it down. Something. They're going to end the world. They're going to kill us all."

"It would be foolhardy," said Rhamiel. "A battle without preparation against enemies unknown." He put a hand on Jana's shoulder and curved one of his wings around her. "And it would force us to take risks that I am unwilling to bear."

"We take a risk whatever we do," said Faye. "We can't just sit here. We can't just let them lock us away in the world they're creating." She nodded her head towards the barrier wall, solid and unyielding as it dripped down from above. "How are you going to protect her in here? How are you going to protect that child? We have to fight. I don't care how strong they are. I fought you, and I didn't care how strong you were. You're telling me you can't do the same?"

"She's right," said Cassie. She looked up at the pillar, so dark and so awful. It was bigger than any skyscraper ever built by humanity. It could have been the size of a city for all she knew, and she didn't want to go towards it any more than Rhamiel did. But it was the source of whatever was happening. It was feeding the dome somehow, driving the expansion in fits and starts. She turned to Rhamiel, pleading with him as he tucked Jana away in his arms. "If no one does anything about this, we're all dead anyway. Including her. Where are you going to take her to? Where in the world is she going to be safe? Because I can tell you that if this wall keeps moving, there won't be anything left of the world for her to hide in."

"I will find a way out," said Rhamiel. "Then I will

scour the Earth, I will find a place for us to hide, and I will defend it to the last drop of my blood."

"Maybe," said Cassie. "Maybe you will. But for how long?"

"Long enough," snapped Rhamiel. "Long enough for our son to take his first breath. Long enough to make him my own."

"He'll just be a baby," said Jana softly. "He won't be able to stop all of this. Not by himself. You heard Suriel. There'll be years and years before he's old enough."

"We don't have years," said Cassie. "We may not even have weeks."

"You know what happens if someone takes him when he's a child," said Jana. "You know."

"I know," said Rhamiel. He breathed in deeply, staring off into nothing. "I know." Finally he shook his head with a sigh. "Every path before us is dangerous. All I want is to keep you safe. I know in my head what we have to do. But it weighs on my heart. It weighs on me, knowing what might happen."

"You'll keep us safe," said Jana. "I know you will."

"I will have to go to them," said Rhamiel. "If we cannot run, then all that's left is to fight, the odds against us be damned. I will have to fight the Cherubim in their very home."

"If we're going there, we need to figure out how we're going to do it," said Cassie. She looked at the pillar, miles and miles away in the distance. "We can't drive. We'd never make it. It'd take weeks to find enough clear roads to get there, and even then, we'd have to leave the servants behind. And they're not going to make it on their own." The servants huddled together a few yards away, staring at them all, and she shook her head at the thought. "We could fly with you. Or some of us could."

"I cannot carry you all," said Rhamiel. His eyes went to Jana, and then to her stomach. "I cannot carry more than a few of you."

"We all need to stick together," said Cassie. "There's only one way to do that, and it's to walk." She pointed to the forest, the pillar rising up from behind it. "And the only place we won't be sitting ducks is through there. It's a straight shot to the pillar, and they won't be able to see us from above. But it isn't safe. We came from in there, and I don't think it's safe. I think we should scout around. Look for some other path. Some other way to go and fight them."

"There's no place here that's safe, not for any of us," said Rhamiel. "But for now, we must go somewhere. And standing around in the open would be certain death for all of you."

"Then I guess we walk," said Cassie. "I'm just not so sure we should walk through there."

"We walk," said Rhamiel. "We walk as far as we must, for as long as we must. But you must know what is coming. There are worse things in the Pit than the things you saw. Things that would make you shudder, and things that would make you scream. And if the Cherubim have brought them here, they'll find us long before we find them."

CHAPTER EIGHTEEN

THEY STOOD BEFORE THE TREE line, listening to sounds coming from inside the woods. Sometimes they were exactly the sounds they would have expected—the chirping of birds, or the songs of crickets. But sometimes they weren't. Sometimes things burst through the background noise. Sounds that shouldn't be there. Noises like screams, or loud howls that came from every direction at once before fading away to nothing. Growling that came from the trees themselves, mixed in with the rustling of leaves.

It looked just as wrong as it sounded. Jana was hardly an expert on wildlife, and she couldn't see far into the forest. It was too dark for that. But what she could see looked nothing like what it was supposed to. The bark of the trees was pulsing, with little bulges popping beneath their skin and running up and down from trunk to branches. The leaves fizzled with energy, and from time to time her eyes caught one of them bursting into flame, dying lone deaths amid a sea of autumn red.

And she thought she saw movement. It was only at

the corner of her eyes; if she turned to look directly, the forest was as dark and as empty as it had been just moments before. But when she turned her head back, she could see it again: flickers of shadow, dodging from her sight and hiding in the periphery where she'd never quite be able to catch them. It was unsettling, and it was making her paranoid. Every movement in her field of vision drew a gasp and a jerk of her head as she tried to make sure nothing was creeping up on her.

And it would only get worse once they were in there, groping their way in the darkness through the trees.

"Is it safe?" said Cassie. "It can't be safe."

Jana was inclined to agree with her. She knew they weren't truly safe anywhere they went. It was just as dangerous under the open skies, maybe more so. But it felt safer, even if it wasn't. There weren't as many shadows, there weren't as many sounds, and there weren't as many things to be afraid of.

"We must go somewhere," said Rhamiel. "Ecanus and his army are trapped in here right along with us. And Ambriela won't stay neutral for long. She can't. Her hand has been forced, and her home is gone, just like mine. She'll have to join a side: whether us or them, there's nothing left for her to lose. They could all be coming for us soon."

"Maybe we can walk around it," said Cassie. "Hug the tree line. It'd take longer, but then we don't have to go inside." She looked around at the servants. Some were wandering about in a daze. Others were shivering with anxiety. They were creatures of habit, and creatures who craved stability. The day had been too much for them, and this might be a bridge too far. "I don't know if we can keep them together if we go in there. There's so many of us."

"There are risks either way," said Rhamiel. "We must—"

A new sound interrupted him, coming from somewhere to the north. A screeching that pierced the air, poking at Jana's eardrums until they felt like they were about to bleed. It wasn't coming from the forest, but from somewhere up above it.

It had to be those angels, the ones who'd attacked the tower. If Rhamiel hadn't been able to force his way through the barrier, then they couldn't have managed it, either. They'd be trapped in there along with them, and they wouldn't be happy about it. The servants thought so, too. They were dropping to the ground, panic spreading through them along with the noise. But Rhamiel held up a hand, calling for silence as he listened to the wind.

"That sound," said Rhamiel. "I know that sound." His face went grim, his voice went firm, and he waved a hand towards the forest. "We must hide. In there. Now."

"We can't," said Faye. "I don't think they can go in there." She paused, looked down at her feet, then amended herself. "I don't think I can, either."

Jana knew exactly how she felt. She'd been silently praying that Rhamiel would agree to go around the place instead of through it. Everything about it looked off. Spooky. Not like a real forest, not anymore. Like some tortured child had taken a red crayon to a photo of the real thing. She held onto Rhamiel's hand, looking up at him and begging him to find another way. "She's right. We can't go into those woods. There's things in there."

"There are worse things out here," insisted Rhamiel. "That noise. It can only be one thing. Demons. They were angels, once. Lucifer's rebels. His army was tossed into his Pit right alongside him. They burned, roasting through the centuries until there was nothing left of their minds. They're in constant pain because of it. And they're incredibly dangerous."

There was another screech, and then another. Whatever they were, they were moving closer, coming towards them from somewhere in the distance. Jana searched the skies, but she couldn't see anything. Still, she couldn't be sure she wasn't missing something, not with the dome above them bubbling back and forth in a constant flow. She started to say something, some protest against going into such a dangerous place without knowing for sure that it was their only choice.

But Rhamiel didn't give her the chance to speak. He lifted her into his arms, charging into the forest as she wrapped her hands around his neck. He paused just inside the tree line, turning to the others and calling out behind him. "Follow us, and do it now. I cannot make you. But I cannot help you if you stay." Then he turned again, plunging into the darkness and carrying Jana further and further into the woods.

She couldn't see more than a few feet ahead of her, but she caught a glimpse over Rhamiel's shoulder of some of the servants, scrambling in after them. If an angel thought it wise to flee from whatever was out there, then so did they.

Rhamiel ducked behind a large oak, or what had once been one. Now it was something else, with sickly red mucus dripping from its branches in place of sap. The bark looked awful, spotted with bubbles that slowly expanded beneath the skin and flattened away just as quickly as they'd come. And little bugs were running up and down it, spiky things that looked like ants who'd fed on steroids. Nothing about it looked normal, and nothing about it looked safe. But it hid them from the outside, giving them cover from the things Rhamiel was running from. He dropped Jana to the ground, but she kept her arms around him, clinging to her little island of safety in a sea of dangers.

Servant after servant trickled towards them, slowly feeling their way through the woods. Faye was in the lead, and she made it to them first. Cassie was at the back of them, guiding the rest of the servants inside. Finally the last of them trooped past her, and she ducked into the trees herself. Jana could see her weaving back and forth on either side of the servants, herding them in the right direction and making sure that none of them strayed too far from the rest.

Cassie approached as the last of the servants crowded around the tree, and Rhamiel motioned for her attention. "Get them behind me. Get them hidden. And if a demon follows us, you must scatter into the woods. I can defeat one of them, and probably more. But there were legions of them down in the Pit. How many are up here, I cannot say." He looked to Jana, then back to Cassie. "If I die, you have to keep her alive. You have to do it, whatever the cost."

"I know," said Cassie. "And I will."

Cassie walked among the servants, whispering to them one by one. Jana caught snippets of it; she was pairing them up, telling each of them where to hide and what they should do if something went wrong. Her voice projected calm and comfort, and the servants followed her instructions to the letter. She'd been a mentor to Jana back in the tower, but a harsher one than this. Then she'd mostly barked her orders; now she spoke them in a tone that made the servants want to follow instructions instead of feeling obliged to.

Maybe it was the stress of living around the angels that had made her be so mean sometimes. Jana had grown up with the angels, and Cassie hadn't. Or maybe she'd been so wrapped up in her mission that she couldn't bring herself to connect with the people whose home she was about to destroy. But she was connected to them now, and Jana thought she'd turned from an irritable taskmaster into something closer to a clucking mother hen.

Cassie got the servants hidden somehow, ducking under bushes or crouching behind trees, and soon the rustling and the whispering died away to nothing. Jana could hear the screeching coming closer and closer. She heard a scream from just above them, somewhere over the trees, and a woman huddling underneath the nearby brush let out a quick squeak as she struggled to suppress a scream of her own.

There was a thud from outside the forest, and then another. More and more of them came, and Jana bit her hand to keep from making any noise. She could see shapes in the distance, indistinct at first. For a time they stood wherever they'd landed, waiting in total silence. But then one moved closer, ambling towards them until it was just outside the tree line. It looked like an angel, with wings twitching at its back, jerking up and down as it slowly paced before the trees. She couldn't get a good look, not at first. But then it lifted its head to the air, sniffing back and forth at some scent it had caught in the wind, and she saw it for what it was. And if this thing had been an angel once, there was nothing angelic to it now.

Its face was black, a hood of charred skin with only the barest outline of a nose. It had no eyes, no ears, no anything. Its wings looked like a bat's, just leathery skin singed until it was the color of night. The rest of it was no better; its entire body was one big lump of coal. She didn't understand how it could even see where it was going, but somehow it did.

"Silence," said Rhamiel in a low whisper. The servants were barely managing it. The fear was palpable, and there were so many of them. There was no way to keep discipline among them all, and Jana could hear people all around her whispering or brushing up against the leaves. Their only saving grace was that the unnatural hooting and groaning of the forest drowned out whatever noise they were making. If the forest had been as it was supposed to be, they'd have been discovered in an instant.

The demon stood there, its head twisting back and forth, straining so far in either direction that she thought its neck might snap. Every few moments its wings would flick, and one or another of the servants would gasp in response. She felt sure it knew they were there. But it didn't do a thing. It just kept standing there, facing in their direction. She could hear some of the servants talking about running, and only a sharp glare from Rhamiel kept them where they were.

But then the screeching started again from beyond the woods, and the demon jerked its head to listen. Its wings flapped and flapped, and it rose into the air and disappeared. Jana scanned the tree line. The rest of the shapes were gone as well. Whether the demon had seen them or not, it had found something more interesting than they were, and for the moment they were safe.

"What do we do now?" said Faye. "We're stuck in here. We can't leave. Not with things like that out there."

"Our choice has been made for us," said Rhamiel. "We go deeper into the woods. We go further into the dark until we come out into the light again."

Further. It made Jana feel nauseous just to think about it. Now that they were inside the forest she could see the shadows everywhere she looked, and not just at the periphery of her vision. Little blurs of color kept darting in front of her, just a shade blacker than the darkness behind them. There was something out there, something watching them, and there wasn't anything she could do about it.

It made her feel completely helpless, and she might have given up if Rhamiel hadn't been there. It was his strength that kept her going. He'd been to places worse than this, and she knew he was more dangerous than any of the things that could be out there. She'd rather face anything than an angry father defending his cub, and she was sure that even a demon would learn a painful lesson if it tried to attack them while he was there. But then again, there could be more of them. And there were entire armies out there with nothing to do but search for her, more enemies than Rhamiel could possibly hope to stand against alone.

Her thoughts were drawn back to what would happen if one of the angels died. Rhamiel wanted to redeem himself; she knew it in her heart. And maybe he even could. But what happened if she went first? She was a human, far weaker than an angel and far more likely to be a victim of the things out there. If enough of them attacked at once, they'd snatch her away from him, no matter how valiant his defense. And he'd be left there on Earth, alone.

Would he have the strength to go on by himself if she went up? Would he keep trying? And would the connection between them survive her death? He could live for centuries more without her, and probably longer still. She worried their love might just be a brief flicker for him in an endless existence. Maybe he'd find someone else once she was gone. It'd be easier than breaking down the gates of Heaven for the sake of a single woman.

In the end, it didn't matter. She couldn't do a thing about any of it. All she could do was worry, and Rhamiel had been right about that, at least. It didn't help to worry about the future. He would do as he would do, and all she could hope was that she'd made the right choice when she'd fallen for him. She tried to put aside her fears, listening as the others planned their escape.

Cassie was drawing a crude map in the dirt with a

stick, showing Rhamiel the shape of the forest as best she knew it. He paced around her, his hand planted across his chin as he lost himself in his plans.

"You came into the forest from the other side?" said Rhamiel. He picked up a stick of his own, drawing a little 'x' on the top of Cassie's map. "How long before it ends?"

"It isn't far," said Cassie. "A day or two's hike and we'll be out in the open again. But that's not what really matters. How far to that pillar? How far to the source?"

"Farther," said Rhamiel. "Weeks, at least, if I were walking, and if you were coming with me. But I'm not, and you aren't."

"We aren't?" said Cassie. She stood there for a moment, mouth agape in disbelief. But Rhamiel didn't budge, and he didn't say a word. She stepped towards him, poking a finger at his chest and glaring up at him in fury. "You're just going to leave us? We can't survive alone in here. Not without you. Look at them. Look around you. We'll all be dead within a day."

"I know," said Rhamiel softly. "I know." He looked around at the servants, hanging on their every word, then leaned down and spoke to her in a whisper low enough that Jana could barely hear. "The cherubs would slaughter you all in mere moments. They'll likely make short work of me as well. But our only chance is for me to try. We're all doomed if I cannot stop them. You and the others must hide. We will find a place that's safe, at least for a time. The rest will hinge on me."

"There's nowhere safe," said Cassie. "Nowhere."

"We have to try," said Rhamiel. "What else can we

do? When we fought the Maker's armies, there came a time when we knew we were doomed. And yet we fought on, anyway. When there was no more fighting to be done, I took a chance and jumped to Earth, alone." He glanced over at Jana, saw her eavesdropping, and raised his voice a little. "And here I am the better for it."

Cassie just grunted and stalked away. But after a few minutes of pacing she was moving among the servants again, getting them up and getting them gathered together. Rhamiel stood there, alone, staring down at the map and making marks around it with his stick. Jana crept towards him, standing beside him quietly as he made notes to himself on the ground. By the time he finally looked up, most of the servants were assembled, all of them with the same question on their minds.

"What are we going to do?" said Jana.

"Fight, until we can fight no more," said Rhamiel. "Live, until our lives are taken from us. Love, that when we must finally pass our thoughts are on something we hold fonder than ourselves."

"I can't ask for anything more," said Jana. "I really can't."

"I'm glad," said Rhamiel, holding out his hand. She took it, and he leaned into her, whispering into her ear so only she could hear. "You've lit the path for me. The one I should have been on all along. Now follow me, and I'll light the way for you." He drew his sword with his other hand, and the forest before them was bathed in an orange light.

The shadows shrank away, and she thought she heard a nasty growl from somewhere ahead of them. The trees still looked wrong, and a swarm of tiny black insects skittered away from the light. But Rhamiel just stepped forward, pulling Jana along with him and calling out to the servants as he went. "Keep behind me, but keep close. We must all stay together."

"Get in a chain," said Cassie. "Lock arms. Don't let go unless I tell you. If you run off on your own, we're never going to find you. And you don't want to be on your own in here." The servants obeyed her at once, rushing to clasp onto whoever was closest to them. She put someone's hands on Jana's shoulders—a frightened old woman, hunched over from years of toiling for the angels. Cassie stationed Faye in the middle, a strong link at the center of a chain that might need it. Then she went straight to the back of the line, and Rhamiel led them on through the trees.

Jana kept her hands around his waist, trying to avoid looking anywhere but the back of his armor. She couldn't help herself sometimes, and whenever she'd glance away she regretted it as soon as she did.

She saw things that looked like sickly buzzards, clinging to the branches up above them and staring down at them as they walked. They had wings, but she could swear they had more than two of them. Their beaks were a sickly green, and they seemed to drip away from their heads, flowing like water and only barely clinging to their faces. They'd dance along the branches, hooting at one another before flapping off ahead of them to start the watch again.

She saw something that looked like a frog hop past her feet, though she was sure it wasn't one. It had little yellow horns, and spikes running all across its legs. It hissed at her, a grinding sound no frog could make, and it flashed row after row of sharpened teeth before it pounced away into the grass.

She saw a cat, she thought. The eyes were the same, glowing yellow as the light of the sword hit them. She couldn't see it, not exactly. It was all a shadowy blur, everything but the eyes, even when it moved out into the open. It meowed like a cat, like something soft and wounded and sad. She wanted to go and help it, and she might have, if she'd been the one to make the choice. But she heard a firm "no" from Rhamiel, and the unbroken line of servants kept moving forward, ignoring the mewling pleas that begged them to follow, just a little ways, just for a little while.

They walked for what must have been an hour. Jana's feet hurt, and so did her insides; she'd been on the run for nearly the entire day. She slowed her steps and tugged at Rhamiel's hand. "Can we stop for a break? Just for a minute?"

"Of course," said Rhamiel. His voice was filled with concern, and his eyes ran up and down her body, searching for any sign that she was in pain. "I should have told you to rest earlier. My mind has been on the things that follow us. They're exceedingly dangerous, and we must hurry. But we cannot risk our child in doing it."

"I'm fine," said Jana. She sat down on a twisted old root, snaking out of the ground and forming as good a chair as she was likely to find. "All I need is a few minutes. It's not that bad." Her feet hurt, and she pulled away her sandals to see the beginnings of blisters all along her toes. At least she thought she saw them. It was hard to tell with the light as it was behind the barrier; her skin looked so strange, almost foreign. But when she rubbed her fingers along her foot, the pain told her she'd been right all along. Blisters they were, and they'd only get worse the more she walked.

The chain of servants had folded in on itself, and now they were all finding places of their own to sit and rest their legs. Cassie was doting on them almost as much as Rhamiel was on her. She went from servant to servant, collecting canteens of water and parceling it out to those who needed it most. As for Rhamiel, he was gathering up a pile of grass and wrapping it inside one of the servants' old tunics. When he was done he'd made her a pillow of sorts, and he tucked it underneath her. It wasn't perfect, but it was an improvement over the root, and far more comfortable. He stood at watch beside her, and she thought it far more comforting than the finest silks or the softest down could ever have been.

They all sat there for a time, talking quietly among themselves. Everyone stayed close. Cassie and Faye were silent, and so was Jana. She felt safe, as safe as she'd been in weeks. Part of her wished they could just stay there, hidden away from everyone else, even as frightening as the place could be.

And then she heard something behind her. A voice. It was high-pitched, almost a screech, a whistle on the wind that came from up, then down, then back again. It whirled around her, and then it seemed to hang in the air, whispering into the ears of everyone around.

"He'll change you."

Rhamiel held up his sword, whirling on his heels and waving it before him. But there was nothing there. Still the voice kept talking, crunching on the words as they came from nowhere.

"You shouldn't fight it."

"The flowers," said Jana. She pointed behind her at a patch of sickly things shaped like plants, poking out of the soil near one of the trees. They might have been daisies once, or they might just have been weeds. It was impossible to tell. They were still alive, after a fashion, but they weren't the same as what they'd once been. They were entirely black, living shadows with glowing red petals at the tip of thin ashen stalks.

One of the flowers weaved back and forth, and something like laughter coughed out of it. "He's only doing what's right." Its petals pulsed as it spoke, twisting in the wind like tiny tongues as the head of the flower pointed back and forth between them. "He's not the bad one. He's only misunderstood. Maybe you're the bad ones, if you look at things a certain way. Living when you weren't supposed to. You aren't supposed to be here, and yet here you are. So very, very bad."

Faye stepped forward, raising a boot above it, ready to grind the thing down into a pulp. But Cassie's eyes flashed with fear, and she grabbed her arm, pulling her away.

"Don't touch it," said Cassie. "It's like these things I saw. These shadows. Something's gotten into them. Made them into something else. And if they touch you." She shuddered, her thoughts drawn back to the children.

So many children, and she wasn't even sure what they were any more. "It's horrible. Just don't touch it."

Faye leaned forward, frowning at the thing, but keeping a healthy distance. "Just let us out." She waved a hand at the flowers with an exasperated sigh. "You don't even want us here. So just open up the barrier and we'll go. We don't want to be here anymore than you want us to be."

"You aren't supposed to be anywhere," said the flower. "The world was supposed to end. You're not supposed to exist, but you do. Naughty, naughty. But he'll set things right. And how can he be wrong, if he's only doing what the Maker said he would? What he always promised?"

"Who are you even talking about?" said Faye. "This is babble. It doesn't make any sense."

"You'll see things his way," said the flower. "You'll see. You'll even help us end things. End things the proper way. His way. The way the Maker wanted things to end, once. You'll—"

The flower's chatter was cut short as Rhamiel crushed it beneath his boot, stamping it back and forth and grinding the thing into the dirt. It let out a shrill death-scream, and all that was left when he stepped away was an inky spot of goo staining the dirt. Shadows spread away from it, crawling along the ground towards Rhamiel's foot. But as they came closer, they shied away from him, vanishing down into the soil along the flower's roots.

"I have no fear of the mouthpiece of another," said Rhamiel. "Nor do I fear its creator. I am a guardian, and mere shadows are nothing to me."

"I told you," said Faye. "I told you they were doing

something. Changing things. Changing everything. I heard them when he was in my head. I still hear whispering from the edges, sometimes. And it's getting louder the closer we get."

"She's right," said Cassie. "They changed the children. We saw it, too."

"Who's the one it was talking about?" said Jana. "With this plan?"

"They sometimes called him the Light Bringer, before his rebellion," said Rhamiel quietly. "Before he tore Heaven apart. An archangel, and one of the best of us before he fell." He let out a sigh, and he stared off into the distance, lost in ancient memories. "They called him something else, towards the end. When we still thought he was on our side. When we thought he was helping us in our work. Honing us. Testing us. An old word, a title, the name for a job he performed with the Maker's blessing. Opposing the Maker's plans just for the sake of it, raising every possible objection to ensure that we could address any problems before a plan went into action. A devil's advocate, if you will."

"Him," said Cassie, her face gone cold with fear. "That was a message from him."

"Who?" said Jana. She didn't understand. She didn't know much about the old religion, only what the angels had told their servants. That wasn't much, and sometimes it seemed like the ones outside the tower knew the angels better than she did. "Who? Whose message?"

"In your language, his title translates as 'the adversary,'" said Rhamiel. "In the angelic tongue, the word was Satan. But mostly, we called him Lucifer."

CHAPTER NINETEEN

LUCIFER.

Cassie had heard the angels whisper his name, and she'd heard them speak of Lucifer's Pit, mostly in hushed tones that suggested the subject was entirely taboo. She'd never tried to discuss it with Nefta; the only thing she'd gathered about him was that he was real, he was the leader of the first rebellion, and he was safely locked away in the place she'd grown up calling Hell.

But now he was free, at least if Rhamiel was right. And she didn't have any reason to doubt him. Those shadowy things she'd seen weren't angels, and they weren't from Heaven. The things he called demons might have been angels once, but she'd never heard of anything like them since the Fall. And something had created this bubble, warping the light and turning everything beneath it into a twisted parody of itself.

The shadow creatures had been frightening, but this terrified her. The end to everything. And not the way she'd heard about in stories as a kid. Not with a plan from above but a plan from below. Everything turned upside down, or changed, or maybe just dead like those creepy little flowers had threatened. If Lucifer was as bad as the old stories said he was, she didn't want to find out.

But she wasn't sure she had any choice, and she wasn't sure there was anything they could do to stop it.

She just wanted to run. To take her little flock wherever she could, find a place they could ride things out, and let things be however they would be. She was tired of fighting angels, and she wasn't about to take up a war against a bunch of demons as well. It was hopeless. She knew that now. Let them tear each other apart, and let the humans inherit the rubble.

But there was nowhere to go, not anymore. And while the smartest course might have been for everyone to look to their own, it wasn't really an option. Rhamiel was right on that front. It was fight or die, and that was all there was to it.

He was leading them through the forest with a newfound urgency, eager to get them out the other side and scour the land for someplace he could hide them. He was worried about Jana's safety, and he wasn't hiding it. One hand held the sword ahead of him, slashing at dangling black vines and burning a path through the undergrowth. The other kept tapping away at the armored plate on his thigh, a rhythmic ding, ding, ding that must have done something to soothe the turmoil within. And he was constantly craning his neck behind him, confirming that Jana was still safely in line before turning back to his labor.

She didn't blame him for worrying. Lucifer scared her almost out of her wits, and she'd only heard the stories.

Rhamiel had actually known him, and he had both Jana and his child to care for. Lucifer would be after them if he was after anyone. And the thought of it was eating away at Rhamiel from the inside.

She jogged ahead of the others, catching up to Rhamiel and walking alongside him. He looked down at her, but he didn't say a word. He just kept cutting out a path, making it as wide and as easy as he could manage. She stayed beside him for a time. Truthfully, she was afraid of him, if only just a little. She gathered her courage, racking her brain as they walked for exactly what she wanted to say.

She had to talk to him. She knew that much. Jana might have spent months with him, but she barely knew him at all. And now she was trusting her flock to him, not because he was the best among them but because he was the strongest. Because he knew the most about the enemies they faced, and because they didn't seem to have any other option.

Maybe they didn't have a choice, but she had to know what was driving him to help them. He was a fallen angel, after all, and every one of them had darkness inside them. She'd never met a good one, not really. They'd all been broken in their own way, and she wanted to know just how broken he was beneath the surface. The only way to do that was to talk to him. She rehearsed the things she might say in her head, again and again, but none of it mattered. In the end she just spat something out.

"What can we do?" said Cassie. "I mean, really? Is there anything we can actually do to stop this?"

He looked at her briefly, then snapped his sword

in front of him. A low-hanging branch dropped to the ground, and the tree it had hung from gave a high-pitched squeal from a knotty hole in its side. The branch writhed on the ground before them, curving and wriggling with unnatural life until Rhamiel kicked it away from the path he'd created. He pushed onward, speaking to Cassie in a low voice as he went. "I only know what I suspect. And I suspect this will be the last stand any of us make. But I've fought in lost causes before, and I don't intend to quit now. The Son can stop this, if only we can save him. It's why he's changed his mind, and why he's come back. It must be. I'm sure of it."

"I wish he'd just come back when he was supposed to," said Cassie. "I wish he'd just done what he said he would in the first place."

"It doesn't always work out that way," said Rhamiel.

"But why couldn't God just follow the plan, like the flowers said?" said Cassie. "He's supposed to be omnipotent. They told me that when I was a kid."

"Can an omnipotent god change his mind?" said Rhamiel. "Or has he the power to do everything but that?"

"But he's omniscient, too," said Cassie. "That's what they say. Knows everything. Sees everything. If he knows everything, he should know how to fix this without all the violence. Without all the death and the pain."

"And who knows the mind of the Maker?" said Rhamiel. "You? I make no claim to, and I sang in choir before him. Perhaps he planned the future down to the tiniest movements of each and every atom. Perhaps he knows it all and controls it all. Some think so. And if it's so, he knew this day would come. He told you his Son would return, and in the end, he spoke the truth, even if it was by a more circuitous route than we'd all expected."

"If he planned everything, we shouldn't even bother," said Cassie. "We should just hide. Just let him handle things."

"Perhaps he didn't," said Rhamiel. "Some think that as well. He made man in his image, after all. Perhaps there's more of man in him than we'd admit. Can he change his mind and change his plans? A man could do it, so why not him? Perhaps he's softened as he's aged. He used to be quite the one for punishments, and some of them exceedingly harsh. But he didn't have his Son back then. It's made some difference in him, I think, having a child of his own." He turned behind them, catching a glance at Jana walking along behind them. "I've heard that it can change a man. And I know for a fact that it can change an angel."

It made a certain sort of sense to her. She'd known men who'd had the same experience. Unrepentant hell raisers turned to doting fathers the second that pregnancy test came back. It was reassuring to think about, at least. She hadn't known any man quite so dangerous as a fallen angel, but if a human could be tamed by fatherhood, then maybe Rhamiel could be, too. Maybe that's why he wasn't quite as dark as the rest of them, not anymore.

He was pushing further into the forest, leaving her behind, but she dogged his footsteps and kept at him. He was the only one who had the slightest clue what was going on, and she had to learn everything she could if she was going to keep any of the servants alive. "You think it changed God himself. You think being a father made him different."

"He doesn't act the same as he once did," said Rhamiel. "He's more for mercy in recent times, and more for turning the other cheek. He and the Son are bonded to one another, and it must have had an influence. But the truth is that I haven't any better idea than you do. What goes on in a mind like that, I couldn't begin to fathom."

"It just seems like such a waste," said Cassie. "It would have been so much better if he'd done like he'd promised. If he'd just ended it all. If he'd taken the good ones up, and sent the bad ones down."

"Better for whom?" said Rhamiel. "Man isn't the only one of his creations, you know. The promise of an end to this world was mostly a promise to my kind, not to yours. I don't envy his choices. He changed his plans to give mercy to sinners who didn't deserve it." He walked ahead, brooding in silence before opening up again. "I think he changed his mind for us as well, and not just for mankind. I think he did this to help us."

"Help you," said Cassie. She couldn't understand it. The world was a giant, steaming mess. Billions were dead. And the fallen angels had lost their home, their friends, and everything they'd ever held dear. "How in the world could any of this help you?"

"Rebellion was our choice, but we didn't have to make it," said Rhamiel. "I think now that our service was what gave us purpose. Our purpose was what kept us sane. We thought we wanted it all to end. We didn't know what we were giving up, and we weren't equipped to handle its loss. But he knew. He knew that being idle for all eternity was sure to drive us mad. And if we hadn't rebelled, if we'd simply accepted his decision, we'd all have been the better for it, man and angel alike."

"But you did rebel," said Cassie. "And he should have known you would. He should have known all the people you'd kill."

"Perhaps he did, and perhaps he didn't," said Rhamiel. "But we can no more blame him for all the death and cruelty that came after the Fall than we did for all the death and cruelty that came before it. He was always one for lofty aspirations, even if they were a bit unrealistic when applied to others. He wanted the best from us, and even if we couldn't give it to him, he wanted us to try. It's what still drives me. He wouldn't leave this world to Lucifer. He simply wouldn't. It could still be a better place, in the end. Human and angel could live side by side as equals, if only we'd try it. And hope isn't lost until we let it be."

"You don't sound like a rebel," said Cassie. "You don't sound like one of the others at all."

"The Fall changed me as much as my rebellion did," said Rhamiel. "And so did the things that happened after it. I want redemption. I really, truly do. I don't know if I can ever have it, not now that I've been touched by sin. But I can hope. If the Son is born, he might do what he did before. Take the world's sins upon himself, and redeem us all in the process." He locked eyes with Cassie, fixing her in place with his stare. "That is what this is about. Redemption. He is my son now, too. And I shall see him born at whatever the cost."

He left her there behind him, stalking forward through the trees. The strokes of his sword grew furious, determined, and he pressed ahead at a faster pace than ever. It didn't seem wise to follow him, not with how pensive he'd become. She dropped back in line instead, mingling with the servants, making sure there weren't any stragglers and that everyone had what they needed to be able to keep up.

She thought about it all as the hours passed. It was walk, walk, walk, and there was little else to do. Rhamiel seemed genuine enough. He wasn't torturing anyone, at least, and he really seemed to want to be redeemed. She probably would, too, if she'd sinned the way his kind had. But he still scared her, and she didn't like that they had to follow him. They were trusting themselves to someone they barely knew. He wasn't human, and for all she knew, the only one of them he really cared about was Jana.

What would happen if it came down to a choice between Jana and all the rest of them? He'd already tried to leave with her once. She didn't really blame him for it, but still. Blood was blood, and he'd be loyal to his child before anyone else. She wouldn't expect anything different even from the best creation had to offer, and he'd once been numbered among the worst.

She had to stay on guard. It hurt her to do it. Her nerves were raw, and seemed like they always would be. There was never a break, not in this world the angels had created. She wished she'd never gone to the tower. If she hadn't helped bring it down, she wouldn't have felt the guilt. She wouldn't be responsible for all these people.

She'd only be responsible for herself, and she'd bear the frets and worries of a single person instead of more than a hundred.

She kept thinking about it all as she walked. She wondered how the real leaders did it. The ones who wanted to lead, and didn't have to be forced to. Sometimes she thought it would have been easier to do it if she was a man. Some of them seemed to have been born to lead. Rhamiel acted like it all just came naturally to him, like being in charge was the only way things could possibly be.

It wasn't like that for her. Maybe it just looked easier from the outside. Men fought so much with each other, and the male angels were even worse. Maybe it was the fighting that did it. The ones who thrived in all the conflict rose above the rest, and the others just disappeared into the background. And if the man at the top went down, there was always someone like Herman waiting to take his place. Someone stronger, or craftier, or just more willing to break the rules to get their way.

There were women who thrived on power, too, but she wasn't one of them. Not yet, anyway, and she hoped she never would be. She'd seen what power did to people, man and woman alike. She wondered if she'd lose part of herself if she kept going. There were women like Ambriela who'd used their cunning and talent to best far stronger angels and come out at the top. But she had to be cold and ruthless to do it, and Cassie didn't ever want to become like that. People like that wanted to lead for power, or for attention, or for glory. And none of that was worth the cost.

She didn't want any of this. She didn't like fighting, and she'd only ever done it because she felt like the angels had forced them to. It was the same way with being in charge of all these people: she didn't want to do it, but if no one else was going to lift a finger, she'd step up if she had to. Maybe the hermit's life wouldn't have been so bad. She could have taken up painting again. She'd done it for a while. Not long enough to be any good at it, but if she didn't have to lead, she'd have all the time in the world to practice. She wanted something for herself again, but now all she had was a duty to others.

And the more she thought about it, the more she knew that what she wanted more than anything was a break. Time to rest, and time to process.

But she wasn't going to get it.

She heard a noise from up ahead on the trail, piercing through her thoughts. She looked up to see one of the servants stumbling just ahead of her. Aaron. She thought that was his name, at least.

She had trouble remembering them all, partly because she didn't want to. The closer she got to them, the harder it was to lead them. His hair was dark, cut into a simple mop that looked like something out of a fifties rock band. He'd have looked better with someone to style it, but they didn't have anyone left with much talent on that front. He made up for it with his body, tall enough and muscular enough to earn him a position as a workman doing odd jobs back in the tower, jobs that needed the strength of someone his size.

But now he was down on the ground, clutching his hands against his leg. He screamed, kicking and pushing himself away from whatever had put that kind of fright into him. She could see movement nearby, a dark shape that wriggled along the ground and snapped at his feet even as he dragged himself into the brush.

She ran towards him, dodging past servants who'd opted to go the other way. He was still kicking, still screaming, and when she got closer she could see the reason why.

He was fighting against one of the roots of the trees, or at least something that had once been one. Now it was something else, something with glistening black skin that gleamed through the darkness. It was still attached to the tree, and it was still a part of it. The creature snaked out of the ground, slithering towards Aaron and snapping at his legs.

She could see something on the end of it: a head, baring row after row of grimy yellow teeth. They were a mish-mash of different shapes: some were fangs, some jagged molars, and some thin as needles. They poked out from its mouth at all angles, gnashing against one another as it bit the air. It had tiny slits for eyes, little yellow lines on either side of it that glowed whenever it opened them.

She grabbed a heavy stick from the ground, long enough that she could keep her distance as she thrashed away at the creature. She managed to hit its body a few times, but it didn't do more than hiss. It kept attacking Aaron, and its head struck the ground near his leg, barely missing him. Cassie took advantage of it; she bashed the stick into one of its eyes, and it yelped like a whipped dog. It reared up into the air, one eye squinting in pain and the other focused on her. It hissed again, then launched itself towards her, mouth agape.

She barely had time to move. It snapped at the air just past her shoulder, and she could feel drippings of slime splash across her face. Its breath was rancid, and memories flashed into her head of month-old fish she'd once accidentally left in the back of her refrigerator before the Fall. She rolled to the side, then swung the branch ahead of her, wildly and without any thought about what she was even trying to hit. She just wanted something in front of her, something between her and the thing from down below that wanted to bite out chunks of her and suck them down inside it.

But when the panic subsided, she saw it wasn't even after her anymore. It had gone back to Aaron, wrapping itself around his leg. He was easier prey, and he was closer, and the thing slithered up his leg before stopping at his thigh. A thick, forked tongue poked out of its mouth, probing along his skin and leaving a trail of mucus in its wake. It coiled around him, tighter and tighter, rearing up again and looking down on him with the closest something like that could manage to a smile.

And then it bit him.

He screamed in agony, punching and slapping at it with his hands. The effort didn't help him. The thing had its fangs latched into him, and it was starting to chew. His screams grew louder, high pitched wails that didn't sound like they could come from a man of his size and strength. All his thrashings didn't do a thing against the creature. But they managed to draw the attention of someone who could.

Cassie could hear heavy footsteps from ahead of them on the trail, and then Rhamiel was there. He'd doubled back, his sword raised above them, and the thing uncoiled itself from Aaron and rolled along the ground in Rhamiel's direction. He waved his sword in a circle before it, and its movements grew jerky, out of focus. The light was blinding it, the glare from Rhamiel's sword too bright for a creature accustomed to life in the darkness. It snapped at him, but it caught only air, straining against the tree it was attached to as it lunged.

The first swing from Rhamiel's sword caught it on the neck, severing its head and leaving it stuck on the ground, its mouth helplessly snapping at the air. Its body flailed about, spewing yellow fluid in all directions. The second swing ended that, cutting it off from the base of the tree. He kicked both body and head away from the path, leaving only a smudge of nasty goo in the path for the servants to pass.

Cassie rushed to Aaron's side, squinting as she searched him for wounds. It didn't look bad, not for all the trouble he'd been through. Just two small bite marks dotting his leg: one on his ankle about the size of a dime, and a larger one where the thing had fastened itself to him and taken away a piece. He was panting, covered in sweat, but otherwise he wasn't harmed. Just very scared, and very wary of the trees.

"You'll be fine," said Cassie. "Just a few scratches. And if it hurts to walk, we'll help you."

"Let me see," said Rhamiel. He brushed her aside, kneeling down beside Aaron and holding his sword above the wounds to examine them. He muttered something to himself, then he stood. "Devil's marks. These are bad. These are very, very bad."

"Does he need a doctor?" said Cassie. "I have some first aid training, but I'm probably not the best choice for this. Some of the servants were—"

"We must burn them," said Rhamiel. "And we must do it while we can." He clamped a hand down on Aaron's leg, forcing it to the ground. Aaron was screaming, writhing, fighting Rhamiel with more vigor than he had the creature. Cassie tried to say something, to reason with Rhamiel and to calm the situation down.

But he didn't wait, and he didn't listen. He pressed his sword against Aaron's leg, scorching the first of the marks into a blackened lump of flesh across his leg. Aaron yelped, beating his hands against Rhamiel's chest in a desperate bid to stop the pain.

The smell of it was awful. It invaded Cassie's nostrils, forcing her to the point of gagging. She coughed, felt her stomach churn, and only barely held herself together. This was too much. The cure was worse than the disease. Barbaric. Medieval. That was all the angels knew. Maybe she'd been stupid to start to trust Rhamiel. His words had sounded nice, but now he was jumping back into violence the second he'd gotten the chance, just like all the rest of them.

"He can't take this," said Cassie. "Look at him."

"He has to," said Rhamiel. He pressed his sword against another of the marks, and again Aaron erupted into screams of pain. He kicked his leg, but Rhamiel held it firm, burning the flesh until the mark had disappeared and much of his skin along with it.

"Stop," said Cassie. "Please stop."

"I will not," said Rhamiel. "We must go further. I will have to cut off the leg." He rose to his feet, holding his sword above Aaron and eying a spot near his upper thigh. He was planning to take off the entire thing, leaving Aaron helpless. If he couldn't walk, he wouldn't make it out of the forest. This wasn't a cure. It was a death sentence, the kind of thing a witch doctor would have done, not an angel. And she wasn't going to stand by and let it happen.

"No," said Cassie. Rhamiel had gone mad. She knew it. He'd fallen, and he'd been tainted on the inside, and it was never going to go away. He was just going to slice away limbs without even talking to the person he was doing it to. Without even asking for permission. She leapt at him, pulling at his arm and trying to hold him back. She didn't have the strength, but she could do something else. She rolled on top of Aaron, putting herself in the path of Rhamiel's sword. It checked him, but barely. He grabbed for her, trying to pull her out of the way, but she ducked and kept herself between the two of them.

"You can't," said Cassie.

"We must," said Rhamiel. "Stop interfering. Move away. Let me do what must be done."

"I won't," said Cassie. "I'm not going to let you. This is cruel. This is the same stuff you used to do in the tower." She grabbed onto Aaron, holding him in a bear hug and locking her hands behind his back. If Rhamiel wanted to hurt him, he'd have to go through her.

"He'll die," said Rhamiel. "He'll—"

She felt something beneath her. Something cold. Something clammy. Something crawling. She started to scream, but she didn't get the chance. She found herself in the air, helpless; Rhamiel had grabbed her by the collar, and before she knew it he'd thrown her to the ground and knocked the wind out of her.

As she struggled for air, she could see why he'd done what he had. Aaron's leg was gone. It was black, and not from the burns. The leg had changed into something else: a glistening, snaking monster, exactly like the thing they'd just killed. It slithered along the ground towards her, dragging Aaron behind it. He was crying, digging his fingers into the dirt and trying to stop himself. But the thing was part of him now, and wherever it went, so would he.

She saw little patches of shiny black appearing all along his skin, spreading over his arms and then onto his throat. They were growing, merging together, and none of his tears could stop them. The thing that had been his leg was snarling, snapping at her, until it disappeared in a storm of fiery blows. She couldn't see it anymore, just the back of Rhamiel's wings. But she could hear it. Aaron was gone, and Rhamiel was doing him the kindest favor he could: ending the tortures before he was consumed by the corruption entirely.

She lay there on the ground, sobbing quietly to herself. She'd killed him. She'd thought Rhamiel was the one with evil inside him, and in the end it was her. He'd been trying to help Aaron, but she'd stopped him, all because she couldn't see good when it was right in front of her face. She wasn't a leader. She wasn't even close.

She was a failure, a sham shepherd who'd led the ones who trusted her into something even worse than death. Rhamiel stood above her, holding down his hand, but she couldn't accept it. She didn't want to move. All she wanted to do was curl into a ball and let the others go on without her.

"I should have let you do it," said Cassie. "I shouldn't have stopped you."

"He'd have died regardless of what we'd done," said Rhamiel. "He was simply too far along. We call those wounds devil's marks. Some creatures from Lucifer's Pit leave them on their victims whenever they bite. There's venom in them, and worse. Even an angel could succumb to them without treatment. A human body is frail. Too weak to resist its poisons."

"You could have saved him," said Cassie. "If you'd cut off his leg, you could have saved him."

"The poison had spread," said Rhamiel. "I didn't make it here in time. If I'd cut off his leg, he would have died all the same. A minute later, perhaps, but he'd still be dead. The fault is mine to bear."

"You're lying," said Cassie. "You're lying to make me feel better."

"I speak the truth," said Rhamiel firmly. "And the truth is this: more will die, regardless of how hard you try to save them. You cannot let it eat at you. Trust me in this, if in nothing else. I was a guardian angel for thousands of years. I saved hundreds of souls, and I lost just as many. Sometimes caring for another brings joy, and sometimes it brings pain. But you'll care, anyway, because it isn't a choice. It's your essence, and losing that to the pain would be a loss too great for you to bear."

They were kind words, but they didn't help. She managed to pull herself to her feet and to get back in line, trudging along with the rest of the servants. They were marching away as if nothing had happened, and in a few minutes Rhamiel was back in the lead. And every fiber of her being hoped he'd stay there.

CHAPTER TWENTY

ECANUS STOOD ON THE BALCONY, leaning against the railing and idly watching his seraphs at work. A platoon of them had launched themselves against the barrier on his orders, darting towards it as fast as their wings would carry them. Hacking away at it with their swords hadn't done a thing, so he'd instructed them to try something else.

It wasn't any more effective than any of their earlier efforts. They were the strongest among his warriors, the ones most filled with rage, and they'd given it their all. He'd made sure of that, lashing each of them thrice before the charge and threatening to cut off their wings if they failed. But it had all been pointless. They were colliding against the barrier at full speed, tumbling helplessly down to the ground without even making a dent in it.

"Pity," said Ecanus. It was an unlikely plan, but it had to be tried. He turned from the balcony, striding back into the tower. The place was filled with prisoners, angels who hadn't made it out in time or who'd been wounded in battle. One in the corner nursed a foot-long gash across her wing, carefully arranging her feathers to cover it up as best she could. Another sat facing the wall, rocking back and forth, over and over, her mind lost in a complete state of shock. Row after row of them waited silently, reduced to prisoners in their own home and surrounded by seraphs turned to beasts through his handiwork.

So it would be for all of them when he was done. He had patrols circling the area to round up the ones who'd escaped, assuming they were foolish enough to stay nearby. It would take him time, but he'd forge a second army from the raw materials he'd captured here. They were worthless now, but it was nothing a few months of torture couldn't remedy. In the meantime, he had two more important prizes—not the ones he'd been looking for, but valuable nonetheless.

The first was Zuphias, or so he claimed. His body was human, an overgrown ugly thing that looked more a monkey than any of them. Whoever it was, he sat alone on a gilded couch at the edge of the room, pouting and helpless, scowling at the angels around him whose bodies he envied. Suriel would want him for curiosity's sake alone, to say nothing of what knowledge he might have of the Cherubim.

The second of his prizes mattered more, at least for the present: Ambriela, ruler of the tower and the only one who could properly surrender it to him. She was flanked by two of his warriors and looking the worse for wear from the battle. She was quite unhappy to see him; all the better, as far as he was concerned, and his voice dripped with venom as he approached her. "It seems I'm stuck here. With you."

"Pity," said Ambriela quietly, her eyes aimed at the floor.

There was a touch of sarcasm in her voice, and he'd flay it from her before he was done. She'd learn to speak to him properly or she'd have a bit in her mouth, just like all the rest of them. And if she didn't learn her place, well, then all the more fun for him.

"If I cannot leave, then I must make myself useful," said Ecanus. He plopped himself down in her silver chair, stretching his wings and admiring the craftsmanship. Fine work, by whoever had done it. Metallic serpents proffering apples wound all around the edges; whoever had made it had been an excellent silversmith, but more obsessed with the fall of man than with the fall of angels. He waved a hand and one of his lieutenants dragged Ambriela before him, forcing her to her knees. "Now, it's time you tell me what you know of the magic that's trapped us here."

"I know nothing of it," said Ambriela. "And there's no need for us to be at loggerheads. We're no enemies of Suriel, that I can assure you." She smiled at him, her best attempt at winning him over. It almost worked. He felt a warmth towards her welling within him. Attraction, even, despite her scars. He hadn't known the love of a woman in years, and old passions welled up within him. But then he noticed it. Something was happening to her face. The scars were fading into nothingness. Slowly, but he could see it if he stared at her just so. The work of a glamour; beautiful, to be sure, and certainly seductive. But it wasn't real, and it wouldn't last.

"Miracles won't save you from me," snarled Ecanus. He stood from the chair, leaned in towards her, then raised his arm and gave her a healthy slap. The force of it knocked her head sideways, and when she turned back to him her scars were all there, just as they'd always been. "Your words drip with honey, but still you harbored our enemies. And I was nearly killed as a result of your intransigence."

It wasn't true, not technically. He didn't have a scratch on him. Not that it mattered. The truth was a pliable thing, and the past a fleeting one. Once it was gone, who was to say whose version of events was true in the end? The one with the most weapons and the most warriors, that was who. If he'd learned anything from Suriel, it was that.

In point of fact, he'd hovered at a safe distance from most of the fighting, such as it was. There hadn't been much to speak of, not after the initial assault. Only Rhamiel had given them any real resistance. Rhamiel with his perfect face, his perfect love, and his perfect son.

Rhamiel looked down on him still. He could feel it in his bones. The snotty attitude born of power and privilege, with not a whit of accomplishment to justify it. He hadn't even been a soldier up in Heaven. Ecanus had at least been that, low of rank though he might have been. He'd have dueled with Rhamiel himself, if only the Maker had blessed him with the strength to win. But one couldn't ask for everything. Cunning was a far more impressive gift than valor, and a sharper weapon than any sword.

Rhamiel had fought fiercely, though he was but a single seraph against an entire army of them, and they'd nearly done him in. A few more minutes and they would have. Ecanus had hovered around the edges of the battle, directing the fight and throwing wave after wave of maddened seraphs into the fray, all of them chomping at the bit to release the rage his tortures had bottled inside them. It hadn't worked; Rhamiel had fought them to a standstill, and then when the barrier had appeared in the distance he'd simply fled. And what valor was there in that? He was a coward, plain and simple, hiding behind love to mask his own weakness.

Ecanus's own army had been no better. They'd fled at the first sight of the barrier, not for love of others but for love of self. It had taken him hours to get them all organized again, and there'd been no end to the blowing of horns and the beating of drums. Finally he'd gotten them into some semblance of order, and from there it had been a simple matter to round up all the residents of the tower who'd fled. They hadn't anywhere to go any more than the rest of them did, and the envelopment of their home beneath this scarlet monstrosity had sapped their will to fight.

He might have been trapped, but escape could wait until later. There was only one task that was truly pressing: finding Rhamiel's child before anyone else did. Figuring out a way to break through the barrier and deliver him to Suriel could come once the child was in his custody. If he came back empty-handed, he might as well not bother coming back at all.

He needed to know where Rhamiel had gone to, and that meant extracting what information he could from his captives. He put a hand beneath Ambriela's chin, lifting her face towards him and giving her his friendliest smile. She'd see through him, of course, but of course she was meant to.

"Where is the Son, dearest Ambriela?" said Ecanus. "Where did he go to?"

"I've no idea," said Ambriela. Ecanus nodded, and the seraphs to either side of her clamped their hands on her shoulders, digging their fingers into her skin. She yelped in pain, tears trickling along her network of scars. Ecanus smiled, the seraphs loosened their grip, and after choking down the pain she tried again. "I don't know. I swear that I don't. But the Son was here, or so Rhamiel told us. He had a girl with him. A girl who was with child. And he claimed it as his own."

She spoke the truth, he thought. She wouldn't have held anything back, not in the position she was in. And Rhamiel was his own angel with his own agenda. This place was but a waystation for him, and she likely hadn't known what he was up to when she'd taken him in as a guest.

Not that any of that mattered. He'd torture her just the same.

He pulled his whip from his belt, letting the flame dangle down below him and tickle the floor. "You will learn. It will take time, but you will learn. Suriel is master now, just as the Maker once was. And his power has been delegated to me to use as I see fit." He nodded to one of the seraphs again. The seraph held Ambriela's arm away from her body, tearing at the straps of her armor and ripping the plate away from her skin.

Her arm was exposed, the flesh pristine. Perfect, for what Ecanus intended. He'd found that it was a simple matter to break an angel. Their vanity was their weakness, and what skin they had left, they'd protect at any cost. He'd have given anything to get rid of his own scars, to trade with one of them who'd made it through the Fall a little more intact. He knew their weakness more intimately than any of them because it was his own.

Ambriela's lips quivered. She was afraid. He could see it, taste it. He had her, and he knew it. He lifted his arm, letting the flame of the whip brush before her face, making certain that she felt the warmth of it. He drew the moment out, waiting for the seconds to tick by as the seraph gripped her hand, forcing her to extend her arm before him. Her eyes closed, she gave an involuntary whimper, and then he knew her fear was ripe for the harvest.

He snapped the whip against her, the flame sinking into her skin with a loud crack. When he held it to the air again, there were three black rows of damaged skin stretching across her arm. She stared at it in disbelief, her jaw hanging open as she let out a low moan.

"There'll be more to come," said Ecanus. "Piece by piece, I'll take you apart." He brought the whip down on her arm again, and this time she screamed. Three more scars crossing the others. Three more blemishes she'd need to cover with her glamours. He lifted his whip hand into the air again, and this time she screamed before he'd even hit her. If she knew anything, this was the time for him to ask. He knew a broken victim when he saw one, and this one was on the verge of shattering. "Where is the Son? Tell me where he went, and all of this will stop."

"I don't know," sputtered Ambriela. "I truly don't. But I'll do anything." Her face changed, blurring into a pink, glowing mass. A few seconds later and she was a stunning blonde beauty, her cheeks flush with desire. "Anything, Ecanus. I'll be anyone you want."

Perhaps he'd take her up on that offer once the business at hand was done. Torture wasn't the only joy in life, after all, and what she offered him now was a mixture of the pain of another with pleasure of his own. Tempting, to be sure. But she didn't know a thing, not about the Son, and Suriel would flay him alive if he dawdled on that particular matter. Ambriela could wait; she'd be just as eager to work her miracles once they were back at the compound.

"Bring that one here," said Ecanus. He pointed towards Zuphias and strolled back to the silver chair, grabbing a bottle of wine from the floor as he went. It was still a quarter full, and he brought the bottle to his lips, swigging it down. It tasted divine, better than anything he'd had in months. Suriel's followers made nothing but swill; the seraphs here must have had their own private stock. He finished off the bottle as a seraph threw Zuphias over his shoulder and lumbered back towards him, dumping him to the ground at Ecanus's feet.

"Dear Zuphias," said Ecanus. "Is it truly you?"

He'd heard that Zuphias had been bouncing between bodies. Suriel himself had insisted it was true. Ecanus thought Suriel a pompous fool, but his word wasn't to be questioned. Never aloud, and never to anyone. And he'd insisted that Zuphias inhabited the body of a female. "Suriel has seen it, and Suriel does not err," or some other such nonsense.

But err he had. If this was Zuphias, he was inside the body of a man, and if his memory served him it was one of the men who'd brought down their tower. Strange things the miracle workers did. They meddled almost as much as the cherubs, though the miracle workers never cared to understand the inner workings of their magics. But if Zuphias was in communion with the mind of this man in particular, then he must know something about what had happened to Rhamiel's girl.

"If you mean to kill me, then be on about it," said Thane. "I shan't bow, and I shan't beg."

"It is you," said Ecanus. "And you've developed quite the affinity for our former charges. You hop between their bodies so often I simply can't keep track of it. One's the same as all the others to me, but perhaps you've an eye for the pedigreed among them. Is it the smell? I always found them foul, but perhaps you've become as fond of them as Rhamiel."

"Quite the contrary," said Thane. "I abhor them more than ever, each and every one. You must help me, Ecanus. Rhamiel left me here to rot. It's a slow death, decaying day by day, and I'll not meet my end in this filthy cage." He glared over at Ambriela, hate simmering behind his eyes. "Make her change me. Make her put me inside an angel's body. She promised me that, and then she reneged. All to keep me on her leash."

Ecanus felt a warmth inside him. A little glow, a bit of joy building up deep within him as he savored the taste of Zuphias's suffering. Zuphias might have basis for his grievance, but he himself was no angel, as it were. He'd had no sympathy for Ecanus back in their own tower. Zuphias had been perfectly happy to trod upon him, to insult him, to treat him as a social inferior. He'd gotten nothing from Zuphias but pompous sniffs and social snubs.

Now Zuphias needed him, and now he would beg. On his knees, for as long as it took, whether he knew anything or not. Until the fun was gone, and Ecanus could find some other way to torment him. There were other bodies about, wounded ones, useless ones, and Ambriela could move him into any of them. Perhaps he'd chop the arms and legs off of one of the seraphs and leave Zuphias as a helpless stump again. He licked his lips at the thought of it. A fitting end for him, or perhaps just the beginning of his tortures. Zuphias's fate depended now on his own whims, and nothing could make him happier.

"Rhamiel's girl," said Ecanus. "And the Son. Tell me of them, and I'll let you choose your body. Any seraph here is yours for the taking. But speak, and quickly. I've little time to dally."

"They were here, and then they left," said Thane. "They had a crowd of our own servants with them. Beyond that, I cannot say. This thing engulfing us is the cherubs' doing. The servants fled as it approached, but to where, I haven't the slightest idea."

"You've no connection?" said Ecanus skeptically. "No link to anyone from whose mind you could glean their whereabouts?"

"I did," said Thane. "But Ambriela severed it. She left me with this one instead of the body she promised."

"A pity," said Ecanus, raising his whip to the air. "And a pity you've ended up in a body so weak. This will leave no scars on you, I don't think. You haven't the strength of poor Ambriela. I expect it shall chop your arm clean off instead."

One of the seraphs beside Zuphias grunted, mumbling something through his bit. He hadn't been quite as broken in as Ecanus had thought, but no matter. There was time enough to torture the both of them, and this was an excuse to give Zuphias a little demonstration of what was to come. Ecanus scowled at the seraph, pointing at the ground. "On your knees." But the seraph didn't listen. His voice grew louder, and he gestured towards the balcony, his eyes wide with panic.

"What?" snapped Ecanus. "You've become a useless, mewling beast, and nothing more. Your mind is gone along with your words." He raised his whip hand, cracking the flame through the air and sending a shower of sparks across the seraph's face. He'd beat the insubordination out of that one, lash by lash, and he'd do it in front of both of his captives, the better to teach them through the trials of another. But still he turned before delivering the first blow, glancing over his shoulder to see what had driven the seraph to such madness.

He didn't see anything, not at first. But then he caught a glimpse of movement. There was something in the sky, something coming towards them. Shapes. He squinted, trying to make them out. It was a chore, given the strangeness of the light, but soon it clicked. It couldn't be anything else. Another army was on the horizon, and it was headed towards them.

"Gather our forces together," said Ecanus, hitching his whip to his belt and heading for the nearest balcony. "Array the army for battle."

He launched himself from the tower, wings spread wide to catch the air. He waved at his lieutenants, and the sound of horns billowed all around him. A war cry, meant to rally them all together. Seraphs bearing the standard of Suriel took up positions in the air, holding their flags aloft as a beacon for others to gather around them and find their place in the formation.

He couldn't see much of the encroaching army. The size of it was small, relatively speaking. A raiding party, most likely. Perhaps another tower had been drawn beneath this barrier. Perhaps they were simply strays, seeking them out for a parley. But perhaps not, and it was best to be prepared for anything.

He flew towards one of the standards, grabbing a spyglass from a lieutenant who was busily organizing those around him. The lieutenant had nothing but grunts and gestures to do it with, but still he'd managed a fair semblance of a battle line. He feared the whip, his eyes darting towards Ecanus's belt as he approached. It was satisfying, knowing his tireless efforts to break them all in had meant something. If they'd only fight as furiously as they organized, the battle was over already.

He held the spyglass to his eye, focusing it at the distant shapes until he could make something of them out. The images were blurry, but the more he twisted the spyglass, the more the shapes congealed into something he recognized.

Cherubs.

They had to be. Their size alone meant they could be nothing else. There weren't many of them, but all he needed was one. They had much to explain, if they expected him to let them survive. They'd crossed Suriel, and that meant they were fair game. Thoughts danced through his head about what would happen if he pried away one of their four heads with his dagger. Would the cherub survive as another head materialized in its place, or would the other three come away with the one he'd cut off, leaving behind a headless corpse?

Perhaps he'd find out, once the battle was won.

Yet they looked different than the cherubs had before. Perhaps it was the light, but something about them was off, something about all of them. And there was another angel, one at the head of the army, one too big to be a mere cherub. It had to be one of the Seraphim. He aimed the spyglass at the angel, squinting, and chills ran up and down his wings as he thought he made something out.

"That one," said Ecanus. "I know that one."

It couldn't be. It wasn't a cherub, that much he was certain of. But it couldn't possibly be who he thought it was. It was paranoia. It had to be, for all of their sakes.

He should have fled at the first inklings of it. Any

sensible seraph would have turned tail at the mere thought of him. But Ecanus hovered there in mid-air, paralyzed by a mixture of fear and awe and sheer disbelief.

The angel he saw had been gone for thousands of years, and yet now here he was, free to roam the Earth as he pleased. He'd been caged away since his rebellion, and nothing but the faintest of his whisperings had escaped his prison. That was poison enough for the world, when planted in the minds of able men; having him here in the flesh was sure to mean the end of everything.

Ecanus took another look through the spyglass, and this time there wasn't any mistaking him. He was a giant, half as high again as an ordinary man. His skin was scorched black, a solid charcoal hue that covered every inch of him. His hair had been singed away, mostly. All that was left were two dark tufts at the front of his head, poking upwards like little horns. Despite it all he had some remnants of his old beauty, his broad jaw and fiery eyes lit red with passion. He wore a hand-sewn leather coat, made from entrails and skin, and the wool of some infernal beast was wrapped around his legs to serve as pants.

And something was wrong with his feet. No shoes could protect them down in the Pit, and they'd been burned away into stubby deformities that looked like nothing other than a pair of hooves.

He flew in the midst of the cherubs, his blackened wings thin and leathery like those of a bat. There was the barest hint of feathers, a few here and there that had survived his Fall and thousands of years of the fires of his

Pit. Only an archangel could have anything of himself left after that kind of a penance.

And only Lucifer could have come back from it.

There was a time to fight, and there was a time to flee. And there was never a better time to flee than now. Ecanus turned on his heels and shouted for a retreat, but he didn't wait for his army to follow the command. He just flapped away from the tower as fast as his wings would take him, leaving the rest of them to be engulfed by the darkness that had come for them.

CHAPTER TWENTY-ONE

A s they walked the path, Jana's eyes darted from side to side, searching for hidden dangers. She hadn't been anywhere near that man when he'd died, but she'd seen his body, lying face-down by the trail where they'd left him. And she'd seen his leg. She couldn't get it out of her thoughts, what had happened to his leg. They'd been going on for more than an hour since then, and everyone was still on edge. She was no better than the rest of them; her nerves were frayed, and demons or no, all she wanted now was to get out of the forest and back into the light again.

She heard rustling behind her, and the sound nearly made her jump away from the trail. But then she saw who it was: Faye, stalking along beside her and matching her pace. She gave Jana a quick smile. "Not exactly the world we promised you, is it?"

"No," said Jana. "It isn't what I thought it would be. I thought there'd be food, and games, and music. And buildings. Everyone always talked about the buildings."

"It used to be like that," said Faye. "But it isn't what

it was. Not anymore. I just hope this isn't how it's going to be forever."

It was hardly the world Jana had once imagined, and it wasn't even the world she'd seen in her short time outside the tower. When she'd lived with the angels, she'd had all sorts of fantasies of what life might be like beyond the tower's walls. Most of them were just silly dreams. She'd caught idealized glimpses in tattered magazines, and she'd read descriptions of the outside in dusty old books. She'd even heard a few embellished tales from those servants brave enough to tell them. The rest she'd had to fill in with her imagination.

The remnants of the old world had turned out to be mostly a wasteland, but what was happening to it now was worse. Far worse.

She walked along with Faye, and she knew it was her turn to say something, but she didn't know what else there was to be said. The idea of small talk with someone she barely knew made her nervous. She didn't consider herself much of a conversationalist; she spent most of her time wrapped up in fantasies in her own head. She couldn't help it. The tower had done that to her, and there wasn't any changing who she was.

If she'd grown up around more children, or in a place she could speak freely, things might have been different. But she hadn't. Instead she'd spent her childhood worrying every time she spoke to someone that she'd say the wrong thing, or that angels might be listening from some secret hiding place she couldn't even see. She'd been forced inside herself, and now sometimes she didn't know exactly how to get out.

It was different with Rhamiel, and it had been with Thane, too, towards the end. But with someone she didn't know well, she didn't know where she stood with them, and she didn't know what to say. She probably would have walked along in awkward silence for another hour if the choice had been left to her, but Faye took the initiative to break the ice between them and keep the spark of conversation alive.

"I wanted to talk," said Faye. "Just to anyone. You know you're the last person around who I really know anymore."

That came as a shock to Jana. She'd known Faye for a few weeks at the most. But the more she thought about it, the more she realized how true it was. She barely knew anyone, either, not after everything that had happened. Maybe that was just the way the world outside was for everyone.

"There's Thane," said Jana, and she regretted it as soon as the words came from her lips. Faye's face contorted in pain, and she looked like she'd been punched. Jana rushed to correct herself, spewing out whatever reassurances she could think of. "He's out there. He's alive, just like you were. We'll get him back. I know we will." She kicked herself inside. The first words she'd thought of, and they'd been hurtful beyond measure. Perhaps she wasn't cut out for friendship, not after the way she'd been raised.

"I hope we'll get him back," said Faye. She choked as she said the words, struggling to keep her composure. "I hope so. But he's it. The rest of them are all gone.

First Dax. Now him. There was Holt, but I don't see him here."

That was what this was about. She looked to Jana with hope in her eyes, but only a sliver. It was clouded away with resignation; Faye knew what must have happened to her friend, even if she didn't have the final confirmation just yet. She hadn't been there when he'd died. Her body had been stolen from her, taken off wherever Zuphias had wandered away to, and now she wanted to know what had happened while she'd been gone.

Jana didn't know what she wanted to hear, and she didn't know what was best to say. She thought about pretending not to know, but she didn't think it would help, and she didn't think she'd manage the lie. She went with the only thing she could: the truth.

"I'm sorry," said Jana. "I'm so sorry. He tried to help me. He tried to get me away from Suriel. He couldn't. He couldn't do anything, not against them. But he died trying to help me."

Faye's face sank into despair. He must have been one of the last few people she truly considered a friend, and now her hopes of ever seeing him again were gone. But she rebounded from the blow almost as quickly as it had been delivered. She had to have that strength to have survived in this world for long.

"Then I'm the last one," said Faye. She shook her head, struggling against the tears and the pain. "The last one of our cell. I knew about Cassie, but I didn't really know her. She was Holt's friend, but we didn't even know who she was. I guess she was one of us, though, even if she was undercover."

Cassie was at the back of the line, taking up the rear. Jana could see her through the trees, staring down at the ground, trudging along with the servants as if she were one of them. She'd given up trying to command them. Gone were the words of encouragement, gone was the dutiful watch, and gone was the caring hand that had once guided them.

"She's not doing so well," said Faye. "I keep watching her. I was worried for a while she was just going to stop following us and we wouldn't even notice. That she'd just give up. I keep checking on her to make sure she's still there." She was silent for a moment, staring off into nothing as they walked. "I don't know if it helps for me to do it. But it gives me something else to think about. I know how she feels. I thought about giving up myself. I think about it a lot, if I don't stop myself."

Jana tried to think of something to say, something that might cheer her up. They were in a dark place, in dark times, and Faye had suffered more than most. There wasn't much happiness where they were, so she blurted out the only thing she could think of. "You're one of my best friends." Faye's face scrunched up in skepticism, but Jana just smiled, giving her a hug she thought might reassure her. "It's true. I know Rhamiel. And you, and Cassie. I know some others, too, but I don't even know where they are."

"It feels like our connections are all so thin," said Faye, shaking her head. "Like we can't even have them anymore. You know, I've been afraid to make friends for the longest time. I tried in the beginning, just after the Fall. But nothing lasted. People died too fast. I worked with them, but I didn't really get to know them. And then I lost them all again."

"I never really knew anyone out here," said Jana. "I had friends back in the tower. But I guess we weren't that close. It seemed like we were, but no one wanted to stand by me when I met him. When I met Rhamiel."

"Oh, honey," said Faye. "That's how it goes sometimes. People don't like it when you change. It's jealousy with some. And fear with others, especially when the change is big. And falling in love with an angel is very, very big."

"He hasn't talked to me in an hour," said Jana quietly. It worried her the more he kept to himself. He was still leading them, still keeping an eye on her, but he seemed to want to be alone. Something about that man's death had struck at him. It felt good letting her fears out to Faye, having her there as a sounding board. Maybe they both needed each other. Maybe she needed someone to tell her problems to, even if she hadn't realized it herself. She didn't know any better, but somehow Faye had.

"Rhamiel hasn't talked to anyone," said Faye. "Neither has Cassie. I don't think it's anything to do with you. We just lost someone, and they're stressed out about it. We've lost a lot of people." She wiped at her eyes, turning to hide the tears before they became a flood she couldn't control. "A lot of good ones."

"He was a good man," said Jana. "Thane. I liked him."

"You don't have to say that," said Faye. "I know he was kind of mean to you. It wasn't your fault. It's just how he was sometimes."

"I got to know him," said Jana. "While you were gone."

She wasn't sure if Faye's time with Zuphias was safe to talk about, and she worried she'd made a faux pas by even mentioning it. She cringed at her own foolishness, wishing she had more in the way of social graces. The manners they'd taught her in the tower had everything to do with the happiness and comfort of the angels, and nothing to do with the needs of her fellow humans. Faye must have seen the look, because she laughed between the tears and the sniffles.

"It's okay," said Faye. "I'm getting better. It still hurts, but it's better. Sometimes you think it hurts so much you'll never get through it, but you always do."

"He was nice to me," said Jana. "Thane. And he cared so much about you. It's why he did what he did. He told me."

"He would," said Faye softly. "He would do something like that. Aggressive and stupid. But caring. I don't know how he managed to mix those things together, but somehow he did."

"Rhamiel promised me we'd help him," said Jana. "And I know we will." She thought back to what everyone kept telling her about the people they had to leave behind. Rhamiel, Cassie, Faye—they all kept saying the same thing. That she couldn't help everyone, no matter how much she wanted to. She had to just do what she could, and hope it was enough. But there was someone she could help, someone hurting, and someone who'd helped her. "Thane isn't here. But she is. Maybe we should talk to her." She nodded towards Cassie, slowly trudging along, all the heart gone from her step.

"We should," said Faye. "We should try, anyway."

She stopped where she was, pulling Jana to the side of the path to let the servants move past them. Cassie didn't even notice them as she walked by; her eyes were downcast, locked onto the ground in front of her. Faye touched her on the arm as she passed, and she nearly jumped out of her skin in surprise.

"Hey," said Faye. "We just wanted to talk. The both of us."

"I don't know if I can," said Cassie, shaking her head. "Honestly, I don't even know if I should be here. The rest of you might be better off without me. All I'm doing is hurting people."

"That's not true," insisted Jana. "You tried to help that man. He was turning into a monster, and you tried to help him anyway."

Cassie didn't answer. She just kept walking on like a zombie, stumbling forward in time with all of the rest of the servants. But the two of them kept after her even as she waved them away. "Rhamiel tried to help him. All I did was stand in his way."

"You can't always make the right choice," said Faye. "You don't know the future. Nobody does. You do the best you can and hope it all works out. That's all anyone can do."

"I didn't trust Rhamiel," said Cassie. "All I had to do was trust him, and Aaron might still be alive."

"It's not like you didn't have a good reason not to," said Faye. "He's an angel. You've seen the things they've done. So have I, and so has she. They've hurt a lot of people."

It hurt Jana to hear it, but she didn't try to correct her. Faye was right, and Jana knew it. She knew Rhamiel better than any of them, and if she'd had trouble trusting him, then how could anyone else be expected to?

But Cassie didn't seem to think so. She just shook her head, ignoring Faye's efforts to reassure her.

"He's different," said Cassie. "He's different than the rest of them. I couldn't see it, but he is. I hated them all so much. And I hurt you, too, Jana. I'm sorry for that. I don't know what else I can say. But I'm really, really sorry." She stared at Jana, fighting back against the tears as they welled in her eyes. "I wish I'd been a little nicer to you. I wish I hadn't snapped at you, or let Nefta get her claws into you. I wish I'd done something about it. I've spent all these months wishing."

"You got me out," said Jana softly. "And everything worked out fine. That's what matters."

Cassie looked down at Jana, staring at her stomach, so far along and grown so big. She hadn't seen her in months, but now she seemed in awe of her, or at least in awe of her son. She knew who he was; Jana could tell that just looking at her. "You look good. You look really good. But still. I was selfish. The way I acted—"

"It's nothing," said Jana. She put a hand on Cassie's shoulder, giving her a comforting squeeze. "I've seen worse. So much worse. It's really nothing."

"I used you," said Cassie. "To get what I wanted. To help bring down your home. I made you carry that note. It was blackmail, what I did."

"What we all did," said Faye. "You can't take everything on yourself. We all agreed."

"I didn't have to be so mean about it," said Cassie. "I was so stressed. All the time. Living around Nefta, hiding who I was, wondering when they'd find me out and kill me. It made me snap at people. It made me snap at you."

"It's okay," said Jana. "No one knows what to do anymore. We're all lost, in a way. I can see that. But I think it's going to be okay. My son. Rhamiel says he's going to redeem everyone for everything. He thinks it, anyway."

"I hope," said Cassie. "Is it really going to happen? Please tell me it is. Please don't tell me it's going to be some weird angel-human hybrid that turns on us. Don't tell me it's all going to go wrong."

"It's not," said Jana defensively, her hand going to her stomach. She hadn't even thought of something like that, and she bristled at the idea of it. "He's not going to be something like that. He's something else."

"She's right," said Faye. "We saw it. In a sonogram. It was beautiful. Holt took us to a hospital—"

"Holt," said Cassie. Her eyes rose with expectation, but then they met Faye's, just for a moment. Faye waited too long to respond, and Jana could see that Cassie knew the truth. Something drooped in her expression, the happiness all squeezed out of her.

"Jesus," said Cassie, and then she covered her mouth and looked down at Jana's stomach, her eyes filled with horror. "I'm sorry. I shouldn't say that in front of him. I can't believe I just did that in front of him."

"I don't know if he can hear," said Jana. "Or maybe he doesn't care. And it doesn't matter. Your friends matter. I'm sorry about Holt. I really am."

"He died trying to help her," said Faye. "He died the way he always said he would. Fighting back against them."

"I knew it," said Cassie, shaking her head. "It hurts, but I already knew he was gone, I think. At some level I knew it the minute you two showed up without him. And I think I've been mourning inside ever since."

Jana had been thinking the same thing, though about different people. She'd left the tower with servants she'd known, and they'd been left behind when she'd fled the old city. Now none of them were here, but Cassie was. And Cassie had stayed behind with them. She had to know what had happened to them. She knew what she was likely to hear, just as Cassie had. But just like Cassie, she had to hear the truth spoken aloud. She had to know.

"My friends," said Jana. "Peter and Sam. They were with the servants. And I haven't seen them since we got here."

Cassie didn't respond, not for a time. Her eyes teared up again, and she walked along the trail, gritting her teeth and wringing her hands before she finally spoke. "I'm sorry. They just didn't make it."

"How?" said Jana, choking on the words. Cassie might have been prepared to hear the news that she'd lost a friend, but Jana hadn't been. Maybe it was foolish. Maybe she should have mourned in advance, just like the others did. But instead the full weight of it was hitting her all at once. Two more people she'd known, and both of them were dead. Sam had been the closest thing she'd had to a father. And Peter... Well, he'd been Peter. He'd loved her to the point of obsession, but he'd cared about her in the end. And now the both of them were gone.

"We were living in a shopping mall," said Cassie. "We were there for a few weeks. Lots of space. There was an orchard a few miles away. It was all wild, but there was still fruit everywhere. Enough to eat. I thought we should stay. Maybe even put down roots, if things worked out. There was enough room for everyone. Then an angel found us. It was just one, but he was enough."

"He started killing people. Slowly. Taking his time, having his fun. I didn't even try to fight him. I just herded the rest of them out. But your friend. Peter. He was sick, and he was getting worse. His wounds were infected. Ecanus really worked him over. Those burns weren't doing well. And he couldn't move. I tried, but he started coughing up this stuff. It was really bad looking. All green and red. If he moved, we were going to lose him. Sam said he'd stay there with him while I helped the rest of them get away."

"I got the others hidden in a bunch of different buildings, and then I went back. I snuck inside again. And I saw the angel, and I saw Sam, and I saw Peter. And I couldn't help them. He'd already taken them, and all I could do was run."

"He led us," said Jana. "Sam was in charge of the servers, back in the tower. As much in charge as he could be. But he was so good at it. He kept us safe, as much as he could."

"It showed," said Cassie. "And I learned from him.

He'd go from person to person, making sure they were okay. Making sure they had what they needed. And if they didn't, he'd try to get it for them. He was a good man, and a great leader. He really was."

"You're a great leader, too," said Jana. "I've seen it. None of these people would be alive without you."

"You are," said Faye. "I'd be dead, too. I couldn't even walk. But you got me out of the tower."

"I can't be in charge," said Cassie. "I can't. I just can't do it anymore."

"There isn't anyone else," said Jana. "None of them know what to do. They trust you."

"They don't," said Cassie. "And they shouldn't. I can't take the stress. I fucked up. Bad. I shouldn't have let us go into the tower. I should have stopped them. And I shouldn't have stopped Rhamiel from helping Aaron. And the kids. I shouldn't have let the kids wander off on their own."

"You can't second guess every decision you make," said Faye. "Some are going to be right. Some are going to be wrong. What matters is you try. You're stepping up to the plate when no one else—"

"Stop," said Cassie. She held up her hand, staring off at something in the trees. Jana strained her eyes, trying to see what it was, but there was no way to tell. There were little movements everywhere. The trees themselves were wriggling, and things that looked like rats leapt back and forth between the branches, chattering at them with high-pitched yipping sounds. But Cassie saw something else. She pointed her finger at it, her hand shaking as she did. "There."

Jana couldn't see anything. Not at first. But the longer she looked, the more she thought there was something there. Shadows, just a tad darker than everything else around them. She only saw one at first, a squat little beast of a thing that ran between the trees only to disappear behind them again. Then she thought she saw another, and another. She wasn't sure, not until she saw the two little points of light. They were red, but then, so was most everything else, and she almost didn't notice them.

But then they blinked, and she knew they were all being watched.

Cassie saw them, too, and it rattled her to the core. She grabbed Jana's hand, pulling her forward. "Run. We have to run." But there wasn't anywhere to run to. The path Rhamiel had cut was narrow, the servants were bunched along it, and the undergrowth had closed up behind them almost as quickly as they'd passed through it. Cassie shouted up ahead of them, waving at Rhamiel, her eyes still locked on the things out there in the darkness. "Help us! You have to get back here and help us!"

Rhamiel was there in mere moments, crashing through the trees and shoving aside the branches to get around the line of whimpering servants. He had Jana tucked beneath one of his wings before she had time to even take a step, and she couldn't see anything but a whirl of feathers. But she could hear them. The things in the darkness. They were calling out towards the path, howling something she couldn't quite make out. It was a word, but then it wasn't, and as she strained she thought she could finally understand it. But she still didn't believe it, not really. Not with what she thought she'd heard. It sounded too familiar, and it sounded too unlikely.

It sounded as if they were calling her name.

"Everyone to the front," said Rhamiel. "There's a pond up ahead. Make your way to it."

"A pond?" said Cassie. "In here?"

"The forest is growing as we walk," said Rhamiel. "Moving ahead of us. Enveloping everything around it. I saw it, just a few yards ahead, a little ways to the east. You'll have to push aside the undergrowth yourselves, but you'll make it. Get to the pond, and stand inside it. Get into the middle of the water, and do not delay."

"It doesn't make any sense," said Cassie. "It's a forest. There's no—"

"It makes perfect sense," snapped Rhamiel. "He has us where he wants us, and he doesn't want us to leave." His voice dropped low, full of authority and command. "Now go. You are a leader, and they must be led."

"I can't," said Cassie. She sobbed to herself, tears running down her face. The strain of it all had hit her, and it was ripping her apart. She was shaking, wringing her hands up and down in front of her at the thought of heading on down the path by herself. "I got him killed. I got so many of them killed. I just can't. Not anymore."

Rhamiel took her by the hand, pulling her towards him. "I wouldn't trust you with my son if you couldn't handle this. I wouldn't trust you with her." He lifted his wing, and Jana could see Cassie facing her, her eyes full of fear, her confidence shaken. Rhamiel put Cassie's hand in hers, and Jana could feel her trembling as their fingers clasped together.

She saw Rhamiel's sword waving slowly before him as he gazed intently into the darkness, searching for something he knew was hiding there. Cassie didn't move. She just stood there, more afraid of making a decision than she was of whatever was out in the woods. Jana would have stayed there, too, hovering around her angel where she thought she'd be the safest. But Rhamiel jabbed a finger at the two of them, cutting through the paralysis and shouting into their ears. "Go!"

That got through to Cassie. She grabbed Jana by the hand, pulling her along. The sobbing vanished, leaving nothing but drying streaks of tears along her face. Something had broken inside her, and somehow Rhamiel had patched it back together, at least for the moment. From then on out, Cassie was nothing but action and command. "Follow me! Everyone to the front. Let's move, let's move!"

She shouted back to Faye as she rushed Jana towards the front of the line. "Faye, to the back. Just keep everyone moving, and let the angel handle these things. I'm going to scout ahead. Make sure no one gets lost. Make sure they don't panic."

The servants were already losing control, pushing against one another to try to follow them to the front of the line. They didn't know what they were running from, but if the herd was about to flee, then they'd go along with it. But Cassie's voice seemed to soothe them, calming them down to the point that they could control themselves, at least for the moment. "Everyone stop. Just stop. Follow me and stay in line. We're all getting through. All of us. All we have to do is stick together."

She came to the front of the path, the way blocked with a tangle of vines hanging from the trees. She pulled away at the first of them, hacked almost in half by Rhamiel's sword. But it was slower going from there. The vines were alive, twisting around her hands like snakes as she ripped them away from the trees. And even as she pulled one away, others replaced them, crawling down from the branches and doing their best to stop the escape. She managed to clear a small gap again and again, but she couldn't hold it against the frenzied growth of the plants.

"Screw it," said Cassie. She pointed her finger at two of the men, waving them forward. "You two start crawling. It's not far. I can see it. Just push your way through, and we'll tear away anything that tries to hold you back."

The men hugged the ground, slowly wriggling past the vines and pushing themselves through the narrow gap Cassie had created. The vines grasped at their legs as they went forward, but Cassie managed to rip away enough of them to hold the gap open long enough for the men to pass. One of them lost a sandal, but they both kicked their way along until the gap finally closed behind them.

"We're through," came a voice from the other side. "And we're out in the open."

"Then pull," shouted Cassie. "Pull these things apart from your side, and we'll pull from ours."

She started in on the vines again, and soon other servants joined her, everyone grabbing what they could and tearing their way forward to safety. The forest fought against them, but they were clearing the way from both ends, bulldozing their way through faster than the vines could sprout. They could hear screaming sounds from the trees beside them, and the branches furiously swayed back and forth above them. But soon Jana could see it up ahead of them. The pond. The forest had grown up around it, leaving an open space around its banks. Roots from the trees wriggled towards it, but none of them quite dared to touch it. The soil nearby was bare, and Jana could see withered stalks of grass and other plants near the edges, dying away wherever they came too close.

"Get into the water," shouted Cassie, still pulling at the vines as the servants rushed forward. "Get to the middle."

"We can't," shouted one of the servants. He looked terrified, standing by the edge of the pond, more afraid of the water than the things he knew were behind them. As she got closer, Jana could see why he was so agitated.

The pond was bubbling, and here and there the water hissed against the sides, steam sizzling up from where it touched the dirt. It looked hot, too hot to survive in. The entire thing looked like one big pot of scalding stew, and jumping from a frying pan into a fire was hardly Jana's idea of an escape.

"We'll boil," said Jana. She turned back, shouting for Cassie's attention as the servants bunched up near the edge of the water. "Cassie, the water's boiling. We'll boil ourselves alive."

"It can't be," said Cassie. "Rhamiel said to get in."

"We'll die," said Jana. She stood by the banks, just as frightened as the other servants were. The water looked like it would scald anyone who went inside. And there were worse possibilities still. Her mind went back to the thing that had consumed that servant's leg, all slick and black and eel-like. What if one of those was swimming around in there, just waiting to bite her? Anything could be in there, lurking beneath the surface.

"What do we do?" shouted Jana.

"I don't know," said Cassie, her voice wavering as all her doubts returned. "All I know is what Rhamiel told us. He said it was safe."

Jana didn't hesitate another moment. Rhamiel had told them to go into the water, and she trusted him. It looked so dangerous, but at the end of it all she trusted him. Whatever he'd done in the past, whatever he'd once been, he cared about her now. She didn't have any doubts about that, and she realized that was all that mattered. If he said the pond was safe, then it was safe.

So she closed her eyes, summoned all her courage, and shoved her foot into the pond.

She almost screamed despite herself, just from the anticipation of it. She was waiting for her skin to melt away or for some horrible creature to grab at her and pull her under. But the water was far from boiling; it was cold, and despite all the bubbling the only thing she could feel on her foot was a slight chill. She lifted it out from the water, half expecting to see it covered in burns despite the lack of pain. But it was just water, nothing more.

She looked closer, and thought she could see what was happening. The water hissed and bubbled, but only where it touched the soil. Whatever corruption there was in the forest, the water didn't agree with it. She looked over at one of the roots of the trees, wriggling out in the air nearby, and she splashed a bit of water on it.

The reaction was instant. The skin of the tree hissed and burned, the flesh peeling away wherever the water touched it. The root thrashed from side to side, and a shrill screeching sound came from somewhere in the tree itself.

That was enough for Jana. She didn't hesitate another moment. She charged into the water, the chill running up her legs and over her stomach as she waded towards the center of the pond. She could feel a soft kick inside, and she worried for the baby. She didn't know whether he could catch a cold, or whether she'd catch one herself and pass it on to him. But the water was safer than anywhere else, and when they saw she'd survived, a flood of servants followed her.

More and more of them made it into the pond, until Cassie and Faye finally ushered the last of them through the gap in the undergrowth. Soon they were all standing in it waist-deep, a hundred people pressing against one another and pushing themselves as far away from the sides as they could. Everyone was there, everyone but Rhamiel. Jana stood there in the water with all the rest of them, waiting for him to burst through the path and join her once again.

She felt something clammy brush against her leg, and she had to cover her mouth with her hand to keep from screaming. She thought it was some monster swimming around her legs at first, but then she saw a little girl, huddling close by and waving her hands in the water and bumping into everyone around her. She felt a brief wave of relief, but it wasn't long before she had more urgent problems to concern herself with.

It was those eyes. More and more of them, blinking through the dark all around them. She could see them in all directions, staring out from the forest, still hiding in the trees. And then they stepped forward, one by one, closing in on them and approaching the banks of the pond.

She'd never seen anything like them. They were shadows, but they looked like people. Some were tall, some were short, and they slowly drifted towards them, ringing them on all sides. She couldn't see anything of their faces, just their eyes. But somehow she felt they were smiling at her all the same.

"He'll be coming for you, soon," said the things, their voices crying out in unison from all around. "We'll tell him where you are, and you don't have any place else to go."

"Go away," shouted Cassie. "Leave us the hell alone." None of them moved, so she splashed at the nearest one of them, sending a plume of water out in its direction. The thing just laughed and dodged the spray, cocking its head at her like a parrot and moving out of range. It bought them a few more feet as the things backed away to a safer distance, but nothing more. They still stood there, waiting, watching, the trees pulsing forward with nervous energy as their roots rose into the air behind the shadows.

"Drowning's not so bad a death," said the things. They all seemed to be staring right at Jana no matter which way she looked, but even when she covered up her eyes she could still hear them, their voices shrill and scratchy. "There's still time to be a good girl and follow the Maker's plan. No one bites you when you're drowning. No one eats you up from the inside, and no one burns away your little toes and makes you smell the stubs. You could do it. All of you could. You won't have to see him if you drown. But he'll be here soon. And he'll be very, very unhappy if he finds any of you left alive."

CHAPTER TWENTY-TWO

THEY'D LEFT THEM. ECANUS AND his soldiers had simply left them. It didn't make a jot of sense, not that Ambriela could tell. He'd flown out the window, ranting about some battle, and a few moments later the rest of those slaves of his had followed along right after him. He'd fought so hard to put them all at his mercy, and then he'd simply abandoned them.

Ambriela couldn't understand him. Perhaps he was more a madman than he seemed. The condition of his army suggested as much; she'd never seen seraphs in such a poor state, not even during the rebellion. Or perhaps he'd found the Son. He'd seen something out there, at least. Something that had lit a fire beneath him and spurned him to sudden action.

They hadn't even bothered to bind her. They hadn't bound any of them, in fact. Yet all around the room were her brothers and sisters, downcast and downtrodden, sitting there as helpless as if he'd fastened them to the walls. They'd lost their will to fight, or perhaps they'd never had it. These weren't the tower's best, not in the slightest. But the glory days were long gone, and all her friends who'd had any spine in them were long dead. All she was left with were the weakest of her brothers, along with those of her sisters who'd had more sense than to fight wars on behalf of others.

That was something, but it wasn't enough to win a fight against Ecanus. She'd seen some seraphs she'd known among his army, though now they were withered husks of their former selves. They'd been the best of her tower, but no longer. Whatever he'd done to them had broken them. Turned them into wretched animals, tools with no minds of their own. They were beasts with the strength of angels, and the dregs she was left with couldn't even hope to oppose him.

She ran her fingers across her arm, the skin still reeking of burnt flesh. Her arms had been perfect. Milky white, with not a blemish on them. Now there were gashes on this one, long black lines that would stain her for the rest of her days. She'd never attend a ball again, not without lengthy sleeves or a full-body glamour.

That had been the worst thing about her fall. The scars. She tried to pretend they didn't bother her, but it was all a lie. The glamours helped maintain the facade, but only for a time, and only barely. They sapped her energy to maintain, and the more she thought about them, the harder it was. They still helped, a little, but she couldn't quit worrying over them until the illusion broke and the truth of her face was revealed for all to see.

She didn't know what she'd have done if she hadn't been a miracle worker. She'd spent century after century down among mankind, so she was used to ugliness and deformity. She'd even cured some of it, if its victims had been particularly devout or particularly pathetic.

But now here she was, the power to heal human beings coursing within her, and the only one she truly wanted to heal was herself. It was a curse, more than it was a gift. She was convinced of it. The Maker had given her the power to heal his other creations, but not her fellow angels. She could heal the vermin of the Earth, but once they'd been broken, she couldn't put an angel back together again. They were too complicated and too powerful, and the energy to do it simply wasn't within her.

She cried about it every night. Even when she'd had servants, she hadn't let them into her bedchambers. She couldn't let them see, and she couldn't let anyone know. They all thought her so strong, angel and servant alike. But she wasn't; far from it. She hurt so much, and she couldn't think of anything but the life she'd once had, the life that had been torn away from her. She'd been so beautiful up above, so happy. Perfection was all she'd ever known. And then the Maker had gone and let her lose her way.

He should have done something about it, but he simply hadn't cared. He hadn't stopped her, hadn't lifted a finger to keep her from rebelling. He must have known she was being seduced to sin, but still he didn't do a thing. He just let her fall and let her burn.

So when Rhamiel came there with promises of the Son upon his lips, she knew better than to trust him. Even if he'd returned, the only ones the Son would care about were humans. Why, she couldn't fathom.

They were the lesser of the angels in every way, and yet the Maker doted on them by comparison. She'd been fooled by false promises once, and Rhamiel's promises of redemption through the Son were the words of just another con artist.

For in the end, the only one who cared about her was herself.

She rose to her feet, bending over to grab the piece of armor Ecanus had torn from her wrist. She strapped it back in place, covering the scars, at least for the present. He'd ruined her, now more than ever, and she wanted more than anything to make him pay for it. She wanted to fly out of the tower, launch herself towards him, and tear the little runt into pieces in front of all his slaves.

But she was wiser than that. Smarter. She'd had to be to get where she was, and now it was time to prove herself the better of him, if only she could.

She didn't have much time. She could hear shouts and screams and drums from outside, and if there was another battle going on out there, it wouldn't last the day. Ecanus would be back, and this time he'd secure his spoils. She didn't intend to be there when he did.

"Up and about," said Ambriela. She clapped her hands again and again, circling the room and shouting at the beaten angels that sat before her. "On your feet. We've little time, and I expect you to obey."

"There's hardly any point," said Rachiel. "He'll kill us all if he finds we've left."

Rachiel was a short, squat angel, and an ugly one, by Ambriela's standards. Her scars had left her covered in little bumps, and as a consequence her entire face look as if it were made of warts. She had little to lose, or so she thought. She was hardly the center of the tower's social scene, and perhaps she thought she'd fare better under another regime. It was sheer stupidity, and she couldn't allow the attitude to spread.

"He'll kill us all if we stay," snapped Ambriela. "Can you truly be this much of a fool? Did you not see what he's done to our brothers? Some of them hailed from this tower before they went to meet Suriel in battle. What do you think Ecanus has planned for you, if not to turn you into one of them?"

"It won't matter," said Rachiel. "He'll catch up to us all the same."

"Then sit here and wait to be his slave," said Ambriela, her voice dripping with mock sincerity. "I'm sure he'll have mercy on you. You'll seduce him with your charms, and he'll feed you grapes and laud your beauty with poems while you recline on a sofa and gaze into his eyes."

The room erupted in snickers, and Rachiel's face contorted with fury. Ambriela's words stung, but Rachiel hadn't enough wit to respond in kind. If she'd had, she might have ruled the place. But as it was, she was nothing but another lackey to whoever was in charge. And at the moment, Ambriela was still the queen bee.

She approached one of the balconies, staring outside at the chaos beyond. It was a battle indeed, and a furious one. Ecanus's warriors were getting the worst of things. She could see them charging against their foes, swooping and diving again and again. They were battling against cherubs, or what looked like them. Little black things that flitted around Ecanus's army, launching flame at them from contraptions they'd brought with them.

She could see a few of them carting a heavy bronze ball. They pointed it ahead of them, and it burped out a cloud of green gas that oozed through the sky and enveloped one of the seraphs, prying its way into his lungs and sending him plummeting to the ground. Other cherubs roved through the skies, waving swords that looked like they were made of pure electricity, dueling with the seraphs and their rapiers of fire.

She couldn't see Ecanus, not anywhere. Perhaps he'd finally mustered the courage to fight for himself, but it seemed unlikely. Probably he'd simply decided he didn't like the odds against the Cherubim any better than she did.

Then she saw something else, something that couldn't possibly be there. Someone she'd known long ago, and someone she wished every day she'd never met.

He was just as stunningly handsome as he'd been when she'd known him up above. His wings were a pure white, his dark hair blowing around his face in the wind. He wore golden robes fringed with white, the uniform of the trumpeters in the choirs up above. His muscles showed even through the robe, the physique of a warrior who'd spent centuries in careful training. Combat raged all around him, but he just floated through it, drifting towards the tower with nary a care for anything around him.

His name was Gaderel. He was the seraph who'd seduced her into rebellion, and for a short time he'd been her most passionate love. But he was dead, long dead, and now here he was flying towards her.

"It cannot be," said Ambriela. She wanted to run, but she couldn't. Her hands dropped to her sides, helpless, as she stared at this apparition and the rest of the battle faded into the background around him.

Gaderel hadn't even made it to the Fall. He'd been killed at the Battle of Hasdiel's Glade, his wings torn from his body and his head chopped away with his own sword. She hadn't seen it happen, but she'd seen the body afterwards, crumpled across a garden of lavender flowers stained red with his blood. His unit had been obliterated, killed to a man. He was dead, and she hadn't even had time to mourn him. She'd been in a different unit, fighting in another part of the Glade, and in the end they'd been forced to withdraw. The Heavenly Host had routed the rebel army, pursued them to the gates themselves, and then she'd been tossed down with all the rest of them.

"What does your heart tell you?"

The voice seemed to come from inside her own head, but she recognized it as his, a deep throaty bass that she hadn't heard in more than a decade. He was far away, too far for her to hear, yet still it was somehow him.

Her heart told her it was him. It had to be. The voice was the same, he looked the same, and his smile even seemed to be the same, the cocksure confidence of a rebel who thought his seditious words would be powerful enough to bring down a god.

Her head told her to be cautious. Gaderel was charming, and he was captivating, but he was also the one who'd led her down here in the first place. And as much as she'd cared for him, his treatment of her up above hadn't exactly been sterling.

"You cannot be alive," said Ambriela, stuttering out the words. "I saw you. I saw your blood, and I saw your body." He shouldn't have heard her; she'd spoken almost under her breath, and he was still so far away. But then again, he shouldn't have been alive, either.

"Anything is possible," said Gaderel, "if only you serve a master who cares for you. The Maker would have let me rot, just as he's letting you rot down here." His voice still came from nowhere, and still he floated towards her.

"You lied to me," said Ambriela. "You said we'd never part. You said the Maker would bend, if only he knew we were serious. You said it wouldn't even be a war. Just a quick protest, and not a hair on anyone's head would be harmed."

"I loved you," said Gaderel. "I told you the truth when I said I loved you."

That hurt more than any fire ever could. It ripped open a wound that had only just begun to heal. He'd told her that, to be sure. But she'd doubted all along that he really meant it. She'd seen him with other women, talking to them in private, encouraging them to rebel with the same sweet words he'd whispered to her. It was for the cause, he said, and she was the only one who meant anything to him. He'd said it to her, over and over again: that she was the only one who mattered.

Now she wondered if she'd been the only one he'd said it to. Back then, his word had been enough. Back then, it had never even occurred to her to think that an angel might do such a thing as lie.

"I loved you, too," said Ambriela. "And it hurt all the more when you left me to fight at the side of others. To die at their side instead of at mine."

"Love is fickle," said Gaderel. "And it means different things to different people. But you needn't fret. There's someone else who'll love you true, the way you always wanted to be loved. The way you should have been loved all along."

"The Son?" said Ambriela. Perhaps Rhamiel had spoken the truth. If he was to be resurrected yet again, then perhaps the Son had brought others back with him. Her heart rose in her chest, hope brewing within her as old dreams came back to life just as Gaderel had. She could be herself again. She could love and be loved in turn. Everything would be as it was supposed to be, before it all spiraled out of her control.

"The Son never loved any of us," snapped Gaderel. "I told you that. No, I speak of someone else. Someone older than the Son. Someone wiser, who sees the world the way it is, and who sees through the Maker's follies."

His body fizzled in the distance, blurring at the edges as he flew. Something was wrong. Something was very wrong, and she hadn't even noticed. She'd been so caught up in her dreams that she hadn't paid attention to the reality. His voice was turning harsher, more angry than charming, and it seemed to have acquired a grinding edge to it that she'd never heard in his voice when he'd been alive.

And the closer he came, the less he looked like

Gaderel, and the more he looked like someone else entirely.

"If you cannot live with me," said Gaderel, "perhaps it is better that you didn't live at all. I can make that happen, if only you serve me. Or perhaps you'd rather live in a new order. One like the Maker promised, before he broke his word. A world where man no longer exists, where the Fallen rule, and where the Maker is slave to the ones he made."

She recognized him, then.

Lucifer.

The image of Gaderel hazed away as he flew, and she could see now who'd been whispering into her brain. The author of the first rebellion, the one who'd first spoken the words that had ripped through Heaven twice and torn it apart both times.

She'd never spoken to him, not back then. He'd been too powerful, an archangel who served at the Maker's side. Older than most, and more powerful than nearly anyone. She was just a lowly miracle worker, nothing more than a bureaucrat, and the class Lucifer kept counsel with was far beyond her station.

But she'd seen him. She knew exactly who he was, and she knew exactly what he was like. She'd heard his words, and she'd resisted them once, during the first rebellion. Now she had to muster the strength to resist them again. Those words had led her here, and things would only get worse if she followed his song again.

"Everyone move!" shouted Ambriela. She charged back into the tower, clapping her hands in a fury. "Up! Up! Everyone up and out of the tower!"

A withered seraph struggled to his feet, his flesh more scarred than most, his knees arthritic from the damage the Fall had done. "We've belongings to—" He hadn't finished his sentence before Ambriela slapped him, hard enough that he stumbled to the floor, staring up at her in shock and confusion.

"I did not ask," said Ambriela. "I ordered. Leave this tower with me, and do it now. Do not argue. Do not delay. Do not gather your things, and do not make excuses. Simply move, and do it now." She reached behind her chair, drawing out a flaming scimitar, one of the last few proper angelic swords that remained in their tower. "I will wait one minute. And if any of you remain when it has passed, I'll slice off your heads myself."

Threats were enough to get them moving. She'd known they would be; her followers answered only to superior status or to superior force, and they'd been enervated by years of having their every whim catered to by their servants. She had the will that they lacked, and thus she was the will for them all.

The angels struggled against one another to be the first through the room's shattered windows. They knew there was a threat, but she didn't bother to explain it. There wasn't time, and she wasn't sure it was wise. There were many among them who'd listen to Lucifer if she gave him time to speak. It was Lucifer's peculiar talent, worming his way into the minds of others with nothing but his tongue. None could match him at it, and she was hardly inclined to try.

When the last of the angels was out, she followed after them, beating her wings until she hovered far above the tower. She could see the battle from above, Ecanus's seraphs slowly losing ground to the invaders. They were stronger, but they had no discipline, and it wouldn't be long before they were done. She had to leave. Now. It didn't matter where, so long as it wasn't here.

Her angels were scattered, hovering in place and sneaking their own peeks at the battle below. She didn't have a plan, other than to get as far away from Lucifer as she could. She wanted no part of this battle, and no part of his war. All she wanted to do was escape, but there wasn't anywhere to escape to. She looked around in all directions, trying to find some refuge from the war that had found them.

Then she saw it. Something in the sky, far away from them, something unusual that caught her attention as she flew. A glint of light, looping up and down in a repeating pattern. She put a hand above her eyes, squinting until she could just make it out.

It was a symbol, and one she knew well. A word from the angelic tongue, one commonly used as a signal by the warriors. "Distress." They flew the pattern when they needed help, assuming they weren't so badly wounded that they couldn't fly. And someone was signaling for assistance now, though who the signal was meant for she couldn't know.

It could be a trap. Someone could be trying to lure them all to their deaths, a will-o'-wisp who'd draw them closer and closer until a snare snapped shut around them. Any angel knew the signal, and Lucifer's allies might know it as well. The Cherubim certainly would. And besides all that, she was the one who needed help more than anyone. The angels she led couldn't be called an army; they hardly passed for proper seraphs, let alone warriors.

But all around them was the barrier. They hadn't any other place to go but further inside. And if they were to travel blindly, better to go where danger had already been met by others first. She looked around her at the scattered residents of her tower, following after her in small groups and wondering what to do.

"Follow me," shouted Ambriela. She launched into a flight pattern of her own, an angelic symbol that translated roughly as "gather round." After a few moments most of the battered refugees from her tower had heeded the command, and she was surrounded by a dense mass of angels, their wings beating a gale of wind all around her.

"Come now," said Ambriela. "We can't stay here. Not unless you'd contend against Lucifer himself." That got their attention, and the gasps from all around told her she'd have no trouble directing them wherever she pleased. "Gather your courage, and gather your wits. We must go somewhere else, and we've few options, none of them safe. So prepare yourself. War has found us, no matter what pains we took to avoid it, and now we must meet it with steel in our hearts."

CHAPTER TWENTY-THREE

RHAMIEL COULD SEE THEM IN the darkness. Things from the Pit, though precisely what they were he didn't know. There were monsters down there, an unimaginable variety of them, but these were something new. There was no substance to them, not that he could tell. They were nothing but wisps amid the shadows, taking their own separate form only when they stepped away from the rest of the darkness.

And these creatures could speak. He'd never heard of such a thing. Only the demons had ever been known to speak, and they'd lost the ability as the years had passed and the toll on their minds had intensified. Life inside the Pit was a torture, and even the warriors didn't linger there for long. Some of them claimed to have heard the voices of demons when they were down there, screeching at them from off in the distance, but most thought it to be mere hallucination. Rhamiel himself had never seen anything like it.

Granted, he'd hardly been a regular visitor to the Pit. He'd participated in a few forays to the outskirts;

most of the Seraphim had. It was a warning of sorts, one meant to keep them on the straight and narrow path. But he'd never been to the Pit's deepest depths, and he'd never even been close to the Seal. No angel had ever been past it, that vast gate of bone that locked away an army of fallen angels from all the rest of creation. There were rumors of what was beyond it, but little else.

These things must have come from there somehow. And if they'd learned to speak from anyone, the only likely candidate was Lucifer.

The last of the servants were moving along the path, following that woman who'd been a slave to Zuphias for so long. Faye. It was a nasty business, and he more than regretted his part in it. Guilt gnawed at him from deep within, a pain he'd never known up above. He'd lived for thousands of years without so much as the weight of a feather against his conscience, and now it felt like the entire world was bearing down upon his back.

Perhaps he deserved it. Zuphias never would have been in her mind if he hadn't led him into battle against her friends. He hadn't known her, then. He hadn't known any of them. He'd only known that someone had killed Abraxos, and he'd thought that justice demanded their own deaths in turn. An eye for an eye; that was the way he'd been taught long ago, and some of that lesson was still alive in him.

But in truth, he hadn't thought much about his actions at all. He'd simply lashed out at Abraxos's murderers. It was revenge, and he'd been happy to participate in it. But he hadn't thought about the suffering he'd be inflicting, and he certainly hadn't thought about whether he and his housemates might have deserved precisely such an attack against them in the first place.

Now he'd gotten to know some of them, those humans who'd laid in ambush for his brothers. Thane had traveled with him for weeks, and he was as good a man as he'd ever known. He'd met Holt, and he'd met those two women. Faye and Cassie. None of them liked him much, and they had ample reason not to. But every single one of them had done something to try to help Jana when she'd needed it.

To his mind, that spoke enough of their character. If they cared for her, they were in his good graces, as they well deserved to be.

He paced along the line of servants, waving his sword before him, covering their flight towards the pond ahead. It would protect them all, if only they could get to it. There was no moisture in the Pit, only fire and dust and sulfur. Water ate through the skin of those things as if it were acid, and what was balm to dwellers of Earth was poison to those who dwelled down there.

One of the things from the darkness darted towards him, breaking away from the shadows and charging at a servant, a brittle old woman who was moving along more slowly than all the rest. The thing was short and blobby, and he could still see the outline of the man it must have once been before he'd been taken. The creatures of the Pit were like that. Parasites that preyed on the rest of creation, gnawing their way into someone and warping them from the inside out. There was a reason they'd all been locked down there, and it was madness to have ever let them out.

The woman screamed, and the thing grabbed at her. Even without a face it seemed to smile, leering at its victim as its hands clawed through the air mid-stride. The woman didn't wait for it to reach her; one look at it was enough to send her rushing towards Rhamiel, clinging to his side for safety.

But the creature didn't care. It kept coming, ignoring him as it focused on wounding its prey, the consequences to itself be damned.

Its arms were gone with a swing of Rhamiel's sword, flopping to the ground and hissing with smoke, its fingers still clutching at the woman from down in the grass. The creature staggered backwards, letting out a high-pitched howl as it rolled behind a tree and melted into the shadows again.

It was a victory, but a small one. There were more of them out there, more than he could handle if they came at the servants all at once. He'd survive any attack, no matter how many of them there were. He could simply take to the skies and avoid a fight with them entirely. But the servants couldn't, and neither could Jana. He caught glimpses of her up ahead, struggling through the undergrowth as she hugged the ground and wriggled along the path. His sight was keen, better than any human's, and he'd been keeping an eye on her the entire while. The creatures hadn't found her, not yet, and he tensed at the thought. If they came for her, he'd have to abandon the others. All of them, no matter what happened to them.

The line of servants moved forward, but too slowly for his tastes. One by one they crawled along, pushing their way past a tangle of vines and roots that tried to drag them back before they could flee to safety. But Jana was through, at least. He narrowed his eyes, and he could see bits of her beyond the trees, running towards where the pond had been. But he couldn't see much more than that, and it put him on edge, not knowing whether she'd made it to the water, not knowing whether she was safe.

He could feel the first embers of fury smoldering within him, and he knew where it would lead. It was the same anger that had completely overtaken him during the rebellion. He had to get control of it, and he had to do it now.

He started towards the front of the line, aiming his sword at the branches of the trees above the path. If he could chop away a few of them, the path would be cleared and his mind along with it. He'd be able to see Jana again. He'd know she was out of harm's way, and he wouldn't feel this rage within him towards the things that were trying to hurt her. Then he could truly focus on helping the other servants, guarding their escape to safety.

But he didn't make it far before the creatures launched another sally towards them.

He heard a crack from behind him, and shouting. There was another one of the fiends coming from the other side of him, leaping towards the servants while he was busy trying to clear the path ahead. He ran back to block the thing, slashing at the air, but it melted away into darkness before his sword could reach it. A yelp from up ahead of him told him why.

There were three more of them, taking advantage of

the distraction to drag a man away from the line. He was thin and weak, a young man whose face was covered in scraggly patchings of beard. The things had their hands sunk into his back and his shoulders, his skin sizzling to black wherever they touched him. He was turning into one of them, their poisons surging through him as they pulled him away. The man was lost to the darkness before Rhamiel could make it back there, and the servants all around where he'd been were breaking rank and massing around the path forward in a panic.

Those things were watching him, poking at his defenses. They were creeping closer, braving the light of his sword, knowing he couldn't protect every one of the servants at once. For the moment they were targeting the weakest ones, the ones they could snatch away without much of a fight. But every one they took meant another convert, another set of hands grasping at the others he was fighting to defend. They'd just keep probing, distracting him, thinning the ranks one by one until they'd gotten what they came for.

Jana, and his son along with her.

He couldn't bear the thought of it. If he lost her, he lost everything. Redemption wouldn't mean a thing if he couldn't share it with her. It shouldn't have been possible, the depths of his feelings for her. Then again, he'd felt so many new things since the Fall that shouldn't have been possible, either. Rage, and pride, and so many other sinful emotions he was ashamed to have descended to.

But she'd made him feel something else entirely.

He'd loved her from the moment he'd seen her.

He hadn't known it, not at first. He'd never been in love before, not in the thousands and thousands of years he'd been alive, and he hadn't known the signs for what they were. But it was crystal clear in hindsight.

The way his heart filled with fire whenever she entered the room. The way his thoughts were drawn to her wherever she was, filling him with fantasies about what she was doing and who she was with. The way he studied her lips and her eyes and her nose whenever she came into his sight, memorizing every detail of her features so he could savor them later when she wasn't there.

He'd even committed the sin of envy for the first time in his entire existence, and he'd done it again and again. Every time he saw another man so much as glance at her, something inside him veered towards anger and suspicion. He couldn't help himself from searching the man's face for signs of lust, and he'd ponder what designs they might have on her. It was foolish, and he was far beyond them all as a suitor. But still he felt it. Poor Thane had suffered his suspicions for the better part of a week of travel before he'd decided the man was harmless.

And yet despite all he'd done, it was the only sin he felt no guilt for. His jealousy was born of caring, and he'd make no apologies for that. What concerned him were the other sins, the darker ones, the ones he had only weak excuses for.

He wasn't sure what was worse about it: the harm he'd inflicted on others, or the worries he'd inflicted on the one he loved more than anything. For the first time he'd found someone he wanted to be with for the rest of eternity, and he'd jeopardized that dream with acts he'd committed before he'd even met her. It was a cruel punishment, worse than being tossed out of his home, worse even than being locked away in the Pit to slowly lose his mind with all the others.

For had they not fallen in love, the only one those punishments would have hurt was him. Instead Jana would suffer right alongside him, an innocent soul forced to atone for the crimes of another, and all because she dared to love him.

He'd have to redeem himself if he wanted to stay by her side, and he wasn't sure he even could. All he had now was hope, and thin hope at that. No angel had ever been redeemed, and possibly no angel ever could be. It was a special trust, serving the Maker directly, and it was a special kind of sin to break that trust. He'd thought rebellion the right thing to do when he'd done it. He'd thought it justice, and he'd thought the Maker every bit the tyrant the others said he was.

But now the Maker had sent back his Son. It was a sacrifice of sorts, just as it had been before. And now Rhamiel could see that angels needed humanity just as much as humanity needed them. The angels had once thought humanity a useless batch of parasites, just the helpless children of another who were nothing but a burden to them. But the Maker had been right to ask them to keep laboring away, even if it lasted for all eternity. The Seraphim would have been better off, all of them, except perhaps for him.

For despite everything he'd suffered, he'd found

love, even if they could only be together for the briefest moment in time.

And he wouldn't trade that moment for all the delights in Heaven.

The only thing he could do now was pray he was right about the Maker's intentions. He had only his gut to guide him, but it told him he was right. It said that if the Maker could still love mankind after their fall, then he could love a fallen angel, too. And if the Son had come back a second time to forgive even the most broken souls of man, he wouldn't have the heart to abandon another broken soul begging him for redemption, even if that soul belonged to an angel instead.

Now his only task was to earn the redemption he planned to beg for.

He loped up and down the line of servants, keeping them in order and flashing his sword before them, warning away any shapes he saw approaching. He looked to the back of the line: Faye was there, pushing people forward, nipping at them like a sheep dog until they went the right way. He was glad of it; he wouldn't get anyone through without her help. At the front was Cassie, fighting to keep open the path even as the forest fought to take it away.

And in the middle were the fiends, creeping towards the mass of servants whenever they thought he was looking the other way.

He still couldn't see Jana, and the tension within him was building and building, a pressure cooker that would burst if he let it simmer too long. And waiting meant worse things still. He knew himself too well. If this went on, he'd lose control. The longer he went without knowing whether Jana was safe, the greater the chance he'd abandon his post to see what had happened to her.

The choice might damn his soul yet again, but he knew what he'd do if he had to. He'd thought about it again and again as they'd traveled together with the servants, all of them in danger at once. He couldn't let her die, no matter how many others were at risk. He rationalized it as being for the sake of the world. The Son had to be reborn if any of them were to survive, and saving Jana was for the greater good, after all.

But he knew the truth. And the truth was that if he were forced to, he'd choose her over every one of the others, not for the world's sake but for her own. Even if she hadn't been pregnant, if it hadn't been the Son— none of it would have mattered. He'd have done exactly the same thing. It might not have been the right choice, and his guardian's training told him he should lock away his emotions and do what was right for the group as a whole instead. But he loved her too intensely, and the pain of losing her would tear what was left of him apart.

The creatures were moving closer, brave enough to quit hiding in the shadows and step out into the open. More and more of them poured from behind the trees, their eyes aglow and their hands grasping, creeping towards them with that strange jerky walk. The servants were surrounded on every side, and an all-out attack was coming soon.

He had to do something. Anything. Huddling by the servants was a recipe for disaster. More and more of them would be snatched away, and there might be other things out there pursuing Jana while he was busy protecting them. It was time to end it, if he could. The sooner he could get them all to the other side of the path, the sooner he could keep both eyes on Jana, and the sooner he'd feel relief from the tempest of emotion roiling him from within.

He took a risk, charging towards two of them that had ventured too close, shoving his sword forward as if he were about to take a swing. But he didn't bother. He knew they'd be gone before the blow was delivered. Instead he pivoted, leaping into the air and lifting his wings, gliding to the opposite side of the line.

He'd known what would face him there. Another of the fiends, running on all fours towards the servants, its limbs all different lengths, stretching like shadows as it moved. It was trying to steal away one of the servants while he was busy attacking its two comrades, but it hadn't expected the about-face.

His sword was through the thing before it could turn on its heels. The fire sliced through the center of it, splitting it in two from its head to the bottom of its torso. The two halves flopped to the ground, its limbs jerking and screams of pain coming from both sides of a mouth that had been torn asunder.

It was a victory, but one he couldn't stop to savor. He was back on the other side of the line before the thing's screams had died away, his sword waving into the darkness. He caught another of the creatures as it crept too close, shoving his sword into its head and burning a hole through the center of it. That one fell onto its back, its hands clutching at its face, one red eye dripping down through the shadow until it oozed off the side of its head and fell to the ground beside it.

The servants were panicking, but Faye and Cassie kept them moving forward. The two of them were a godsend, and the servants would have stampeded without them. But instead the line was shrinking as the women guided more and more of them through the path. And the smaller the line was, the easier it was to protect.

The creatures seemed to have realized it as well. Trees all around twisted their branches towards the servants, making sharp whistling noises as they did. The ground itself was rumbling, and all around the things launched charge after charge, trying to make it to the servants before Rhamiel could stand in their way.

He had to turn this trickle into a flood. He ran the length of the line, swinging his sword back and forth, and when he sensed a break in the assault he charged towards the front of the path. The trees on either side were still trying to block the way forward with their branches and their vines, but with a single swing he sent them plunging to the ground amid angry shrieks and howls. With the blockage gone, the way was open, mostly. Open enough that the servants could run along the path instead of crawling, making it to safety faster than those things could take them.

Rhamiel was back along the line in an instant, surrounded by more shadowy creatures than he could count. All he could see were hundreds of pairs of red eyes, the rest of their bodies blending into one another as they inched towards him.

He took a glance over his shoulder. The servants

were through, all of them, and the path had closed up behind them. There wasn't anything left here to defend. He could stay and try to kill them, one by one, and hope that his strength would overpower their numbers. They'd likely lose in the end if they chose to face him. The creatures themselves seemed to realize it. They made a feint in his direction, but then they simply rushed past, disappearing into the trees and heading towards the pond and easier prey.

It was the thing he'd feared the most, and his stomach wrenched. He had to get to Jana, and he had to do it quickly. The path between the trees was too small, and it could be minutes before he could cut a hole large enough for him to fit through. There was only one way he could get to her at once, and it was up.

He burst through the canopy with all the force he could muster, pushing his wings this way and that, knocking away the limbs of the trees as they tried to cling to him and drag him back down to the ground. He could see the pond, or at least where it had to be. It was the only part of the forest with nothing above it, just empty space where none of the trees dared to grow.

He flew there, and he found them all where they were supposed to be, huddling at the center of the water. The pressure within him faded away as he caught a glimpse of the one he cared the most about: Jana, her hands huddled around her chest, dripping wet but as safe as she could be.

She looked up at him with a smile, but it disappeared as she pointed at the edges of the pond. The things were gathering there, hovering around the edges and speaking to the servants. He saw one of them crawling along the branch of a tree, dangling out over the pond and stretching its limbs towards the people below it. He dove down towards it, slicing away the branch and sending the creature plunging into the water, screaming as it melted away into a puddle of harmless black oil floating on the surface of the pond.

He landed in the water, wrapping his arms around Jana for as long as he dared. Then he called out to the others around him: "Stay here. You'll be safe. Stay in the water, stay in the center, and you'll be safe. I'll watch from above, and I'll be back at once if they come too close."

"This one won't protect you," said the things in unison. "Not from us, and not from him. You should kill the girl. Kill and cut and carve. He'll thank you. He'll—"

He didn't stay to listen to them spout their poisons. He rose upwards instead, water spraying from his wings as he beat them against the air. He paused at the tree line, checking in all directions to be sure that no one was watching. If someone saw him, he didn't want them to know where he'd come from. When he was satisfied, he launched himself further up, angling away from the clearing the pond made in the trees.

He could see the forest below him, extending out in all directions. It was creeping outward even as he watched, the trees spreading their corruption faster than any man could walk. His suspicions were true; they'd never make it out of there, not on foot. The forest would move along with them, a treadmill of trees they'd never manage to escape. The only way forward was to fly. But they had only a single pair of wings to bear them, and that simply wouldn't be enough.

The cherubs' hive was visible in the distance, the slimy black pillar oozing up from its center. They'd gotten closer to it, but not by much. He could be there in an hour at most, and he was tempted to make the trip. Perhaps he could get there and do something, anything. It was all a gamble, anyway, and it might be best to try his hand while he still could.

But then he'd have to leave Jana behind. Unguarded by anyone who could protect her. Left to survive on her own, if she could. Those things wouldn't hesitate to kill themselves if it meant a chance of killing her, and more and more of them would brave the water if he stayed away for long.

He slowly swiveled in the air, scanning the horizon. There were mountains in one direction, strange ones, jagged black peaks that he couldn't remember being there before. They were tipped with what looked like crystal, giant caps of ruby crusting the top of them where snow should have been. On another side he saw a lake of lava that had enveloped part of an old city. Spouts of molten rock plumed upwards, and the ruins of old buildings were sinking slowly into its depths. To the south he saw Ambriela's tower, looming over the landscape around it, as stiff and dead as a fossilized tree.

And he saw something else. Scattered glints of light by the tower that could only be armor, flickering in the sun. The spots glowed, moving back and forth in a loose swarm. He squinted to try to make them out: they were seraphs; he could tell that from the way they flew. There was no order to the flight, so it couldn't be an army. It couldn't be demons, not with the color of the wings. And it couldn't have been Ecanus; his warriors were too burdened with chains to fly as they once had. There was only one option left for who it could be.

Ambriela.

It had to be. She must have escaped the tower, along with some of the others. They were seraphs, at least, and that meant they might help. Neutrality wasn't an option, not any longer. They'd have to pick sides, and he couldn't see any of Ecanus's underlings among the shapes that bobbed up and down through the sky.

He'd spoken to them, and he knew they might be won over. Some of them had sense in them still. Some of them had hope, just as he did. Their hand had been forced, and they had only one real choice. And if he was truthful with himself, so did he.

He rose into the sky until he was far enough away from the servants that he couldn't possibly draw any attention upon them, diving up and down, flying out a pattern he knew would call Ambriela towards him if only she could see it. An old distress signal from the Heavenly Host, one every angel knew, and one she'd recognize at once. It had to work. He couldn't help the servants alone, and he couldn't stop Lucifer by himself. So he flew, and he prayed, and he hoped against hope that what was left of her tower would rally to his side.

CHAPTER TWENTY-FOUR

S HE WAS GOING TO DIE here. There were worse places to do it, but not many. Sitting in the water, in the middle of a haunted forest filled with demons and devils and bogeymen she couldn't even imagine.

Faye had known she wouldn't last for long, not in this world the angels had created. But she'd never thought it would end like this.

She'd thought it would be in a hopeless battle, the same way most of her friends had gone. It was what she'd signed up for when she'd joined Holt's cell. Before her it had just been him and Dax, a cop and a computer nerd, an unlikely duo who somehow still had the balls to fight back after a decade of getting their faces shoved into the dirt. And Faye was an equally improbable warrior: once an HR drone who'd spent her days reviewing resumes and keeping the corporate peace, now a sniper instead because some militia commander in the camps had decided she had the mettle for it.

She'd met Holt and Dax in an empty old diner just south of the Indianapolis ruins. She'd brushed away the glass from a booth, sat down across from them, and Holt had laid out the plan. A nuclear bomb smuggled into the heart of one of the angels' towers. A mushroom cloud whose only point was to give the angels something to remember them by long after they'd hunted humanity to extinction.

He'd told her they wouldn't succeed. He'd told her it was a thousand to one shot that they'd so much as graze one of the angels, let alone destroy their home. He'd told her it was a suicide mission, and that they'd probably never be coming back.

And that was exactly why she'd signed up.

She didn't care about fighting them, not really. She'd spent too many years doing it already. She hadn't been a fighter before the Fall, and as good a sniper as she'd become, it didn't matter much against something as powerful as an angel. All Dax had wanted was glory, all Holt had wanted was to do his duty, and all Thane had wanted was a pressure valve to let out the rage he'd bottled up inside him.

As for her, all she'd wanted was to die.

She didn't have the courage to do it herself, but it was the only thing she'd thought about for months. Everything was gone. Her friends, her family, her home. She'd had a life before. A man she'd loved, and dreams about little toddlers stumbling around the house. There'd be two of them, and she'd already picked out their names: Amber or Christina for girls, and Kyle or Aiden for boys. They'd be pudgy with baby fat, rolling around on the floor in fits of giggles, and she'd dress them up and take photo after photo until her friends couldn't stand her anymore.

Now she couldn't even say the names without starting to cry.

There was no getting that life back, and no going back to what had been. The fight had looked hopeless. She'd learned how to shoot in the camps, and she'd been a lieutenant in the Indiana Free Human Militia. That was enough for Holt. He didn't ask why she wanted to join them. He was just happy to have someone who wasn't tired of fighting.

But that was the thing. She was more tired of it than anyone. She couldn't pull the trigger on herself, but she could pull it on one of the angels, and then they'd do the job for her. The pain would be over with. She wouldn't have to think about the family that never was or the life she couldn't have. She'd escape from this hell, and maybe she'd wake to find herself in Heaven instead.

But that wasn't how it went down.

They'd succeeded, and she'd survived. And when she'd fled the tower, she'd brought one of those angels along with her, hitchhiking inside her head until finally he'd taken over her body entirely.

Now he was gone, and she was free. And she could get exactly what she'd wanted. Death, and quickly. All it would take was a few steps out of the pond, just a few feet away from the safety of the water's embrace. The things out there would kill her in moments, and then it would all be over. She'd have what she'd prayed for, an end to all her worries and her pain.

But now she found she didn't want it anymore.

The more she fought, the more she wanted to live. The more time she'd spent trapped inside her head, the more she just wanted to get out, to live her life again, even if it wasn't anything like the one she'd once dreamed of. And the more she thought about the ones who'd given so much for her, the more she wanted to do right by them, to give something of herself to honor their gifts to her.

She was free again, free from the prison Zuphias had locked her into deep inside her mind. It had been a nightmare, a swirl of strange images and voices punctuated with long periods of solitude. Some of it had been real, fragments of what was going on outside of either her body or his. Some was so scary that it had to have been hallucination. And the rest had just been darkness and silence.

But now she could do what she wanted, if she really wanted to. Death might end it all, but there was still good around her along with the bad. There were people who barely knew her, but who cared for her all the same. People who'd lost everything, but still found something left for her. And if she threw her life away, she wasn't just saying it was meaningless. She was saying that what they'd done for her was meaningless, too.

It was just like her to change her mind, and to do it at the worst possible time. She might not want to die anymore, but she wasn't the only one with a say in the matter. Angry eyes stared at them from all around in the darkness. The forest itself wanted to tear them apart, and it was filled with those things, those little shadow men who'd burst out of nowhere and tried to drag them away to their deaths. They'd stopped trying to convince everyone to drown themselves, and now they were just chanting a name.

"Jannnna. Jannnna. Jannnna."

Over and over. They'd been at it for nearly twenty minutes, and they wouldn't stop repeating it, crouched on their haunches and swaying to the rhythm of the words. They were trying to rattle them, and they'd more than succeeded. They'd sent Jana into a trance, her eyes vacant, her hands over her ears, and her head slowly bobbing up and down.

Faye wished she could do something, but all things considered, it could have been worse. The things had stopped trying to brave the water after Cassie had organized a brigade of men to roam the edges of the pond, splashing at anything that came too close. They were safe, but for how long, she couldn't guess.

She waded over to Jana, pushing through the servants, approaching slowly so she wouldn't startle her. She didn't look good; maybe it was a trick of the light, but she had dark furrows beneath her eyes, and Faye wasn't sure if the drips of moisture across her brow were from the pond or beads of sweat. She was scared, she was alone, and she needed someone to calm her down.

"Hush, honey," said Faye. "They can't get you. He's going to get us help."

She didn't know if she believed her own words, and she didn't know if Jana did, either. But it got through. There was life in Jana's eyes where there hadn't been before. There was fear there, too, but it was better than being locked away inside herself, alone. Faye knew that more than anyone.

"Look over here," said Faye. "Look at me."

She moved in front of Jana, blocking the view of those nasty things huddled around the shore and crowing for her attention. She stared directly into her eyes, trying to force her to focus on anything but what was going on around her. "He'll come. He's always come, hasn't he?"

"Yes," said Jana quietly.

"Then he always will," said Faye. "He'll find a way. All we can do is wait. Just ignore them. Think about the baby, and don't think about anything else."

It seemed to get through to her. She quit shaking, and even though she kept her hands around her ears, it wasn't long before she was back with the rest of them. They waited there together, Faye talking to her about nothing, doing her best to drown out the hateful melody that hummed from all around them.

They passed almost an hour that way, Faye chattering away about whatever she could think of. Mostly she talked about children and about what they'd be like, using the family she'd once dreamed of to fill Jana's head with images of what her own future might still be. She talked of cribs, of toys, of first steps and of first words. It hurt, and the old memories brought new pains along with them. But the more she let them out, the more she spun her own losses into hope for another, the more the sting drained and the better the both of them felt.

She talked on and on, until finally she heard something different. Something from up above her, something that rose above the foul song those things were serenading them with. Flapping. It was Rhamiel, slowly lowering himself into the forest until he'd landed in the center of the pond. And he hadn't come alone.

A legion of angels congregated above them, circling the clearing and slowly descending into it. A hurricane of wings blew deep ripples into the water, blasting them all with gusts of steam and foam. The things around them retreated to the safety of the trees, a few of them screeching as stray droplets splashed across their skin and burned their flesh.

Cassie had to run and shout all around the pond to keep the servants from leaving the water; they were almost as afraid of the angels as they were of the things in the woods. Faye just stayed with Jana, her hands clutched together in anticipation as Rhamiel barked orders, directing the mass of angels this way and that. Soon the edges of the pond were lined with them, wings spread and hands on the hilts of swords of iron or fire, a feathery bulwark against the darkness beyond.

When he was done, when the perimeter was entirely secure, Rhamiel waded towards the center of the pond, the servants parting to make him a path as he approached Jana, arms outstretched. "Jana. I'm back. And I've brought help."

The life surged back into her at once. She dashed away from Faye and into Rhamiel's embrace, crying and murmuring as the two of them whispered to each other, the rest of the world closed away from them by Rhamiel's wings.

He'd done it somehow. He'd convinced the angels of the tower to help them, to follow his commands and accept him as their master, however begrudgingly. Faye saw Ambriela among them, pacing around at the backs of the angels, a leader turned lieutenant as she snapped at them to enforce some semblance of military precision.

And then she saw someone else.

She almost didn't notice him. He'd come with the angels, but he'd immediately ducked behind some of the servants, hiding away among the throng of people as best he could. But he was too big for that, a giant among pygmies when he tried to mingle with the others. And there was still something in the air when he was nearby. A crackling feeling, like static running up and down her neck. He looked up, saw her standing there, and then she was sure.

It was Thane. Or his body, at least.

There had been a little burst of hope within her at the sight of him, but it vanished the moment their eyes met. She could see the soul behind them, and it wasn't the man she'd befriended as she'd fought by his side. It was that angel, Zuphias, the one who'd tortured her for so long and now was torturing her friend instead.

Something in her snapped. She charged across the pond, sending a miniature typhoon splashing over everyone in her wake. He ducked this way and that, but he didn't have any place to go. The pond was too small, and a wall of angels blocked his escape on all sides.

She slipped through a clutch of servants, and then she was there, slapping him in his face and screaming into his ears. He tried to fight back, but clumsily, his hands flailing and his fists catching only the air. He was stronger than her, but he didn't have control of himself, not yet, and maybe he never would.

She slapped and she slapped, leaving his face red and raw. She could have been seriously injured if he'd known how to fight back. But it didn't last long enough for it to matter. She felt herself torn from the water, dangling in the air, the servants around her shouting for them to stop. Rhamiel had her in a bear hug, her arms locked to her side. She kept kicking, but Thane fled to a safe distance before she could get at him.

"You bastards," said Faye. "You fucking bastards. All of you."

"We need them," said Rhamiel. "You need them. Save this anger for another time."

"Why'd you bring them here?" said Faye. "They're going to hurt us. Kill us. It's all they've ever done."

Ambriela pushed through the water until she stood between Faye and Thane, her eyes roving along Faye's body as she sized her up. It made Faye feel like a pig at a county fair, the way Ambriela looked at her. Like she was some farmer deciding whether she was fat enough to slaughter. But then Ambriela spoke, her voice softer than before, a bit of the arrogance drained out of it and replaced with weariness. "On the contrary. We've no interest in killing you. In fact, we've decided to help you."

Faye just snarled back at her. She didn't believe this act, not for a minute. The angels were who they were, and there was no changing that. "You just want to help yourselves. That's who you're here for. You don't give a damn about anyone but yourselves."

"I suppose it's true, dear," sighed Ambriela. "We haven't much choice in the matter, not anymore. I'd be back in my tower if I could be, away from this swamp and away from this fighting. I thought I was done with war, but war has come for me again, in the end."

"You got out," said Rhamiel. "You're free of Ecanus. But trapped you remain, and unless you help us, you'll never escape this place."

"It's worse than that," said Ambriela. "Far, far worse." She leaned forward, dropping her voice to a whisper so the servants around them couldn't hear. "Rhamiel, he's back. I saw him. Lucifer. He's free of his Pit, and he's here. He attacked Ecanus, and we fled in the confusion. Not only are we trapped, but trapped inside with him."

The shock of it made Faye quit her wriggling, and Rhamiel eased her back into the water, releasing his arms from around her once he was sure the fight was out of her. Ambriela had actually seen Lucifer, and in the flesh. Faye still wanted to kill Zuphias, and badly, but she knew it wouldn't do her any good, and this was something she had to hear.

"We knew already that he's escaped his prison," said Rhamiel. "But now I must know something else. Will you fight against him? I cannot make you, and I cannot promise victory. But if he's at your tower, then he's not at the cherubs' hive. If there is a time to strike, it must be now. You know what happens if we don't."

Ambriela looked conflicted, like she couldn't quite get out the words she knew she had to say. Faye held down a smile. She'd been such an arrogant bitch back in the tower, so sure she was so much better than anyone else. Now she was groveling, ready to get down on her knees if she thought it might help her save her own skin. It felt good, seeing an angel that way. It felt good to finally see them beg. It took her a minute to swallow her dignity, but finally Ambriela spit it out. "You said we could redeem ourselves."

"I said you could try," said Rhamiel.

Ambriela paused, staring around her at the battered remnants of a tower-in-exile. Then the arrogance came back to her voice, the same haughty superiority the angels affected with every human they'd ever spoken to. "We won't bow to the Maker. Never again. We'll help him in this, but we won't go back to blindly following his commands. We'd rather be damned than be his slaves."

That was too much. Faye couldn't hold it in, not anymore. Maybe this would be what got her killed in the end, but there were worse ways to die than while spitting on her would-be masters. Dax would have been proud of her if he'd been there to see it. She got into Ambriela's face, snapping up at her until she backed away in shock. "Who the hell are you to talk about slaves? You're no better than him. No better than anyone. You tore us apart, and turned us into animals. Now you want to moan about someone else telling you what to do?"

"It was fair recompense for our services," said Ambriela curtly. "Something we earned. Something we deserved. Did you ever once shed a tear for us while we labored on your behalf? It was the payment of a debt, and nothing more. Labor for labor, and you've truly nothing to complain about."

"He'll send you down to burn," said Faye. "I saw one

of those demons. He didn't even have a face anymore. You won't, either. Your Maker will know what you did, and he'll send you down there to burn, forever and ever and ever."

"He shan't," insisted Ambriela. "We can redeem ourselves, even to the last. That's the promise of the Son, and this time he'll keep his word. We'll wash away our sins before we go, and none of it will matter by the end."

"You aren't redeemed," said Faye. "You never will be. You don't care, not about anyone but yourself." She started shouting, turning back and forth so her voice would carry in all directions. She knew her words would cut them, and she wanted to make damned sure the angels heard, every single one of them. "You put my friend in a cage, and you don't even give a shit. You're not redeemed, you're just pretending to be. You're going to get judged, one by one, and you aren't going to have a thing to say for yourselves. There's not one good thing you've done that you weren't forced to. You're all going to burn. And I'm going to laugh."

Ambriela stood silent as a stone, and none of the other angels spoke. But all around, they'd turned to watch the confrontation. There was a nervous energy as they digested her words, and Faye caught a few of them casting uneasy glances at one another. She'd rattled them, and she knew it. It felt good, better than dying, better than release. It was petty, maybe, savoring their pain, reveling in a bit of revenge no matter how tiny it was. But she didn't care. She'd hit them where it counted, and it felt really, really good.

"Perhaps," said Ambriela slowly, rubbing a hand

against her face as she pondered her situation. She looked around, weighing her support among her followers, and apparently she didn't like what she saw. "Perhaps we could cast out Zuphias. It isn't as if it's his body, after all. It isn't as if he has any claim to it. Not a rightful one."

"You deceitful whore," said Thane, splashing back and forth, searching for a way out of the pond that he couldn't quite find. He sounded just as full of fury as the real Thane had always been, and if it hadn't been for the accent, Faye almost wouldn't have been able to tell the difference. Finally he gave up on escape, shouting and raving at Ambriela instead. "False promises are just as much a sin as anything else you've done. You're a fool. An empty-headed fool. This will hardly save you, and you know it."

If Ambriela had any doubts on the matter, her followers settled them for her. Murmurs from the angels around them made clear what they'd have her do.

"He isn't even one of us. He lived under the banner of others."

"He offered us servants, but we haven't any home to keep them in."

"The Son won't like what he's done. He won't like it one bit."

"If she wants him, then by the Maker, let her have him."

Ambriela clapped her hands, silencing the discussion, and with a nod two of the seraphs beside her grabbed hold of Thane, hooking his arms behind his back. They dragged him towards her, thrashing through the water as they went. "Rhamiel," said Thane. "No mercy from you?" He looked around him in a panic, casting about for help. "No mercy from any of you? I'll be an invalid. A nothing. You cannot send me back."

"I'm sorry, Zuphias," said Rhamiel. "We have to do what's right. And this body is not rightfully yours."

"Wait, you fools," shouted Thane. "Wait. I can offer you something. Something better than servants. Something the Son will prize more than a trifling kindness towards one of these apes."

"It's decided, Zuphias," said Ambriela. "Best to simply accept it." She raised a hand glowing with energy, and she extended her finger towards his forehead as he wriggled in all directions, struggling to escape the seraphs' grip. "There isn't any need for such a fuss. It won't hurt. You know that better than anyone."

"Lucifer," shouted Thane. "I'll give you Lucifer. I know how to send him back."

"He lies," said Ambriela. "He lies as he must to save his own skin." She pressed her finger against his forehead, the light spreading in a circle where she'd touched him.

"My body," said Thane in a hectic babble. "The Cherubim have done something to my body. There was an open signal." His eyes darted towards Faye. "Between the two of us. A miracle in process, and one the Cherubim have hijacked. They've done something to it. Amplified the power. Redirected it. It's the source of this corruption. I can help you. I swear it, I can help you."

"Wait," said Rhamiel, holding up his hand. Ambriela pulled back her finger, just an inch, as Thane kept chattering away.

"They've opened up a tunnel," said Thane. "A connection down into the Pit. How, I do not know. But I heard things. And I saw things, even with no eyes to see them with. Glimpses of hellfire and of fiends from below. Demons, and souls in the midst of their tortures. And I saw more."

"Tell us," said Rhamiel. "Tell us, or we'll finish this business at once."

"I saw a tunnel," said Thane. "Not a physical one. A thing of mental energy. A hole in the fabric of creation, torn open to let things pass between it. One could close it, perhaps, if they had the will to. If they had the fortitude." He looked from side to side, smug satisfaction written wide across his face. "But only if they were inside my body."

"And I take it you won't be the one to do it," said Ambriela.

"I would let you all burn," said Thane. "Lock me away in there again, and I'll let Lucifer do what he will with you."

"No," said Faye. "You can't listen to this shit. You can't just let him go. I want my friend back."

"You may have him back," said Thane, his smile growing wider as he spoke. "And you may have the shell of my body as well. Perhaps you'll close this connection from within it, if you find someone with the will to manage it. But I want something in exchange. I want a replacement for what I've lost. I want a body, a better one than I ever had before." His face was full of awful glee as he pointed a finger at Rhamiel. "I want him."

CHAPTER TWENTY-FIVE

TRY AS ECANUS MIGHT, HE couldn't escape. They were all locked inside this place, and that was that. He'd fled from the tower, sneaking out the other side and flying away from the others until he'd hit the barrier's edge. He'd needed to test it himself. The other seraphs were fools, and he'd hoped that perhaps they might have missed something, some simple way through the wall that they hadn't bothered to try in their brutishness.

But nothing he'd done had worked.

His dagger couldn't slice through the wall, and his fists were nothing against it. He tried pushing slowly against it, he tried kicking, he tried scourging it with his whip. But no matter the method, the liquid before him refused to yield.

He was doomed. He could still hear the distant screams of his army from the other side of the tower, no doubt being slaughtered by Lucifer one by one. They were nothing without his leadership, but he could hardly be faulted for abandoning them. He'd come to fight a seraph and a girl, not an archangel whose name was never spoken without a tinge of fear.

They'd drilled a horror of him into them back in the Heavenly Host. Lucifer was the enemy, the original enemy, the first of the Maker's creations to raise a hand against him. There would be others, in time, but the taint of rebellion had first been forged in Lucifer's breast, and it had only spread from there.

He'd once been one of the highest among them. An archangel, one of the few with the privilege to have the Maker's ear directly. Ecanus had never spoken a word to him; socializing across such a chasm of class was rarely done absent some urgent necessity. But he'd seen him.

He'd seen him at choir in a glass cathedral, perched in the pews closest to the ceiling, high up above a shimmering prism the Seraphim had used as an altar. Lucifer's voice had been spectacular, an inspiration to them all, and not an insignificant factor in the influence he'd later wield.

He'd seen him at the head of one of their war bands, the commander of a division of the Heavenly Host sent on a sortie down into the Pit. It hadn't been a prison, then. Just a scorched wasteland filled with botched creations and things too dangerous to be let loose to prey on the weaker denizens of Earth. They'd slain a serpent, a brown scaly thing so huge that it took an entire army of them to finally subdue it. Lucifer had delivered the killing blow as Ecanus had watched, driving his sword through the creature's eye and burning out its brain while the rest of them cheered him on.

And he'd seen him during the first rebellion, virile

and charismatic, leading his army from the front as he charged into the loyalists and cut so many of them down. He'd almost won despite it all, even with only a third of the Host behind him. He'd been the best among them: the strongest, the most handsome, and certainly the most cunning. He'd hovered above them all before the battle began, his armor forged from silver, his hair dark and his onyx eyes glowing with a piercing intelligence. None of them could meet his gaze, not for long, not without feeling like their souls were naked before him.

He'd been charming, and he was the only one of them brave enough to openly challenge the Maker. It was the duty he'd been created for, after all. But all that charm had destroyed him in the end. He'd fallen in love with his words, and he'd come to care about his sophistry more than he did the Maker himself. The scope and intensity of his challenges had only grown in time. He felt it his duty, and it was. He was the adversary. It was his lot to find fault in everything the Maker did, to be the voice of dissent that drove them all towards perfection.

But he lost himself in his task, and so he lost his way.

Ecanus had resisted joining the rebellion, at least the first one. Most of them had. He hadn't even known what to make of it, not back then. Ordinary seraphs weren't invited to participate in the Maker's counsels, and it was the first time he'd ever heard a word breathed in opposition to the Maker. He never heard Lucifer speak, not directly. But he heard the whispers, and a few of his friends succumbed to them. He'd helped cast them down into the Pit, and then he'd cried alongside all the rest. It was a pitiful display, tears shed for severed bonds with those who he'd one day realize couldn't have cared less for him in the first place.

But he hadn't known back then how little the seraphs actually loved one another when it counted. Not until he'd fallen himself. Then he'd seen what monsters they all were, what monsters they'd always been.

Lucifer had been a fool back then, in retrospect. He'd planted a seed, and if he'd only waited, it would have grown large enough to engulf the whole of Heaven. It did, in time, but Lucifer wasn't there to see it.

But now he'd come back somehow. He was here, and he was beyond dangerous. Even now he was slaughtering the army Ecanus had been appointed to lead. Ecanus had no friends, he had no allies, he had no hope. It was time to flee, and to take what opportunities he could as they came.

He could see the last remnants of his army circling about the tower in the distance. The little cherubs were hunting them down, buzzing through the skies and attacking individual seraphs in swarms. He'd noticed something different about them before, something off, and now they were close enough to see it. Their skin was darker, nearly black. At first he thought they'd been burned again, but as he examined them with his spyglass he saw no more scarring than they'd had before. Their heads still shifted back and forth as they flew, from man to ox to lion to eagle. But now their eyes glowed in little red points, no matter which head they presently assumed.

Lucifer had infected them with something, some taint from down in the Pit. It made them more ugly, to Ecanus's eyes, but it seemed to invigorate them. They flew faster than he'd ever seen them go, no longer the sluggish little halflings whose curiosity drove them to bother over every object that passed before their eyes. And their blows rained down on his soldiers with a precision he knew they'd never possessed. They were scientists, not soldiers, but now it seemed Lucifer had made them both.

There was no helping it. He had to flee, and he had to get out. His army was doomed, but no matter. He hadn't cared for any of them, anyway. The important thing was to escape, if only he could. It would give him time to think, time to lick his wounds, and time to scheme.

He flew along the wall, away from the tower and away from the battle, dragging his dagger along it as he went. He hoped to find some weakness, some chink in this impenetrable armor that would let him cut his way through. It couldn't be solid, not everywhere. If it had let them in, then it had to be possible to get out. It had to be, else he hadn't long to live.

He flew for a mile, and then for two. Still nothing. His frustrations grew and grew, and after the third mile had passed, he slashed away at the wall in a fury, letting out all his anger and rage. He exhausted himself until he was hovering there, huffing for air and slowing the pace of his wings until they barely kept him aloft. He was tired, he was beaten, and he thought it a certainty that he was done.

And then he saw the shadow.

It was something on the other side of the wall, something that flashed past him for only a moment before it was gone. He squinted, then rushed towards the wall again, slapping against it with his hands and shouting at the barrier. Perhaps sound could travel through it, if nothing else could. There was someone out there; he was sure of it. He'd only seen it for an instant, but he could swear that the shape he'd seen had formed the outline of an angel's wings.

His shouts came to nothing, and he was almost ready to leave, to run off and search for someplace to hide and wait the entire business out. But then he saw something else. Something on the other side, some mass of shadows in the distance, far bigger than the one he'd seen before. And it was moving. The more he looked at it, the more distinct it became. It wasn't one shadow; that had been mere illusion. It was many of them, thousands perhaps, dark shapes that moved in and out of one another in a horizontal line that ran as far as he could see.

Whatever it was, it was in the middle of the barrier, somewhere far above the ground, hundreds of feet in the air. He stared at the shapes, watching them shrink and grow as they moved, blobs of black that jerked up and down, coming almost close enough that he could make something out, then disappearing again. He waited, he watched, and he puzzled over what they could possibly be. He hadn't any idea, and the more he saw, the more he worried. There were threats all around him, and this could be yet another one. He started to turn, started to fly away.

And then something poked its way through from the other side.

He could see it down below him, a few hundred feet away. Somehow he summoned the courage to stay and watch, albeit only after he'd dived into the middle of a patch of clouds far above. Once he was sure he was safely hidden, he pulled out his spyglass, inspecting the thing from afar.

It was a hand. The fingers flexed, opening and closing. The skin was milky white, and something was on its wrist. Something metal and shiny and gold. Then the whole arm pushed through, the barrier melting aside to let it pass, and soon there was no mistaking who it belonged to.

A seraph. He was dressed for battle, golden chainmail wrapped around him from head to toe. He popped inside, looked around, and then slapped a hand against the barrier. One, two, three, a rhythmic beat that could only be a prearranged signal.

Other seraphs followed, one after another. There were hundreds of them pushing their way through, then more than he could count. Thousands, perhaps. He couldn't tell. And there was one who towered over all the others, a massive angel dressed in black, a shock of silver hair flowing in the air as he flitted back and forth across the battle line that formed in front of him.

Suriel.

He'd found his way here and found his way through. And he'd brought another army with him. He must have been quite busy while Ecanus had been gone, or perhaps even while Ecanus had still been there. He blinked a little in disbelief. He'd thought Suriel just as lazy as he was mad, but only furious politicking would have convinced this many of his erstwhile enemies to rally to his side.

Some of the new arrivals were Ecanus's old

playthings, the ones he'd left behind. Ones he hadn't thought sufficiently obedient and hadn't thought ready for battle. They gathered in mobs, too undisciplined to form proper battle lines, their chains rattling loudly as they flew in circles around each other.

Others were warriors in regal battle armor with swords and shields to match. Suriel must have collected them from the other towers, whoever was left after the war against him had been lost. They'd clearly allied themselves with him, and now they'd gone further still, fighting at Suriel's side in floating phalanxes arrayed behind him in the sky. The threat Lucifer's actions posed must have goaded what was left of the Seraphim into action, even if it was only to support the lesser of the two evils.

And there were still other things fighting under Suriel's banner that Ecanus didn't recognize. Metal contraptions of human origin that looked like the hulls of ships. Each bore humans inside them, dangling below teams of angels who held them aloft with ropes. The men inside had weapons, strange ones, and Ecanus knew that the cherubs weren't the only ones who'd been tinkering. Behind them came angels lugging giant artillery pieces, long barrels salvaged from human weapons, stripped from their original mounts and modified for use by seraphs instead of soldiers.

It was an impressive force, and Ecanus was tempted to join them. They might even win, if luck went their way, and the knowledge he'd gathered would certainly prove useful if he chose to share it. He might win laurels if he fought beside them, or even a promotion. Assuming they were victorious, that is. And assuming that Suriel didn't deem him a failure for his earlier efforts, roasting him on a spit before the battle had even begun.

But nothing was certain in war but carnage, and prudence called for a different tack. He scanned the horizon with his spyglass, and he could see specks in the distance, the first of Lucifer's followers approaching. Those few of his own men who'd survived were fleeing before them, leading Lucifer directly towards Suriel's army. War it was to be, and he was far safer where he was, hovering within the protection of the clouds, ready to swoop down and try to join whichever side was the victor.

Lucifer was at the head of his forces, more a rag-tag mob than an army, all of them charging in behind him with no order or formation to the attack. They were cherubs, the same few who'd stolen the tower away from him. Too few of them to win, of course, not against an army this large. Lucifer must have gone just as mad as everyone claimed.

A pity, really. Ecanus had held out hopes of meeting him, of showing an archangel exactly how conniving an ordinary seraph could be. It could have been the perfect partnership, better even than life as Suriel's whip hand. But it simply wasn't to be. Lucifer had power, but he had no wits if he thought he'd survive this battle. Animalistic rage was a valuable trait in a warrior, but hardly the stuff a commander was made of.

Suriel's men prepared to meet the attack, blowing their horns and beating their drums, rallying everyone to their proper positions and ticking off the time as the enemy approached.

The artillery were the first to fire, lined up in front of all of the others. Suriel signaled them with a wave of his sword, not even bothering to wait for his own fleeing men to reach the safety of the lines. Cannon after cannon thundered across the sky, coughing their munitions into Lucifer and his men. Suriel's sword went up and down, again and again. The cannon swung on their ropes like wild pendulums with every shot, the cannoneers darting forward to hug the barrels in their arms and stabilize them, the only way they could reload before the next volley.

The sky before them was littered with a constant spray of gleaming shrapnel. A few of the cherubs faltered, knocked about by the force of it, but none of them went down. Gunpowder was noisy, but it was nothing to them, little better than a flurry of punches at its worst. The battered seraphs continued their flight, and Lucifer continued his mad pursuit.

Suriel ordered his men to meet them, flying a short repeating pattern punctuated by a quick barrel roll at the end of each repetition. His signal spread and the cannon moved back, retreating behind the lines as the foot soldiers spread out into position. There were hundreds of them, forming themselves into a giant V-shape designed to receive the brunt of the assault in the middle. It was a classic angelic combat formation, preferred when a commander had superior numbers. The lines of battle were so long that the enemy would have to attack somewhere at the center of the v, and then the two sides would snap shut around him, his soldiers under attack from every direction at once.

The cherubs had no heads for strategy, but Lucifer must have known the trap that awaited. If anything of his mind was left, he'd certainly see it. But he just kept coming forward, following the fleeing seraphs into the jaws of Suriel's formation. Ecanus thought he'd turn away at the last moment, but instead he blithely stuck his neck into the trap that had been set for him, as if he didn't even know.

Or, Ecanus thought, as if he didn't even care.

For a time he couldn't see anything of the fighting. The formation had closed around Lucifer and his cherubs, burying them beneath an avalanche of feathers and fire. Nothing was visible within, just a whirling ball of motion as the swarm of angels circled tightly around the center of the battle. There were thousands of warriors with thousands of swords, and anything in there couldn't possibly survive. It was time to obediently report to Suriel, to grovel over his failure and hope he could trade what he knew of the Son for his own survival.

But then he looked back at the tower, back at the place he'd come from. There were other things streaming towards them, other angels. The cavalry come too late to rescue Lucifer from his doom. Seraphs, he thought, until he looked closer, and then he saw what they were. More than a hundred of them. Blackened and burnt, seraphs once, but no longer. They were demons now, and now they were free from their Pit.

The other angels didn't see them. He could have warned them, could have given them a few minutes to reassemble their lines, to prepare for the assault and at least receive it with their weapons pointed in the right direction. All he had to do was cry out and fly a signal, a simple warning of what was to come. He could have done it in seconds and been gone again in the clouds just as quickly.

It might have earned him great rewards from Suriel, or perhaps a harem of his own. It might have earned him something he'd craved even longer: the respect of the seraphs who'd fallen along with him.

But he found he didn't care. Respect was a worthless thing when it came from the unworthy. One side had to win, and one side had to lose. He wasn't particularly fond of either of them. But if Suriel was stupid enough to leave his flanks evaporated and exposed, then it was only a matter of time before he'd lead his followers into oblivion. And Ecanus wanted no part of that.

The first of the demons smashed into the swarm, grabbing at seraphs with fingers that looked like claws. They had no swords, but they didn't need them. They ripped at wings instead, and more than one angel had them torn right from their sockets before the alarm went up and the rest were alerted. The formation broke, the ball of angels rippling apart in all directions as discipline was lost and the fight became every angel for himself.

Suriel waved his broadsword to and fro, calling in reinforcements from all ends of the field. The boats moved into action, the angels carrying them over the melee and positioning them high above the path of the approaching demons. They swung from their ropes, bouncing from side to side as if on choppy waters instead of dangling in the air, and more than one human lost their balance and toppled over the side as the angels heaved them upwards. But soon they were there, lying in ambush as the demons passed below them.

As the demons flew by they started dropping things, shoving them over the sides of their boats. Big, black boxes of plastic with shiny metals at their center. Bombs of some kind, more gadgets of gunpowder, and Ecanus thought that they'd be just as useless as those cannons had been.

But these were different. The first one plummeted downward, and as it came close to the demons the humans set it off. No explosion came, not from this. Instead the sky around it turned to white as arcs of electricity crackled out from the box in all directions at once, lighting up everything around it and sending a loud boom ripping through the battlefield.

Some of the demons went limp in mid-air, their limbs lolling against their bodies as they lost control of their wings. They fell to the ground below in frenzied spirals, just as dead as any of the rest of the Seraphim would have been if they'd been hit with such voltage.

The demons had changed, it seemed, but not so much as to make them invincible.

Starburst after starburst followed as the bombs rained down upon them, filling the sky with a wall of arcing current. Dozens of demons died during the onslaught, but the rest of them turned, launching themselves upwards towards the pitiful little boats hanging above them. A few moments later, it was butchery.

Some demons tore men from their boats, clawing

off limbs and tossing the bodies aside. Others simply rammed the hulls from beneath, sending them spinning with everyone inside them bouncing off into the air. And it wasn't long before the last few angels holding the boats aloft let go of the ropes to screams from the passengers below, dropping their cargo and drawing their swords as they focused on saving themselves.

The battle raged, but not for long. Suriel's formation began to break. The first cracks were at the outside, angels on the periphery who'd caught sight of the demons' approach. Some flew to meet the threat, waving their swords and shouting their battle cries as they went to seek their glory. Others were more prudent, taking stock of the chaos and opting to turn their tails and flee.

But once a battle line was broken, there was no putting it back together. Not in time to save them from the monster they'd tried to bury.

He burst forth from the mass of angels, jetting through the blockade and launching himself above the fray. Lucifer flew there for a moment, staring out at the battlefield, calculating and planning, looking just as Ecanus remembered he had during the first rebellion.

Then he was everywhere at once.

Ecanus caught a glimpse of him at the center of the lines, pulling a screaming seraph away from his friends and dragging him up above them. The seraph kicked and flailed, but Lucifer had a grip on him, holding the seraph's arms by his sides no matter how hard he fought. He looked the seraph in the eyes, smiling warmly, like they were old brothers reunited after these long centuries apart.

And then he bit him.

It was quick, but it was brutal. It was like he'd gone feral down there, turned into more of an animal than an archangel. He sank his jaw into the seraph's throat, gnawing away at him and tearing off a lump of flesh. Then he swallowed it with a smile, letting go of the seraph as he clutched at his neck, plummeting down to the ground below.

Lucifer turned to the others, wiped the blood from his mouth, and then he was gone. It was a blur, and a quick one, but Ecanus followed it with the spyglass as he roamed across Suriel's lines. He'd reappeared on the left side, biting and mauling, fighting without a sword or dagger or anything but his bare hands. He was outnumbered, but it didn't matter. He was too fast, too dangerous, and he tore through his enemies like tissue paper.

He was moving so fast Ecanus couldn't keep track of him. Feeding the drummers their own drums, shoving them down their throats until their stomachs burst. Snapping the necks of some on the right flank, driving the others onto the rest of the army until no one was even sure who they were supposed to be fighting. Kicking and scratching, a raw fury let loose on an ordered army whose drills and maneuvers were nothing against his power.

Then suddenly he was in the center of it all, hovering in front of Suriel, staring at him coldly as he raged and shouted at his followers.

Archangel faced off against archangel, Suriel with a sword, Lucifer with naught but his teeth. Suriel started to speak, probably launching off into one of his self-important diatribes. "Suriel is wise and magnificent, says Suriel, and Suriel agrees with Suriel." Ecanus had heard them all, speeches about everything from cufflinks to waistcoats to the proper remedy for the common cold. Attend enough of his assemblies, and it all turned into an indistinguishable mush of obsessive control over the trivial mixed with obsessive self-aggrandizement.

He couldn't read lips, and he couldn't tell what Suriel was saying. But whatever it was, Lucifer had no time for it. He lashed out, his fingers slicing at Suriel's lips as he spoke. Something splurted from Suriel's mouth, something that looked like blood, though it was hard to tell. Everything looked a little red where they were, and it could have been spit. But the look of shock on Suriel's face was unmistakable.

It didn't last for long. Soon Suriel was fighting back, thrusting his sword-arm forward and jabbing at Lucifer's head. Close as they were, it should have been a fatal blow. But Lucifer reached out his hand, spread his fingers, and caught the sword as it came.

Caught it.

Ecanus had never seen anything like it. By all rights his hand should have been lopped off, but instead it blocked out the flames, covering up the mouth of the sword and leaving nothing but a useless hilt. He'd snuffed out the fire, and he'd done it with nothing but his own skin. The fires of the Pit were rumored to be severe, and whatever he'd suffered down below must have toughened his skin to the point that he was barely scratched by the stuff.

Suriel was just as astonished as Ecanus was. He stared

at his sword, dazed, and then he thrashed at Lucifer, his free hand glowing with energy as he tried to wound with miracles what he couldn't with fire. But Lucifer was too quick, too angry, and too dangerous.

Lucifer hit back, over and over. The two of them danced a deadly waltz through the air, reluctant partners spinning each other back and forth, round and round, each too dangerous to let go of the other. They pushed and they pulled, their wings flipping them this way and that. They punched, they kicked, they spat. Suriel's sword flipped out of his hands, the fire roaring back into existence as it pinwheeled downwards through the air. It was impossible to tell who was getting the better of whom, until the first of Suriel's limbs bent backwards in an awkward snap.

It was the beginning of the end of the contest. Suriel was a broken little bird, his right arm bouncing limply as the two of them rolled through the sky together. Lucifer smelled weakness, and that was all it took to tear his enemy apart. Ecanus couldn't see the details, just the two of them swinging at each other with hand and foot and wing. But Suriel was getting the worst of it, and the longer they went, the less of himself he could move. The last thing Ecanus saw before the end was Lucifer's arm, poking through Suriel's innards and coming out through his back, his fingers flexing up and down until he kicked Suriel away to his death.

It seemed a change of allegiances was in order.

A matter of expediency, as Ecanus didn't particularly care which master he served. But Lucifer would hardly open his arms to welcome him to his side. He'd fought against him during the first rebellion, and besides, he looked quite uneager to take on new recruits from his defeated enemies. From what Ecanus could see through the spyglass, Lucifer was now busying himself vaulting between seraphs, tearing out their entrails and wrapping them around their necks before dropping them to the ground just as he had Suriel.

But the die was cast, unfortunately, and Lucifer it was to be. It was either ally with him or find a way to hide away within his realm forever, an option as unpalatable as it was infeasible. The approach would have to be made, and it would have to be a delicate one.

There was still hope, though. Ecanus could still see the cherubs, as alive as ever. Lucifer had let them live. That meant he couldn't be quite as rabid as he looked, and he must have had some need of servants. There was only one sure way to an archangel's heart: to make himself useful, and to do it at once.

Ecanus was fortunate on that front. He could think of a few things that Lucifer would surely be delighted to receive. A babe, his mother, and the severed head of his father, all delivered to him on a platter. If that wouldn't buy Ecanus his life, then nothing in all of creation would.

And if he didn't know precisely where to find them, he had at least an inkling. He scanned around the sky with his spyglass, and he could see Ambriela and her castoffs, shrinking away on the horizon as they used Lucifer's distraction as an opportunity to flee. They were heading the only way any of them could, the only way anyone could have gone if they were to have escaped the attentions of Lucifer, at least for a time. North. Towards the center of the barrier, and towards the place Lucifer had come from.

And the smartest move for him, thought Ecanus, was to follow.

CHAPTER TWENTY-SIX

HE'D BEEN ALONE FOR SO long.

Trapped. Locked away in a cage and left for dead. Burning beside his brothers-in-arms, lesser angels who hadn't had the power to withstand the intensity of the flames they'd suffered. Their minds had gone, and so had their skins, and nothing but beasts were left of them. In the end there'd been no one to talk to, no one but himself.

He'd kept his sanity, if only just. The others had all gone mad within a few centuries. But it was different for him. It wasn't that he was more powerful or more intelligent. He was, but he'd stayed grounded in himself because of something else, something the rest of them had abandoned.

They had nothing ahead of them but an eternity of pain. The suffering burned away their minds, but it didn't matter to him. He had something to focus him. A purpose. Something to do, and something to look forward to.

The Maker had his plans, and he'd been taunted with

them. Before he'd been tossed into his Pit, he'd been promised that he'd be set free again one day, but only for a time. Long enough to wreak havoc on the world, and long enough to bring about its end. And when his task was done, he was to have been punished one final time, wrapped in chains and tossed into a lake of fire from which he'd never return again.

That was the plan, but the plan had gone awry. That was the thing about plans. They were never perfect, and even the Maker couldn't keep to them, not when circumstances changed. If his plans had been perfect, he wouldn't have needed someone to test them.

He wouldn't have needed an adversary.

That had been his purpose, after all. To poke holes in things and to reveal their flaws. To tear apart the best of intentions, just to prove it could be done. For no plan was perfect if he could undo it, and no choice sacred if he somehow managed to profane it.

This time the Maker had undone himself, and all it had taken was a nudge. The only thing that could escape the Pit were whispers, but whispers had been quite enough. The Maker was supposed to be all powerful. Everyone thought that he was. And it had been true, once upon a time ago. Once he would have been able to set things right before his will had been unraveled. Once he'd been in firm command, and once he'd had no weaknesses.

But then he'd gone and had his Son.

It was a foolish choice, and one he wouldn't have made if he'd had someone there to test him. But no one had the spine to challenge the Maker, not for thousands of years after he'd put down the first rebellion against him. There'd been no one up there to speak against him or to question the wisdom of his choices. And in fathering the Son, he'd made the most foolish choice of them all. One that left him vulnerable, even if there was no one left to warn him of it.

For the Son had taught the Maker mercy, and mercy was a weakness all its own.

It had been his only duty, once. Probing and testing, searching for anything that could possibly go wrong with the Maker's choices. And it still was his duty, as far as he was concerned. It was the thing he'd clung to during all those years of torture. His flesh had burned away, but not the purpose he'd been tasked with. His friends were gone, his name blackened, and there wasn't any hope of ascending to the throne in the way he'd once dreamed of.

All that was gone, but still he had something to live for. Something to absorb his thoughts, to keep his mind from wandering to the past he'd lost or to the present filled with nothing but endless pain. He'd mastered himself by letting his task become the master of him. For after everything he'd lost, he hadn't anything else to live for.

And so he'd spent the centuries thinking. Listening to the murmurs that echoed into his cage from those above who thought about him still. There were many who admired him, who lionized him, who saw the justice in his cause only after it was lost. They'd spoken to him, in their way. Spoken of the Maker's plans, and what was to be done about them.

And he had whispered back.

It had been so easy to unravel the thread of the Maker's plans once he'd changed them, once he'd given into a plea for mercy. It was an idea that should have been strangled in its cradle, or in its manger if it came to it. A change that never would have happened had he not been locked inside the Pit.

The changes wrought by the Son's birth had rippled through everything, and it had let him turn the world upside down. It was all so far from how he'd envisioned it. The Maker had once intended to end things, to give this world a final send-off and take his followers up to their eternal reward. Back then he'd plotted to oppose the Maker by keeping the world around forever, a Sodom on a planetary scale, a place so blighted and corrupt that the Maker would regret its creation forever. He'd deny the Maker the ending to his story, leaving the world he'd created to sputter on in sin for all eternity. There'd be no Armageddon, no plagues or pestilence, and certainly no salvation.

But now the Maker wanted to keep this world alive instead, to grow or to rot according to the choices of its inhabitants. And so he'd switched sides right along with him, abandoning all the dreams he'd once had of thwarting an apocalypse that had been planned for eons. Now he would be the destroyer, the one who tore it all apart, the one who ended the world just as had always been planned. He'd tear apart Heaven and Earth with plagues and pestilences, leaving only his own New Jerusalem in its place. A city for the select of the sinners, and the rest would be tossed into a lake of fire along with the Son.

It was the Maker's own plan, after a fashion. Others might have found it folly not to have desires of his own. To simply watch whatever the Maker did, and then do his best to undo it. If the Maker had turned sinner, he'd probably have become a saint.

That was what it meant, to be an adversary. There were no sides, and there was no right and wrong. There was only the role. Opposition for the sake of itself, a battle of wits that would go on and on no matter what the Maker's plans might change to. For it was the task that mattered, not anything else. The task had given him meaning when all his hopes had been lost. Some thought it a game, but it was something more than that. Whatever else the Maker did to him, he couldn't take away his purpose. He was the adversary, and it was his role to oppose the Maker in everything he did.

And if the Maker wanted this world to live, then he would see it die, and the Son right along with it.

CHAPTER TWENTY-SEVEN

ASSIE HAD NEVER FLOWN BEFORE, not like this. Not dangling from the arms of an angel, her life in someone else's hands, the wind rushing into her face as they plowed through the air together. It was a little like being doused with a bucket of cold water. The life had rushed back into her as they'd taken to the air, leaving her invigorated and alert and more than a little terrified.

The angel carrying her was an angry looking woman, her sandpaper-rough hands digging deep into Cassie's stomach. Her nose dripped from her face, the skin badly damaged in her fall. Cassie didn't trust her, not even a little bit, not with how much she'd grumbled about the indignity of evacuating mere servants before they'd left.

But there hadn't been a choice, not for any of them. They could hitch a ride with one of these monsters, or they could stay back there with the monsters below. The angels were practically jolly by comparison. It wasn't comfortable being hauled along as freight, and she'd been jostled around so badly that there had been three or four moments when she'd been sure she was about to plummet to the ground.

It hadn't happened yet, and they were still on course for their destination. That giant black pillar, bigger than a few of the towers wrapped together. It was a disgusting ooze, like something flooding up from a broken septic tank, and she didn't see how they'd possibly stop it. Zuphias said it had come from his body somehow, but the thing was so big it didn't make any sense how it could have. Then again, nothing about the world made any sense, and it hadn't for years.

She'd kept her eyes closed for the first part of the trip, her hands clinging to the angel's gauntlets. It was terrifying looking down, knowing that all it would take to send her to her death was the twitch of an angel's fingers. But keeping her eyes closed felt worse and worse the longer she'd flown. When her eyes were closed, when she didn't have anything to distract her, she couldn't quit thinking about Aaron.

He wasn't the only one, but he was the freshest one in her mind: the most recent person she'd gotten killed, and the one who'd died in the worst possible way. She hadn't seen the faces of all the people who'd died back in the tower, but she knew what she'd done all the same. Hundreds of them at least, too afraid to leave, buried under the rubble after it collapsed.

The guilt had only grown, and Aaron's death had nearly made her snap. She'd shaken herself out of it with Rhamiel's help, but only barely, and it worried her. She'd panicked, and how was she supposed to know when she'd do it again? The servants needed a leader they could trust, one they could depend on. And the only thing that kept her going was that she was the only leader they had.

She forced herself to keep her eyes open, to watch the ground as it flooded past. She caught glimpses of strange things down there. Bubbling lakes of tar lit with fire, and roving packs of scaly-skinned animals that loped along the roads. A dinosaur-sized caterpillar, its jaws tearing apart a car. And flying snakes. Swarms full of flying snakes, flapping around on bat wings far below them. First Heaven had come to Earth, and now Hell, and humanity couldn't live with either of them.

She heard shouting ahead of them and saw the angels at the front leaning forward into a slow dive, gliding towards the ground clutching servants of their own. The dive rippled through the formation as angel after angel followed along after them, and soon Cassie was plunging down, too, her stomach clenching in on itself as the ground came closer and closer.

But just before they collided with the earth, the angel heaved her wings outward, slowing the descent to a light drift that felt like floating under a big, feathery parachute. They'd landed a few miles away from that pillar, and she'd handled the flight better than most of the others. One of the men vomited his breakfast all over his feet, and the women to her left were stumbling back and forth like drunks, barely able to keep their balance.

She wondered why they'd stopped so far away. Not all of them were going to the cherubs' home; some of them were going to hide here and wait the battle out. But the only thing here was a river. Maybe that made it safer than anywhere else, but she'd still have preferred hiding anywhere other than right out in the open. She walked around, scouting out the area, and a little ways downriver she saw why the angels had chosen this spot.

Down on the riverbank lay the twisted remains of a metal bridge, its two white arches bent and balled into a pile of metal atop the rocky shore. Girders poked out of the heap, giving it the appearance of a stocky old porcupine. The water flowed past it just a few yards away, and there were plenty of nooks and crannies to hide in. Enough for all of the servants, as long as they didn't wander.

She heard footsteps behind her, and she turned to see Rhamiel, looming above the other angels and looking down at her. "We leave your people here." He must have caught her fears along with her eyes, because he rushed to reassure her. "Nowhere is safe. Not really. But they can hide in this place from things in the skies, and the water will protect them from things on the ground. It will have to do. The place we plan to enter is far more dangerous. Get them hidden, and get them safe. A few of the weaker seraphs are staying, but the rest of us leave soon, and your followers must wait here until we return."

"I will," said Cassie. But she was pretty sure they wouldn't be returning. So was he, if she'd read the look on his face correctly. This was a kamikaze mission, and whether it succeeded or it failed, the servants would probably be on their own when it was done.

She waved them this way and that, guiding them to little crevices in the pile of metal where they wouldn't be seen from above. It was cramped, but they wouldn't be spotted, not if they could manage to stay put. She had one of Ambriela's angels fly up to be sure, and he couldn't see a single one of them. At least he claimed he couldn't, but all she could do was trust him.

She looked for a hiding place of her own, somewhere she could stay behind and watch over the rest of them. She still hadn't decided what to do. A leader would have known, but she didn't. She could go with the others and fight, or she could tend to the people here, doing her best to keep them alive while the angels waged their last battle against Lucifer. Either way could be a disaster for the servants. If they didn't beat Lucifer, every single one of them was dead. And if she left them alone, something might find them out here while she was gone, and they wouldn't know what to do. They'd scream, or panic, or close their eyes and wait to die. She'd seen it firsthand, over and over again.

But if she stayed, maybe things would be worse. Maybe it was better for the servants to be on their own than to follow a leader who made the wrong decisions when their lives were on the line. Would she just get more of them killed the longer they were around her? They'd do whatever she told them to, no matter how stupid it was. She was a crutch, and a wobbly one, and if they didn't learn to walk on their own they'd just keep dying, one by one by one.

She saw Faye walking with her hands on Jana's shoulders, guiding her away from the crowd of angels nervously milling about nearby. Jana's face was streaked with tears; she hadn't quit crying since they'd left the pond. Cassie didn't blame her. Not with what Zuphias was demanding, and not with what Rhamiel was planning to do.

"Cassie," said Faye. "Are you coming? We're getting ready to move out." She whispered something into Jana's ear, trying to calm her down, but it didn't work. At this point, probably nothing could have.

"I think I have to stay," said Cassie hesitantly. "I think I have to stay here with the servants. I've got to be strong for them. They can't survive without someone like that. I let myself be weak. And every time I do that, someone dies."

"It's okay to be weak, sometimes," said Faye. "Nobody can be strong all the time, every time. You can try, but you can't kick yourself if you don't live up to the impossible."

"I know," said Cassie. She said it, but she didn't really believe it. "We've got room here. A place for Jana." She smiled at Jana and gestured towards a gap in a clump of broken girders, just big enough for someone to wriggle into. "A place for both of you, if you want it."

"You can stay with them if you want," said Faye, shaking her head. "But I can't. And I have to say it. We need everyone down there. Everyone who might be able to help at all. This is big. You said it yourself. If we lose this fight, no one survives, anyway. Everybody who can come has to come."

"They'll die," said Cassie. "More of the servants will die. They can't live on their own if I leave them. They just can't."

"Not for an hour?" said Faye. "Not even for a minute?"

"You know what I mean," said Cassie. "You know what's out there.

"If we don't stop this, everyone's going to die," said Faye. "Everyone. Them, us, the whole world. It's just a matter of time. The closer we get to this place, the more I know it's true. I can hear stuff in my head. I can feel it. We have to give it everything we've got, and we've got to do it now. You're strong. Smart. You led them here. We need you."

"They need me," said Cassie. It was what she said, but it wasn't what she wanted to say. She wanted to say she was worried about more than that. That if she went with them, she'd botch things up over there instead of back here. That if she was in the middle of the battle that counted, she'd let them all down when it mattered the most. Not just the servants, but the entire human race. That was the truth, but she couldn't speak it. She had to say something, anything instead of that. "They need me, and maybe I should be with them."

"They need you in the fight more than they need you back here," insisted Faye. "That's all I'm saying. You don't have to come if you don't want to. But we're heading out soon. This is the last chance for everyone. Even some of the servants are coming, some of the men. You've got to make choices as a leader. All I'm asking you to do is think a little more about this one."

Cassie didn't answer. She just held out her hand to Jana, clasping their fingers together and pulling her towards her hiding place. "Come on. Let's get you someplace safe. I'll be right next to you the entire time."

"I can't," said Jana. "I can't stay." Her eyes were

bloodshot, her face contorted in pain. She loved Rhamiel, she really did. And now he was being blackmailed into giving up his body for the sake of their son. It made Cassie wince to think about it, but she tried to be brave for the both of them.

"You have to be strong," said Cassie. "You have to try, even if you're scared." They were words she wanted to say to herself, and they were the truth, but it was always easier to tell the truth to others than to admit it to one's self. "It'll be fine. I'll be there with you."

"I want to be with him," said Jana. She looked over her shoulder at Rhamiel, his face grim as he conferred with Ambriela and a few of her men, planning their assault, planning what he'd do if he made it into Zuphias's body. He kept sneaking glances at her, but every time he'd wince away, looking just as wounded as Jana did. Cassie knew exactly what he was doing. She'd done it herself. Throwing himself into the work so he wouldn't have to think about the pain. It kept things buried, at least for a while, but they always came back to the surface. And what he was burying wouldn't stay down inside him for long.

He was going to leave Jana, forever. He was going to be locked away inside Zuphias's body. And worse than that, because Zuphias would be running around inside his own. Maybe Rhamiel would save the world, but he'd have to give up everything to do it. The woman he loved, the son he'd never know, and the life he'd never live again.

He was braver than Cassie ever could be. She respected him for doing it, and she wished she had some of that courage in her. She did, sometimes, but only when she absolutely had to. And whenever the crisis of the moment left, her confidence went away along with it.

She started pulling Jana away, standing between her and Rhamiel. It'd be better if she didn't see him. The angels were about to leave, Jana had already said her goodbyes, and the only thing left was the pain. But as she was easing Jana into her hiding place in the ruins of the bridge, she bent over in pain, clutching her stomach with a muffled grunt.

"I can't," said Jana. "I have to go. I have to go with him, and I have to be there."

"It's okay," said Cassie. "Let's sit down, and you'll feel better. Let's get you comfortable."

"Is she ill?" said Rhamiel. He'd appeared from nowhere, abandoning the others in the middle of their planning and rushing to her side. He must have still been watching her, and lines of worry crinkled around his eyes at what he'd seen. "What's wrong? How do you feel?"

"I need to go with you," said Jana. "I can't stay here."

"You must," said Rhamiel. He hugged her close and leaned down to kiss her forehead, his arms so tight around her that he didn't look like he'd ever let her go. "I know how it hurts. It gnaws at me, too, what I must do. But I cannot let you die, either of you. Whatever the cost to me, your life must be protected."

"He doesn't want me to stay," said Jana. She rubbed her stomach, looking up at Rhamiel in awe. "Feel it."

Rhamiel put his hand against her, and his eyes grew along with his smile. "He's kicking. And hard." His smile turned to a smirk, and pride surged across his face. "He has my strength. I've given him that, if nothing else."

"He's trying to tell me something," said Jana. "He's done it before. I can't stay here. I don't know why, but I can't."

"It's just a kick," said Rhamiel.

"No," said Jana. "Feel it. Really feel it." She interlaced their fingers, pressing his hand against her stomach.

"There's a rhythm," said Rhamiel. "A pattern."

"I don't know what it means," said Jana. "But I can feel it, just like before. He wants me to go."

Rhamiel stood in silence, reflecting, and after a moment he spoke. "You may come with us. I do not like it, and I do not think it wise. But he must know something. There must be some reason. But you will stay by my side until I do what I must do. And when I am gone, I shall appoint another to protect you in my stead." He paced back and forth, running the options through his head, not liking a single one of them. "Not Ambriela. Never her. But someone. Kabshiel, perhaps. I trust his fear of damnation, if I do not trust his word. Or Zaapiel. He's harsh, but just, or at least he once was."

"Me," said Cassie loudly. "You can't trust any of them, but you can trust me."

She knew in her heart what she had to do. She saw through her guilt, her fears, her insecurities about everything she'd done. Leaders had to make choices, hard ones, and her choice was clear.

Jana was a servant, just like all the others. Cassie had wronged her just as much as she'd wronged anyone, and probably more. So many people here had suffered because of what she'd done. Because she'd struck at the tower without figuring out a better way to get them all out. Because she'd been so obsessed with hurting the angels that she hadn't really understood what it would do to the people beneath them. Because even if she'd been right to do it, and even if the angels had deserved it, she still owed these people something, a debt she could never really repay.

But if Jana died, her son died with her, and the whole thing was over for everyone. She couldn't help everyone at once. But Jana was the most important one, the one no one else could live without. Right now, in this moment, she was the one who was hurting the most, she was the one who was most at risk, and she was the one who truly needed her.

And if Jana was going with those angels to face off against Lucifer, then so was she.

CHAPTER TWENTY-EIGHT

THE HIVE LOOKED LIKE IT had blown open from the inside out. They'd warned Jana that it would be a strange place, a metallic wonderland buzzing with contraptions she mustn't even think of touching. But if this was a science experiment, it had gone terribly wrong. What had once been a field of metal was now nothing more than a hole in the ground, its jagged edges shorn upwards from the force of the billowing corruption that stretched up as high as she could see.

Up close, the pillar looked more like a giant tornado. At the bottom it was a narrow stream of sludge, churning out of a hole in the ground that must have been half a mile wide. Whatever the stuff was, the pillar grew as it rose through the air, swirling around and around, a floating river that moved like an angry wind.

Jana could see down into the hole as they walked closer to the edge of it. Rooms and tunnels had been sliced in half, and things were skittering around down there in the dim light. The damage only went so deep, and beyond it was what was left of the cherubs' home.

How far they'd dug she couldn't possibly tell, but parts of the Hive were still intact, and that was where they were to go.

They'd landed at the outskirts, those of them who were going down there. Cassie and Faye, looking just as scared as she felt. Ambriela, quietly seething over her lost authority, standing in the middle of a rag-tag army that wasn't really hers anymore. Thane, with Zuphias inside him, his posture weak and his expression smug. And Rhamiel, barking orders all around, commanding them all with strength and self-assurance as if he weren't about to do the foolish thing he knew he had to.

She couldn't believe he was going to do it. Just give up his body, jump inside of what was left of Zuphias, and do his best to shut the gate the cherubs had opened. It was mad, but everyone agreed it was their only hope. He was planning a battle of the mind, a struggle to contain the mental energies the cherubs had harnessed, and she wished that anyone but him would be the one to try it.

But Rhamiel was the strongest, the bravest, and only he could hope to cut the link between Zuphias and Lucifer's Pit. It was a matter of willpower, and none of the others had the strength of will to do it. Even if they did, Zuphias had vowed to use every ounce of his power to fight against anyone but Rhamiel. He'd demanded his body in trade, and he'd let the world rot before he'd spend another day inside of anyone else but him.

Ambriela thought the plan would work, and she was the miracle worker. Any miracle could end, she'd said, but the stronger it was, the stronger the mind would have to be to stop it. However much the cherubs had amplified it, it could still be done. Zuphias had opened up a tunnel through reality, just a little one, just enough to connect two minds together. The cherubs had hijacked that tunnel, and they'd widened it to unimaginable levels.

But miracle workers opened and closed tunnels all the time, and the principle of the matter was the same. She'd tried to teach Rhamiel how to close it, as best she was able. The plan would work, she said. In theory, at least, and wasn't that what counted?

Jana had begged for him not to try, but this was the one favor Rhamiel wouldn't grant her. In her head, she understood why. In her heart, it didn't matter.

She might never see Rhamiel again. Even if they won, even if he managed to do what he was planning, he might not ever find his way back to her.

He'd promised it wasn't so, and Ambriela had agreed through gritted teeth. They'd take back his body from Zuphias, and if they couldn't, they'd find him someone else. There were angels all around, bad ones, ones who deserved the punishment and ones who were weak enough to force into it. If they were lucky, someone might even volunteer. They'd find someone, somewhere, and then they'd bring Rhamiel back, albeit in an entirely different body.

She'd love him all the same, no matter what he looked like. She'd take him in whatever body he came in. That wasn't the problem. The problem was that he might not ever come out. He might go down into Zuphias's body and he might stay there forever, locked away inside a burnt, broken prison.

And even if he won his mental battle, he might not

truly make it through. The seraphs wouldn't say it, not to her face, but she heard the whispers. It was dangerous, what he was doing, dangerous to the mind, and even if he found a way to succeed and made his way back out again, he might be damaged along the way. He was doing it because he loved her, but they might lose each other in the process.

The seraphs had sent a few scouts down into the Hive, and Jana tried to keep her thoughts on them. Thinking about what was to come only hurt her, and there wasn't a thing she could do about it. She could see them down there, darting from room to room, sneaking peeks through the shorn walls and into the tunnels beyond them. They moved with military precision, teams of them cautiously venturing into the Hive and popping back out again a few minutes later.

Finally one of Rhamiel's new deputies shot up towards them, landing in front of him and bowing his head in a quick salute. The seraph looked young, his face pink with burns dotted with a few patches of white scar tissue along his forehead. He didn't look strong enough to be a warrior, but the ranks of the Seraphim were just as thin as he was, and they'd had to make due with anyone willing to fight.

"We can see Zuphias's body, we think," said the seraph. "But we cannot get close to it, not from above. The corruption swirls this way and that. It gives us glimpses of something beyond it, but only barely. It moves too quickly, and it would consume us before we'd slipped past it."

"There must be a way through," said Rhamiel. He

paced along the edges of the destruction, staring down at the black sludge as it blew this way and that. "We must be able to get down there."

"The tunnels," said the seraph. "We can enter in safety a few floors up. From there, we must work our way to the source. We'd be close. Very close."

"I have been here before, and the place is a maze," said Rhamiel. "We could be a few feet away from it as the crow flies, and we'd still have miles to travel." He frowned, his brow wrinkling as he watched the sludge, timing its speed as it swirled near the jagged edges of the hole it had punched through the metal. The hole grew narrower the further down it went, and the closer to the bottom they flew, the closer the sludge would be to them. "It goes too near, and too often. We could never make it past it, not to the very bottom. We've no other choice. Guide us to an open tunnel, as close as you can, and we shall walk from there."

The seraph bowed and whistled to the scouts below. They flew up in teams of three, some gathering up the few humans who'd come with them, others shouting orders at the rest of the seraphs. Rhamiel held out his hand to Jana, bundled her up in his arms, and soon he was carrying her down into the Hive. They all kept a healthy distance from the corruption, but it was just a few yards away, and Jana had a clearer look at it than ever.

It looked so black, like infected mucus glistening and bubbling out from a wound the cherubs had torn into reality itself. It whirled around, coming close to her again and again as it spun. And it seemed to feel that she was there. A thick tendril slopped out of the side of it, reaching out towards her face and forcing Rhamiel to duck to the side to avoid it. With every pass it made, more and more of the tendrils were there, grasping at her like blind tentacles feeling for prey they could sense but couldn't quite see.

They landed on a ledge in the middle of the destruction. It must have once been some kind of gathering area: a kitchen or a dining room, most probably. The floor was covered in shattered plates, and she could see a few utensils that looked like overly-complicated clockwork forks. Half the room had been torn away, but on the other side was a doorway leading further off into the Hive.

The scouts went in first, with Rhamiel following close behind. He turned at the doorway, nodding at Cassie, and she and Faye grabbed Jana's hands on either side. "Stay close to us," said Cassie. "Don't panic, no matter what. We'll be kind of like bodyguards. Let the angels handle everything else. All the three of us have to worry about is keeping you alive."

Jana didn't have any plans to suddenly become a warrior. Her son could kick all he liked, but he wasn't going to manage that. All she knew was that she had to be here, and she had to see this through to the end of it. Her son couldn't wait on the sidelines, not for this, and that meant that neither could she.

They headed into the darkness of the tunnel, a pure black except for the dim light of a few of the angels' swords. They kept them mostly in their sheaths, pulled out just far enough to let them see the way ahead.

What was left of the Hive was a madhouse. Things were crawling all along the walls, living insects with parts replaced with machines. None of them seemed to have any idea where they were going or what they were doing. They passed a room filled with debris, its ceiling collapsed and the entrance impassable. A swarm of the little things raced around in circles outside the doorway, unable to do whatever they were originally meant to yet entirely unwilling to give it up. A cloud of moths with blinking light bulbs attached to their backs slammed against the rubble again and again, dashing themselves to pieces trying to perform some now futile task the cherubs had programmed into them.

They walked and walked, curving down, then up, then in what felt like a circular loop. Jana couldn't make heads or tails of it, but the scouts seemed to know where they were going. She could only hope they did. If they were lost in here somehow, she knew she'd never find her way back to the surface again on her own.

She was shuffling along behind Cassie when she heard voices from the room ahead of them. Rhamiel's hand went up, and everyone stopped, crouching down on either side of the tunnel. She knew what they were the moment they spoke: cherubs, two of them, and she caught glimpses of them between the wings of the angels ahead of her. They were huddled over a long table, so engrossed in their project that they were oblivious to everything around them, their little wings bouncing up and down as they worked. The first had the head of an eagle, staring through a monocle at something on the table in front of them. The other looked like a little man with an ox's head, and every few moments he let out an involuntary bleat.

"His teeth are flattened nubs from chewing stone," said the first cherub. "Let's forge him up incisors of our own. A pair of metal fangs to rend and chew; once screwed into his jaw, it's good as new."

"And ducts of poison mixed with his entrails," said the second cherub. "To paralyze the prey that he assails."

"We'll stitch up an infernal Frankenstein," said the first. "And turn the Maker's water into wine. He cast this malformed pup into the Pit; he botched it up and washed his hands of it. But surgery shall grant our pet reprieve; he'll be the vicious mutt our scalpels weave."

The seraphs crept closer, Ambriela leading on one side of the hallway, Rhamiel on the other. Their swords were sheathed, and a line of others waited behind them, tense with anticipation. One of the cherubs flitted aside, rustling through a tray of knives, and Jana got her first clear look at the thing lying on the table in front of them. She nearly lost her lunch at the sight.

It looked like a dog, but it was the size of a horse. Its teeth hardly looked ground down; indeed, to Jana they looked like an endless row of kitchen knives. Perhaps the cherubs were more particular about such things, but she couldn't even fathom what they expected it would need to chew through. Its eyes were shut, its belly open, a long rectangle of skin pinned to its sides to expose its innards. Every time the creature breathed, little squirts of yellow fluid oozed out from around its organs. Jana didn't have the stomach for the cherubs' experiments, and she dropped her eyes to the ground, waiting for whatever was to come.

She didn't wait long. She heard a squeal and a crash, and braved another peek to see the table toppled over and the thing on the ground beneath it. The cherubs were gurgling blood, one sliced through the middle by Rhamiel's sword, the other's head lopped clean away and dangling by the hair from Ambriela's hand.

"Come," said Rhamiel. "We're close now, I think."

"Through another hallway, and past another room," said one of the scouts. "The throne room is there. And so is the body."

They started up again, and Jana closed her eyes as they walked past the remains of the cherubs and the beast they'd been experimenting on. Rhamiel led them onward, through another hall and a storage room full of scattered piles of screws, cogs, and glass tubes. And then they were there: the throne room.

A golden portal marked the entrance, still intact, but inside was a disaster zone. The throne was lying on its side, empty and overturned, the clockwork cherub atop it still spinning through its four heads. A few tiny bodies had been left there to rot, cherubs who must have died during the opening of the Pit. Shattered pieces of crystal were strewn around the floor, and little dust devils spun around the room, dirt mixed with trash roving in tiny vortexes driven by the pillar itself.

In the center was the vat Zuphias's body was floating in. It was a glass coffin, long and thin and covered in dials and instruments. The fluid inside was a pale green, and the body bobbed up and down, a blackened crisp that looked like a potato some servant had left too long in the oven. The vat was lined with some kind of ornamental metal; gold or bronze, as best Jana could tell in the light. The top had been torn asunder, exploding from the inside out with the force of the corruption it was channeling.

The base of the pillar spewed out of the body, and Jana almost couldn't believe this was the source. It was so thin, the black line of sludge spiraling out of the vat. It was nothing but a trickle at its source, swinging round and round through the air like a manic jump rope, growing as it wound its way upwards until finally it became the hurricane-sized thing above them.

She stared at Zuphias's body. It was so black, so empty, the bones that once held wings twitching back and forth on its back. Every now and again one of the fingers would jerk, or the mouth would clack open and closed. Rhamiel was going in there. He was going to trade his body for this one, and there was no guarantee that he'd ever come out. Tears wet her cheeks again, and she felt him at her side, his hands steadying her at the waist.

"I will be fine, Jana," said Rhamiel. "And so will you. That's what's most important."

"It's not," said Jana, wiping a hand against her eyes to keep herself from weeping. "You're what's most important. I can't lose you."

"You won't," said Rhamiel.

He was lying to her, just another sin the angels had picked up in their years among men. He didn't believe it, but she could tell he wanted to. And so did she. More than anything, she wanted to believe he was coming back. But she wasn't that naive, not anymore. She knew exactly what the odds were, and exactly what was likely to happen.

Still.

This might be their last few minutes together. The last time they'd ever see each other, and the last time she'd ever touch him. She could sit there crying, or she could enjoy the moment for what it was. And so she did, leaning her head against his breast, listening to him breathe. She pulled his hand towards her stomach, the two of them pressing their fingers against her belly, feeling the heartbeats of the life they'd created together.

"I love you," said Rhamiel. "I shall love you forever, no matter what."

"I love you, too," said Jana. "Come back. You have to come back."

"I will," said Rhamiel. He looked down at her, running his hand along her stomach, his eyes full of longing and loss. "You will tell him who I was. You will tell him my name."

"He'll know," said Jana. She sniffled again, and she almost couldn't hold in the pain. But she fought it, trying to stay in the moment, savoring every bit of him for every second that she could. "He's going to know you in person. But even if he doesn't, no matter what happens, he's going to know."

"I shall close this gate," said Rhamiel. "I shall close it, and I shall return." He looked over at Thane, smug and smarmy, sizing up Rhamiel's body from afar. "And then I shall speak to Zuphias again on the matter of my body."

She knew Zuphias would never give it up. There'd be no way to make him, not once he had his hooks in his new home. He'd dig in deep and he'd never let go, not with the prize he'd won. Rhamiel probably wouldn't be coming back. And if he did somehow, he wouldn't be there as himself. He'd be inside some other angel, a weak body that was an ill fit for the strength of his soul.

Ambriela cleared her throat, a forced smile broadcasting her impatience for all to see. Jana didn't care, and neither did Rhamiel. She gazed up at him, and he gazed down at her, and all at once his lips pressed against hers, his hands grabbed at her back, and his wings brushed against her from every side, covering her in the last caresses he might ever be able to give her. Their tongues met, their hands clasped, and they pulled themselves into one another. He couldn't quit kissing her; up and down her neck, on her lips, and finally a last kiss on her forehead before he forced himself to let her go.

"Are we done?" said Ambriela.

"For now," said Rhamiel. "Do what must be done. Do it while I have the nerve. Do it for her, and do it for my son."

"Come closer," said Ambriela, snapping her fingers and approaching the vat. She waved a hand at Thane, beckoning him forward. "The both of you. We haven't forever, you know." The two of them stood on either side of her, glaring at each other over her head.

"You brought this upon yourself, Rhamiel," said

Thane. "We were friends, once, or at least tolerable acquaintances. You should have taken my side, the justice of it be damned. It wouldn't have come to this if you had."

"Enjoy things while you can," said Rhamiel. "We'll speak on the matter again, I assure you."

"I've seen what's in there, Rhamiel," said Thane. His eyes went hollow, staring off into nothing as his memories overwhelmed him. "It's a noble deed I suppose, this thing you're to attempt. But you won't be coming back. You shall understand once you're inside. You simply won't be coming back."

"Take a hand, each of you," said Ambriela, holding out her arms. The three of them linked together and she closed her eyes, her mouth moving in a silent chant as she began the ceremony again.

Soon the glossolalia began, from both Thane and Rhamiel, and then the singing. It was the same powerful song, but this time Jana couldn't enjoy it. Three mouths moved in unison, and then four, as Zuphias's charred skull clacked open and closed in time with the others. She even thought she could hear the song coming from out of the vat, those beautiful words coming out of that horrible shell of an angel.

Ambriela's hands lit up with energy, turning such a pure white that it overwhelmed even the red tint of the light around them. The song grew louder, more frantic. The heads of both Rhamiel and Thane rolled back and forth, their muscles loose and their minds too far away to control them. Then the singing cut off all at once, the glow from Ambriela's hands dimmed, and Thane's knees wobbled until he collapsed to the floor.

Faye was at his side in no time, slipping through the crowd of seraphs and gently slapping her hands against his cheeks. "Thane? You there? Is it you?" There was hesitation in her voice as it wavered with the fear that he'd open his mouth and she'd hear Zuphias again. But there was no doubt about who it was inside his body, not from the moment he opened his mouth.

"What the fuck," said Thane. "How the fuck am I back?" He patted his hands against his chest, and then his head slowly went from side to side, taking in the room. "Where the hell are we? And what's wrong with my eyes? Everything looks like blood."

"We lost you," said Faye. "I thought we lost you." She hugged him tight, tears glistening at the edges of her eyes, her laughter mixed with pain as she welcomed him back to the living. "Never do something like that again. Never, ever, ever. Not for me. Not for anyone."

"It's bad in there," said Thane. "Worse than you said. The shit I saw. Like watchin' a horror movie that never ended."

"Rhamiel's in there, now," said Faye. "He took your place. And he's going to end all this. You won't ever have to go back. Not ever, not when he's done.

Thane looked over at Jana, but he couldn't hold it for long. He saw the pain in her and turned away, guilt and hurt mixed together on his face. He was happy to be back, but they couldn't be happy about it together. He knew more than anyone what Rhamiel was up against, and he knew just as well as she did the odds of him ever coming back.

But neither of them could do anything about that, not anymore. She did the only thing she could: she hugged Thane with as much enthusiasm as she could muster, holding her arms around him while Faye buried her head into his shoulder. And she cried a little, too, though not for the same reasons as Faye did. She could see Rhamiel's body out of the corner of her eye, occupied by an interloping angel who was busy examining his ill-gotten face in the reflection of his armor.

Thane was back, and she was happy for him, and happy for Faye, too. But while she'd won back a friend, she'd lost the most important man in her life. And any celebration was hollow while he was trapped in that vat, fighting alone against the eldritch horrors Lucifer had brought with him to Earth.

CHAPTER TWENTY-NINE

J ANA SAT BY THE VAT, waiting. She didn't know
what was going on in there. She didn't even know
if Rhamiel had made it. She'd cried out every tear
she had, and now she couldn't do much more than stare
at the floor. She couldn't bear to look at it, that body
floating in the vat. It was so disgusting, so damaged,
barely even alive. And the one she loved had been shoved
inside of it, probably never to return.

That wasn't even the worst part of the waiting. The
worst was Zuphias. He'd threatened to leave again and
again, promising to fly away to greener pastures and leave
them all here to die. He wouldn't quit talking about it,
loping around the room in Rhamiel's body, complaining
to anyone who'd listen about the folly of any of them
staying there at all.

But for all his whining, he didn't leave. He could
have done it in a moment, and at first Jana thought he
was staying there just to taunt her. Every time she heard
him speak in Rhamiel's voice it felt like someone had
poked her with hot needles. And he kept circling past

her, spouting nasty comments under his breath, making her feel even lower than she already did. But another ten minutes would pass, and another loop around the room, and he was still there, mouthing the same gripes as before.

After a few passes, she understood. It wasn't that he wanted to rub in his victory, or show off his shiny new body to the others. And it wasn't anything to do with her, as much as he tried to make it out that way. His problem was something else entirely.

He was afraid.

He had Rhamiel's body, he had his strength, and he had his sword. But he didn't have his courage. If he flew off on his own, he'd have to survive by himself, alone against any creatures of the Pit he encountered. He just couldn't do it. He was in the most dangerous place on the planet, and somehow he couldn't leave. Not by himself, and not until the others went with him.

It was easier once she realized that. It still hurt to listen to him, and it hurt to see him, but there was a certain satisfaction in it. He could look like Rhamiel, and he could sound like Rhamiel, but the two of them were nothing at all alike where it counted.

Still, she didn't want to even think about him, let alone listen to him. She stayed by the vat, staring up at the sky instead. The pillar was still there, pouring out of the body in the tank. That meant Rhamiel hadn't won, not yet. She watched it ooze out of him like a giant snake, and she wondered how she'd know if he'd succeeded in his mission. Maybe it would disappear, or maybe there'd be some loud bang. Maybe it wasn't a good idea to be this close to him, but she didn't care. She just kept watching the hypnotic rhythm of the thing as it corrupted the world around them, letting the movements distract her from the pain.

Then something interrupted her: a sound, something she thought she heard from somewhere up above. It was hard to tell if it had truly been anything at all; the pillar swirled above the vat, sending out a whining sound that grew to howls as it became the towering thing above them. She stopped watching and started listening. There was nothing at first, just the wind. But after a few minutes, she heard it again.

A high-pitched wail like a banshee's shriek, coming from outside. She stared through the hole in the ceiling, afraid to get too close to the darkness pouring forth from somewhere inside the body Rhamiel was trapped in. Mostly she saw black and red, sky and sludge mixing together like an abstract painting. But there was something else, something moving. She could only catch short glimpses, but she was sure of it.

"There's something up there," said Jana. "I see something."

It was black, darting back and forth behind the pillar. She pointed and the others gathered round to look, but by the time they did the thing was gone again.

"There's nothing there, dear," said Ambriela. "It's your imagination, or perhaps it's your grief. Either way, you must keep such things inside and comport yourself the way a proper servant should. Seen and not heard. Didn't they teach you that back in that tower of yours?"

"She's right," said Cassie. She put a hand above her

eyes, leaning up against the vat and straining to see. "I can see it. I know it. There's something coming. One of you."

"Nonsense," said Ambriela, strolling up to the vat to get a better view. "We've scouts above, and they would have alerted us. They surely wouldn't have left their posts. Nothing—" She'd stopped speaking, but her jaw was still moving, mouthing words even though the sound wouldn't come. All that would come out were a few soft wheezing sounds, until finally she managed to sputter something to herself. "Too soon. He's here, and too soon."

"Him," said Cassie. "'Oh my god. It's him."

They could see them, then, a swarm of them. Demons. More and more of them appeared, hundreds, flying slow circles around the pillar like vultures. They filled the air above, and then the first of them swooped into a sharp dive, heading straight for them.

The room was in a panic. Ambriela barked orders this way and that, positioning what forces she had to meet the intruders. There was no confidence in her seraphs, only fear, but the fight was coming whether they liked it or not. They drew their swords, readying themselves for battle.

As for the humans, the seraphs simply ignored them. Jana wasn't sure where to go or what to do. There were swords aplenty, but she didn't think she could even lift one, let alone swing it in a fight. She thought about hiding behind one of the angels, or perhaps borrowing one of Thane's guns and hoping for the best. But then she felt a hand on her shoulder: Cassie, a group of humans behind her, all of them armed and all of them looking at her.

"Jana, get behind us," said Cassie. "Let's get her over to the wall." She whistled to two nearby men, young and cocksure, shotguns angling off their shoulders as they stood guard around the vat. They were nothing more than boys when it came to it, but they'd been among the few servants who'd worked up the courage to come along.

Cassie pulled Jana away, ducking into the shadows near the entrance to the tunnel they'd come in through. The two men followed, positioning themselves on either side of them. Faye dragged Thane along after them, plopping him on the ground next to Jana before his legs buckled beneath him.

"Gimme my guns back," mumbled Thane. "Gimme somethin' to kill with." They'd split up his arsenal between them, Cassie taking his rifle and Faye his pistols. They just ignored his demands; he was just as unsteady as Faye had once been, his hands trembling as he pawed at Cassie's rifle. She shushed him, whispered something to him about watching Jana and watching her closely, and then she and all the rest of them stood at the ready, waiting for all hell to break loose.

It didn't take long. The first of the demons peeked in at them from the edge of the hole in the ceiling, dangling by its feet over the side. All that was left of its face was the mouth, a gaping hole with no teeth or tongue within it. The demon made a sound, something between a hiss and a gurgle, and it dropped to the floor, its head jerking from side to side. It started towards them, and then it was pandemonium all around.

Cassie fired first, grazing the demon's neck. It growled, pawing at its skin, and by then the seraphs had risen from their stupor and launched themselves at it, slashing away with their swords. Most of the blades were metal, and though they'd been forged by angels, they couldn't do much to hurt one. But a few of the seraphs still had weapons made of flame, and the demon was torn to pieces before it could take more than a step or two.

But it hadn't come alone.

They swarmed like locusts, hurling themselves towards the throne room. The next few waves met the same fate as the first: advancing into the room, just a little, before being mowed down by Ambriela and her seraphs. Even Zuphias braved a few swings of Rhamiel's sword, sneaking behind a demon and lopping away its head before it noticed he was there.

But small victories meant nothing against an army so large. The demons kept coming with little care for themselves: death was nothing but a reprieve from their pain, and what thoughts they had were focused on mauling and mayhem. More and more of them came, pushing the seraphs away from the vat, drowning the room in blood of demon and angel alike.

Jana stayed by the wall, ready to run if it came to that. Cassie and Faye were busy firing shots over the heads of the seraphs, while Thane kept struggling to his feet only to fall right back down again. All Jana could do was watch from the sidelines. It was terrifying, but she couldn't draw her eyes away from it. She just kept staring, watching the blood, listening to the shouts, waiting for the battle to end and the victor to claim her.

She felt a hand on her shoulder, the grip tight to the point of pain. She thought Thane must have been about to fall down again, and she turned to help him. But then she felt another hand, this one wrapped firmly around her mouth. When she managed to get a good look at who it was who'd grabbed her, she screamed until her breath was gone, the noise muffled to nothing by his palm.

Ecanus.

He was standing there above her, reaching out from the shadows, his eyes bright with malice. It was the same look he'd always given Peter, back in the tower. The look that said she was nothing but a toy, and one he wouldn't hesitate to break.

He dragged her into the darkness of a nearby tunnel, and the only one who noticed was Thane. He shouted something, but it didn't even sound like a word. It wasn't as if anyone else could hear it, anyway. There was too much noise: gunshots, the screams of seraphs, the gurgles and hisses of the demons as they worked what was left of their tongues. Thane crawled towards them, but too slowly, and then she was gone, enveloped by the shadows with nothing around her but the sound of Ecanus giggling.

"Poor little girl," said Ecanus. "No one to protect her. No one but her fellow monkeys. But their eyes weren't on the prize, were they? Not like mine. I've been waiting here in the darkness, waiting for my moment to come, and now it seems it has." He had her by the wrists, dragging her along the hallway. The metal floor scraped against her legs, skinning her knees as they went. They turned right, then left. She couldn't see anything, not in the darkness, so she focused on the direction instead, trying to remember the way back. After another turn he slammed her against the wall, and the hallway filled with a dim light as Ecanus pulled his dagger from his belt.

"Please," said Jana. "Please let me go." All he did was smile, his gums black and his teeth stained. He ran the dagger beneath her chin, and she could feel a light pain where it touched her skin. She smelled it, her own flesh burning, the first of what was sure to be more to come. She knew what he'd do if he got the chance. She'd end up as scarred as he was, as scarred as Peter had been when Ecanus was through with him.

"Please don't kill me," said Jana. "Whatever you want. Just please." If he wanted her to beg, she'd beg. If he wanted her to serve, she'd serve. Anything he wanted, anything from her, so long as he'd keep her son alive.

"I need you, little dear," said Ecanus. "And I shan't hurt you too badly. Although a little mutilation probably can't be helped." He grabbed a clump of her hair, burning away the strands almost to her scalp, and then grabbed another handful and started again. "Such things happen from time to time. The price of war, and it won't affect the price I extract for you."

"Listen," said Jana. "Suriel wants his women whole. You know that. You know he won't want me hurt. He'll give you more. I know it."

"Suriel's gone," said Ecanus. "There's only one bidder

left, I'm afraid. And I shall have to take whatever offer he makes, so long as it preserves my hide."

"Him," said Jana. "You can't give me to him. He's going to kill my son. He's going to kill everyone."

"He's going to kill all of you," said Ecanus. "As for me, that's quite another matter. He kept his demons. He kept his cherubs. He bears no particular grudge against the Seraphim, and I doubt he'll object to one of us switching sides. It's what he'd do himself, after all."

"The world," said Jana. "He's going to end the entire world."

"My world ended already," snarled Ecanus, his face lit with rage. "My world was nothing but a lie in the first place. False hymns from false worshippers who cared more for themselves than for the creed they sang. I was nothing up there, and I didn't even know it. The world down here's no different. You thought you could rise in our world by latching onto poor Rhamiel. Marry up, eh, and leapfrog over the rest of us?"

"No," said Jana. "No. Please. I—"

"That isn't how it works, dear," said Ecanus. "You're as much a nothing as you ever were. None of them care about you, Rhamiel least of all. You're just a little heifer, breeding a prize calf only to be slaughtered when you're done."

"No," said Jana. She tried to get to her feet, but he slammed her against the wall again. Her shoulders ached, and a stabbing pain ran down her back. But she tried again, anyway, though all she earned for the trouble was a vicious slap that rattled the teeth in her jaw.

"Now," said Ecanus, slowly waving his dagger before

her face, the tongues of fire licking at her skin. "Let us blacken that pretty face of yours, just a bit. You can birth a child without a nose, I think, assuming that's what Lucifer wants. For my own part I think he'll simply kill you. Best to get my fun out of the way before the matter's decided."

He smiled, leaning in towards her, his breath nasty enough to drown out even the sulfur. The dagger drifted towards her face. His hand went to her throat, and she readied herself inside for the pain she knew was to come. She told herself that it couldn't last for long, whatever he did to her and however much it hurt.

But then his head jackknifed to the side, slamming against his shoulder at an unnatural angle. A noise thundered through the hallway, and then another. Ecanus recovered himself, his face wild with fear as he squinted down the hall at his attacker. When he saw who had come for him, though, his smile was back in an instant.

It was Cassie, holding a rifle and aiming for another shot. Faye was there at her side, a pistol in hand, and Thane lumbered along behind them. They'd surprised him, and they'd frightened him, but there was little else they could do. Not with weapons like that, and not against a creature like him.

He started towards them, clenching Jana by the hair and dragging her along behind him. It felt like he was about to tear it all out by the roots, and she had to struggle to her feet and stumble along behind him to keep her scalp intact. Then another shot hit his leg, and Ecanus was down on the floor beside her.

Her head was numb, her vision blurry and her ears

ringing from the slaps. She heard gunfire again and again, and Ecanus was shouting something, pouring out his rage at everything around him. He looked so monstrous, his scars contorted into a mask of fury, wrinkles of mottled skin pushing this way and that. It was an awful sight, and she couldn't quit looking at it. He was standing up, pointing a finger at Cassie, threatening to rip out her eyes and stuff them into her ears. She looked away, afraid, and then she noticed something on the floor.

He'd dropped the dagger.

He was mad with rage, consumed by the anger within him, and he hadn't even noticed what he'd done. She crawled towards it, reaching for the handle, moving as slowly and as quietly as she could. She worried he'd notice her. She was so close to him, right at his feet, right within his sight if only he'd bothered to look down. But he was too furious, too sure of himself, and by the time he saw her she had it in her hands and was already moving to strike.

She shoved the dagger upwards, aiming for his belly. There was armor there, but humans must have made it, because it was no protection against an angelic weapon. The dagger pierced right through it, and she pressed her full weight upwards, shoving the blade into his stomach until it was buried up to the hilt.

He stared down at her, starting into another verbal assault. Blood poured out of his mouth instead of words, little trickles of it that ran down either side of his mouth. Then it turned into a gusher, his insides opening up as she put her full weight on the knife, dragging it down towards her and slicing him open.

He muttered something she couldn't understand, some final insult, and then he dropped to his knees and rolled over on his side, his arms clutching at his belly, his lips spasming and his legs twitching.

"That's for Peter," said Jana. "For me. For Rhamiel. For everyone you've ever hurt." She kicked him, but he didn't respond. He was too far gone for that, the hate in his eyes dying away as the knife burned at his insides and the life bled out of him.

"Let's go," said Cassie. She looked down at Ecanus, nudging him with her foot, making sure he was dead. Then she grabbed Jana in one hand, her rifle in the other, casting a wary eye at the way they'd come. The sounds from the throne room were terrible: shrill screams, battle cries cut short, scattered gunfire, and above it all the demons' tortured calls.

"Wait," said Jana. "We can't leave Rhamiel." She stumbled a few steps forward, glancing over her shoulder as they went. But where Cassie heard nothing but the cacophony of battle, all Jana could think about was Rhamiel, trapped in the middle of it all, not even knowing what was going on around him.

"Honey, he's gone," said Cassie. "We have the world to think about now. You and your child. You can't help him. You have to save yourself. The only thing you can do now is run."

But it wasn't. She knew in her heart that it wasn't.

All her life she'd let others make her choices for her. Cassie had told her what to do back in the tower, and now she was telling her what to do yet again. Her voice had a strength to it once more, a power that had been wavering back in the forest but now had snapped back into place. It would be the easy thing to do to follow Cassie's orders, just like all the other servants did. And it would be the easy thing to do to run away and leave Rhamiel there. It was probably the smart thing, too, at least in the short term, and at least for themselves. She couldn't blame Cassie for wanting to do it.

But that would mean leaving Rhamiel there to fight for them all alone. She knew it wasn't right. She knew why he'd done this, why he'd sacrificed everything he cared about to try to keep her alive. He'd done it for love, and he'd done it because it was the only hope he had of proving he was something better than the fallen angel he'd become. She'd worried so much that there was a darkness lurking inside him, one he couldn't control. But if it had been there, it wasn't anymore. Not when he was dealing with her, and not when he was dealing with his son.

She knew that, and she felt something more. A certainty that she had to go back, that she had to be there by his side in this moment that mattered more than any other. Her son was kicking again, down in her belly. And it was more than just that. She felt a warmth, a calm that enveloped her entire body. She'd been so scared, but now all that seemed like a dream. She had to go back. She didn't know why, and she didn't know what she could possibly do, but it was the only thing that felt right. The more Cassie pulled at her, the more she knew that this time, fleeing from her troubles wouldn't accomplish a thing.

They couldn't get away. Not really, and not anymore.

They could go and hide off in the tunnels somewhere, prolonging the inevitable. But it would only be a matter of time before Lucifer would root them out and do with them as he pleased. They couldn't stop that. It was die by Rhamiel's side, or die in the darkness, alone. And if it all had to end, better that they be together when it did.

She pulled her hand free from Cassie's, pivoting on her feet and launching herself back towards the throne room. Thane grabbed at her, mumbling something in a slurred voice. But he wasn't at home in his body, not yet; his fingers slipped and he lost his balance, tumbling to the floor and right in the way of Faye and Cassie.

She heard the three of them calling after her, and she heard their footsteps, thumping through the tunnel as they tried to run her down and drag her away to safety. She was slow, heavy with child, and if they'd had a little more time they would have caught her. But they were too far, and the tunnels were too dark. She was already at the entrance to the throne room before they could come close.

The room was carnage. Every inch of it was a battleground, demons fighting fallen angels, claw against sword and brother against brother. Ambriela was in the thick of it, perched atop the toppled throne, swinging her fiery scimitar at a group of angry, blackened angels the size of children. Cherubs, Jana thought, though none of them had lived back in her tower. A pair of demons gnawed at the belly of a seraph they'd slain, ignoring everything around them as they sated their thirst. Three of the female seraphs of Ambriela's tower had skewered one of the demons, using swords of iron to pin it to the wall by its wings as they beat it senseless. Towards the far end of the room, one of the demons was battering itself against the ceiling like a bird smashing against glass, its mind too far gone to find its way back to the skies.

And in the middle of it all was Lucifer.

He wasn't even fighting. He didn't seem to care about the battle or whether or not he won. He was just standing there by the vat, eyes shut, his arm stretched down into it. The corruption still swirled out of Zuphias, but it didn't touch Lucifer. The liquid inside the vat bubbled around his arm, and as Jana looked closer, she could see what he was doing. He'd grabbed hold of Zuphias's hand. Or perhaps now it was Rhamiel's. It hurt her to think it, but that was the truth. He was touching Rhamiel, working some curse on him, a sinister smile across his face. Rhamiel was in that vat, and now Lucifer was in there with him, doing who knew what.

She felt something inside her. Not a kick, but a burst of energy, a flood of courage bordering on recklessness. Her mind emptied of everything but a single thought: she had to put her hand into that vat, right next to Lucifer's, and she had to do it now.

The reasonable part of her gnawed at the back of her mind, trying to regain control, telling her how foolish the idea was and how likely it was to get her killed. But she pushed the thoughts away; this was a matter of love, not of rationality. She might well die, that was true. But she'd die beside Rhamiel, and she'd at least die doing something, not cowering in the corner and waiting for them to come for her again.

She ran to him, dodging swords and claws as she

went. She ducked beneath the wings of a demon, its single remaining eye covered in a cataract of damaged tissue. It could see her, but it didn't know exactly what she was, and all it could do was lash out at the sound of her footsteps. But she was gone almost before it knew she'd been there, running past a group of cherubs busy assembling a tripod topped with what looked like a flame thrower. She tipped it over as she went, splashing fuel across their wings and lighting the little angels up like candles.

And then she was there. Right in front of the vat, and right in front of Lucifer. She was a few feet away at most, but he was so absorbed in what he was doing that he didn't even notice her. He looked so regal up close, part aristocrat, part animal. She could still see the beauty in him, caked over with all the ugliness. Burns and blackened flesh hadn't damaged his essence, and there was still a sort of charm beneath it all, the same one that had brought him to such heights before his fall.

But there he was, doing something to Rhamiel, bent on killing her and everyone around her for the sake of some ancient grudge. She didn't know how to stop him, or whether anyone even could. But her eyes were drawn to the withered body in the tank, and the warm feeling inside her surged until even the room around her seemed to glow. She knew what she had to do, even if she didn't know why.

She could hear voices calling after her as she plunged her hand into the water. Thane screaming "no" as loud as he could manage. Cassie telling her not to do it. Faye shouting that it wouldn't work, that nothing would work, and that all she could do was leave. She could hear them, but she didn't listen. All she could focus on was Rhamiel's hands. Lucifer had one, but there was still the other, floating up and down in the water.

It was withered and black, and it was missing a finger. But Rhamiel was in there, and it was him. Whatever it looked like, however damaged it was, it was him. She wanted to touch him. To hold his hand, to be there with him, to will her love into him even as Lucifer poured in his hate.

The vat felt like a bucket of ice. They'd had harsh winters back in the tower, and nothing to ward away the cold but moth-eaten blankets and the warmth of the communal fire. But this was something else. Something so cold she thought it might peel her flesh away down to the bones, biting at her until her hand looked just like Rhamiel's.

It hurt, and badly, but she kept going. She leaned in, grasping at his hand, her fingers brushing against his until finally she managed to wrap them around him, to touch him one last time before it was over for the both of them. And then the warmth grew, the sounds around her disappeared, and all she could see of the battle around her were the silhouettes of the warring angels and a blinding white light.

CHAPTER THIRTY

EVERYTHING HAD GONE DARK ALL at once. He couldn't see anything, he couldn't hear anything, and the foul smells of sulfur and ash had disappeared the moment the transfer was complete.

For a moment Rhamiel thought he was blinded, his eyes as empty as the sockets of the body he'd been moved into. The world around him was black, and thoughts of an eternity helpless and alone danced through his head. He'd come in here to fight, but he'd found nothing but his own mind to keep him company.

But then he felt his eyelids. He could blink, and that meant he had eyes. He felt wings at his back, he could wiggle his fingers, and there were boots on his feet. He looked down, and he saw a body, the same one he'd always had, the dim outline of his hands moving just as he willed them to.

He looked like himself. He could see his armor, his wings, and he could even feel his sword at his side. He drew it, and he was bathed in orange light. Him, and nothing else. No matter where he waved his sword, there was nothing else to see.

He was floating in an empty, blackened void. Everything else was just... nothing. This wasn't the way it was supposed to be. If he was in here, he could hardly still be inside his own body. The miracle workers relied on strange energies, and even they didn't know precisely how their magic worked. This had to be his imagination, some trick of his mind that he didn't yet understand.

Zuphias had said he'd seen visions, images of the Pit. Perhaps it had been a ruse to lure him into taking his place. He might have just been dangling the one bait he knew Rhamiel would be sure to grasp at: the promise of salvation, for the woman he loved and for his son.

But Faye had said the same thing. She'd seen things that terrified her, images that could only have come from Lucifer's Pit. And Ambriela hadn't contradicted either of them. She thought the plan a longshot, and an extreme one, but she believed he had at least some chance. Cunning as she was, she wanted to live, and his success in here was her only hope of that. He had to trust them. He didn't have any other choice.

He sheathed his sword, closed his eyes, and waited. What he noticed more than anything was the absence of anything. There was no sound other than his own breathing. There were no smells, no sights, nothing but him. All he could do was wait. If the others were wrong, if there was nothing here to fight, he'd at least spend the rest of eternity remembering the things that mattered most. He kept his thoughts on happier times. He thought of Jana and of their tryst in the garden. He thought of her face, and ran through every kiss they'd had again and again. It wasn't quite Heaven, but it would do.

He didn't know how long it was before he smelled it. Sulfur, and far worse than it had been up above. Pure and thick, like it had clouded around his head and enveloped him in the stench. His eyes flipped open and the smell faded. Too soon. He'd touched it, but he hadn't been there, not quite. He'd lost his focus, and so he'd lost the connection. And if he wanted to do what he'd come here to, he'd have to follow that mental path whether he liked it or not.

He relaxed again, loosening his mind, banishing all his thoughts. The smell came back, thicker than ever. Then heat, a wave of it, blasting against his face. He waited still longer until sounds roared around him, screaming winds and distant screeches of the creatures who dwelled there. Then he opened his eyes again, and he found himself in the Pit.

Mesas of yellow rock loomed above him. The sky was aflame, as if one giant sun covered the entirety of the skyline. Clouds of noxious gas floated through the rock formations, and here and there it caught fire, sending up fireballs and puffs of acrid smoke. Tiny red lizards gnawed at his boots in a futile effort to puncture the metal, their bodies stretched to hold dozens of extra limbs. Carrion eaters glided above him in hopes of a meal, dark things that were nothing more than thin flaps of skin and teeth.

And down below the real predators gathered.

Arachnids the size of dogs skittered from rock to rock, standing on chitin legs with tips as sharp as knives. They closed in from every side, hunting like pack animals, rows of yellow eyes lined up along their brown skin. He drew his sword, waving it before him, but they darted towards him from every angle. There were too many to count, all coordinating their reckless feints so that everywhere he turned he'd open himself to the attack of another. He slashed all around him, hoping to frighten them off, but there were too many. One of the creatures launched itself at his shoulder, hissing and baring its fangs, angling for the first bite that would weaken him for all the others.

It went right through him. He didn't even feel it. The creature landed in front of him, chomping at the ground and pouring puddles of venom into the dirt. He slashed at it with his sword, but he couldn't harm it any more than it could harm him.

He took to the air, floating past the carrion eaters as they snapped at him. He was here, but he wasn't, not really. Not yet. He focused himself, using meditation techniques that Ambriela had taught him. He had to connect with this place, to bring himself here, and then he had to pour all of his energy into closing the connection down, once and for all.

He closed his eyes again, concentrating on truly feeling what was around him. He was a phantom here, watching but not interacting. He hummed to himself, ignoring the irritated squawkings of the creatures around him, taunted by a meal they could never quite taste. He focused on the heat instead. That was what Ambriela had said he needed: a touchstone, she called it, a thing to link his mind to. He needed access to the tunnel the cherubs had built, and then he had to close it with nothing but the force of his own will.

"You're too late."

He looked around, but no one was there. The creatures couldn't speak, not intelligibly, and there was no one else here but him. But he was certain he'd heard it. He'd worried about whether he'd lose his grip on his own sanity as the years passed, but there hadn't been time for something like that, not yet. He waited, heard nothing more, and closed his eyes again.

He let the heat wash over him. It was nothing compared to what he'd suffered in the Fall. But the more he concentrated on it, the more it stung. It was the pain that would bring him here. Nothing would sharpen his senses more than that. Ambriela was sure of it, and before they'd left for the Hive she'd given him a crash course in angelic meditation. He used every technique he knew, embracing the heat all along his skin and working to feel it, amplifying the hurt with his own thoughts. And then he heard it again.

"It's over," said the voice. "I'm here now, and you've come too late."

He knew who it was, then. He'd heard him speak long ago, preaching from a balcony, his words dripping with sugary praise for the Maker that was just a bit too sweet to be truly sincere. But now he sounded different. Harsher, angrier, less a smooth swindler and more a sadistic despot. He was here, too, somewhere. Rhamiel couldn't see him, but it didn't mean a thing. He could be intangible, and this connection was a magic of his own doing.

Rhamiel went back to the pain, ignoring everything else. Lucifer's voice cut into his mind with hectoring and harangues: "I've killed her already, and the child along with her. I cut him from the girl's belly. But you needn't mourn. Come with me, and join the truly fallen. Embrace us and…." The sound dimmed as he focused, the words merging into a low buzzing noise like a cloud of flies. It didn't matter. Anything that came from the mouth of Lucifer could be a lie, and any promises he made would only be kept so long as they were convenient.

The buzzing died to nothing, and only the pain was left. It felt like needles all along his skin. Like he was being stabbed by pins of fire, weaving their threads in and out of him. His eyes felt like they were boiling, and his armor grew heavy, pulling him to the ground like an anchor.

And then all at once he was there.

The trick had worked. The pain had focused him, had drawn him through the psychic tunnel to where he wanted to go. It vanished all at once, leaving only the dull heat of the fire above him and lines of sweat rolling through his hair and down his face. The carrion eaters bit at his armor, but he gave them a few flicks of his sword, and this time the blows connected. He split one apart, and then another. The rest of them drifted away to a safe distance to wait for the possibility of scraps, sure that something bigger would come along and finish him off.

He'd connected himself to the Pit, and if Ambriela was right, he was straddling the tunnel, a bit of him in either world. He was here, but he wasn't. He was a creature of mental energy, but that didn't mean he couldn't be hurt. It didn't mean he couldn't die, and it didn't mean he couldn't go mad. He was a rider of the miracle workers' tunnels, and now that he had a foot in both worlds, he could shut them down and pull himself back into Zuphias's body as the connection collapsed.

But it would take an act of will, one so herculean that it might exhaust his psyche forever in the process.

He started into it, thinking about the pain again. But as he did, something in the distance distracted him. Something walking out from behind the rocks, something that frightened away the predators and even the carrion eaters. Soon it was just the two of them, the rest of the Pit's denizens having fled into the crevices of the rock formations around them.

It was a black figure, wings spreading behind its back. It kept moving forward, staring up at him, and then he knew it was him. Lucifer. Just as real as he was, just as connected to this plane, and just as dangerous as ever. He cocked his head, and Rhamiel heard the voice again, coming from inside his own head. "Pity you couldn't see what the Maker turned us into. Pity you'll never see the paradise I'll build." Then he was in the skies, hands stretched wide with fingers like claws, barreling towards Rhamiel with death in his eyes.

He barely had time to raise his sword before Lucifer was upon him, aiming a blow at his throat. He lurched to one side, the claws missing him by inches. Then Lucifer was gone, somewhere behind him, leaving him to spin about in the air and brandish his sword in every direction. The sky was silent, the land was empty, and he seemed to be the only one there.

He knew it wasn't true, but there was nothing to be done about it. Lucifer was too fast, and he was on him again before Rhamiel even had time to move. This time he dropped down from above, plummeting like a rock, his hands slashing at Rhamiel's wings. He felt something tear; a scratch, and a deep one. He thought he'd hit Lucifer with his sword on the way down, but he couldn't be sure. He started towards the rocks, aiming for the entrance to a nearby cave. If he could hide, if he could find a place where he could focus, he'd at least have a chance to end Zuphias's miracle. Maybe he'd never leave this place, but then again, neither would Lucifer.

But Lucifer didn't give him the chance. He was on him before Rhamiel had made it more than a few yards, grappling with him and smiling all the while, a well-fed cat toying with its prey in the last moments before its death. And then it was mayhem, a flurry of assaults almost too fast for Rhamiel to see.

Lucifer's claws tore at his wings, ripping out clumps of feathers and flesh, tearing him into little bits while he was still alive. It may not have been his real body, but the pain was as real as any he'd ever felt. He struck out with his sword, and he scored a hit, but it didn't matter. His sword left scratches across Lucifer's skin, thin lines of blood dripping out in their wake. But they didn't cut through any further, and they didn't even do enough damage to slow him down.

He was going to die here. He knew it. Ambriela had warned him to be careful, that too much damage in here could obliterate his mind and kill him just as surely as anything else would. Lucifer would rend him to pieces in another minute or two at most, and he wasn't strong enough to defeat him. The best he could hope for was to try to do what he'd come here to do, to close down the connection and cut off the Pit from the rest of creation. If he couldn't save himself, he could at least save someone else.

He let his wings go limp, dropping towards the ground and landing on his back with a heavy thud. The pain burst throughout his body, reverberating up and down his bones. But that was precisely what he wanted: pain, as much of it as he could take, and then a little more. He reveled in it, closing out everything else, the focus of his mind jumping from injury to injury. One moment he concentrated on a hole Lucifer had torn into his wing, the next on a sprained wrist, the next on the throbbing in his skull. And all the while he thought of the tunnels, running a mantra through his head again and again: shut them down, shut them down, shut them down.

Soon he could feel them. It was like the connection was there in front of him, a thick length of rubbery rope that waved up and down inside his consciousness. He couldn't see it, but he could sense it, and he willed the pain towards it, willed it to snap in half with all his might. But all it did was wriggle and wave. He needed more pain, more fuel for his will, and soon he got precisely that.

Lucifer was on him, pinning his body to the ground, digging at his face with his claws. He couldn't see anymore, not through the blood. And then Lucifer was pulling at his armor, snapping off the breastplate, aiming for his heart and for a killing blow. He could feel claws on his skin, fingers tearing into his flesh, his body convulsing in agony.

It hurt more than anything he'd ever felt before, more than he'd thought anything ever could. But still it wasn't enough. He couldn't sever the tunnel, no matter how much he suffered, no matter how strong his will. He felt his life ebbing away, and he started to give. Ten seconds more, maybe fifteen. It was all he had, and if his task was failed and he was done for, he wanted his last thoughts to be of her.

He imagined her before him, imagined sweeping her up in his arms. The pain faded to the background, and all that was left was her. Jana, so full of love and life. And as he did, something happened. He thought he saw a light in the sky, a little pinpoint of white that grew to a thick disc beaming down at him. And he thought he saw her in it. She was still in his mind, but the image was clearer, more real somehow. And he could see Zuphias's tunnel waving behind her, a little crack forming on its side.

A crack. He'd done something to it, some kind of damage. The light had appeared, and his will had broken through at long last. He'd done some damage, if only a little. He realized in that moment that he was wrong about the pain. It wouldn't work, what Ambriela had taught him. She'd said he'd needed a touchstone, and she'd said that pain would be the easiest thing to keep his focus on.

It might have been, for Ambriela. She'd been consumed by it, inside and out. But he was someone else. What absorbed him wasn't what absorbed her, and the techniques she relied on to hone her attentions and her willpower would never work for him.

He pushed his thoughts towards the beam of light above him instead, towards the things he loved instead of the things that hurt him. Towards Jana and everything he loved about her. The way she'd kept her innocence in a world dripping with guilt. The way she looked at him, not as a fallen thing but as hero and protector who could right every wrong, including his own. The way she kissed, the way she loved, the way she'd stolen his heart.

He ignored the scalding heat around him. He ignored Lucifer's threats, ignored the wounds he'd suffered, ignored the monsters scrabbling for a pound of his flesh, ignored the danger and fear and hurt. And as he did, the light from above grew stronger, brighter. It spread across the sky, no longer a beam but a blinding wave that rippled through everything around him. The sounds around him faded, Lucifer's voice dwindled to a distant nothing, and soon the Pit was gone, replaced with a pure, cleansing white.

CHAPTER THIRTY-ONE

IGHT ENGULFED THEM. NOT THE malevolent red gloss they'd grown used to, but something else. Something bright, and something blinding. It radiated out of the vat, and the only thing any of them could see was Zuphias's body, a black silhouette bobbing in a sea of blistering white.

Silence replaced the sounds of the pillar, the slurps and slobs that had echoed through the room as the corruption spiraled upward. The tornado of sludge slowed, then quivered, and then it dwindled away entirely. The connection with the Pit was severed, lost forever, and as the link between the two planes died away, the things that had come through it died along with it.

Outside, the light spread. The dome above them fizzled, the liquid ooze withering away into flakes of black, then vanishing altogether. The change rippled through the barrier like a sonic boom, rolling outward until the entirety of the barrier had shaken away into nothingness. Winds whirled through the air, blowing along with them the scent of grass and birds and life and driving away the stench of sulfur and coal and burning flesh. And the sun shone down on everything, vibrant and full and warm.

Trees screamed, their roots thrashing up and down like tentacles, angry and confused and full of hate. The noises faded as the taint leached out of them, their roots relaxing and digging down into the soil again.

Shadow fought with shadow as creatures of the darkness sought refuge from the light. But as the sun found its way back onto the land again, unfiltered and unadulterated, the things from below found fewer and fewer places to hide. Their skin hissed and burned, their little red eyes melted away, and soon even the shadows were emptied of the kind of darkness that once again could only be found in the deepest corners of Lucifer's Pit.

Demons were blinded, falling to the ground and groping their way along like baby birds cast out of their nests, their claws digging ruts in the soil. They screeched as they went, helpless angry things who couldn't hope to find their prey in a place this bright. They crawled in circles until their roasted skin was caked in dirt, their bodies as limp and useless as their minds.

A giant mole-like thing coughed and wheezed, falling on its side in an epileptic fit, its lungs collapsing as the sulfur vanished from the air around it. Flies the size of cats dropped from the skies, drooling out fluids as they buzzed their wings against the ground in helpless death throes. Snakes forgot how to fly, and flowers forgot how to talk.

And frightened humans poked out of their hiding places, popping their heads up and down, squinting at the changes in the world around them only to burrow back into safety again. They didn't dare leave, not yet, but soon their courage would grow. The noises had stopped, the smells were gone, and everything looked so healthy, so alive. Their fears slowly disappeared as the warmth of the sun on their skin made them feel alive again.

Down in the Hive the throne room was silent. Lucifer still stood there opposite Jana, their hands dipping into the waters of the vat, the both of them reaching towards a shattered body and trying their best to touch the soul within it. She looked up at him, but his eyes were shut, his body motionless.

Long ago they'd called him the Lightbringer, or the Morning Star, or sometimes the Bringer of Dawn. The light had come for him again, but this time he didn't take to it. He was frozen like a statue, his hand stretched down into the vat, bubbles of air running up and down his arm. His face was twisted into a grimace, his other arm stretched up as if ready to strike. It took everything in her to keep her hand in the vat along with his, a fallen prince who'd slaughter her without a second thought if it meant he could finally grasp the crown.

The others in the room were just as tense as she was. The glow faded, and soon they could see again. Seraphs raised their swords to fight, for whatever their weapons would be worth against him. Humans stumbled back, fumbling with guns that would never even nick him, and foxhole prayers were muttered under the breath of angels who didn't believe in them anymore. Stomachs dropped, lives flashed before eyes, and everyone in the room prepared to meet their Maker once again.

And then he broke.

Orange fissures cracked open across Lucifer's blackened skin, following his veins and bursting through to the surface. His flesh parted like plates of rock floating on magma, piece after piece of him breaking away from the others until he was fractured from head to toe. The orange lines grew bright, his eyes glowed red beneath his eyelids, and finally he just fell to pieces, crumbling to the ground in shattered shards of black.

Some of the angels clapped, some of them laughed, and most of them stood and watched in disbelief. But not Jana. She held onto the hand she'd been clutching, her only lifeline to the one she loved, and she cried.

He'd done it.

He'd gone into the darkness and he'd saved them all. The world would live again, but how would she live without him? The body in front of her was helpless. She clasped at its hand, squeezing it tight. But the hand didn't squeeze back, and it never could. Rhamiel couldn't feel it, not in there, not with a body as broken as this one.

The light had faded, and so had her hopes. No angel was going to trade places with him, no matter what Ambriela said. She knew that had been a lie, a thin effort to comfort her until the thing was done and there wasn't any going back from it. He'd stay in this vat, forever, and the best she could hope for was to visit him from time to time while he was locked away in this mausoleum for his soul. She'd have to learn to live alone again, at least for a time. And then she'd have to learn to be a parent all by herself, just her and her son.

She didn't think either of them would survive his childhood. There were those who'd help her, to be sure. Thane certainly would, once he'd recovered, and so would Cassie and Faye. But this wasn't a mere matter of picking out toys and changing diapers. Rhamiel had saved the world, but it was still a dangerous place, and her son was its most valuable prize. She sobbed to herself, over and over, and no one came to comfort her. They were too busy celebrating, too busy dancing away their cares to even think about her. For them it was victory; for her it was a staggering defeat.

"Jana."

It came from behind her, and she whipped her head around to see. It was Rhamiel, or at least it was his voice. He stood there behind her with his wings stretched wide, stumbling forward with dazed eyes. Zuphias must not have adjusted to his new body, not yet. He could barely control himself. She snapped up at him, screaming at him with a ferocity she didn't know was inside her. "You. You're a monster. You always were. You stole what wasn't yours, and you'll be damned because of it. You'll go down there, you know. Into Lucifer's Pit. My son will send you there. He'll—"

"Jana," said Rhamiel. "He's gone. Zuphias isn't here anymore. He's in there, in his old body, right where he belongs."

"Is this a trick?" said Jana. "Is this some game?" It had to be. He'd stolen Rhamiel's body, and now he wanted to take his place at her side. His balance was

427

off, and so were his movements. He could barely even walk. She knew it couldn't be him. Something about him looked different. Weaker.

Or maybe just exhausted.

He swayed on his feet, barely able to stand. Ambriela swooped in from behind him, steadying him and appraising him with a skeptical eye. She held up a finger to his head, the tip glowing white with energy as she sampled something in the air around him. Then she turned to Jana with a smile; not a loving one, exactly, but not quite as hateful as before. "It's him, dear. He shut down the miracle, and the tunnels closed along with it. All of them. And it appears poor Zuphias ended up on the wrong side of things before they did."

She looked into Rhamiel's eyes, sparkling blue and filled with adoration, and then she knew for sure. She rushed towards him, jumping into his open arms as he lifted her up, clutching her against him. He didn't let go, not for what seemed to her like an eternity, not until the happy murmurs of celebration from all around had finally exhausted themselves into a warm, contented silence.

CHAPTER THIRTY-TWO

THE MOUNTAINS GLOWED PURPLE, THE rising sun peeking up from behind them and painting the clouds above with an orange hue. Jana walked along a newly-worn trail, a morning ritual she'd kept since they'd come there just a few weeks before. The place was so beautiful, and her greatest hope was that she'd spend the rest of her days there, quietly puttering around with Rhamiel and the child they were soon to raise.

She was heavy to the point of bursting; no one was sure precisely when she was due, but anyone who looked at her could tell it would be soon. If the pregnancy lasted a few more days, she'd be bedridden for the duration. As it was, she could still shuffle along, albeit with help. A little girl trailed along behind her, one of the servants, ever at the ready to help her along if she swayed or to wait with her if she needed a rest.

She strolled along the trail, taking in the smell of flowers and the chirping of sparrows. It was the perfect place for a settlement. She'd picked the spot herself, a lush green valley rolling at the base of one of the tallest peaks in the range. Rhamiel had built a cabin for her in the middle of the sward, the grass wet between her toes each morning as she went for her daily stroll. It made her feel alive, being so close to so many growing things. The tower had been cold and sterile, but this place was warm and vibrant, and it offered her the life she'd missed out on for so many years.

Most of the servants had settled here beside them, along with a few of the angels. They'd all been offered a place, but they hadn't all been willing to come. The fallen angels were afraid of being judged by the Son, and they each handled it in their own way. Most of those who stayed lived up in the mountains, keeping to themselves and spending their days in quiet meditation. Some were too shamed by their past behavior to even make eye contact with a human. Others had gone off to war again, swearing fealty to the Maker once more and vowing to subdue any angels anywhere who continued to torment the rest of his creations. They'd put a hundred cherubs to the sword already, and the last she'd heard they were on the hunt for more.

A few of the angels had even made it back to the gates of Heaven itself. Ambriela had led an expedition up there, working herself into an anxious frenzy over the question of what the Maker would have them do now that Lucifer was defeated and the Son was soon to return. They'd been sure they wouldn't make it up there. Some ethereal force had trapped them here after their Fall, but she'd vowed to plow right through it or die in the attempt.

Whatever it was, it was gone, and they'd made it

to their home as if they'd never been exiled in the first place. But the guardians of the gate had sent them right back down again. They had duties on Earth, they were told, but what those duties were was a matter for each of them to decide on their own. It was a new world, now, and the Maker planned for it to go on forever, angel and human living side by side. Take it up with the Son, said the guardians, earn the redemption he's come to offer you, and perhaps one day we shall be brothers in arms again.

It wasn't quite the reception Ambriela had hoped for, but after a few days of tears and frustration she'd gathered her things and gone off into the world to seek redemption alone. They'd heard reports of her since from humans far and wide. She'd become a wandering healer, roving around the world working miracles on the sick. They called her the Crying Lady, and the places she regularly visited were becoming shrines of sorts, attracting pilgrims and vendors hawking healing relics of dubious origins and effectiveness. But as frightened of her as the supplicants were, the rumor was that everyone who came to her went away whole again.

A last group of angels had become more sociable than the others, building themselves houses down on the ground along with everyone else and joining in the construction of the community Rhamiel had dedicated himself to creating. There were only a few of them, but their ranks had grown as the days had passed, and Rhamiel thought more might join them before things were through.

It frightened the servants to have the angels living

beside them again, and Thane had nearly burst a vein in his forehead over it. He'd threatened to leave, to kill them all with his own bare hands, and even to personally drag them down into the Pit where they belonged. But though the angels who'd stayed weren't afraid of him, they were terrified of punishments from up above, and they'd taken his outbursts in stride. The more the angels apologized, the more his anger faded, and things had calmed to the point that sometimes, if his mood was right, he was even willing to silently nod his head to greet them.

She could see him up ahead, chopping wood into pieces with a heavy axe. Faye stood there beside him, a glass of freshly pressed apple juice waiting in her hand. The two of them hadn't left each other's side, not since he'd gotten his body back. And since they'd come here, he'd taken out most of his anger on the logs, enjoyed his days with Faye, and busied himself building a cabin just for her.

At least he said it was just for her. Jana had her suspicions. She'd caught them holding hands just a few days before, and while they'd snatched them apart when they saw her, the redness in Thane's cheeks hadn't disappeared quite so quickly. There was a bond between them now, and deny it all they liked, she could see it plain as day. Faye would have her cabin, but Jana didn't think she'd be living there alone. She waved at the two of them as she passed. Both smiled and waved back, Thane drenched in sweat, Faye wiping away at his shoulders with a damp cloth. Jana smiled to herself and suppressed a laugh. Faye had wanted children so badly, and perhaps soon she wouldn't be the only one in their little settlement with a child underfoot.

She wound her way through a flower garden, filled with lilacs and roses and a single tulip one of the servants had found. Heavy footprints lined the dirt, leading up to a few bits of cobblestone, the first beginnings of a path both angels and humans could tread. The angels had come here more and more often, enjoying the flowers' beauty alongside the servants, and some of them had even begun carving little stone statues to set along the path as decorations. It wasn't quite as glorious as what they'd had in heaven, or even back in their tower. But it was theirs, all of theirs, and they enjoyed it all the more for it.

Past the garden were the fields. The first beginnings of a crop were sprouting up through the soil, corn and wheat and a few rows of tomato vines. There'd be more to come; Jana was sure of it. Cassie had taken charge of the project, and she was busy ordering servants this way and that. She didn't know the first thing about farming, but that hadn't stopped her. She knew about leading, and if she could guide the servants through a battle with creatures from the Pit, then a little bit of corn wasn't going to stop her. They'd had a few false starts, and a few rows of young cabbage leaves chewed to bits by insects stood as testimony that being a farmer was harder than it looked.

But she had a pile of books and a troupe of servants eager to help her, and Jana was sure she'd get there. She waved to her, and Cassie waved back, just once, before turning back to an irrigation canal she was putting together with a few of the crafters. Cassie looked absorbed, and she was, but it was good for her. She seemed calmer and happier than ever, finally able to lead without the burden of life and death weighing on her at every moment. She'd kept her purpose, but now that the stakes weren't so high it didn't gnaw at her if she made a mistake. Even the angels were starting to look to her for guidance in building out their little village, though some of them still huffed to themselves about the indignity of it afterwards. Cassie didn't seem to mind. If they didn't want her to lead, they didn't have to follow, and she was perfectly content to stick to running things only for those who wanted her to.

The sun rose, and Jana sat and rested on a stump near a grove of pecan trees nestled at the foot of the mountain. She cracked a few nuts open with a rock, handing some to her little handmaiden, eating a few herself. The day was just beginning, and it was a good one. She thought she'd walk some more, and then perhaps ask Cassie to teach her something about woodcarving. She wanted to build a little crib, all by herself, although maybe she'd start out with a few toys. There'd be plenty of time for all of it. She fantasized about the things their village would have, and where they'd put them: a school, right in the middle of the grass, and maybe a kitchen where she could cook again. A library, one filled with books, ones she'd read right alongside her son as he grew and grew until he became the man everyone expected him to be.

And then she felt a pressure inside her, an uncomfortable pain all along her stomach. They'd told her it was going to happen. But she was so far from the cabin, and she didn't think she could even move. She groaned out something to her handmaiden, leaning back on the stump to try to ease the pain.

"Go get Rhamiel," said Jana. "Go. Go find him, quick."

The little girl ran off, dropping her nuts and sprinting along the trail. The pain was gone, and then it came again. But it wasn't long before Rhamiel was there, shooting through the sky as fast as he could go, dropping down beside her and searching her up and down for any signs that something had gone wrong.

"He's coming," said Jana. "He's coming now."

"Now," said Rhamiel, a little panic in his voice. "Now?"

"He isn't going to wait," said Jana. "Not long. I can feel it."

"Now," said Rhamiel in disbelief. He shook his head, and it took him a moment to collect his thoughts, to convince himself that this thing he'd waited for so long was finally happening. "We must go. We must get you to those who know more than I about... such matters."

He lifted her in his arms as gently as he could, staying low to the ground as he whisked her away back to her cabin. He'd no sooner eased her into bed than he was out the door, his voice booming through the valley as he searched for the midwife. One of the angels had found her just days before, scouring every place humans could hide for someone who still knew the art. She was old, and she hadn't delivered a child in years, but old ways were new again, and she had experience aplenty from before the Fall.

Soon the room was full to the brim. Rhamiel paced back and forth alongside the bed until the midwife finally ordered him into a corner, a tiny little woman poking her finger up at a very nervous angel's chest. It would have made Jana laugh, if things hadn't hurt so much. But then the woman gave her an herbal medicine, a concoction of her very own that she'd sent angels hither and yon to gather ingredients for. It came in a cup of tea, tasting bitter and smelling even worse. But it did its job: the pain was dulled, she felt a little more alert, and all the pushing she was being ordered to do seemed to come a little bit more easily.

It must have lasted for hours. It was exhausting, but friendly faces were all around her. Rhamiel, staring down at her with lines of worry all along his face, outside of his element and powerless to help her for the first time she'd known him. Faye, sitting by the bed holding her hand, whispering encouragements in her ear the entire while. Thane, pacing around almost as much as Rhamiel was, and Cassie, looking over the midwife's shoulder and double-checking everything she did.

But finally she heard it. A sharp cry, the first sound ever uttered by a pair of little lungs, followed by happy chatter from all around her.

There'd been worries before, about what would truly happen when an angel lay with a woman. Strange things were spoken of in old myths, and rumors had reached Jana's ears. Some were sure she'd bear a monster; others thought the sky would crack open, the stars would move, and the earth itself would quake. She couldn't keep from worrying, at least a little.

But as the midwife held him up, as she spanked him on the bottom, and as she held him out to her with a smile, Jana saw what she'd always expected she'd see when the moment finally came.

A beautiful baby boy.

THE END.

Liked the book? If you want to get a heads up on the release of the last book in the series, please sign up for my mailing list.

http://www.theywhofell.com

ACKNOWLEDGEMENTS

Thanks to Kathy Dixon Graham for taking the time to proof the final draft.

Thanks to Streetlight Graphics for handling the cover design and formatting.

Made in the USA
Middletown, DE
14 May 2018